DRAGON'S CLAW

A. C. EDWARDS

ISBN: 9780-6458-6732-9
A PDS record for this book is available at the National Library of Australia

Dragon's Claw: 'Dragon' Series Book 2

Cover Design by Red Tally

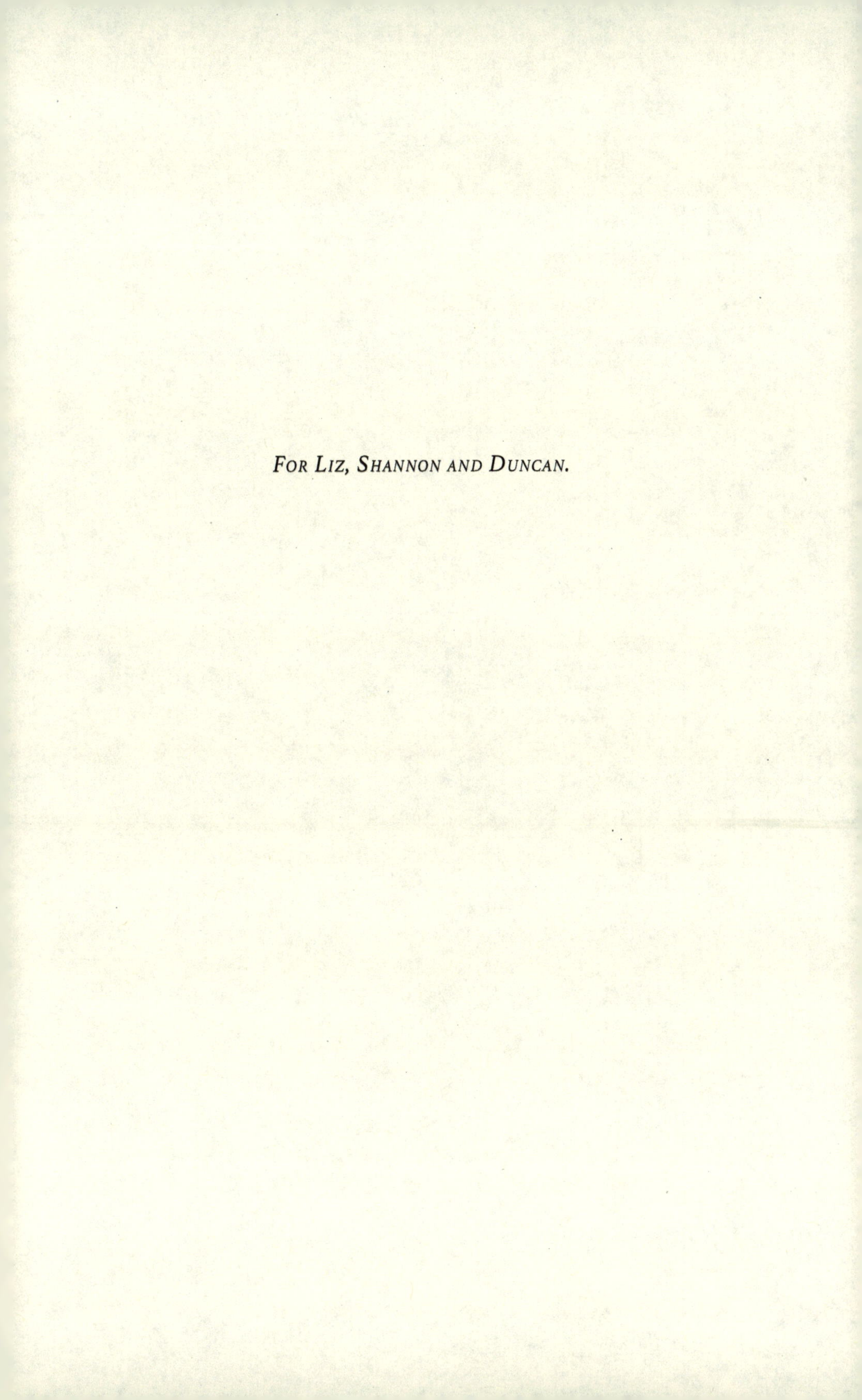

For Liz, Shannon and Duncan.

When a man is no longer afraid of death, there is no use threatening him with it.

Chinese Proverb

I'm a bad person.

But you know that by now.

First you flicked through the journal now you're reading it. You couldn't resist. You're reading everything I have to say.

Have I shocked you? Disgusted you? If we could meet and you could look me in the eye and tell me what you see, would you? Without flinching, would you really look? I've looked inside and know what I am. I have seen. I'm not a good person - I'm not even sure I am *a person. Perhaps I am after all, for in Nietzsche's words "Man is the cruellest animal" and I'm nothing if not cruel. I'm your worst nightmare, your deepest fear.*

I'm inevitable death, stalking your every move, waiting to reach out and tap your shoulder.

I'm the crawling feeling at the back of your neck when you walk alone in the forest at night. I'm the panic that grips your heart and rises to choke you, unfightable.

I am the shadow across the sand as you swim beyond the shore-break; the footsteps behind you in the dark alley; the monster that lurks under your bed and the flitting night-bat of terror.

I'm the horror that grips you when your heart cramps, when the x-ray shows a shadow on your lung.

I'm the cut rope when you climb, the tangled parachute.

I'm the snake in your sleeping bag, the black wolf in the dark of night.

You are shifting uncomfortably in your chair. I know it. I can see you. Be honest. It's not what I've done, is it? Not really. The scariest thing for you, the most terrifying of all, is the thought that, deep down inside, you and I are alike. It horrifies you to think that we have the same tastes, the same...passions. You tremble and your face flushes to think that you could do what I have done and, yes, enjoy it.

There! Your pupils dilate at the thought. You would not look me in the eye, even if you could. It's not that you're disgusted, appalled, and shocked. It's the terrible, earth-shaking truth that you are jealous of me. You want to be *me.*

How did we come to be here, you and I, in this room so close I can smell your desire? Read on and I'll tell you.

1

I DROPPED TO ONE KNEE, my ears ringing, and shook my head. The blow had rattled my brain and shaken my teeth. It hurt but what really worried me was the knowledge my assailant had pulled the blow and there was more to come.

It had been going like this for over five minutes and I didn't know how much more I could take. I rose slowly to my feet, breathing hard, and cuffed away the sweat that flowed freely into my eyes. My attacker moved in, low and fast giving me no time to throw up my guard. I had always been an orthodox boxer, with a slight preference toward a crouching stance given my height, but I knew it was completely ineffective in the face of the relentless attack.

Stepping back, I rolled my left shoulder and dropped my hand in the "Philly Shell" guard to protect my gut and groin as I saw the blur of the strike coming in. I was too slow. In the instant before the blow hit home, the thought went through my mind that I had been a fool to make the challenge. Boxing versus Kung Fu... What was I thinking?

Steel-hard fingers stabbed home deep into my pubis and the pain was instant and excruciating. My eyes blurred and I threw out a jab that connected with nothing but thin air as my assailant danced aside, scything a leg out to sweep me off my feet. I was airborne for an instant before thudding onto my back with a grunt. My attacker moved in to finish me off, eyes glittering and jaw set...

'Joey,' I gasped, raising a gloved hand. 'For Christ's sake, *stop*. Enough.' I spat out my mouthguard as a slender, brown hand reached down to help me from the canvas.

'Sorry boss,' she said without a shred of sorrow in her voice. Josephine Hu-yung Loh stood back and watched me, her head cocked to one side and a slight grin curling the corners of her mouth. I noticed with mounting irritation she was barely perspiring, and her lean 160-centimetre frame looked fresh and ready to go.

'You okay?' she asked solicitously. 'I mean, you're not going to die on me, are you?

'Don't be a smartarse. It's unbecoming,' I said as I snatched a towel down from the ropes of the boxing ring and wiped my face. 'You know I was only a heartbeat away from knocking you flat.'

Joey's laugh rang out in the gym, an old industrial warehouse tucked away in the Tai Ping Shan suburb of Hong Kong's Central District.

'Boxing against Kung Fu! What were you thinking?' She shook her head and turned to her gym bag in the corner of the ring to draw out a sports drink that she popped and guzzled.

I took the opportunity, in between dragging in ragged breaths, to study her more closely. Joey had been Hong Kong Police Force, and it had been nearly four years since she had joined me after leaving the HKPF VIP Protection Unit under a cloud following her brief fling with the wife of one of her Principals, a very senior member of the Hong Kong Government. It had also been two years since our case to crack a sex-trafficking ring had ended with me being shot in the head. Two years since Joey had saved my life more than once. Two years since she had killed her first man. She had changed then. Gone, forever, was the annoying millennial skater-girl I had first employed, and in her place was a tough, resilient woman. Joey also had a healthy dislike for authority. I think I liked that the most about her.

Her flash tattoos shimmered on the glistening skin of her arms that were damp with perspiration. She pulled a towel from her gym bag and dabbed her face before rubbing her arms down. I could see her breathing was deep but controlled as she flicked an errant strand of the bob-cut, jet-black hair from her eyes.

Joey was an adept at Wing Chun – a form of Kung Fu particular to Hong Kong that emphasised strong legs and a relaxed style of flashing arm movements. In fact, she had been made *Sifu*, a master, only a few months earlier and had taken on her first apprentice. Typically of Joey, her apprentice was a young girl, a nobody street kid and orphan from the back of Shek Kip Mei. She was sponsoring the kid through school and the kid roomed in Joey's apartment in between stays in St Christopher's residential childcare. I admired that but didn't think it would end well. The kid was bound to disappoint. As a copper, I'd seen it dozens of times before, but I kept my own counsel on that one. I loved Joey like a sister and admired her immensely as a tough and relentless investigator, a thorough professional. She was half my age and probably the closest friend I had. I didn't have many friends.

A faint memory came back to me from lying on my back, stars dancing before my eyes.

'You know,' I said. 'You shouldn't call me "boss" anymore, Jo. We're partners now. "Jones and Loh" remember?'

She stuffed the towel back into her bag and turned to face me. 'Yeah,' she shrugged.

'Old habits, hey?' She took another pull on her sports drink and shrugged. 'It just feels weird calling you by your first name. You know... it's like calling my dad by his first name.'

I pulled a face and threw my towel over my shoulder. 'Well, "unweird" it.... Also fuck you, I'm not that old.'

'You're *older* than my dad. Just sayin'...'

I sighed. She was right. I had recently turned 47 and, although still fit, had started to spread out across the middle and the running times over my favourite 10-kilometre track in the hills above Wan Chai were slowing. I was still training a few times a week, both in the boxing and weights gym and was holding my own. But I was also still drinking too much, and my dark hair was salted with grey. In my favour, I had recently decided to give up smoking. I wasn't sure yet whether that was a blessing or a curse as my well-worn, leather tobacco pouch and the nicotine cravings still called to me much of the day and night.

I ducked through the ropes of the ring and stepped gingerly down onto the concrete floor of the gym. Out of the corner of my eye I saw Joey grasp the top rope and somersault out of the ring, sticking a perfectly balanced landing before pirouetting gracefully to grab her bag. I absently rubbed an old injury in my right knee. I loved Joey but sometimes I really hated her.

After we had showered and changed, we met at the front door of the gym and stepped out into the bustling activity of the street. It was mid-November and getting colder, but the day was crisp and clear, the late-afternoon sky a cloudless deep blue. Hong Kongers hurried by wrapped in designer puffer jackets and scarves; sneakers had been swapped for boots and hand-held fans for gloves. After the unceasing heat and humidity of summer and Typhoon Season, winter in Hong Kong is a special time. Hong Kongers seem to come alive with the first real drop in temperature, sometime in October. They quickly turn their eyes to Christmas and the feel on the streets is somehow different, calmer. I turned the collar of my own jacket up and blew into my hands, casting about for a taxi. In moments, one of the city's legendary red cabs pulled up to the kerb and Joey and I leapt in. I checked my G-Shock.

'Nearly half four,' I observed. 'It's Friday. How about a beer and some noodles?'

Joey shook her head. 'Sorry boss...I mean *Galahad*. I'm taking Penny out to the movies tonight. She got a report at school yesterday and she's really improving – not to mention actually attending – so it's a movie and hot pot as this week's reward. Another time, huh?'

I was mildly disappointed but not unused to drinking and eating alone so I took the rejection in my stride. Penny, Joey's young apprentice, was everything to Joey and she threw herself into guiding and nurturing the kid. Who was I to get in the way of that? I smiled my agreement and directed the driver to drop her at the office in Sheung Wan before turning him around to Wan Chai, and my small apartment not far from Happy Valley Racecourse. After the usual routine of sluggish crawl and frenetic dash through Hong Kong traffic, the taxi pulled up outside my building.

I stepped out as a tram clanked by; its sides covered in advertising calling on me to buy an apartment in yet another development in the eastern reaches of Victoria Harbour. I keyed in the door code, summoned the elevator, and stood patiently while it trudged its way down to me. With a mechanical sigh, it arrived, and I stepped in, pressing the button to my floor. After what seemed an age, the lift came to a stop with a bounce. I stepped out onto the landing, turned left to my apartment door, ran my hand over the electronic lock to activate it, then swiped my door card. The door opened with a satisfying click, and I walked in. Moments later I was shoved back hard against the door as my giant black and tan dog leapt up to greet me, his paws against my chest.

Bors had grown quickly after I had adopted him as a worm-ridden pup. Now, two years on, he really was a monster – part dog, part bear – and I was actively considering a move out of my small Wan Chai apartment and into a house and garden in the leafy village of Sai Kung on the edge of Port Shelter. I knew Bors had been walked once that day by the dog-sitter, but we enjoyed our time together and I liked the peace of a sedate stroll around the outside of Happy Valley Racecourse, so I clipped on his collar and leash and we hit the streets. An hour later, with Bors walked, watered, fed, and snoring in his bed, I showered and threw on some jeans, my worn desert boots and a fresh T-shirt. Zipping up my puffer jacket, I put on my favourite baseball cap and headed out into Wan Chai for a bowl of wanton noodle soup and a beer. Just the one I promised myself.

I whistled as I took the short walk down Morrison Hill Road toward Hennessy Road and my local noodle joint. With money in the bank and the investigations business doing well – largely on the back of contract protection work we had picked up with HKPF courtesy of Joey's old contacts – life looked good. I was happy. I had been happy for months, and that was an unusual state of mind for me. Within minutes I reached the noodle joint. Its yellow and red neon lights shone brightly into the lowering gloom, lighting the faces of passers-by. I walked in and took a seat at a small, laminate table.

The walls of the restaurant were plastered with pictures of the meals on the menu with their names and descriptions in Cantonese. I ran my eyes over them thinking, perhaps, to take a larger dish but decided on my go-to. Raising a hand at a passing waiter I ordered the soup and a beer. Minutes later a steaming hot bowl of wanton noodle soup arrived at the table accompanied by a tall bottle Tsing Tao beer. I looked at my meal as I organised the chilli oil and soy, and selected two black, plastic chopsticks. The hand-made wantons were the size of large oysters and floated enticingly in a rich chicken broth, tangled in a net of thin egg noodles. Quick, warm, and hearty, it was no wonder this dish was favoured by Hong Kongers, summer or winter. I took a pull at the beer and sighed in contentment before taking up my chopsticks and curved *tong chi* soup spoon and tucking in with noisy satisfaction.

An hour later, I was home in the warmth of my apartment. I poured a whisky and headed out onto the terrace – larger than the apartment itself and the place I spent most of my time. Switching on the Bluetooth speaker, I thumbed through a playlist on my phone and soon the sounds of Alvin Youngblood Hart's raspy voice and tin guitar were murmuring 'Big Mama's Door' into the dark. I settled back into one of the comfortable outdoor chairs, sipped at the whisky and looked up. The night was clear and cold. The stars above The Peak and Mount Cameron winked and shimmered like shards of ice, and the waxing crescent moon was a silver scythe that cut the black cloth of night.

Bors sat at my feet, turning his head now and then at the sound of a night bird or a cricket, and I scratched his ears absently, lost in thought. Yes, life was good and things looked to be getting better. I sighed and sipped again at the whisky, pushing down on the nicotine craving that hit my brain at times like this. The past two years had been good, the weekend lay before me, and I was at peace.

Bitter experience should have taught me not to tempt the gods, but I did. My happiness was a poke in their eye, and I was completely unaware of the dramatic turn my life, and the lives of everyone around me, was soon to take. I hummed along to the soft Blues drifting from my terrace and drank my whisky. Meanwhile, the gods laid their plans, and the world began to tilt.

2

MONDAY MORNING DAWNED bright and cold, and I shivered as I stepped from the taxi and into the grimy block off Ko Shing Street in Sheung Wan that housed the offices of Jones & Loh Investigations. The narrow street was lined on both sides by Chinese herbal stores. It was busy. Sweet, pungent smells wafted the air from the wooden shelves, glass cabinets and bags of exotic herbs and traditional medicines. Greeting a shop owner, I stepped into the building. The ancient lift was out again so I trudged up the three flights of stairs, each step in the cold stairwell further dampening the sour mood I had inherited along with the mild hangover with which I had woken. I juggled the tray of two take-out coffees and keyed in the door code. I took a deep breath and forced a smile onto my face, knocked open the door with my hip, and stepped in. I took in the office at a glance.

It was still small, fitting only three small desks and office chairs, but it was a different place from that of two years ago. Courtesy of a great deal of money I had, unbeknownst to anyone, 'come into', the office had been renovated and was a much cheerier place than it had been. The old and cracked windows had been pulled out and replaced with black, aluminium-framed bifold windows. The grimy and streaked wallpaper had been torn down and the walls had been stripped back to their bare brick. The linoleum had been pulled up to reveal classic dark hardwood floors that had been polished to a black-brown shine and the office furniture had been replaced with stylish flat pack pieces that had taken me three days, and two bottles of good whisky, to construct.

My favourite worn and over-stuffed brown Chesterfield chair still took pride of place against the wall by the door, but my tattered storage boxes had been replaced with steel filing cabinets in which, for the first time, my files were catalogued and stored in a neat and logical order. Adele had done that and had taken a fortnight to teach me the system when all I wanted was my old storage boxes back. The battered electric kettle was gone and, in its place, a chrome espresso machine glimmered in the soft lighting of the room. The cheap oil painting I had bought years ago from Stanley Markets hung on the wall, above the Chesterfield, and threw a splash of colour into the semi-industrial aesthetic of the place.

The addition of a new Class B high-security safe, in which sat two Glock 19s, four 15-round magazines and two cleaning kits, completed the picture. All in all, the office was a much more agreeable place to work and I had managed to retain much of its old-world charm, given my distaste for modernity. I still felt guiltless at taking that cash and had long ago made peace with myself over the dubious morality of that particular life choice. "Fuck 'em" as they say in the classics...

The door swung shut behind me and Adele Chung looked up from her morning newspaper. With the paper in hand and fine China cup and teapot, filled with her favourite Pu'er tea, by her elbow Adele was a woman of habit. Now in her mid-sixties, Adele was the widow of a Sergeant who had worked for me years before in the Hong Kong Police Force. She had 'adopted' me not long after I had left the force, hounded out by the ghost of my father and his reputation, and given her a job in my new investigations business. She still dressed like the headmistress of an elite girls' school and still ruled the office, and me, with an iron fist cloaked in a velvet glove. She was keenly observant, had an acerbic wit and, as I told anyone who cared to listen, took no shit from anyone – least of all me. I called Adele "auntie" but, in truth, she had long ago taken the place of own dead mother. I was a little scared of her and I loved her dearly.

'Jou-san, Galahad. *Good morning,*' she said brightly looking at her watch. 'Again, you surprise me with your arrival before noon. I *am* impressed!'

I had my back to her as I put the coffees down on my desk, so I risked an eye roll before crossing the room to kiss her lightly on the forehead.

'Jou-san a-yi. *Good morning, auntie,*' I said leaning over her shoulder to top up her teacup. 'I have been coming in at 8.00 on the knocker, every day for nearly two years now. When will you stop taking roll on me, huh?'

'Never. Without me you'd still be the half-drunken bum you were when we first met.' She wagged a finger at me. 'You know this zai-zi. *Son*'

I nodded, conceding the point. She was probably right. Adele Chung was rarely far from the mark when it came to me. She looked up and studied me closely, sniffing the air slightly like a tiny, wrinkled gun dog.

'Your eyes are bleary, and you smell of alcohol,' she pronounced. Right again. 'You have a hangover, and you drink too much. *Still!*' Again right. I grimaced apologetically but she went on. 'At least your shirt is ironed, and your shoes and suit pants are clean – but *when* will you stop drinking?'

I wandered back to my desk and flipped the lid off one of the coffees, taking a sip before I replied.

'Jesus, Adele, I gave up smoking! Isn't that enough? It bloody well is for *me*. I can't do both at the same time.' I grinned sheepishly. 'A man has to have some joy in his life...'

She made a huffing, hissing sound like water being thrown on a fire, then flicked up her newspaper and retreated behind it. Knowing that was about all I'd be getting from her for the rest of the morning, I opened my laptop and scrolled slowly through the new emails before checking my calendar for the week.

I had just deleted an email calling on me to sign up for the latest

Human Resources Workplace Counselling Course – where did these people find me, and why would they think I cared? – when the office door clicked open, and Joey walked in. I held the other coffee up toward her and she strode across the office, taking it eagerly. She flipped the lid off into my bin and took a long pull on the lukewarm brew.

'Ahh diu, *fuck*, that's good,' she moaned, collapsing on the dented and scratched leather of the Chesterfield. 'Oh... jou-san Adele.' Adele lifted a hand above the newspaper and winkled her fingers.

'Big night?' I inquired.

Joey shook her head, her bob-cut rotating around her slender neck. 'No, not at all. But a *very* long and busy weekend with Penny.' She ticked off her fingers. 'Movie and hot pot Friday, Disneyland Saturday and PMQ Sunday,' she said, the last referring to the old Hollywood Road Police Married Quarters, now a trendy mixed-use arts and design venue. 'I tell you; the girl is wearing me out!'

'You love it, don't give me that "poor me" bullshit.'

Joey grinned and sighed happily. 'Yeah, I do.'

'How's her training going? You know, the actual Wing Chun apprenticeship?'

Joey shrugged. 'Slowly. It's not as if we jump straight into fighting techniques. I must start up here,' she said, tapping the side of her head. 'I have to get her mentally prepared before she even looks at the practice dummy, let alone learns a technique. Discipline: that's what she needs.'

I recalled the first time I had visited Joey's apartment, at the time still stupidly attracted to her and feeling like a blundering, embarrassed elephant in her traditional and stylishly designed apartment. There had been an obviously well-used, wooden Kung Fu training dummy standing in the corner of her bedroom, and it was clear the lacquer on its arms and the rope bindings at its head were stained with years of sweat and rusty, dried blood. Then I remembered her belting me around the boxing ring the previous Friday and gave an involuntary shudder.

Joey finished her coffee and crossed to her desk to sit down and flick on her laptop.

'No need checking the calendar,' I said, pointing at my laptop screen. 'You'll remember we have that VIP Protection Task this afternoon. 1600 'til whenever. I have a sneaking suspicion it will be a long night.'

Joey nodded. 'Me too,' she said and toed her black kit bag from under her desk. 'I'm ready to go. Advances all done,' she added, referring to the detailed advanced reconnaissance and planning essential to the performance of an effective VIPP job. 'I was back at the venue briefly on Saturday on the way back from Lantau. It all checks out.' She glanced briefly at her phone. 'I think we should do a final clean and check of the handguns, say, about 14:00?'

I knew the weapons were clean and serviceable but approved of Joey's meticulous preparation of all our operational tools, so I nodded my agreement.

'There's just one more thing,' I said. Joey raised her head; an inquiring look on her face. 'The small matter of the final report you're doing on that insurance fraud case last month. It's due today and I can't *wait* to read it ...'

Joey made a similar sound to Adele – it's quite common among Hong Kong women when they're annoyed – and turned to her laptop while I reclined in my chair, hands clasped behind my head, and closed my eyes against the hangover that was finally starting to recede.

3

I FINISHED KNOTTING the dark blue, silk tie and slid my hand down the front of my shirt aligning the buttons, before running my thumbs around my beltline to ensure a secure and neat tuck of my shirt. Old uniform habits die hard and, looking in the full-length mirror behind Adele's desk, I was pleased with what I saw. I turned around as Joey walked across the room from the gun safe. She wore a slim-fit, black suit, open-neck white shirt and black court shoes. A fine gold chain glinted at the open neck of her shirt and disappeared into her cleavage. A small Longines dress watch was visible in front of her left shirt cuff. Her makeup was subdued, and her lustrous black hair shone in the warm orange glow of the office downlights. She looked sensational, and every bit the professional she was.

'We look bloody good, don't we?' I said with a grin.

Joey grinned back and tossed something at me. 'You'll look better wearing that.'

I caught the black Fobus holster and slipped the rubberised paddle between my waistband and right hip, giving it a slight tug to test it was fitted securely. Joey dropped a Glock into her holster, and I did the same, clicking the trigger guard home before shrugging into my suit jacket.

After so many years it was a strange, and not unpleasant, feeling to be again wearing a firearm for work. Our contacts having secured us a role as contract protection agents with the HKPF, the next step had been to obtain firearms licences and licences to carry on duty. That had been easy for Joey, given she had remained licenced for a time after leaving the job, but less so for me. I later found out that concerns had been expressed at some levels about my triad connections, but I had calmed the horses during a long interview at Police Headquarters in Admiralty, at which I presented a convincing, if not entirely truthful, argument that my "connections" were in fact Confidential Informants.

The licence had been duly issued but I could tell by the look on the Inspector's face as he stamped the document and handed it to me, that he was less than impressed. Nonetheless, I adhered strictly to the conditions of the licence and never carried a firearm on any job but our protection tasks with HKPF. Given my past, I really did not want to fight Town Hall on that issue.

Tonight's job was a simple one. As contractors, we were never allocated protection on any senior members of the Hong Kong Government or visiting Mainland dignitaries. Nothing risky. We got the small fish; the ones who really shouldn't have had a protection detail but whose connections or money, or both, had swung it in their favour. In the scheme of things, they were nobodies and, as their protection team, we were even less. That's certainly how the professionals in the VIP Protection Unit played it. They knew Joey from her time on the team and still liked her and engaged with her whenever we were in a briefing or on a task. Me, with thinly veiled disdain, they barely tolerated.

My past – or more to the point, my father's – still stuck to me like a dog turd on the sole of my shoe but I had learned to live with it. All I cared about was that my father's name had been cleared two years previously after Joey and I cracked the sex trafficking case, when new evidence emerged proving my father had been, after all, not guilty of criminal association with a triad. The man who had planted that seed into the HKPF was now dead and had, except for deeply buried records, been excised in an example of *Damnatio Memoriae* the Romans would have been proud of. Still, there in the briefing room, we were the unwanted uncle at Christmas as far as the VIP Protection team were concerned, but I didn't care. The money was excellent, and tonight's job was a simple one.

4

VICTORIA HARBOUR WAS a deep blue and shimmered in the late-afternoon sun.

A blue and white Star Ferry surged across the water from Wan Chai pier, it's bow wave frothing and shining and a gaggle of crying gulls swooped and dived into its wake in search of food. The sun was slowly setting but its rays still glinted powerfully off the building glass across the water in Tsim Sha Tsui and I raised a hand to shield my eyes as I took in the scene up and down the harbour. To the west, some low cloud was beginning to light up in golden yellow and red as the sun started its drop below the peaks of Lantau Island. The glass facades of The Center and the Bank of China Building turned molten and looked to ooze down the sides of the giant skyscrapers. Closer in, a lone Black Kite soared and circled above the harbour, its head swivelling this way and that in search of floating carrion, feathered wing tips adjusting its lift and glide. To the east, two tugs muscled land reclamation barges down the harbour, steering clear of a People's Liberation Army (Navy) Type 056 Corvette steaming into her home harbour, while an ancient sampan bobbed about as two straw-hatted fishermen cast their nets hopefully into the deep.

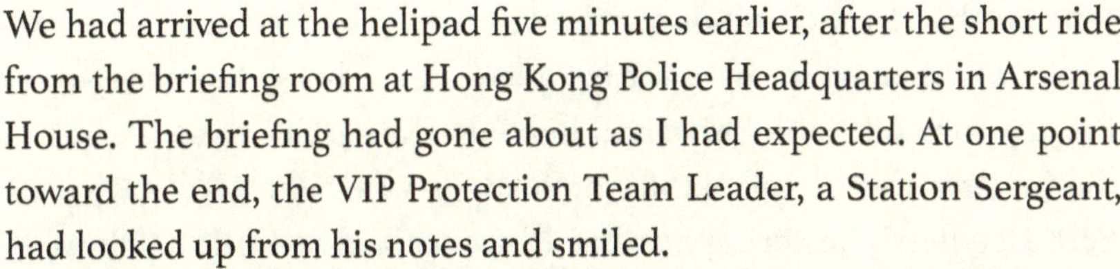

We had arrived at the helipad five minutes earlier, after the short ride from the briefing room at Hong Kong Police Headquarters in Arsenal House. The briefing had gone about as I had expected. At one point toward the end, the VIP Protection Team Leader, a Station Sergeant, had looked up from his notes and smiled.

'Welcome again to Joey and her big side-kick,' he said to the group of men and women gathered in the room. They had chuckled appreciatively and, leaning against a wall at the back of the room, I had smiled tightly back.

'No, seriously, welcome back *former* Senior Inspector Galahad Jones,' he said, not at all seriously and with a poorly disguised sneer. I nodded back graciously, and the briefing wrapped up. 'Usual routine for tonight's task, people. No intelligence to indicate a present threat to Number One and Number Two,' he went on referring to the team's nicknames for the Hong Kong Government's Chief Executive and Chief Secretary respectively. I had to agree. Given what I knew about the Chief Secretary – a secret I wished I didn't share with someone I wished I didn't know – I thought a "threat" was highly unlikely.

'So, it's the usual drill. We arrive, pre drinks, dinner, speeches, we leave. Nice and easy. Timings, routes, seating plan, venue map, communications all in the Operational Order on your tablets.' The Station Sergeant had looked back down at his notes then.

'Oh, just one more thing. Joey...' he said. 'Your assignment has had a shift in transport. Limo occupancies have been shuffled about so the big boys can talk, and your guy has won the lottery. He gets a chopper. So do you and Mr Jones. Enjoy...'

Joey glanced over at me and rolled her eyes. She knew I hated helicopters – there was just too much that could go wrong with them, and I would never voluntarily step into one. I had shrugged back at her as if I didn't care, but my stomach had clenched, and my bowels felt suddenly hot and watery.

~

The whine of two powerful engines snapped my attention back to the helipad as two Pratt & Whitney turboshaft engines came to life, causing the H-175 Cheetah to vibrate on its pad. I glanced at my G-Shock and looked to my right in time to see a black Mercedes-Benz E-Class turn off Expo Drive and head up the service road leading to the Government Flying Service helipad. Joey saw it too and gave me a nod. Needlessly lowering our heads, we walked toward the chopper and positioned ourselves to welcome the Merc. It arrived, pulling up to a smooth stop, and Joey stepped forward to open the rear door while I received a thumbs-up from the pilot and waved Joey in. In minutes, we had seated and secured the VIP and his assistant – a scrawny young man who looked like a weasel – giving them each a headset, slid the wide passenger door shut and taken our own rear-facing seats behind the pilot. I toggled the Push-To-Talk on my headset and told the pilot we were clear to go. With a roar of the engines that bounced the aircraft, the Cheetah lifted smoothly off the helipad and pointed north for a moment before swooping off to the west and our destination. I felt sick and swallowed down hard.

I wanted to look out of the window and take in the scene flying over a darkening Hong Kong, the cars and trucks like Matchbox toys below us, the major roads lit like branches of a Christmas tree, but as I was facing the VIP I decided to go to straight-face-eyes-forward mode. I noticed Joey was sitting rock still with her sunglasses on – I suspected her eyes were closed as she took a short rest; she'd seen this all a hundred times before.

We were a minute into the short trip when the VIP's assistant opened a briefcase and handed his boss a copy of the day's South China Herald. The VIP nodded his thanks, flicked open the paper and thumbed straight to the business section. The newspaper was raised in front of his face, at eye level to me, so I decided to pass the time by scanning the front page. My eyes took in the headlines, passing quickly from one to another. *"Bus overturn in Tsuen Wan." "HKD drops to lowest in 6 months." "Chief Exec to outline economic plan at dinner tonight."* Seeing nothing of interest, I was about to glance away when a headline in the bottom right of the page caught my eye.

"Gruesome murder in Tai Mo Shan – hikers find body." The story was brief, so I read on.

"The mutilated body of what is believed to be a young man was yesterday found in Tai Mo Shan Country Park. Two hikers on a remote hiking section off the Maclehose Trail came across the remains in thick vegetation, alerted to its presence by the smell as they passed by. They contacted Police and the area was quickly sealed off and a crime scene established.

Police have yet to comment on the case. "It was absolutely horrible" said one of the hikers, Mr Lam Gang-fa. "The body was so mutilated we couldn't tell what it was. I thought it was maybe a wild pig at first. Then we saw the ropes... it was a nightmare." Mr Lam's companion was too distraught to speak to The Herald. Police investigations continue and a statement from Arsenal House is expected soon."

That *was* news. While murder wasn't unknown in Hong Kong, it was rare and particularly violent murders were even rarer. With a shudder I recalled the charnel house inside an apartment two years before, the bloodied and brutalised human remains derailing my hunt for a trafficking gang. Rare but not unheard of... I gave a mental shrug. It was tragic, someone's son was dead in what looked like violent circumstances, but it had nothing to do with me and I wasn't prepared to give it any more thought. My life was sailing along nicely I thought, as the chopper skimmed smoothly toward a landing pad on top of a Kowloon-side skyscraper. No lonely death on a hiking trail was going to change that.

The chopper touched gently down, and I eased a sigh of relief, offering a slight grin to Joey. We quickly disembarked and I was thankful to see the hotel reception committee waiting for us to the side of the helipad. The last-minute change of transportation meant neither Joey nor I had any idea how to exit the roof and locate the function venue from that approach. Joey stepped back behind the VIP and The Weasel, while I moved in front, allowing the hotel staff to greet our man and lead him off the roof. We entered a wide stair-well, well-lit and, like every skyscraper stairwell in Hong Kong, smelling of the rich earth aroma of clean concrete. The person in charge of the hotel team, a small, rotund man with a round, cheery face, directed me down and gave me the number of the floor into which we should emerge. After only two flights I pushed open a door and we entered a thickly carpeted, softly lit corridor lined with valuable works of Chinese porcelain. Chinese traditional music played quietly through the corridor, and we stepped up to the bank of lifts. Cheery Face – who according to his nametag was 'Clarence' – ushered us all into a lift and pressed a button. I glanced at Joey.

'Why are we going to Ground, Clarence?' I asked in Cantonese. 'Can we not go straight to the functions floor?'

Clarence looked up at me in mild surprise. Despite being mixed-race, I look only very faintly Chinese, inheriting my Hong Kong-born English father's Anglo-Celt green eyes and skin complexion; while my mother, herself a mixed-race Hong Konger, had given me her dark hair and a very slight curvature to my eyes. Clarence was surprised and amused by what appeared to be a *Gweilo* speaking to him in fluent Cantonese. He answered me politely.

'Oh, I am so sorry. We have two elevator towers, so to access the functions floors we need to first go to Ground then change lift lobbies to go back up.'

I nodded and shrugged. No problems. The lift hummed quietly downwards, and I studied the closed doors waiting for them to open which they did with no warning, so smooth had been the ride. I stepped out, allowing Joey to move around me. She had done the advances and knew exactly where the correct lift tower was, so she cut her way across the crowded hotel lobby with the rest of us in tow.

Large chandeliers hung overhead and threw a bright light over the lobby, their teardrop crystals clinking faintly in the air conditioning. The room was filled with the well-heeled of Hong Kong: business leaders, politicians, influencers; the men in bespoke dark suits, tailored shirts, cuffs shot and pinned with expensive cufflinks. The women in diaphanous, low-cut and backless creations drifted and flowed across the lobby to the delicate tic-tack of Louboutin and Valentino heels. Over it all settled a loud hum of conversation, broken now and then by laughter. The vibe was up and, for these people, it was time to party. From the corner of my eye I saw another team with their VIP enter, with yet another behind them. The heavy hitters were starting to arrive by limo which presaged the grand arrival of both the Chief Executive and Chief Secretary.

We had not gone more than five metres when the loud buzz of the lobby crowd was disturbed by another, sharper sound. A name had been screamed out and it took me a second to realise it was the name of our VIP. As I began to turn, I saw Joey spin on her heels and look back past me. Our VIP's mouth was open in shock, and I caught a glimpse of his eyes, the flare of recognition clear on his face for a split second before Joey covered him up. The lobby was suddenly chaos. Women were screaming and chairs were overturned as people scrambled away from a threat they could not see but instinctively knew was coming. The sound of breaking glass rose sharp in the air as a hotel concierge was shouldered aside and through a large windowpane by the front doors of the hotel. The two protection teams were covering their VIPs, concerned only with getting them out of the way of whatever trouble was coming in. Suddenly the seething, panicked crowd parted, and I was face to face with a lone man who shouted the name again.

'Chan! *Chaaaan,* you *bastard*!' He launched himself forward, a wicked butcher's knife gleaming in his right hand. I heard Joey shout behind me, and a scuffle as she hustled the VIP away from danger. The attacker was two metres from me, and slightly to my right, when I moved. I ran in hard and low, taking him in a rugby tackle that lifted him from the ground and slammed him down onto the marble floor of the lobby.

Despite the wind being knocked from him, he flailed with his arm and the edge of the knife blade bit into the shoulder of my suit jacket and scored a slash across my shirt, slicing open the skin on my chest. I grabbed the hand holding the knife and crashed it onto the floor, then twisted as savagely as I could. The attacker screamed, but more in frustration than in pain, and bucked hard under me to throw me off. I grabbed the fringe of his hair and lifted his head, slamming it into the floor. Still he fought. I was reaching for my holster when the muzzle of a Glock jammed into the attacker's forehead, and he froze.

'Go on,' Joey breathed seductively into his ear. 'Move. Make me do it.'

The air seemed to go out of him then and he sagged beneath me. I let go of the grip of my handgun and was readying to punch him between the eyes when I saw the tears. He was gently crying. Quietly and with great dignity, he wept. I lowered my arm and stood up while Joey flipped the attacker onto his stomach, pulled his arms behind his back and handcuffed him.

Slowly, things returned to some sanity in the lobby. Guests re-entered the room – many looking shamefaced – and watched on with interest, muttering amongst themselves. I swivelled my head and saw the VIP Team Leader moving from a side room toward us.

'You okay?' Joey asked, looking at my bloodied chest.

I glanced down. It stung but I didn't think any major damage had been done. 'Yeah, okay.' I let out a long breath. 'Jesus, that was close.'

'What the *fuck* was...' Joey began but was interrupted as the Team Leader reached us. He looked down at the immobile and silent attacker and toed the butcher's knife with his shoe. He looked me in the eye and a grim smile broke his face.

'*Diu*, man! That was some work. Great job.'

I nodded but didn't smile back. 'Thanks. Our guy was the target, but I don't think it's political.'

'Oh? That's an amazingly quick conclusion, Mr Jones. Why?'

I indicated the miserable form on the floor with a nod of my head. 'Take a look at him,' I said. 'Middle-aged. Flip-flops, threadbare shirt and pants, no jacket. It's winter and freezing out there. He's hungry and filthy. Can you smell him?'

The Team Leader took a deep sniff. 'Yes, he stinks. He needs a bath.'

I shook my head. 'No not *that*... well, yes, that but also what's all over his clothes and skin? It's old cooking oil. See the rice and bits of meat stuck to his pants?' I pointed at the knife. 'That's his butcher's knife. He's a street stall cook. Since when are street stall cooks hired for a political assassination?' I remembered the tears on the man's face and the abject sadness in his eyes. I shook my head again. 'No. I don't doubt he meant to carry the attack through, but this is personal somehow. He may even just be a nutcase who needs to be tucked up between clean sheets in Castle Peak,' I added, referring to Hong Kong's oldest psychiatric hospital.

'Well, either way, he's for the jump after this little show.' The Team Leader gestured over his shoulder with his thumb to the sound of sirens outside. 'The uniforms are here now so they'll deal with it. Meanwhile we carry on... We've got a dinner to go to.' He paused looking at me again. 'But *you* don't; you're a mess. Joey can cover your man. Get yourself patched up then go home and take rest.'

I began to object but he held up his hand. 'No. Hospital, *now* please. Get a uniform to drive you.'

I nodded silently and turned to leave the lobby.

'Mr Jones, sir!' the Team Leader called out. I turned. 'Thanks. Really. Great work and welcome to the team.' I nodded again, waved briefly over his shoulder to Joey, and left the hotel.

5

A WEEK later I sat at the front table of a small Italian bar in Soho, facing out onto the intersection of Staunton and Aberdeen streets, and grimaced as I sipped a beer.

'I don't want to,' I said.

'You sound like a whining child,' the woman next to me replied. 'And besides, you don't have a choice. You're doing it.'

I scratched absently at the stitches on my chest. The knife blade had torn the cloth of my jacket at the left shoulder and had cut a deep gouge across my left breast that had required six stitches. It itched annoyingly. The fact I had lost my suit jacket and a tailored white shirt had hurt me more than the wound. The cost of replacing both, when I visited my tailor just off Des Voeux Road in Central, would hurt more still. I gave my sister a hard stare, an "I've-made-my-decision-and-you-won't-change-it" stare, but she didn't flinch.

'Gal, when was the last time I asked anything of you? Meanwhile, you've borrowed a huge splodge of cash from me – only recently repaid I might add – wrecked my car – and yes, the new car was very much appreciated and I still ask myself where you found the money for *that* – *and* I had to throw out my sofa after you bled all over it. Do you recall all that...?'

It was all true. Two years ago I had turned to my younger sister, Prudence, after a savage beating over a large gambling debt I had owed to Jade Tooth, the triad-connected owner of an illegal Mahjong club in Yau Ma Tei, and one of Hong Kong's most violent men. She had treated my wounds then had loaned me the entire sum of 325,000 Hong Kong Dollars with which I had paid my way out of what was, almost certainly, a gruesome death and watery grave somewhere off Lamma Island.

Her new Mini Cooper S had been badly damaged when it had been shot out by a rogue cop, acting on the orders of his boss who I had been tracking at the time in connection to a sex-trafficking ring. I had bled heavily in the car, having taken a round in my right arm. I also had a faint recollection of urinating in the car, at some stage, as heavy rain had poured in through the shattered windows while I staked out a house. To cap it all off, I had totalled the car when I had driven around a blind corner and into my target's parked car on a dark and rainy Shek O Road.

I pulled again at my beer and glanced sideways at Pru. She was sipping an Aperol Spritz, watching me closely.

She had inherited our mother's jaw-dropping, classic beauty and looked much more Chinese than I did – me looking far more like our father. She was almost as tall as me, as slim as an Egret and twice as graceful. Her long obsidian-black hair framed a heart-shaped face from which a pair of dark, perfectly formed almond eyes viewed the world with keen interest, a degree of amusement and a good dose of healthy cynicism. A former model, her marriage to the son of one of Hong Kong's wealthiest families had gone belly up after her husband had been found, himself belly up, in a mistress's apartment with a needle in his arm. She had inherited his wealth and was now one of Hong Kong's leading art dealers and socialites. Prudence was strong, confident and accomplished. I had said it many times over the years and thought it again now: she was everything I was not. She rarely asked me for a favour but now she was asking that I meet her new boyfriend. I sighed and put my beer down.

'Okay, Pru,' I said with a grin. 'Sure. Why not?' She clapped her hands and laughed happily, the sound like a soft wind tinkling through temple chimes. She leaned across the gap between our bar stools and kissed my cheek.

'Thank you daaih lo, *big brother*,' she said, eyes shining. 'Honestly, you'll *love* him.'

I winced. 'I doubt that. So, what's the story with this guy? Start with his name.'

Pru put down her drink and slapped her legs. 'Well, let's see... he's name is Giles, he's English. He's some sort of senior guy in a private bank.' I rolled my eyes. Bankers were right up there for me with used-car salesmen, reality TV stars and politicians. Pru jabbed me in the ribs. 'Stop it, baak ci, *idiot*! He's lovely.' She sighed deeply, her eyes taking on a wistful, faraway look. I shuddered.

'He's just so... *beautiful*. He's handsome – my *God* he's good looking – intelligent, well-spoken, well-dressed. He's a *great* lover; exciting and daring...' I put my face in my hands at that. '... Oh, and did I mention he's rich?'

I frowned. 'Pru, you're one of the richest people I know. You don't need the money. That's not a reason...'

She held up her hand. 'Chill, brother. I'm just kidding.' She tapped her red lips with a superbly manicured finger and glanced up. 'Mind you, it doesn't hurt does it. At least he won't be sponging off me...'

I nodded. 'Yes, good point. So, what else? Previous relationships? How long has he been in this job? Where does he come from in England and how long has he been in Hong Kong? Where does he live? Any family?' I realised I was slipping into type and grinned. Lighten up! 'Oh, and which club does he follow?' I asked, referring to Hong Kong's hard-fought domestic rugby competition.

'I shall answer that last one, but you can save your police interrogation for when you meet him. He is training now with Valley.' I snorted. As a Hong Kong Scottish member and former player, I didn't like anyone outside of 'The Rock', our home ground in Shek Kip Mei. I had a special disdain for 'Valley'. I couldn't resist Pru's excitement, so I relented and gave her a hug.

'Are you happy sai mui, *younger sister*?' I asked quietly. 'You've been alone for a while now so that's all that matters to me...'

She squeezed my hand. I looked down and saw our mother's slim gold ring, with a small ruby inlay, on the ring finger of her right hand. She never took it off. '*Deliriously*, my darling!' she said. 'He is so attentive, polite, honourable... he treats me with respect and kindness.'

We both looked at each other for a long minute, the silence stretching comfortably before us. We were all that was left of our close-knit and loving family after the death of our father and subsequent suicide of our heart-broken mother. Pru was all I had in the world – at least until my on-again, off-again girlfriend, Angel, returned from wherever she was. I was glad Prudence had finally found someone. Still, I hated the idea of any man coming close to my kid sister. I'm old-fashioned that way.

I moved back to the bar and signalled the barman for another two drinks. While I waited, I bit down on the ever-present urge for a cigarette that was especially acute when I drank. I missed my old leather tobacco pouch and the scent of the double-cherry tobacco like an old friend who had left town and never wrote. I sighed deeply and tried to think of something else. I was sure meeting Pru's new boyfriend would make me want to drink and smoke but I would just have to be mature about it – I was fairly sure I could manage that.

I was waiting for the drinks, leaned back casually on the bar, when I glanced out onto Staunton Street. Across the road, on the corner with Aberdeen Street, stood a man.

He was mid-thirties, slightly above average height, overweight and balding. He was looking straight into the bar at me. As I caught his eye he pushed his glasses up his nose and smiled. I realised I knew him – at least I knew *of* him. He was an expat, a trader on the money market and was a known loose cannon. Rumour had it he was a cocaine addict and had particularly deviant sexual preferences. I frowned as I turned back to the bar. His name was Toby something. I had met him, briefly, perhaps twice but had barely spoken to him other than to note he seemed to have an unhealthy fascination with me and what I did for a living. He was a loner and, as far as I knew, had not a single friend in Hong Kong. I looked back and he was gone so I shrugged it off. Toby was a little unhinged but basically harmless. The fact he was standing outside a popular bar in Soho meant nothing.

The barman slid the drinks across to me and I took them back to our table. Pru and I sipped at them, chatting for two more hours as the sun went down over Hong Kong and the restaurant lights came on in Soho, shining bright red, yellow, blue and green into the narrow streets as the late-afternoon drinks crowd milled sedately about in the cool evening air. There were dogs on leashes everywhere and fit young things springing by in gym gear, despite the cold. Staunton Street was its usual chaotic jam of impatient taxis, delivery vans and luxury cars that always just seems to work itself out without too many tempers fraying. Up and down the street, over the noise of the car exhausts and honking horns, laughter and clinking glasses rang out into the purple twilight. The sound system in the bar played Led Zeppelin's "Babe, I'm Gonna Leave You". Page's hard riffs and Bonham's crashing drums had me nodding along as Pru and I chatted. It was a good place to be.

Eventually, Prudence kissed me on the cheek with a parting 'See you soon. Don't be late,' and hailed a cab to her apartment only a few hundred metres up the hill in Mid-Levels. I finished my beer, paid the bill and walked off down Staunton Street toward the Mid-Levels escalators, having decided to walk the three kilometres home through the back streets of Wan Chai.

6

It had been a mild day for November and now, with the coming of night, the temperature was dropping rapidly and I could feel the chill in my lungs as I breathed in deeply. Once I left Central, I headed uphill and into the maze of small streets and laneways that I often took when walking home. I wasn't sure they were a short cut, but they were often deserted and I enjoyed the peace. Stuffing my hands into the pockets of my jeans, I headed along a darkened Moon Street toward the stairs down to Queen's Road East.

As I walked, I noticed a fog descending around me, cloaking the street and shopfronts in a thin white gauze that was slowly thickening, swirling about like a wraith, insubstantial and faintly menacing. I shrugged. Fog was rare in Winter, being much more likely to appear in Hong Kong in Spring, but fog it was and it sent a chill through me as I pulled up the collar of my denim jacket and tightened the thin scarf about my neck.

I had reached the top of the steep stairs and was about to step down when I paused. The hair prickled on the back of my neck. Behind me footsteps suddenly stopped. I turned my head and listened intently. The laneway was silent except for the scuffle of a rat and the far-off piping of a Scops Owl. Far below me the traffic on

Queen's Road was a soft hum. The laneway was dark. I stood in a patch of yellow streetlight at the top of the stairs. Fifty metres away, through a tunnel of darkened fog, stood another streetlight.

I could see nothing. I leaned forward slightly and squinted my eyes, peering through the dark. There, on the other side of the distant streetlight I could make out a figure, immobile and indistinct in the dark. I stood perfectly still and watched. The figure didn't move, and I was beginning to think I was imagining things when it shuffled slightly and began, it seemed, to step slowly backwards.

'Who's there?' I shouted, annoyed that my voice cracked slightly. There was no answer.

The figure began to move back more quickly, and I could hear its footsteps retreating down the lane. I sprang forward and ran after it, quickly closing the gap to the next streetlight and the dark beyond its golden penumbra where I stopped. I controlled my breathing and listened.

All was silence and the figure was gone. Turning quickly on my heel I retraced my steps and ran smoothly down the stairs, took an alley off to the right and, in moments, emerged out into the light of St Francis Street where I stopped and looked back. Seeing nothing, I moved slowly downhill and onto Queen's Road East. There was no doubt in my mind: I had been followed and that was never a good sign. The question was by whom and why?

I couldn't immediately think of any reason why someone would have been stalking me down a darkened laneway and run off when challenged. I had kept my nose clean in the two years since the Dragon's Back case, owed no one money and had avoided almost all contact with both of Hong Kong's main triads, 14K and Sun Yee On. How did the figure know I would be there? *I* didn't even know I would take that route until I had. That meant he – I assumed it to have been a 'he' from the sound of the footsteps – had to have been following me long before that. Had he watched as Prudence and I had sat and drank together? Did he know where Prudence lived? I shivered at the thought.

Pulling out my phone, I tapped on my sister's contact. She

answered after two rings, and I heaved a sigh of relief to hear her voice.

'What's up?' she said.

'Nothing Pru. Just wanted to say "goodnight".'

She chuckled. 'Well *goodnight,* Gal. Again.'

I hung up. It was puzzling, although I wasn't alarmed. I told myself I was jumping, literally, at shadows. It could have been anyone and I had probably scared them as much as they had me. But a stab of doubt pricked at me – my instincts told me something was amiss, and I had learnt long ago to trust my instincts. In the excitement of the moment, I had completely forgotten about Toby whoever-he-was. I was still wrestling with the problem when I toed open the door to my apartment to be greeted by Bors surging out of his dog bed and across my tiny loungeroom. The events of the evening were still on my mind when I finally collapsed into bed. Perhaps it was the beer but, despite the nagging feeling that something was closing in on me, I soon drifted off into a deep, dreamless sleep.

7

You want to know about the young man at Tai Mo Shan. I chose him because he was there – of course I knew I had to have a partner, but I didn't care who or where. He was there and then... he wasn't. I've come a long way since the early day. My skills are really quite advanced. I prolonged that young man's agony for hours: cutting, pulling, and stretching. He wouldn't let go. He kept living and screaming, screaming into the night and the longer he lasted, the more he screamed, the longer I lasted until I could hold myself no longer. When I had taken the last of the skin from his face he started to slip away. I held my breath waiting for the instant he drew his last. When it came, so did I. I carved the letters in his back, and I took his watch.

8

The next day dawned bright and clear, and the apartment terrace was shadowed and frigid when I stepped out, barefoot, in my shorts to drink an espresso.

Above me, Mount Cameron and The Peak shone dark green in the rising sun, stark against a deep blue and cloudless sky. I scratched at Bors' ears while I contemplated the scene, breathing deep at the fresh morning air and running over in my mind the plan for the day.

The events of the week before had played on me and I couldn't shake them. I was convinced there was more to the attack on my VIP than met the eye – and that the assassination angle just didn't stack up. I was also certain our man had recognised the attacker, even though, at that stage, he had heard only his voice and not seen his face. More than anything, I was called by the image of the attacker's face, rumpled in despair with tears coursing down his weathered cheeks. It had nagged me for a week. I had finally decided to do something about it and had put two calls in to Hong Kong Police Headquarters at Arsenal House the previous afternoon.

I shaved carefully that morning and caught myself frowning at my reflection in the mirror. My green eyes looked back at me, clear but from whites that were flecked with red. The crow's feet in their corners were slowly turning from "lines of experience" into deep wrinkles and I pinched and stretched at them with one hand while prodding the bags under my eyes with another. Age was catching up with me and my "lifestyle choices" – as Adele loved to call them at every possible opportunity – weren't helping. I glanced down at my gut and pulled miserably at the roll that had been developing around my middle the past few months. Angel liked to poke it and I hated when she did. My right knee ached, as it always did in the morning, and my neck was stiff. All in all, I was finding being 47 wasn't all that it's cracked up to be.

Having shaved and showered, I pulled on a pair of navy chinos then slipped on a crisp, white shirt, tucking it in smoothly. A brown leather belt, pair of desert boots and tan jacket completed the picture. I nodded at myself in the mirror, threw some food into Bors' bowl, grabbed a banana from the bowl in the kitchen and let myself out.

Out on Morrison Hill Road I was immediately hit by the din of the traffic and buffeted by the warm exhaust of close-passing double-decker buses. The footpath was packed as the neighbourhood bustled it's way on and off buses or joined the steady stream of humanity that flowed down through the wet markets towards Causeway Bay MTR Station. I peeled the banana and stuffed it into my mouth, then looked up toward Happy Valley Racecourse just in time to see a red taxi round the bend and the driver nod at my raised hand. He pulled in against the double yellows and I leapt in, slamming the door behind me and we surged off into the peak hour traffic.

The calls I had made the day before had been to my old friend, Station Sergeant Billy Wong, and the Team Leader on the VIPP team Joey and I were contracted to. The former had been pleased to hear from me, but the latter less so – he had sounded unimpressed when I had put my request to him but had agreed, grudgingly, to help nonetheless. In a little over 30 minutes, having taken a short cut that landed us in gridlock, the taxi pulled up and I stepped out onto the footpath.

Arsenal House loomed over me, heavily secured and imposing. It was the last piece in the development of HKPHQ that had begun in the '80s and ended up in a rambling compound in Wan Chai, with several wings and the old Caine House where my own office had once been. I stepped through the large double glass doors and the old police station smell of boot polish, floor wax and Brasso wafted comfortingly over me.

I had first smelt that heady brew as a child when my father had taken me into the old Wan Chai Police Station, and it never failed to wrap me in gentle, nostalgic arms. I thought ruefully, and not for the first time, that I really was getting old. I pulled out my new contractor ID and approached the front desk constable in the bright and airy foyer. Buried somewhere deep in the recruiting manual is guidance for the recruitment and selection of front desk constables: unsmiling, taciturn to the point of vow-of-silence, while still being brusque bordering on rude. The young female constable on the desk that morning was a perfect fit, and I made a mental note to drop a congratulatory note to the recruiting OIC. She looked at me, one eyebrow cocked, her hands motionless on the desk in front of her.

'Galahad Jones to see Station Sergeant Wong and Station Sergeant Li,' I said in Cantonese, smiling warmly and handing over my ID. 'I have an appointment at 10,' I added, glancing at my G-Shock. The constable glared at my ID then back at a screen in front of her, her face immobile. She tapped a few keys of the computer then picked up a phone and spoke softly into it.

'Yes, sir,' she said finally, looking back at me. 'I see that here. Sergeant's Wong and Li are waiting. Ground floor, Meeting Room Three, just to the left past security.' She handed back my ID and gestured with a nod of her head toward the security guard standing by the bag scanner and security gates. I thanked her and, not having a bag, bypassed the scanner, swiped my ID on the gate and passed through, turning left into a brightly lit corridor. The meeting room was two down on the left and I paused briefly before knocking on the door and stepping in.

Billy Wong was the first to stand and he moved across the room, his hand extended and a broad grin on his round face. I noticed he had put on more weight since I had last seen him some 12 months earlier at the conclusion of the reopened inquiry into my father's conduct and death. He was short, round, stuffed into his uniform like an overripe fruit, and unceasingly happy. Billy and I went back many years, to a time before he was injured in a gunfight in Tsuen Wan and, after his recovery, relegated to office duties for the rest of his career. I liked him a great deal and was secretly envious of his balanced and content approach to life. He shook my hand vigorously and slapped my shoulder.

'*Diu*, Mr Jones, it's good to see you sir! It's been, what, a year?'

I nodded. 'About that Billy... and you can drop the "Mr Jones" and "sir" thing now I think.'

He shook his head, his face serious. 'Never! You were always my ranking officer and that you shall stay.'

I decided it was pointless to pursue that, so switched tack. 'How's Mandy and the family?'

Billy winced and his face seemed to sag 'Mandy's not good, Mr Jones. Cancer...'

'Shit, Billy. I'm sorry...'

'No need. No need,' he said hurriedly. 'She's comfortable and not in too much pain. The kids spend as much time with her as they can and I'm on regular day shifts so I'm with her every afternoon and night.' He sighed and blinked rapidly. 'So many years together, to come to this...'

I recalled that both of Billy and Mandy's children were criminal lawyers in the city – it had been a joke of ours that Billy had to keep quiet about having lawyers in his family. I also hadn't forgotten that Billy's nephew, Michael, had replaced my oldest friend, Peter Toh, as Chief Inspector in the OCTB – Organised Crime and Triad Bureau – after Peter had murdered a fellow corrupt cop and tried to do the same to me before disappearing. I knew Michael Wong didn't like me and I had been expecting that to come to a head for two years. There was an uncomfortable silence in the room before Billy broke it with a clap of his hands and his ever-present grin.

'So, of course, you know Sergeant Caesar Li.'

I nodded. 'Station Sergeant,' I said in greeting. Li sat erect, and slim, in a chair at the head of the table and nodded back. His hair was greying and cut short in a buzz cut that accentuated his angular face and high cheek bones. His eyes, brown and bright, regarded me openly with a hint of amusement that crinkled the lines of his mouth. He surprised me again by addressing me as "sir". Things had certainly changed in the VIPP Team since I had tackled the attacker at the reception the week before.

'So,' Li said. 'Shall we get down to it?'

I sat in a chair and addressed the two men in front of me. 'It's pretty simple really,' I began in Cantonese. 'I want to visit the man who attacked Chan Yi-chen.'

Li's eyebrows shot up. 'Guo Yu-xuan? Why? I mean, he's banged up in Stanley and I'm pretty sure he's on a "no visitation" card. He's possibly facing terrorism charges, Mr Jones and that could mean life... 15 to 20 minimum I'd say. In case you forget, you're the man who brought him down. Why would you want to see him? What's the point?'

'I agree,' I said mildly. 'Like I said on the night, and in my statement, I don't deny that Chan was the target, but I just don't think it's political. I'm convinced there's something more here...' I shrugged. 'It could mean something lesser than a terrorism charge and that could mean the difference of a few decades in high security,' I said, thinking of Stanley Prison, one of the six maximum security facilities in Hong Kong. It was also the oldest and had been the location of the brutal Stanley Internment Camp during the Japanese occupation of Hong Kong. 'I've got an itch on this one that I need to scratch... all it will take is one visit, half an hour, tops. That's all I'll need: my hunch will either be wrong or right and surely it's worth it if we can get to the bottom of what happened and why...'

Li looked sceptical. 'Counter Terror investigators from 'A' Department *and* homicide investigators from 'B' Department have interviewed the guy. He made admissions. Chan was his target, he intended to kill him.'

'Anything else?'

Li shifted a little in his chair. 'No. He's not giving on his motive or who's behind him. He's prepared to take the fall so whoever hired him must be very heavy indeed...'

'*If* someone hired him...'

'Mr Jones, come *on* ... sometimes things are just what they seem. My advice: drop it.'

I couldn't help myself. 'My father was considered a corrupt copper from the time of his murder in 1987 to just last year after the new inquest cleared him. *That* wasn't what it seemed, now was it...?

Li winced and nodded. He knew all about the human trafficking case that had led me and Joey through a maze of corrupt senior police and government officials and, possibly, knew of the triad entanglements that had snared me during the case The case had ended in a trail of bodies and irrefutable proof of my father's innocence after decades of family shame. Li sighed.

'Yes, okay. Point taken. So, assuming I agree, the question is *how* do we swing it? I mean, you are nothing to the investigation but a witness, you're not even the arresting officer. No offence, but you're a *private investigator* for God's sake! You have no entitlement to interview the suspect – as a witness, you shouldn't even really be *seeing* him – and no reason to be permitted entry to Stanley...'

Billy Wong spoke up, tapping an index finger against his lips. 'I think I can help there.' We both turned to look at him. 'Yes. My cousin is a Senior Superintendent in CSD,' he said, referring to the Hong Kong Correctional Services Department. 'I'm sure approval for a half hour visit is possible.'

I laughed out loud. 'You see, Billy? *This* is why I called you! I knew if anyone could get me in you could... or possibly Michael.'

Billy grimaced. 'Mr Jones, Michael is *much* too busy on ...something else.' I was about to ask what could be demanding the attention of a Chief Inspector in OCTB when Billy went on. 'Besides he is more likely to want to see you *resident* inside Stanley than let you visit an inmate.'

Billy was right about that, and I shivered slightly. 'Okay. Fair point. So, when can we set this up?

The three of us spoke for another five minutes, during which we agreed on the process to obtain the visit pass. After much argument, Li refused to let me go in alone and said that he would escort me to Stanley and would sit in on the meeting – that way we could, however tenuously, at least link the visit to the investigation. In a way, that was exactly what I was trying to do. Billy was confident we could achieve this within the week but urged me to exercise patience.

'For which you are not well known, Mr Jones, but do please try.'

We had wrapped up and were walking back out through the corridor when Li turned to me. 'I almost forgot, he said. 'I need to debrief Chan – he hasn't been available until tomorrow afternoon – so you had better come along. Your perspective will be useful in the debrief.' I nodded and Li went on. '*But* you will sit there, shut your mouth, and not offer an opinion unless asked and you *certainly* won't ask any questions. Okay?'

'Sure,' I said. 'Eyes and ears open, mouth shut. I can do that.'

Li shook his head glumly. 'Somehow I doubt that Mr Jones.'

9

I PASSED the rest of the afternoon in the office catching up on paperwork. Adele was away visiting a cousin in Shantou, on the eastern coast of Guangdong, and Joey was interviewing a prospective client in what was shaping up to be another reasonably interesting insurance fraud job. I had the office to myself. I switched on the Bluetooth sound system, made an espresso, and settled back in my chair as the brassy funk of Kenny Wayne Shepherd's "Diamonds & Gold" filled the room. As Adele was away, I turned the music up – I would never have dared done that had she been in the office. I sat sipping at the coffee, shuffling the papers on my desk when a section of lyrics sounded clear in my consciousness.

I felt my heart thump a little harder and my face redden as the lyrics, warning of selling your soul for diamonds and gold, pointed a finger accusingly at me. It was the money of course. Two years before, with a bullet wound to my temple, left arm pinned and in a cast, and my right arm aching badly from another gunshot wound, I had scrabbled around in the vegetation hanging off a cliff near Shek O and come away with a large duffle bag. The bag had held bundles of US $100-dollar notes, neatly secured in ziplock bags. Two and a half million in US of cleanly laundered triad cash, to be precise. I had dragged the bag home and kept the money. Not a person in the world knew at the time I had it and now, nearly three years later, that still seemed to be the case. My conscience hadn't troubled me then and still didn't, but every now and then it pricked at me – less out of a sense of guilt at what I had done, but more in a rising fear that one day, soon, I would be rumbled.

I swallowed the last of the coffee as Kenny Wayne sang on about reaping what you sew. It sounded like a dark prognostication, and I shivered superstitiously and killed the music, listening to the sound of my heart hammering in my ears in the sudden silence of the office. With an effort I pushed down on the demons that swirled around me. I turned to the papers on my desk and shuffled through a series of bills and invoices, piling them up for Adele to deal with when she got back, then read through Joey's final report on the fraud case we had completed a month before.

I couldn't concentrate as the song lyrics reverberated in my mind. I turned to my statement into the incident at the hotel – I wanted to be across that before I met the suspect and, in particular, the VIP Walter Chan. Still, I couldn't focus. I rubbed my eyes and physically shook myself.

'Jesus Christ,' I muttered. 'Get a *grip*, Galahad!'

Everything was fine. Hell, I had only stolen from thieves! The money was mine. I deserved it and what it had brought to me, and others. Life was good, I told myself, and nothing would get in my way. My old English teacher at St. Paul's College would have called that hubris and he would have been right. I didn't know it then, but, true to the finest tradition of Greek tragedy, my pride and defiance of the gods was leading me inexorably into the cold, vengeful arms of Nemesis.

10

Later that same afternoon, I sat at a table of a small bar high up in Mid-Levels. The outdoor heaters were burning, and I had shrugged out of my puffer jacket as I sipped at the beer in front of me. The last, weak rays of the sun shone pleasantly on my face, dappled through the leaves of the big trees of Jamia Mosque. The mosque's gardens, encircled by high rise apartment towers, were a call back to a quieter, simpler past and I had always enjoyed the sense of calm they brought.

By now, I had dismissed the fears and doubts that had nearly consumed me in the office – I'd always been able to juggle moral dilemmas to my advantage – and was enjoying the peace of the late afternoon.

On the way up through Soho and Mid-Levels I had had the feeling I was being followed. It was a familiar, crawling feeling on the back of my neck – a feeling I had long trusted – and it had been with me almost from the moment I stepped out of my office in Sheung Wan. I had used every counter-surveillance trick I knew to spot the tail. I had checked my reflection in shop windows pretending to fix my hair and had turned suddenly on my heels as if forgetting something. I had entered shops and watched out the front windows for anyone propping nearby and had wandered down deserted alleys. I had seen nothing, but the feeling had stayed with me until I had sat at the bar when it suddenly disappeared. The experience had left me a little rattled and, not for the first time, I had unconsciously patted my pockets for my tobacco pouch and sighed when I came up empty.

I wasn't thinking much in particular when I suddenly tuned in to the conversation of two expats at a table to my left. After a few vulgar references to a woman and what had transpired the previous Friday evening, their conversation changed tack.

'So, did you see The Herald this morning? There's been another murder...'

'Shit! Really?'

'Yes, another *bad* one, up on a hiking trail again but this time on The Island. Somewhere along the Hong Kong Trail, above Pok Fu Lam. Looks like the same M.O – the victim had been butchered. A young woman this time. Bloody *awful*. The paper is pushing a "serial killer" angle, but the cops are hosing that down.'

'Well two in, how long is it... two weeks? Looks like a pattern to me.'

'What the fuck would you know? You're an accountant...'

'I don't need to be Sherlock Holmes to work out two victims, similarly murdered, both on hiking trails, in two weeks, looks like a pattern...'

'Anyway, what the hell... another beer?'

I sat still for a moment. The accountant was right – while it had a long way to go to being a serial killer there was certainly a pattern to these crimes and there was every likelihood they were connected. My professional interest was piqued, and I found myself working through what would be going on among the team of investigators assigned to the case.

They would be trying to draw connections between the crime scenes, establish similarities between the victims, identify common aspects in the method of the attack, the positioning of the bodies, the weapons used. Had any physical evidence – other than the bodies – been found at the scenes? Had DNA samples been adequate and had they revealed anything? Were there any witnesses? Was there any indication from the killer that they would strike again...? I shrugged and stood up, collecting my empty beer glass. It was an interesting mental exercise, to be sure, but I couldn't care less. The killings had nothing to do with me and, as I had decided in the helicopter when reading the news of the first killing, I wasn't prepared to give it any more thought.

I had only just sat back down and placed the fresh beer on the table in front of me when I noticed the hum of the two men's conversation suddenly stop, and I started as two, cool hands gently covered my eyes. Before she spoke, I knew who it was – her scent was unmistakable.

'I knew I would find you here,' she whispered, her breath warm in my ear.

I gently removed the hands and turned in my chair. The accountant and his friend were staring, their mouths slightly open. I stood and wrapped my arms around Angel's waist as she leaned in and kissed me hungrily. We broke our clinch, and I caught the accountant's eye as he guiltily shifted his gaze.

Angel was wearing slim-fit jeans and black Louboutins with impossibly sharp heels. Her coat was black wool cashmere Shanghai Tang, underneath which she wore a white shirt, collar snapped up and unbuttoned to reveal her deep cleavage and the swell of her breasts. A double strand of pearls that I doubted sold for a cent under $100,000 Hong Kong, wound around her throat and screamed 'Look at me' to the world. Her makeup was discreet and professional, and highlighted her magnificent dark, almond-shaped eyes. Her long, dark hair was casually ruffled and messed in a way only four hours at the salon could achieve.

The breath caught in my throat as I watched her sit and wave her hand at the waitress who appeared seconds later with a glass of champagne. Angel cupped her chin in her hands.

'I've missed you Galahad Jones,' she said quietly, before taking a long sip of the effervescent yellow contents of the glass.

Angel Yeung Mei-ying was every bit as beautiful as when I had first met her. It had been over two years since we literally bumped into each other in the supermarket beneath Times Square, both reaching for the same bunch of pak choy.

She had worked in a high-end cocktail bar in Wan Chai that was a cross between Cirque du Soleil and a 19th century opium den where she had danced – or, more accurately, had lounged seductively on a large shelf behind the bar – clad in a figure-hugging Cheongsam. I had fallen for her instantly and that, as I later found out, had been the plan. Angel had been tasked to seek me out and reel me in – which she had done effortlessly. Rather than being the struggling dancer I thought she was, Angel was a senior member of 14K Triad.

She was, in fact the Straw Sandal, Liaison Officer, to Lee Pak-chun, the triad's 489, or Mountain Master, the man at the very top of the pole. And so had started my close, and fraught, relationship with 14K triad that had, admittedly, been useful to me but that I had worked very hard the past two years to put behind me.

With a shudder I recalled Lee's words in the back of his Mercedes during a meet to swap information: "No one is ever out, Mr Jones," he had said. "And, most certainly, none of us is ever clean."

While I had tried to distance myself from Lee and the triad, I had done the opposite with Angel Yeung. I wasn't blind to the dubious moral choice of associating with a senior triad member, but I was powerless to act. She had her claws deep in me and we both knew it. Angel was tall, glamorous, stunningly beautiful, and very dangerous. It was a heady mix and a drug I couldn't get enough of.

She sat silently while all this played through my mind as I ran my eyes over her. She stared back at me, much like a tigress would eye a limping goat.

I finally spoke. 'So, how did you know I would be here, my beautiful flower?' I said, using the English translation of her first name.

'You're a creature of habit, Gal,' She replied. 'I keep telling you not to be – it's not good for your health – but you are. It's Wednesday...' she checked the vintage Omega watch at her wrist. 'It's nearly 5:00 so, for you, that means Beer Time. I checked the two places you would be. When I saw you weren't at that little Italian bar on Staunton, I knew you would be up here. I knew you would be sitting outside because you always like to look at that tree...' She pointed over her shoulder with a thumb and grinned, her perfect white teeth gleaming. 'I'd make a good detective, no?'

I scratched the back of my neck. 'I think you *would*, Angel, but let's just say that your career choice to this point probably rules you out.'

She pouted and drank again at the champagne.

'So, where have you been the past three weeks?' I asked, feigning disinterest.

I noticed her eyes flicked away momentarily as she answered. 'Indonesia. Business trip,' she said dismissively.

I didn't doubt she had been to Indonesia and I was sure her caginess was due to the agreement we had made some time ago: I didn't need to know about her "business" dealings and I didn't *want* to know. I decided to press her, nonetheless.

'Indonesia is a big place, Angel. Where did you go... anywhere fun?'

'Jakarta...' Then offhandedly. 'Megamendung,' she added with a slight shrug. 'About 50 kilometres south of the capital.'

Something about that name rang a bell with me but I couldn't pick it. I suddenly remembered the Cambodian girl Joey had rescued two years previously and who Angel had taken in. It was rare to see Angel without the serious young woman in tow.

'Where's Chaya?' I asked, sipping at my beer to soften the question.

Angel wagged her finger. 'Ah, Galahad, you have me. Your devious police mind is too clever for a simple country girl like me.'

'You were born in Shanghai.'

She waved a slender hand as if brushing away a fly. 'Whatever. If you *must* know, Chaya accompanied me to Indonesia. The purpose of the trip was to settle her into a training course. She is still there.'

'Training course? What training would that be, I wonder.'

'*Business* training, my love. Books, reports, spreadsheets. Fucking

PowerPoint. Boring stuff, but everything I need her to be able to do as my assistant at YunCorp.'

YunCorp was Lee Pak-chun's legitimate business and one of Hong Kong's mightiest corporations. It dominated shipping, finance and industry in the SAR and a very large slice of Guangdong and Hunan provinces. I supposed it kept him busy, when he wasn't masterminding a criminal society that had its fingers in almost every level of Hong Kong society.

I have a particular knack of knowing when someone is lying. It comes from years of experience as a Hong Kong copper and as a Private Investigator, and probably because I am a fairly accomplished liar myself. Angel was lying to me. I decided to let it go – it was none of my business what Angel had Chaya doing in Jakarta; although I was certain it would be triad business, so I definitely did not want to know.

I sipped at the beer. 'When did you get back?'

'Only a few hours ago. I dropped my bags at home, freshened up then came hunting for you.'

There was something about the thought of being hunted by Angel that both excited and frightened me. I had to admit, I didn't make for an elusive prey when it came to her.

I checked my watch. 'Want to grab a bite?' I asked.

Angel smiled that predatory smile again. 'And then what...?'

I shrugged. 'Maybe we both get lucky...' I suggested.

Angel gently bit her lower lip. 'Well, according to the horoscope, today is an auspicious day for dining... and for love.'

I raised an eyebrow. 'Is it? I didn't realise...'

She swallowed back the last half of the glass of champagne and gave a contented sigh. '*Every* day in Hong Kong is an auspicious day for eating and for loving, Galahad. You should know that by now.'

11

Caesar Li and I had been sitting in the waiting room to Walter Chan's offices for an hour and my mind was wandering. The West Wing of the Central Government Complex in Admiralty was richly appointed, and political staffers moved silently about the carpeted corridors. Their stern efficiency so identical in each that it must have been issued to them on joining, along with their pencils, laptops, and mobile phones. I checked my watch and sighed impatiently. Li shot me a look like an annoyed teacher during a class exam, so I sat back in the chair and closed my eyes, letting the previous night replay in my mind.

Angel and I had had a few more drinks at the bar, our conversation flowing like the friends and lovers we were. It was free and easy, with the occasional friendly jibe, but I couldn't avoid the feeling that Angel had been holding something back. She hadn't told me the whole truth about the Indonesia trip, that much was clear, and she had danced aside whenever I tried to raise the subject. The more she equivocated, the more I was convinced she had been in Indonesia on triad business but just what that was I had no idea. In fact, everything I knew told me there was no Chinese transnational organised crime in Indonesia – the distinct undercurrent of anti-Chinese feeling in the country, together with the extremely powerful local organised crime families simply didn't allow it. So, that being the case, what had she been doing? I had shaken it off as we re-acquainted ourselves after a three-week separation.

Angel's eyes had sparkled, and the rich red of her lips softly caressed the words she spoke that floated across the table and stroked my skin. Her jet-black hair was long and lustrous and seemed to shimmer with greens and purples like the wings of a dragonfly. Every now and then, she would take up a strand and twirl it absently in her fingers as her eyes stabbed into me and my throat would constrict, my tongue thick in my mouth, heart pounding, like a gormless high-school boy.

I don't think she had ever deliberately manipulated me, except for the first time we had "met" – she didn't have to; I was a willing subject – but her every expression and gesture, her shape and scent, the satin smoothness of her skin and the velvet caress of her voice had me bound and helpless. It always had and probably always will.

Our love making that night had been frenzied, but strangely silent as we explored every curve and every inch of each other's bodies as if we had just discovered one another. Angel had taken control and I did as I was bid, trying hard to keep up with a woman 12 years my junior. During one of the many pauses while we drank some water and quietly chatted, Angel had run her fingers lightly over my many scars, her eyes serious, then had leaned in and gently kissed each one before rolling across and mounting me, taking me into her in an ecstatic embrace. As she moved against me, her back arched, head thrown back, I had gasped for air and fought against a blackness that lowered over my eyes like a fighter pilot struggling against g-LOC.

Much later, Angel had snuggled warm and sweat damp against me as she slept while Bors snored loudly from his bed in the lounge-room completely oblivious to the moment. I had lain for a while with

Angel's head in the crook of my arm, while I stared at the ceiling, my mind racing as a dark sense of foreboding pressed down on me. I could not shake the feeling that something was coming. I could not see it, but I could sense it, just out of reach but close. Very close. After a while, Angel murmured something and rolled over to kiss me lightly on the cheek. Exhaustion, then sleep, finally took me and feverish, fragmented dreams took over where my consciousness had left off.

I felt a sharp jab in the ribs, and I snapped out of my thoughts, glancing at Li. He nodded to the doorway in front of us, in which stood an attractive young woman in a well-cut grey suit.

'Sergeant Li and...' she glanced at the iPad in her hand. '...Mr Jones. Mr Chan will see you both now. Do please come in.' She stepped aside from the doorway and gestured us in with a formal sweep of her arm. I stood and adjusted the knot of my tie and, gesturing for Li to go ahead, we walked in.

The office was large, probably bigger than my apartment. The room was well lit by a floor-to-ceiling window that faced north across Tamar Park and Victoria Harbour, and the afternoon sun cast a golden light over everything.

The floor was carpeted, but a large Persian rug stretched across much of it and floating shelves dotted the walls, upon which stood several expensive-looking Chinese porcelain pieces – I recognised one immediately, having seen it on show in my sister Prudence's gallery years before. It wasn't old but it was an original Li You-yu and probably worth more than my annual salary. Four traditional Guo Hua paintings, each discreetly spot lit, hung on the walls, their brush and ink on paper beautifully depicting landscapes, birds and flowers.

All in all, the office looked less like that of a government minister and more that of a wealthy business tycoon – which, in a sense, Walter Chan was. I turned my attention to the occupant of the office.

Walter Chan Yi-chen had risen behind his desk as we entered. He was short and podgy. His eyes peered myopically out at us through thick spectacles that perched on a bulbous nose beneath a fringe of thinning, grey hair. His presence was almost comical beside that of his enormous six-drawer, mahogany desk – he looked like a puffed-up kid standing next to his father's car.

I hadn't paid much attention to him during the protection job and was mildly surprised at the unassuming, grey man I saw before me. Everything told me this guy was harmless, inconsequential.

Surely this wasn't the target of a political assassination attempt, so why had Guo attacked him? Chan stepped forward and offered his hand in greeting. Li and Chan greeted each other in formal Cantonese, and I shook Chan's hand silently, with a polite nod. He studied me with his head tilted.

'Mr Jones...' he said, the voice fleshy to match its physical shell. 'You are the man who tackled that lunatic at the reception. Are you not?'

I nodded. 'Yes, sir. I also sat directly across from you on the helicopter ride across from Wan Chai. As I recall, you were busy with the newspaper.'

Chan, frowned slightly, wondering if I was being a gu wac zai, *smart arse.* I kept my face expressionless.

'Mmm, yes,' he said finally. 'Taking in the news when one has the opportunity...' He moved back behind his desk and motioned us to both sit, which we did in chairs placed in front of the huge slab of dark timber. Chan sat and I half expected him to be perched on a kid's booster seat.

'I must thank you, Mr Jones,' Chan said. 'Without your quick actions I might not be here today.'

I nodded. 'Yes, well, Mr Chan that's what I wanted to...'

Li quickly interrupted. '*What* Mr Jones means to say is that *I* am here today, sir, to take a quick statement so I can wrap up our paperwork. Quite routine, really.'

'But Sergeant Li, I gave my statement to the investigators a few days ago. I really have nothing to add.'

Li feigned regret and shrugged slightly. 'Yes, sir, so sorry but as we are a different section, responsible at the time for your protection, we have our own processes to complete. We are not investigating the assault on you but conducting an internal review as we do after all such incidents involving one of our Principals.' Li looked across at me, a tight grin on his face. 'Mr Jones is here,' he said through gritted teeth 'as a *courtesy only* given his role in the incident. He will *not* be questioning you.'

Chan nodded and seemed unfazed by whoever was to speak with him. He made a show of checking his watch.

'Yes, well, let's get on with it please. I have a meeting in 30 minutes.'

Li nodded, pulled a standard issue black police notebook from inside his jacket pocket then started by recapping the events leading up to the attack.

He described Chan's pickup from the office and movement to the Government Flying Service helipad, embarkation on the chopper then the short flight to Kowloon. He stepped Chan through the move through the hotel from the rooftop helipad to the lobby.

'Was there anything bothering you at that time, Mr Chan?' Li asked.

Chan had been affecting to be supremely bored with proceedings and seemed surprised to be asked a question. Chan put down the pen with which he had been doodling on a notepad. 'Pardon? *Bothering* me...?' He tapped his fleshy lower lip with the tip of a podgy finger. 'No, not that I recall. I wasn't really paying much attention to be honest... I had a meeting coming up over dinner that I was concentrating on. My aide certainly didn't seem concerned by anything.'

I remembered the scrawny young man I had nicknamed "The Weasel". He and Chan made a great pair. Your tax dollars at work.

Li nodded and made a notation in his pad then went on, taking Chan step by step through his movements that night. Only half listening, I turned my attention to a painting on the wall behind Chan. It was a seal, a yin jian, or "chop" as its more commonly called, painted in bright red on rough, off-white parchment and framed in dark timber. The yin jian is a seal used to sign documents or artworks and, while they are mostly company seals, they are also commonly used by individuals with their family chop or personal name.

The one on the wall behind Chan was the traditional Chinese characters for his name. I did not think much about it; chop paintings are everywhere in Hong Kong, and it would not be at all unusual for a senior politician to display his in his office. I was staring at it when something Li said broke in on my thoughts.

'...called your name. What happened then?'

Chan shifted in his seat and frowned. 'No. I don't think so. I didn't hear my name called.'

'You *didn't*? Several witnesses state the offender called your name. The first time when he came through the door to the hotel and the second time just prior to launching his attack.'

Chan shook his head. 'Well... perhaps he did, but I certainly did *not* hear it. I was too focussed on getting to the function. And besides, it was very noisy in the lobby...'

Li scratched his chin. 'Have you seen the offender at any time, either before or in the aftermath of the attack. Could you identify him?'

Chan shook his head. 'No,' he said, his voice firm. 'I have not seen him at any time, I do not know who he is, I would not recognise him if I saw him again.'

'I'm sorry sir,' Li said. 'But if you did not see him how, may I ask, would you say you do not know him?'

Chan sat rock still, unblinking. 'It is a figure of speech *Sergeant*,' he finally said. 'Nothing more.'

After he made another note Li looked up. 'Last question, sir, and this will help with our future threat assessments. Do you have any idea what might have prompted this attack? Have you received any threats recently? Would you say you had enemies?'

'That's *three* questions, Sergeant. But let me answer each in turn.' Chan ticked them off on his fingers.

'One: I have no idea what may have prompted this. I assume it is a totally random attack by some disturbed person.' He rolled his eyes dramatically. 'Who *knows* what crazy stories he has told your investigators! Two: I have received no threats recently nor, to my recollection, at any time in the past. Last: I can't say I have *no* enemies – I hold the number two position here in the Development Bureau and we make many decisions concerning urban planning, land administration and infrastructure development every single day. Sometimes those decisions do not go the way of "vested interests."'

Chan paused as if he had just had an idea. 'Yes, you know... that *could* be it. It could be related to a recent planning decision I have made, but I honestly could not say which or why.'

12

THE INTERVIEW COMPLETE, Li and I had left the building and bought a takeaway coffee before taking a bench in Tamar Park. The sun shone on our faces as we sipped our brews and gazed out across Victoria Harbour toward Kowloon. Li lit a cigarette and exhaled loudly, emitting a deep sigh of contentment. I tried to ignore the smell of the smoke wafting around me.

'You know he's lying, right?' I said.

Li grunted. 'I don't *know* that, nor do you.'

We sat in silence for a minute or two before I spoke again. 'I know it. Chan's lying but I can't figure out why...'

'Okay,' Li sighed again, this time not so contentedly. 'I'll play. Where's the lie?'

'He heard his name being called. Not only that, but he knew *who* was calling him. It was only a split second, but I saw his eyes. The look wasn't surprise at being called, it was recognition and fear. He knew who was shouting his name and he knew why.'

'And...?'

'There's only one reason he would lie about that: he doesn't want us to know he knows Guo, and that's because that would lead us to their connection and the reason for the attack. If he's lying about it, he wants to cover up Guo's motivation because, somehow, it won't be good for him.'

Li dragged on his cigarette. 'Okay, assuming you're right – and I'm *not* saying you are – what possible connection could a government minister and a street stall cook have that Chan wants to hide? I mean, it's not as if the recipe for Char Siu is a state secret,' he chuckled, referring to the ubiquitous Cantonese barbecued pork.

I sucked at my teeth and shrugged. 'That's what I intend to find out as soon as Billy can get me into Stanley.'

'Good luck with that! Guo isn't talking. He's the strong silent type… or too scared or stupid to say anything.' Li flicked the butt of the cigarette away and drained his coffee. 'Anyway, I must get back to the office. I'll drop a copy of the review in your pigeonhole.'

We stood and nodded our farewells. As he was walking away, Li turned back and called out.

'Well done on keeping your mouth shut in there, Galahad. It's not at all what I had been told about you and I really was quite impressed.'

I just rolled my eyes and stalked off toward Central with my hands stuffed into my coat pocket and my mind deep in thought.

13

The first two weren't the first of course. No, far from it. I can't remember exactly when *my first was, it was so long ago. I do remember the* how *of it. It was like a boy's first kiss, the first clumsy fumbling under a bra, the first ejaculation into the sink at his own hands. My first was the neighbour's cat. A small thing. Maybe I was 10 or 11... or was I younger? One day when the neighbours were out, I caught it and took it to the park, a place in the trees. It was raining and no one was about. I tied its neck to a tree, nice and tight then I took the kitchen knife out of my school satchel. How it shone, even in the gloom, and the raindrops rolled and glistened along the blade like tears. The stupid animal was squirming, so I started cutting. Short nicks at first. Not too deep. But as the cat squealed then started to scream, I cut longer and deeper, pulling back the flaps of fur and working the blade through flesh and muscle. The blood. I could never have imagined so much blood from such a tiny beast. It flowed hot onto the leaf much, steaming in the cold air. It covered my hands and my clothes, and I could taste it on my lips. With every drop my delight, my ecstasy, increased. The cat died slowly but not slowly enough. Once it rattled out its last pathetic breath my pleasure seemed to evaporate with its spirit. Gone. Lights out. I realised then it was in the doing, the work of the knife on a living being, that gave me a thrill greater than any disgusting magazine or frantic masturbation into a Kleenex in the school bathrooms. I knew it was my future and I knew I would never, ever, want for partners. I wore that animal's skin like a hat all the way home and no one seemed to notice, or care.*

14

Two days later, the high, grey walls of Stanley Prison loomed over me as Station Sergeant Li pulled the car into the security checkpoint off Tung Tau Wan Road.

The walls, topped with rolls of tightly strung razor wire, were dotted at regular intervals by powerful perimeter lights and at each corner of the large fortification that jutted out to the sea south-east of Stanley Village, stood a manned guard tower, linked to another by elevated walkways. We were still only at the vehicle checkpoint, but the place gave off an air of dark menace; a walled encampment in which the inhabitants knew neither freedom nor peace. I shrugged off the feeling of dread. Every inmate in Stanley was there for a reason, and those reasons were serious enough to warrant incarceration in maximum security. I had no sympathy for them, but I felt a chill as the car drove through the gates that slid shut behind us with an ominous metallic clang.

Li parked the car, and we moved down the clearly marked path to reception. He nudged me as we walked. 'Have you been here before?'

I shook my head. 'No. Never. Shek Pik a few times when I was in the job, but never here.' I shivered slightly again. It was cold and the weak sun barely warmed the interior of the prison, but I knew that wasn't the reason for my sudden chills.

'You know, my father was born here,' I said conversationally.

Li did a mental calculation and turned to me. 'During the war? *Diu*, the stories we hear about the place then…'

'Not "stories", it's all fact. Japanese brutality and indifference to civilian interns – women and children – is a matter of record. My grandmother nearly died for want of any medical care following the birth of my father, and both nearly starved on several occasions.' I frowned, shaking my head. 'Anyway, that's a story for another time…'

Pushing open the doors to reception we walked in, and I stood back slightly while Li presented the paperwork we had been issued the day before by Billy Wong's cousin. The place smelled of carbolic but that couldn't mask the stink of human sweat and ordure that drifted in from the main prison compound and seemed to cling to everything inside the walls. Li wrinkled his nose.

'I've always hated the smell of this place,' he said. 'Imagine living it every day for twenty years. *Diu*!'

He unclipped the holster from his belt and handed it and the Glock to the Corrections officer across the desk who secured it in a safe and issued Li with a receipt. After the obligatory five minutes studying the two-page pass document, and stamping it numerous times, the officer handed back the paperwork with a scowl. With a final glare he buzzed us into the next secure compartment where we were met by an armed guard dressed in a uniform of dark green pants and olive drab shirt. He nodded through the glass at the counter officer and buzzed the external door that swung open with a faint hiss. We stepped out and followed the guard along a covered walkway that dog-legged to the left before emerging out into the main yard of the prison. I stopped briefly to take it in.

To the east lay a row of six, three-storied cell blocks that ran from a large exercise yard in the north of the compound to the prison walls on the southern cliff of the promontory. A large building that I took to be the mess hall hunkered between two of the cell blocks and, to the west of the compound sat more buildings housing the remand cells, guard barracks and administration offices. The low buzz of thousands of male voices was hive-like, the drone broken now and then by a shout or the solid metallic thunk of a cell door shutting. Apart from the guards, there was no one in sight. I glanced at Li, and he rolled his eyes, giving a comic shiver of apprehension as we turned in the direction of the remand cells.

Three more doors, two signatures and a pat-down later, we were seated in two steel chairs in an interview room, across from a metal table that had been anchored to the polished concrete floor. Manacles were bolted to the surface of the table. A single, tin ashtray was screwed to the tabletop. Like every prison interview room I had ever been in, this one was painted a weak vomit green – the *couleur du jour* of every government institution I had ever entered – and smelled of a pugnacious blend of cigarette smoke, carbolic, and fear. We didn't have long to wait.

A steel door at the other end of the room opened and in shuffled a figure I had last seen weeping on the floor of a 5-star hotel lobby. Dressed in one-piece prison overalls, the same colour as the walls, Guo Yu-xuan seemed to disappear as he walked across the room toward us, only his head and face visible as they levitated toward us in a strange optical illusion.

His face was blank, and his eyes betrayed nothing – neither anxiety nor fear nor, even, curiosity. He was void of emotion, vacant, and for a moment I thought he must have been drugged. The escorting guard gently sat Guo in the chair across from us and swiftly, efficiently, connected the prisoner's handcuffs to the manacles, drawing in the connecting chain so there was just enough slack for the Guo to raise his hands to his face. The guard took up a position in the corner of the room and Li looked at him.

'We have authorisation for a private interview…'

The guard shook his head. 'No. Standing Orders state….'

'And *my* papers, from Senior Superintendent Wong, specifically state "unescorted interview…"' Li snapped back. 'Out!'

The guard scowled then shrugged. 'I'll be just outside… I'm going to check on your authority.'

'You do that,' Li said, looking nonchalantly into his jacket as he drew out his notebook. The door clanged shut and we were alone with Guo.

Handcuffed and manacled to the table, the prisoner sat silently, looking from Li to me, taking us in as if committing us to memory. I realised that his face wasn't blank after all. It seemed to me Guo was calm. More than accepting of his fate – which a man in his situation is best to be, for the sake of his sanity – he was calm, as if he had not a worry in the world. He looked to me to have had an insight into the true nature of mind and was deeply happy in the discovery of that. He certainly looked different to the weeping creature I had dragged off the floor of the hotel. It was all very Zen.

'Do you have a cigarette?' Guo asked quietly in Cantonese.

Li rummaged in his suit jacket and tossed his packet, and a lighter, onto the table along with a business card. We watched while Guo fumbled with the pack. The cigarette finally wedged between two fingers, he held up his hands, the manacle chain pulling taut, and nodded to the lighter on the table.

'Would you mind? It's a little difficult...'

Li leaned in and lit the smoke. Guo dragged deep then exhaled slowly and very deliberately. His hands cuffed closely together; he pointed the cigarette at me.

'I know you,' he said.

I nodded. 'We've met. The hotel. The night you attacked Chan Yi-chen.'

'Ah, yes,' Guo said. 'The big policeman. The rugby player.' He chuckled slightly, the sound strangely warm in the chill of the interview room. 'You speak very good Cantonese, big policeman. What brings you here today?'

'My name is Jones. I'm no longer a policeman, Mr Guo. Nor do I still play rugby – my knees won't permit it.' Guo chuckled again and dragged on the cigarette. 'My colleague, however, *is* Police,' I added. 'And I would like to talk to you about Chan.'

Guo ashed the smoke and sat back. 'I have told the detectives everything there is to know about that...'

'Humour me.'

Guo studied me for a moment. 'You don't want to know *how*, do you Mr Jones? You were there after all.' He sighed. 'You want to know the *why* of it all, do you not?' I nodded and he went on. 'I told the detectives, and I will tell you: my motivation for the attack is my business. I will tell no one of it.'

'Even if it might mean the difference between a life sentence and, perhaps, seeing your family again before you die? You've been told you are facing terrorism and sedition charges, have you not?'

'I have.'

'There is no coming back from that, Yu-xuan,' I said. 'You will spend the rest of your life in maximum security, in solitary 23 hours a day, staring at the bare, green walls until they drive you insane.'

I could see the muscles at his jaw working. Outwardly, Guo was imperturbable. 'That is my fate, Mr Jones, and I am resigned to it.'

I decided to try another approach. 'You really are a sorry, selfish bastard Guo,' I said mildly. He looked shocked and I pushed on. 'You failed in your pathetic attempt to murder a government minister, and you and I both know this wasn't political. You're too *ordinary* to be triad or, even more laughably, a professional assassin. This was personal wasn't it...? And now, for your own selfish reasons you have abandoned your wife and your daughter...What's her name?' I pretended to search my memory then shrugged. 11 years old and now fatherless.' I shook my head. 'What a failure you are...' There was something there, I thought. The moment I had mentioned Guo's daughter his façade had cracked.

Guo scowled. I had finally lifted his mask. 'You know *nothing* of my daughter, Mr Jones. Nothing!'

'I know she's lost her dad,' I snapped. Guo's shoulder slumped and he lowered his head, chin to chest. I softened my voice. 'You know Chan, don't you Yu-xuan? I saw it in his eyes when you shouted his name.'

'I don't know him,' Guo whispered.

'He knows *you*...'

'No.'

Li interrupted by picking up the pack of cigarettes. 'This is a waste of time,' he said standing up. 'You can't help him, and he doesn't want your help. "Guilty, Your Honour." Let the bastard stew, Galahad.'

I tried one last time as I stood. 'Call the number on the card if you change your mind,' I said, tapping the card on the table. 'Think of your daughter.'

Li knocked on the door and a guard swung it open. We were stepping out when I heard Guo whisper from inside the soulless, green room.

'I am...' he muttered, his voice husky and broken.

15

THE MAIN ENTRANCE door to Stanley Prison closed shut behind us and Caesar Li and I were standing outside, the cold grey walls at our backs.

The sun seemed to shine brighter, and I could hear birds in the trees that greened the Stanley promontory. The air smelled fresh and clean, and I drew deeply on it, cleansing myself, as Li lit a cigarette. After the last hour inside Stanley, I desperately felt the need, but I resisted. Li puffed out a lungful of smoke.

'Happy now, Galahad? I tried to tell you that would go nowhere. Guo is protecting someone and is too sacred to give him, or them, up. It's probably triad. You saw how he reacted to the mention of his daughter, right? He's obviously been threatened – the girl dies if he talks.'

I took a deep breath and puffed out my cheeks. 'Yeah, I guess you're right. I don't know why I thought it was personal... just a hunch, but I was so *sure*.' I shrugged. 'I was wrong.'

Li slapped my shoulder. 'Don't beat yourself up. Even *I* get things wrong now and then... although I cannot remember the last time I did.' He grinned and fished out his car keys.

I looked around and, across the carpark, I saw a figure leaning against a dark sedan, his arms crossed. He wore sunglasses but I knew him instantly. My stomach dropped. I had not seen Michael Wong for over a year and now here he was, out of the blue, waiting for me in a prison carpark. This couldn't be good. He pushed himself upright and walked towards us.

'I want to talk to you, Mr Jones,' he called. Li looked up and swore as Michael Wong strode across the carpark. He stopped in front of me, ignoring Li, and slowly took off his sunglasses, meticulously folding them and slipping inside his jacket.

'I won't ask why you're here, Jones,' he said. 'I already know that – and Uncle Billy will have some explaining to do.'

I wanted to shoulder my way past him but a long-silent voice in my head warned against that. 'What, no small talk Chief Inspector?' I said.

Caesar Li drew in a breath – even in-service officers didn't fuck with OCTB, and it wasn't a good idea for a discredited, former Senior Inspector to do it.

Michael looked at Li. 'I'll take this from here, Sergeant Li,' he snapped. Li turned to leave, having rolled his eyes at me. Michael called out at Li's departing back. 'You're lucky Jones is an approved contractor, Station Sergeant, or I'd be reporting this breach to your chain of command. I may yet...'

Li stopped and I saw his shoulders tense. He didn't turn around or utter a word, but carried on to his car, opened it, gunned the engine, and drove off. Michael Wong turned back to me.

'You and I are taking a drive, *Mr* Jones,' he said turning on his heels and gesturing toward his car with a sweep of his hand. There was nothing I could do --, so I decided silence was my best strategy, I crossed the carpark and got into the rear seat of the car. Michael climbed in beside me and tapped the driver on the shoulder. With a spin of the wheel the driver flicked the car out onto Tung Tau Wan Road. Turning to me, Michael spoke, his voice tense.

'You know I don't like you, right?' he said.

'I have been told that, yes.'

'While your reckless disregard for most procedures is an annoyance, and the smug certainty of your own brilliance is irksome, it's your deep, personal attachments into 14K that I *really* don't like. Your *friends* are known criminals, Mr Jones. In my books that makes *you* a criminal.' He always called me "Mister" because he couldn't bring himself to call me by my first name, let alone my former rank.

'You are consorting with an organised criminal gang, an organisation responsible for a great deal of the violent crime in the SAR, official corruption, extortion, gambling, drugs, and illegal prostitution. We both know that Consorting is an offence. Yet, for reasons known apparently only to you, that's all just fine. Just so long as whatever you're up to benefits Galahad Jones...'

'I'm not up to anything, Michael.'

'You'll address me as *Chief Inspector...*'

'I don't think so, Michael. You were a snot-nosed kid when I first met you and, while you've come far – and on your own merit, I'll give you that – you're still not my senior in any way. You clearly don't like me so why should I bother trying to fluff up a professional and courteous relationship with you?'

It was childish, I knew that, but Michael Wong was pushing my buttons and I reacted the best way I knew; by lashing out. Michael spluttered then drew a very deep breath, visibly controlling himself. It turns out that, although younger, Michael Wong was a great deal more mature than me.

'Well,' he said. 'I guess that makes things clear.'

I shrugged. 'I'm still not up to anything with 14K...'

'Lee Pak-chun...?'

'Helped me identify a corrupt policeman and flush out another – who, incidentally, you have taken over from. He also helped me clear my father's name – again, something you had a big part in. I recall you may have got the credit for that one... Anyway, I haven't seen Lee in over two years, and I don't intend to.'

'The Panda...'

'A Confidential Informant. That's how and why I know him.' That was a lie but a good one. The Panda and I had become friends over the past two years since he and Joey had rescued me on the cliffs near

Shek O. 'As a C.I, I associate with him but only to obtain information of use to me and, on occasion, the Police where appropriate. To be honest, I also enjoy his company – he's quite the raconteur.'

'Appropriate? What the hell is *appropriate* where these people are concerned? Everything they *do* is police business... Also, you hang out with a known violent criminal because he's fun to have a *beer* with?'

'He doesn't drink.'

Michael sighed in exasperation. I raised an eyebrow. 'And before you throw Angel Yeung at me, yes, I know what she is. But, you know, "love is love." What can I say?' I grinned.

To his credit, Michael Wong smiled back, ever so slightly. It looked like a hairline crack in a concrete wall. I gazed out the window to watch as the lush, green hills above Repulse Bay Road sped by as we headed west toward Deep Water Bay. The forest of these hills had changed little in centuries, and local lore still had them as home to a thunder of dragons who would sweep out over the sea when called upon, to protect Hong Kong and the islands to her south. I believed in dragons. Why not?

Michael broke the silence. 'Just so you are clear: This isn't a social call. Got it?'

I nodded, still gazing out the window.

'I find, to my profound regret, that I need to consult you on a professional matter.'

That got my attention. I turned my head to look at him.

'First, I have a question about Guo Yu-xuan,' he said.

I shrugged. 'Shoot.'

'I know you were the VIPP agent that took him down, but your statement is in and there's no call to visit him in prison. So, what's your interest? The Galahad Jones I know *always* has an angle...'

'That's unfair. Not *always*...'

'So...?'

I gave a sigh. 'I was bothered by everything to do with the attack. It just didn't seem to stack up to me. I could have sworn it was personal, not political, and I'm still sure Chan knows Guo somehow...

As it turns out, it seems Guo is the fall guy for someone else. He's been frightened into remaining silent. Probably a threat against his family.'

'Triads?' Michael asked.

'Could be,' I agreed. 'But that puts the ball squarely back into Chan's court. If it's triads, why? What's Chan mixed up in?'

Michael nodded. 'True. But nothing as far as we know. We run checks on all of them in LegCo at some time or other – mostly soft touch and cursory, but checks nonetheless. Nothing on Chan. Ever. Still, you could be right... I'll look into it.'

'You can thank me later.'

Michael looked out his window as Deep Water Bay Beach passed by and the opulent surrounds of The Hong Kong Country Club hove into view. He was thinking about something, working himself up to a decision. He made it quickly.

'What do you know about these murders?' he asked, turning to face me.

'The hiking trail murders?'

He nodded. 'Nothing,' I said. 'Well, nothing beyond what I read in the papers or hear in bars...' My skin began to crawl and the hairs on the back of neck prickled. '*Should* I know something?'

Michael studied me for a long moment. 'A taskforce has been formed from OCTB and homicide. I'm heading it,' he said. 'The commissioner is hot on this, and we are taking it *very* seriously. As part of the investigation so far, we've reviewed violent killings the past ten years – the very few there have been. Naturally, I've been back over the files of the Thomas Murders two years ago,' he paused briefly to draw breath. 'There are striking similarities between those murders and the ...method used by this killer.'

Again, I was thrown back into the bloody scene in the Thomas' apartment. The ruined bodies, sadistically taken apart, the gore spattered walls and ocean of blood on the floor, the stench of shit and piss and blood that had nearly choked me. I had been shocked more than I could have believed by the sight and shocked, also, by my reaction to it. I had been angrier at the spanner their deaths had thrown into my trafficking case than I had been at the Thomas' brutal murders. It had taken a lot of drinking over a lot of hours to even begin to wash that horror, and shame, away...

'Go on,' I said.

'It's early days yet, but while they are by no means identical, the sheer ferocity of the attacks, the sadism with which the victims have been executed, is pointing to a connection.'

'Can you be more specific?'

'No.'

I asked the question that was on everyone's lips. 'Is it a serial killer?'

Michael sighed. 'We're not there yet – and thankfully the media have shut-up about it to this point – but I just don't think this is gang-related. I've seen some pretty brutal triad executions but this is *way* beyond that. So, yes, we're working on the assumption we've got a serial killer loose in Hong Kong.'

I nodded slowly. 'So, what does this have to do with me?'

'I just thought you might be able to offer some insights on the Thomas case. Nothing more...' He said that too casually. Lie.

'Me?' I said, surprised. 'I had nothing to do with it other than a tour of the crime scene conducted by Peter Toh who, I assume, wrote it up as a triad murder case...' I had almost finished my sentence when a thought, a memory, hit me like a bolt of lightning so vivid that I flinched in the seat. Michael saw it.

'Jesus,' I breathed. Peter Toh's words, uttered in the dark clearing ringed by storm-ripped trees, a bloodied body slumped in the mud, flashed back into my consciousness. *I had help on that one. Someone I've been keeping for just such an ...occasion. Someone particularly skilled in that sort of thing.*

'Toh told me he had "help" with Thomas and his wife... Someone "particularly skilled," he said.'

Michael frowned. 'That's not in your statement following your shooting. Why?'

'Forgive me, Michael. I had just been shot in the head by my best friend, I had a broken arm and a bullet wound in the other arm. Maybe I wasn't thinking too clearly...'

'Granted,' he said grudgingly. 'Well, thinking back to that time then, do you think Toh was involved in the actual killings?'

'Definitely not,' I replied, with a shake of my head. 'He's a cunning, manipulative, cold-hearted bastard but that sort of thing isn't him. He won't hesitate to put a bullet in your brain, but the up-close-and-personal touch required for knife work – in particular the ferocity of the Thomas Murders – isn't his style. Might he have organised them, however...?' I shrugged. 'What makes you think Peter Toh is involved in the hiking trail killings? Have you got something pointing that way?'

Michael looked at me for a long moment before speaking. 'No, we don't have anything that points to Toh, or a connection to anyone involved with Thomas and his wife, other than similarities in the killing modus.'

'There's something else you aren't asking me Michael... Why?'

He shrugged. 'Oh, it's just standard but as you raise it, I *will* ask: have you noticed anything unusual lately?'

'Unusual...? You mean UFOs-over-Lion Rock-Unusual or something more specific to me?'

'Anything out of the ordinary as far as you are concerned.'

For a moment I considered telling him about my sense of being followed recently and the shadowy encounter in Wan Chai. I decided against it.

'Nothing,' I said. 'Why do you ask?'

Michael shrugged. 'No reason, really. Just a standard question. One never knows...'

I nodded and turned back to the window, not wanting him to see my face while I thought that through. Michael Wong hadn't driven all the way to Stanley, after we had spent 14 months avoiding each other, just to ask if I had any "insights" on the Thomas case, or if anything strange had been happening in my life. He could have done that over the phone. Michael was lying to me. I could not think on what level or why, but it had to have something to do with evidence they had from the recent murders. Had the Taskforce picked up something at each crime scene that was pointing in a certain direction? Michael's questions to me smelled a lot like a line of inquiry – and I was disturbed to think that, somehow, my name was tangled up in that. The car sped into the Aberdeen Tunnel, heading to the north of The Island, the silent driver focused on the traffic ahead.

I turned to Michael. 'Why do I still get the feeling you're not telling me something?' I asked.

He shrugged. 'I really have no idea...'

'Well, if you're not going to play straight with me, I think we can say this interview is over.' I leaned forward and tapped the driver on the shoulder. 'I assume you know where I live. Drop me there.'

The driver's eyes flicked up to the rear-vison mirror, questioning Michael who nodded and waved his hand with a disinterested flick.

'Yes. Drop Mr Jones home. We're done.'

It was silent and sullen in the car for the last few minutes of the trip down Wong Nai Chung Gap Flyover, past Happy Valley Racecourse. We soon turned onto Morrison Hill Road, and I was dropped without another word.

Standing in the growing shadows of the late afternoon, feeling the chill of evening coming on, I watched as the taillights of Michael Wong's car turned left onto Wan Chai Road and out of sight. It had been quite a day and I had a lot to think about. I needed a drink.

16

'Do I know you?' I asked the young woman who had pulled up a stool next to me. The bar was heaving, and I slid across a little to make space. Joey Loh held up one finger to the barman and turned to face me.

'That's not very welcoming,' she said. 'I spotted Bors and you in here on the way home from the office, so I thought you'd enjoy the company.'

'You know I hate company,' I said. 'Or is it company hates me? I can never work out which it is...'

She shrugged. 'A little from Column A, a little from Column B...'

I acknowledged that with a slow nod. Joey's beer arrived. She took a sip of the beer and wiped foam from her top lip with the back of her hand.

'When I saw you, I thought I'd drop in and say "hi". I mean, we've been a bit like junks passing in the fog lately. Sorry about that...'

'No, don't worry about it,' I said. 'I've been doing a bit of running around and I know you're busy with Penny...'

I didn't say what I was thinking but Joey read my mind.

'And I could do with a bit more focus on the job... right?'

I shrugged. 'Maybe. Look, I know you're fully invested in Penny –

and that's great...' I didn't really think that. 'But you need to turn your eye back on the main game. Just a bit.'

Joey nodded and smiled. 'Yeah, I know. I will.' She sighed. 'That girl really is taking up a lot of my time – she needs it and I love it – but it's all about balance. My yin and yang are imbalanced and that can only mean bad things ahead. I need to readjust.' She sighed again and took a long drink of her beer.

'So,' she said. 'What has the all-knowing Galahad Jones been up to lately?'

I guffawed loudly. 'The only thing I *do* know, Joey, is how little I know. Especially lately.' Joey cocked an eyebrow. 'You remember the attack on Walter Chan, of course...'

She nodded.

'Well, I've had a nagging feeling something isn't right with it. It just doesn't seem to be what it looks like.'

'Your instincts are usually right on this stuff,' Joey said.

'Not this time. I sat in on Caesar Li's debrief of Chan and it was all very boring... but I still came away convinced Chan was lying about knowing the attacker. His name is "Guo" by the way...'

Joey rolled her eyes. 'I know that. I typed your statement for the arrest brief, remember?'

'Oh...right. Anyway, somehow Chan knows Guo – I'm sure of it. At least I *was*. Now I think I'm just imagining things. Li and I visited Guo in Stanley, and he isn't talking. It looks like someone has got to him. That means he did what he did on someone's orders and *that* means it probably all is just what it looks like: a hit, with Guo as the fall guy.'

I ordered two more beers, and we sat in silence until they arrived, swallowed up by the noise of the bar patrons that competed with to a Deep Purple track blasting out over the small, crowded space. I looked down at my feet where Bors lay watchfully, his ears slightly pricked, glancing up now and then to check in with me, or to eyeball a reveller who had got too close. I leaned down and scratched his ears.

'Hey,' I heard Joey say. 'Something strange happened the other day.'

I felt a slight prickle at the back of my neck as I sat up and faced her.

'Yes. Strange. Penny and I were walking back from an early dinner in Mong Kok, and I got the sense we were being followed.'

I swallowed hard. 'Go on,' I said as mildly as I could, feeling my heart banging at my chest. The chilled air from the street seemed to flood into the hot bar and wrap itself around me.

Joey shrugged. 'To begin with it was just a feeling, you know. But it wouldn't go away so I started to pay more attention. I caught the reflection through a shop window of a man across the road. He was standing still and watching us, I'm sure. When I turned around, he was gone.'

'What did he look like?'

Joey shook her head. 'No idea. It was all too quick. There was traffic moving between us, the light was poor...' She shrugged again.

'When was this?'

Joey told me and my pulse raced. It was the same night I had been followed back from Wan Chai. We *were* being followed, and by two different people in different parts of Hong Kong. There could only be one reason for that, and I had a vision of a duffle bag stuffed full of US Dollars. Whoever owned that money knew I had it and they were closing in. I had no choice now, so I made a decision.

'Joey,' I said, leaning in close. 'I was being followed the same night. In Wan Chai. I nearly got a look at whoever it was, but he was gone in the dark before I could get close enough. I'm pretty sure I know the reason we are both being tailed...'

'And that would be?' Joey asked, sitting stone still, her eyes hardening.

'You remember a couple of years ago, after the trafficking case and I paid you and Adele two months' back pay, then I got the office renovated? Joey nodded. 'It was triad money. Millions of dollars of it that I took from Zhou before he was shot by Peter Toh.'

Joey let out a hiss. 'Jesus *Christ*, Gal!' She shook her head. 'I had a feeling about where that expenditure but how could I have even *suspected* you had access to a hoard like that, or where it came from?' She paused, thinking.

'Zhou had it when he tried to run, right?'

I nodded.

'You're right then,' she whispered. 'That's who is following us. It's dirty money. It's SYO's money,' she said, referring to Sun Yee On triad for whom David Zhou had been working. 'It's *their* cash and they want it back. *Fuck*!'

I rubbed my chin, feeling two day's growth scratching under my palm. 'Yeah, it would seem so. I'm sorry, Jo...'

'Sorry barely cuts it, Gal... *Jesus*! You stole proceeds of crime, from a *very* dangerous group of people. That was money from gambling, prostitution, drug sales, extortion... It makes you no better than *them*!' She stopped suddenly and gripped my elbow. 'How much of it do you still have.'

I did a mental calculation. With what I had spent in the aftermath of the find, less a recent hit in the foreign exchange rate, there was a little over the equivalent of 1.9 million US dollars sitting in my account. I was sweating just thinking about it.

'A lot,' I replied.

'*Fuck*!'

'Will you stop *saying* that?'

'To be honest Gal, I really don't know what else *to* say...'

'Look,' I said. 'We don't *really* know who is following us. Yes, the cash would seem to be the reason but why now after so long? Why you? If it's SYO, why didn't they connect the dots sooner? And why would they even think you were involved?' I shrugged, a little uselessly. 'When you consider our recent cases and the number of people I've pissed off in this city, it could be anyone.'

'If it's SYO,' Joey replied, 'they'll be looking to get to you through me. That's what I would do.' She sipped her beer and gave a slight belch. 'Still, what you say *could* be true. We're both pretty unpopular in certain circles. But we should still take precautions on the assumption it's SYO. But God knows what *those* should be. If they want us, they can reach out and take us any time.'

We sat sipping at our beers, each wrapped in their own thoughts. I had no idea what Joey was thinking but I could guess. She was singularly unimpressed with what I had done – and probably even more so by my apparent lack of guilt or concern. *I* was thinking the bar was getting rowdy, Bors was hungry, and it was time to leave.

I *was* also thinking about the money. Of the amount I had spent, only a fraction had been for my own benefit – two new shirts, a now-ruined suit and a new G-Shock was hardly living the high life! What I had used had been anonymously donated to help a dog shelter in Wan Chai, trying to get my informant Fat Johnny Tong out of the gutter, spent on a new car for Prudence, back pay for Joey and Adele, and on renovating the office. I had also paid Prudence back the HKD325,000 she had loaned me to get out from under my near-fatal debt to Jade Tooth. I really had no idea what I would do with the HKD15.6 million still sitting in my bank account, but I was sure of two things: I wasn't telling anyone about it, and I wasn't giving it back.

Our conversation died and, thirty minutes later, after we had finished our beers, Joey and I wished each other luck and left the bar. She didn't look me in the eye when she walked away, and I felt the first sting of regret and guilt.

17

It was cold in the streets and a gentle mist hung in the darkness like a light silk sheet.

My breath fogged and looking down at Bors on the end of his leash, I could see his breath puffing as he padded happily along. Crowds surged up and down the footpaths, carrying bags from department stores and boutiques as they set about Christmas shopping, and the city was decked out in string lights that winked and sparkled gaily over all. A department store Santa stood on Queen's Road, ringing his bell loudly and ho-hoing at passers-by, and Christmas trees adorned with lights and tinsel shone into the upturned faces of delighted children. I walked on, oblivious to the joy and beauty around me, head down, my left hand stuffed into my jacket pocket, and right hand gripping Bors' leash.

Christmas is a time for happiness, giving and forgiveness, and I was feeling none of those. The Ghost of Christmas Yet to Come stalked me, "...a solemn Phantom, draped and hooded, coming, like a mist along the ground", its grey and tattered shroud bringing fear and death back into my life.

In those last minutes with Joey, and as I walked home through Central, I had made two decisions. I was thrilled with neither.

First, I would contact Tommy Ho and enlist his help to run counter-surveillance for Joey and me. I would have to tell Angel – she would find out in a heartbeat anyway. The good news was The Panda could be trusted to keep unwanted tails off us and, if necessary, take care of them in a way only Tommy Ho could. The bad news was this meant re-establishing formal ties with 14K and *that* was something I did not want to do. I had managed to avoid direct contact with the triad for over two years and now, at a time when it looked like Michael Wong was closely watching me, I was about to run back to them with open arms.

The second decision was to confront Jade Tooth about the tails and learn what he knew about the money. The triad-connected club owner was a very nasty piece of work. If SYO turned to anyone to get their cash back it would be Jade Tooth. I didn't relish stepping into his lair, but it was the only way to confirm the tails were SYO and were related to the missing cash. I considered taking Tommy Ho with me but quickly dismissed that - taking a 14K hardman into an SYO club was like lighting a fire and tipping a bucket of kerosene onto it. No, that wouldn't do. It would have to be a solo job and I thought back two years to the last time I had paid a visit to Jade Tooth. On that occasion, I had narrowly escaped a one-way trip to somewhere off Lamma Island and had managed to hospitalise two of Jade Tooth's thugs. On reflection, I thought with a faint smile, it had been quite a successful visit. Still, I didn't like the idea of journeying back into the 'Lucky Dragon Social Club' and I shivered slightly. It wasn't the cold.

Lost in thought I had blundered on toward home, unaware of my surroundings when I suddenly stopped and looked about. For a moment I had no idea where I was.

Slowly, it dawned on me that I had left Queen's Road East and was walking down a deserted Tai Wong Road. The street was grave silent, except for the occasional scurry of a rat and the faint hum of traffic from Johnston Road up ahead, and it was dark. Very dark. Not a single streetlight shone, and the shadows were deep and menacing. I cocked my head and listened. Silence.

I gave Bors a pat and walked on, angry at myself for dropping my guard so completely. I was almost at the light and noise of Johnston Road when Bors stopped, turned about and growled, the sound low and threatening from deep in his chest. I squinted into the dark, turning my head slowly from left to right to use the vision at the corners of my eyes. Bors strained at his leash. The street was silent.

After a minute or two I could see nothing and was about to turn away when, 35 metres away, I caught sight of a darker blob against the gloom of the unlit street. It appeared to be leaning against a wall. I stared directly at it and the shape disappeared, then reappeared as I turned my head. The figure didn't move or utter a sound. Bors continued to growl and strain at the leash, his hackles now bristling the length of this back.

'I know who sent you!' I shouted. 'You can tell Jade Tooth he can stop this charade. I'm coming to see him...'

Nothing. The figure remained perfectly still and silent. Had I imagined it after all? I certainly had not imagined Bors' reaction that was now becoming more savage as he clawed at the pavement. I took a step forward and as I did a low, throaty chuckle came from the dark. I froze. The laugh was mocking. It was humourless, dry and bitter. A shiver ran the length of my spine, and I reached down to finger the clasp of Bors' leash. As I did the figure spoke.

'You have no idea,' it rasped, the voice chilling; the sound of a body being dragged through gravel. I didn't recognise it – I hadn't expected to – yet it was familiar somehow. I racked my brain searching for a match that hovered tantalizingly close but just out of reach.

'You do not know what you are facing,' the voice said. 'You have no idea...'

I wanted the phantom to keep speaking. I wanted him distracted when I loosed Bors.

'It's almost laughable,' it said, the figure still immobile against the wall. 'How can one man be so arrogant and ignorant at the same time...?'

At that, I pulled back on the snap clasp of Bors' leash. The leash dropped away and Bors surged into darkness with a howl. I sprinted after him. I soon lost what little illumination I had at my back from Johnson Road, and I ran on in the dark like a blind man running full tilt into the unknown.

Up ahead I heard Bors baying as he charged up the street and I homed in on the sound. I stumbled into a styrofoam box and staggered forward as empty bottles shattered on the road around me. I tripped again and fell to my knee, slamming it painfully into the concrete. Swearing loudly, I stood and ran on. A tunnel of light at the Queen's Road East end started to grow. I could see Bors skitter to a halt near the end of the street, then turn around and trot back towards me. I sprinted on, my left knee screeching in protest, and soon reached Bors. I patted his head and reached down to take a hold of his collar, both of us panting furiously.

I spun my head left and right up and down Queen's Road East. The crowded footpath made it impossible to identify anyone and the tail obviously wasn't stupid – he wouldn't be running and drawing attention to himself.

After throwing us off at the end of the street he would have casually strolled away, blending with the sea of humanity that flowed around him. I turned around to look back down Tai Wong Road. The figure had been standing about 100 metres down the street and we had been about 35 metres further on. I frowned as I looked back at the scene.

Bors was a big dog – built more like a black and tan lion than your run-of-the-mill Hong Kong rescue mutt – but he could run. Fast. The phantom could not possibly have got only a 35-metre head start on Bors then outpaced him to the end of the road 100 metres away. I clicked my fingers and tugged on Bors' collar.

'Come here, boy,' I said quietly as I turned around and started walking slowly down the street.

The darkness quickly enveloped me again, but I knew what I was looking for. I found it when we had walked to about 40 metres from where I thought the shadow had been standing. An open doorway, leading into a darkened and rundown apartment building. Looking up the darkened stairwell of the tenement I winced; I really could have used a torch. I gave my knee another rub and stepped into the inky blackness of the stairwell, the sound of Bors' nails clicking reassuringly behind me as I climbed.

Walking into the abandoned building was like walking into a tomb; it was dark, dank, and utterly silent but for the occasional crack of grit under my shoes, the thudding of my pulse in my ears.

I stepped slowly and carefully up each step, peering ahead into the dark expecting a figure to surge down onto me at any moment. Bors' snuffled panting sounded loud in the stairwell. I opened my mouth slightly to try and quieten my breathing and focus my hearing. We came to the first floor and two open apartment doors, hanging off their hinges, gaped wide and dark. I peered into one. It was hopeless. I was blundering around, literally, in the dark. The phantom could be in any room, and he held all the cards. Up and up, around the corner of each landing, Bors and I stalked.

Suddenly, a metallic clang sounded over our heads as the door to the roof was flung open to slam against the outside wall.

'Come, on!' I hissed and ran the last flight of stairs to the top landing.

The door was swinging gently, squeaking on rusty hinges, and I stepped out. The rooftop was faintly lit by the lights of neighbouring buildings, and I scanned around, searching for the man I knew had to be there with me. Noticing a length of steel pipe at my feet I bent and picked it, hefting it for grip and balance. It wasn't great but it would do.

I was deciding which direction around the rooftop to walk when I heard scrabbling in the gravel and footsteps took off away to my right. I spun and ran after the fleeing figure, catching a faint silhouette of him as he ran toward the roof edge. I had him now and I noted with satisfaction that Bors had surged ahead of me in pursuit and would be on his prey in an instant.

I skidded to a halt as, with Bors within striking range, the figure ran straight at the low wall around the rooftop edge and, without pausing, leapt over and out of sight. Bors howled in frustration and for a terrifying moment I thought he would follow over the edge. He slid into the wall, then stood on his hind legs to bark furiously into the night.

I stepped up next to him in time to see the darkened figure of a man stop on a lower rooftop and turn back to look at me. He was there for only an instant before he turned and walked casually to the roof edge and lowered himself over the side and down.

With a jolt of recognition, I realised I knew that silhouette - or thought I did. It was only a momentary glimpse in the dark, so I could not be sure. A name screamed in my mind, and I shuddered to think what it meant for my life, and those around me, if I was right.

I patted Bors on the head and headed back to the rooftop door and down the staircase, as black as a dragon's maw, soon emerging back on Tai Wong Road. Glancing around, I secured Bors to his leash and walked out into the light and noise of Johnson Road. I was shaking as I negotiated the brightly lit street, the shop touts calling on me to buy everything from smartphones and copy watches to Chinese herbal remedies and sui mei on a stick.

Without really thinking, I stepped into a gaudily lit shop, its bright red and green neon dragons colouring my face and spoke to the tattooed hipster behind the counter. Five minutes later I walked out with a package in a brown paper bag burning a hole in the back pocket of my jeans.

18

In 20 minutes, I had walked down Johnson Road, onto Hennessy then turned right onto Tin Tok Lane, pausing only briefly at the food stall on Wan Chai Road to buy some takeaway Char Siu and rice.

My dinner gripped in my hand in its white plastic bag, I crossed back over the street and was soon at the front door to my apartment. The lift took its usual time to clank and grind its way to the ground floor then back up to the floor on which I lived. Bors pawed impatiently at my front door as I engaged the coded lock then barged his way in as soon as he heard the distinct click of the door opening. I elbowed my way in with my bagged dinner that I dropped on the kitchen bench.

The front door swung shut and locked behind me. The first order of business was to feed Bors – he had earned his meal tonight – so I dumped some food in his bowl and cracked an egg over it, then poured myself a stiff whisky and walked out onto the terrace.

I hit the button on the Bluetooth speaker and pulled out my phone to thumb through my playlists. Prudence had once accused me of having an 'anti-inclusive' taste in music and, looking at my playlists, and at the collection of vinyl inside beside my treasured turntable, she was right. It was Blues and nothing much else. I tapped on a track and soon Preacher Boy's rough vocals and the ringing sound of his slide-guitar was dropping a languid cover of "Baby, Please Don't Go" across my terrace and into the night around my part of Wan Chai.

I took a long pull at the whisky and sat on the terrace lounge, looking down at the brown paper bag on the table in front me. I leaned across and tipped out the contents and sipped again at the whisky while I contemplated the 50-gram pouch of double-cherry flavoured tobacco, packet of cigarette papers and a small bag of filters. I had done so well the past months and, in truth, did feel better for it, but the cravings were a constant, demanding companion and the latest developments easily passed in my mind as a case of "Break Glass in Emergency".

I tore open the pack, rolled a cigarette and lit it with the barbecue lighter. I coughed once, deeply, as the smoke hit my lungs then rinsed the ash taste from my mouth with another pull on the whisky. In seconds the nicotine hit my system and I settled back on the lounge with my eyes closed and a light smile of ecstasy on my face. I would worry about my health and my lack of self-discipline at another time.

Above me, the jet-black night sky was cloudless and dotted with a million pinpricks of light, as if a great hand had scattered diamonds across a bolt of black velvet. The familiar outlines of The Peak and Mount Cameron were invisible against the dark of night but, over the hum of traffic, I could hear the shrieks and warbles of night birds in the jungle far above me.

It was cold and I pulled my jacket tighter as I sipped the whisky. I dragged on the cigarette, desperate like the embrace of a lost lover, and exhaled a cloud of cherry-scented smoke into the night. Bors sat by my side, and I tossed him a treat – a length of biltong – that he noisily and enthusiastically devoured.

It was a peaceful scene, and I was almost lulled into riding along with it, but dark and confused thoughts whirled through my mind. The music track had changed and Dan Auerbach's jangle rock guitar vibed its way over and around the lyrics that told me of the terrible choices I had made, and of the heartbreak to come.

I *had* made many terrible choices in my life but the most terrible of all had been stealing the triad money. Even now, thinking about it in those terms, "triad money", I felt no guilt at what I had done. I was trapped now anyway – if I tried to give it back, I'd be giving them my life into the bargain. What stabbed at my conscience were the consequences my actions now appeared to have brought into the lives of those around me.

If, as I dreaded, the figure I had fleetingly seen, in the dark, on the run, was Peter Toh, the man who had tried to murder me two years earlier, that meant it was him who had been following me, not Jade Tooth's boys. *Was* it Peter? It certainly had not sounded like his voice, and I had known him for over 20 years. But *if* it was him, that meant SYO were not on to me over the missing millions – at least not to the extent they were telegraphing it by trailing me all over Hong Kong. That was the good news.

The bad news was, if all this were true, Peter Toh had returned from whatever hole he had crawled into two years ago and was stalking me. Why? What did he want and why was Joey also being followed and by whom? The thought of Peter back in my life and on my heels made me shudder. I swilled back the last of the whisky and rolled and lit another cigarette.

My dinner forgotten and cold, I poured another long measure and gazed up at the stars, dragging on the smoke.

How did I know which scenario was true here? Was it Toh or was it Jade Tooth, and how the hell did I figure that out? Despite an earlier resolution, I now had no intention of bumbling into Jade Tooth's place trying to test the level of his knowledge of the stolen cash. If he didn't know, he didn't need me to tell him. But the question remained: who was following us? The only plan I could conjure up was to stake myself out like a goat and see who arrived first: Peter Toh or Jade Tooth. It wasn't much of a plan, and the outcomes didn't look great, but it was all I had.

One thing *was* clear: I had to get Joey out of the way somehow. She was not going to take kindly to me locking her up somewhere while I sorted out the problem I had brought upon her. Still, I needed her safe and out of the way so I could concentrate on whatever was coming at me.

Perhaps I could ask Angel to take Joey in for a while – Angel's protection team would see that Joey was safe and sound. I laughed out loud at the thought and Bors looked up sharply, his head cocked. Neither of them much liked the other – Joey because Angel was triad, and Angel because Joey was a beautiful young woman with whom I spent most of my time; never mind that Joey's tastes didn't run to middle-aged men like me (*any* men really). I chuckled again at the thought of locking them together in a house. But Angel could certainly help me get some protection for Joey at arm's length so I would not have to deal directly with the heavies in 14K.

I decided I would call Angel in the morning and raise it with her – then all I had to do was convince Joey. I sat back, sipping slowly at the whisky, feeling its rich warmth through me and tried to clear my mind. I closed my eyes.

Getting in touch with The Panda seemed like a better idea now than it had earlier in the evening. Having Tommy Ho at my back was definitely something I would need in the coming days until the shit really hit the fan and I knew where I stood. I shook my head. There was every chance Peter Toh was back and SYO were hunting their money, I was back in bed with 14K triad, and I was smoking again. It was turning out to be quite a night.

19

THE WOMAN in Pok Fu Lam was a delight. I gripped myself at the same time I entered her with the steel. I think her screams against the tape were perhaps the sweetest I have heard in... forever. She loved it. She wanted me to hurt her. I squeezed and tugged at myself while I cut her and bit her. I tore at her with my teeth and every gush of her hot blood into my mouth was orgasmic. It made me harder. The more she writhed and screamed, gagging against the tape across her mouth, the harder I got, the closer I came. It was sublime. All the while working the knife in under her ribs and taking off a breast. That was when I began to eat her alive. Her eyes stood out on stalks as I chewed her hot, raw flesh and swallowed it. She wasn't the first of course – I've been eating pieces of my partners for years – but I remember her as the sweetest. Like a succulent little piggy raised on the tastiest of forest acorns. Are you alright? You look ill? Anyway, as usual, it was over too soon and I came in my underwear – no DNA that way, you see. I carved the initials across her belly then I lay beside her for a while, the ground soft on my back. After a while, I went home. I took her necklace; a dreadful, cheap thing.

20

My knee groaned as I turned off Kennedy Road and up the steep incline of the Wan Chai Green Trail. Bors ran effortlessly beside me, taking the hill in his stride, as I leaned into the slope and slogged my way up. I had woken early and thrown on my running gear and headed out to clear my head after making two calls. The first had been to Angel and it had gone pretty much as I had expected. Angel didn't like being woken early – and for her that was before 9:00 – and she did not like surprises. Asking her to provide protection to Joey was a surprise.

'Why are you calling me at this ungodly hour, Gal?' she had croaked sleepily. I could imagine her lying in bed, her long black hair ruffled and eyes droopy with sleep.

'It's 7:30,' I replied. 'Most normal people are up and at it by now.'

'I'm not "normal". You know this...'

I had chuckled and sipped the espresso from the small glass in my hand. 'True,' I said. 'Look, I have a favour to ask.'

Angel groaned, and I heard the duvet rustle as she sat up in bed. 'Go on...'

'Joey and I are being followed. I'm not sure who it is but I *think* it's Jade Tooth's boys,' I said, deciding against telling Angel of my fleeting half-glimpse of a shadowy figure I thought might have been Peter Toh. 'I'm going to call on Tommy Ho to run some counter-surveillance for me, but I was hoping you might be able to tuck Joey away somewhere safe for a while.'

Angel was silent for a moment then: 'You want protection for your little trollope, and you want *me* to organise it?'

I sighed. 'Angel don't be an idiot. Joey is neither a trollope, nor is she "mine". She's being followed and I have a bad feeling about it. I want her protected and you're the best person to do that. Can you?'

She heaved a dramatic sigh. 'Okay, my love. For you, yes. But first, tell me why. Why is Jade Tooth tailing you and *that* girl?'

There was no point lying to Angel about it. She was going to find out sooner or later, so I decided to come clean. I took a deep breath and dived in.

'That night I tracked David Zhou he was carrying a duffle bag. It was full of US hundred-dollar notes; 2.5 million of it to be exact. I threw it over the cliff before Peter shot me. When I got out of hospital I went back and retrieved the bag and kept the cash. I think SYO have finally worked out where their missing money went and have got Jade Tooth on the job to get it back...' The phone was silent, and I checked we had not been cut off. 'You still there, Angel?'

'You took a bag of cash belonging to SYO,' she said quietly.

'Yes...'

'And you kept it.'

'Yes.'

'*Diu*, Galahad,' she laughed. 'That's both very naughty and *very* stupid of you. What on *earth* made you think you would get away with that?

I shrugged, staring off at the hills above my terrace. 'It seemed like a good idea at the time.'

'Well, never mind,' Angel replied lightly. 'It's done now. We just have to make sure SYO don't get their hands on you and that little bimbo.'

'She's not a ...

'And...' Angel went on, thinking two steps ahead 'we have to make sure SYO don't connect us with you and the missing money. It could start a war if they think we took it.' Her voice changed as she pondered that dilemma. 'Not sure how we do that, but I'll think of a way...' she said to herself. 'Maybe we just get rid of you, hey? No more you, no more problem...'

'Angel, that's not funny.'

'Who said I was joking...?'

I really hoped she was joking. The thing about Angel was you never really knew if she was about to kiss you or slip a knife between your ribs. It was what made our relationship so addictive.

'Look, can you help out or not?' I asked, a little huffily.

She chuckled again, throaty and dangerously sexy. 'Of course, babe. *She* I can do without but whatever would I do if I lost *you*?

I sighed. 'Thanks Angel, I owe you...'

'I shall add that to the growing list of things you owe me. Now, how do we do this? I mean Hello Kitty is not going to just let me lock her up somewhere, now is she.'

'Her name's "Josephine" ...'

'Yes, yes... How do we protect your little biker moll?'

I sighed. Angel was never going to let up baiting me over Joey. It was like a sport for her. 'I agree she won't go into hiding,' I said. 'She's too independent and tough for that.' Angel snorted down the line. 'So, can you put a team on her? Cover her at home, the office, when she's moving about...?'

'Can,' Angel replied. 'You said you're calling The Panda, right? Well, when you do, tell him I give the okay to put a four-man team on Gidget. You've got two weeks, that's all.'

'Done. Two weeks will have this all sorted out,' I said not believing myself. I had a nasty feeling whatever was behind all this was going to stretch into our lives far beyond the next fortnight.

Angel had hung up after extracting a promise from me to take her to dinner that weekend and I had quickly called Tommy Ho while I laced up my trainers.

Typically, The Panda had shown no interest in the reason behind the request – if he had he would never show it. He had agreed to put a team on Joey immediately and to start following me about from mid-afternoon that day after he had finished another job that called for his particular talents. I shuddered to think what that job might be or who the poor soul was that was about to experience one of the Panda's "chastisements". That done I had snapped the leash to Bors' collar, and headed out.

I was sweating freely by the time I got to the top of the Green Trail and turned left along Bowen Road Fitness Trail, despite the chill in the clear winter morning. My lungs burned for the first time in months, and I was beginning to regret buying that pouch of tobacco. I wiped the sweat from my eyes and ran on. Below me, beyond the jungle covered slopes of the hill, the city spread out in a shimmering blanket of towers and buildings that spread from Happy Valley to the Harbour, glinting in the bright blue sky of a Hong Kong winter day.

Joggers and walkers passed me by, heading the opposite way along the trail, most careful to give Bors a wide berth. Except for the kids. Children, I had found, loved Bors and were attracted to him like they are to a teddy bear. Much to the horror of their parents, young kids would often come in close to pat or hug Bors and he always replied with rumble of delight from deep in his chest and a wet lick from his impossibly long, black tongue.

As I ran, I considered what lay before me. There was so much that seemed tangled up and I couldn't unravel the knot.

Despite it still nagging at me I decided to put Walter Chan and Guo aside for a later date. Doing that bothered me – I itched to get to the bottom of that mystery – but there seemed to be more serious matters pressing in on me.

Why had Michael Wong appeared out of nowhere to ask me about the Hiking Trail Murders? I did not believe for a moment he considered me a person of interest, but I was sure I was somehow tied up in his Taskforce's inquiries. The question was how? What was it that had aroused Michael's interest in me? Or was it simply just a case of him back-checking on the Thomas Murders and my recollection of them? If that was so, what similarities were there between the Thomas' and the most recent killings? Come to that, why had I suddenly remembered Peter Toh's confession only days before I thought I caught a fleeting glimpse of him running from me across Wan Chai rooftops? I simply could not believe that Peter Toh was back in Hong Kong, involved in the recent murders and was stalking me. It was all just too improbable.

I spat into the vegetation on the side of the track and ran on, checking my pulse rate on the G-Shock at my wrist. It was ticking along at a steady 133 and I felt good, in my stride, my mind and body cruising in harmony as I entered the runner's zone. For his part, Bors padded along in a distance-eating trot that didn't waver, kilometre after kilometre.

The murders were horrific, but they had nothing to do with me and I really didn't care. I had my own problems. At the top of that list was Jade Tooth and his gang on the hunt for SYO's money that they, somehow, had figured out I possessed. The question there was how did I stay ahead of them and out of their clutches? I told myself that once Jade Tooth saw The Panda was at my back he would give up and look elsewhere for the money. I had barely framed that thought when a voice in my head told me I was kidding myself. No, things really did not look good. To cap it all off, I had to meet Prudence's new boyfriend the next night in Central and I was definitely not looking forward to that.

I got the end of the fitness trail, darted across Tai Hang Road, and headed up to the steep descent of Blue Pool Road. Bors and I plunged down, each step a grinding agony on my knees until we finally emerged at the bottom of the hill by Happy Valley Racecourse. I pulled Bors up momentarily as I rubbed at my knees, and he eyed me with what looked like disappointment before we trotted off again for the last stretch around the racecourse to home.

As I hit my stride, I turned inward to my thoughts. Pru's new boyfriend was an unwelcome wrinkle as far as I was concerned. Selfishly, I was annoyed at having to meet and be civil to a total stranger – one who was dating my kid sister – when I had bigger problems on my plate. I snorted as I ran. An attitude like that was probably the reason I had very few friends, but I couldn't help it. I just didn't like people very much.

Bors and I slipped across Leighton Road against a red and, in moments, pulled up outside my apartment building. I glanced up and down the road then settled my gaze on a kid sitting outside the convenience store, drinking a Coke and smoking. He looked up, sensing my eyes on him, and gave me a thumbs up. I had long ago enlisted the neighbourhood kids as my early warning and they did a good job, covering two blocks around my apartment day and night for a small payment each month. Angel had once told me – only half-jokingly – she wanted to recruit them to the triad and that had just made me all the more determined to keep them in my employ, even when I didn't really need them. But I needed them now.

I nodded at my sentry, keyed in the code to the building door and stepped in, summoning the lift with a stab of my finger. I checked my G-Shock. Nearly 10:00. I decided I was safe enough in my neighbourhood to drop off some laundry and pick up groceries. It was hours until Tommy Ho was free to cover my back while I went about trying to earn a quid for "Jones & Loh", so I decided on a leisurely morning of domestic chores while Hong Kong went about its business.

Half an hour later, showered and changed with Bors asleep in his bed, I stepped back out into the street with a bag of laundry slung over my shoulder.

The hot exhaust of a stopping bus blew over me, warming against the chill of the day and I sidestepped the passengers disembarking into the hectic footpath flow. On its tracks, free of the vans, cars and taxis that crawled up and down the road, a Shau Kei Wan-bound tram rattled and clanked its way past. Its sides were plastered with a huge poster of a beautiful woman smiling delightedly up at a handsome young man. None of the passengers onboard looked remotely delighted.

I crossed the road and entered Sharp Street West, the narrow street on which my laundry lady had her thriving business. The street was clear. As I passed the entrance to Chan Tong Lane, I spotted another of my sentries and raised my hand in greeting.

The kid stood and gave me a smile that instantly changed to a look of horror. I had barely registered the shocked look on his face when a bag went over my head. My legs gave way as I was struck behind the left ear and I was bundled into the back of a van that roared away up the street with me pinned to the floor by a pair of heavy-booted feet. The van swung hard to the left and I was thrown across the floor to strike my head on a hard, sharp edge. I grunted in pain and a dark curtain descended slowly over my eyes as I lost consciousness.

21

FAINT LIGHT FILTERED through the course weave of the bag over my head. It was a hessian bag and smelled of rotten vegetables.

I sat perfectly still, my head slumped, as I tried to gather my thoughts. I was sitting in a metal chair and my hands were bound at the wrist behind the chair. My ankles were tied to the chair legs. I could hear soft clinking sounds off to my left, like someone tapping a glass before a wedding speech. The room was warm and, apart from the glass clinking, completely silent. I could sense someone standing behind me and, as I concentrated, I could hear breathing, laboured as though through a broken nose.

My head ached and I could feel dry blood, cracked and itchy, behind my ear. Whoever was in the room was waiting for me to come around, so I decided to get on with it. I groaned and raised my head, looking blindly around me. I heard a click of fingers, and the bag was whipped from my head. I blinked my eyes in the sudden brightness of a desk lamp and found myself looking into a face I had hoped never to see again. Jade Tooth.

The gangster sat perched on the edge of a table in front of me, his arms crossed. He was wearing his favourite black mesh T-shirt and skinny jeans, and the black-shaded tattoo of a dragon writhed the length of his right arm. The fingers of his right hand were studded with gold rings, and I noted he had moved on in the last two years from a massive gold watch in favour of an equally large stainless-steel Hublot with mesh bracelet. One thing about Jade Tooth: he was a madman but he knew his watches.

Without taking his eyes off me he reached back and pulled a cigarette from the packet on the table. Still watching me, his black eyes cold and reptilian, he struck a match and lit the smoke, slowly waving the match out. He sucked his teeth. I saw they were brilliant white, and he had obviously had work. I swore one day soon I'd hammer those expensive, white teeth down his throat.

'You don't seem surprised to see me, Galahad,' he said quietly.

'I am a little, Jade Tooth,' I croaked. 'It's been, what? Two years. To what do I owe the pleasure...?'

Jade Tooth chuckled. It sounded like death, and I shivered involuntarily. 'I have not seen you at Mahjong for, like, *ages* man. Why is that?'

'I don't gamble anymore.'

He laughed outright at that. '*Diu*, man! You're a gambler – not a good one but a gambler. You want it. No, you *need* it. And here...' he swept an arm around the grimy surrounds of the "The Lucky Dragon", his den deep in Yau Ma Tei. 'I can meet your needs.'

I realised then that the clinking sound I had heard was two old ladies putting out ashtrays and glasses in readiness for the evening's illicit Mahjong school. They carried on around us as if there wasn't a man tied to a chair in the middle of the room. I shook my head.

'I have other interests now, Jade Tooth.'

He dragged hard at the cigarette, held delicately between two long, finely manicured fingers.

Jade Tooth had always looked and acted like a Bond villain, but I wasn't lulled by that. He was still one of the most violent men in Hong Kong and SYO's number one enforcer. He was a very dangerous, and slightly unhinged, person. I wasn't sure I would get - out of this in one piece and my mind worked frantically.

By now I had figured out why I was tied to a chair, facing the man

I least wanted to see. It was the stolen SYO cash. One thing about that: it ruled out my feverish imaginings of Peter Toh returning to Hong Kong to stalk me through its streets and murder people on our hiking trails. Peter was God knows where, but he wasn't in Hong Kong. Joey and I were being followed by SYO and now there would be a reckoning.

Jade Tooth lifted up his T-shirt and pulled out the matt black form of a QSZ-92 and placed the handgun carefully on the table beside him.

'Are you not going to ask why you are here, Mr Jones?' he asked, sounding a little miffed.

'I figured *you'd* get to that.'

He wagged a finger at me, smiling. 'Oh I admire you, I really do,' he said. 'You must *know* you're not getting out of here alive, but you're cool. *Diu* man, you're cool like George fucking Clooney!'

I sat silently and he went on. 'The strong silent type you are. You're not going to beg me, are you?' He scratched his chin. 'Damn, I wish you *would* beg.' He flicked the butt of his cigarette onto the floor and an old lady swept down on it with her dustpan and broom. 'Okay, let's get on with it, shall we?'

Jade Tooth nodded at the figure behind me and lit another cigarette. As he stepped around to face me, I saw the man behind me was one of Jade Tooth's soldiers who I had kicked in the face two years earlier. That explained the flattened nose and the laboured breathing. I was mid-way through congratulating myself when the soldier's right fist lashed out and slammed into my mouth.

My lips split and blood exploded over my chin. He punched me again, this time flush on the nose. The pain was an explosion in my head, too intense for me to even make a sound. The bridge of my nose shattered, and the cartilage tore. Blood flowed freely over my shirt. I groaned and my eyes flickered. That was the signal for Jade Tooth's boy to really get to work.

Blow after blow rained down on me, thudding into my face, my jaw and my stomach. At one point he got creative and lifted a leg to slam the heel of his shoe into my groin. The pain was indescribable, and I could hear someone screaming loud in the room. I was vaguely worried for the old ladies who were witnessing this, but I needn't have been: they were too busy making teas and it was me doing the screaming.

After what seemed an age, and an endless wave of pain, the beating finally stopped. My eyes were swollen and near shut but I could see Jade Tooth as he studied the fingernails of his right hand. The iron-tang of blood in the room was overpowering. Somewhere behind me I could hear the old ladies laying out teacups and filling the hot water urns.

'Where is the money, Galahad?' he asked quietly, like a parent asking a child what he had done with his socks.

I spat on the floor, the clotted blood splatting onto the sticky carpet with a wet slap. 'I don't know want you're talking about,' I mumbled.

Jade Tooth sighed dramatically. 'Galahad, you're being tiresome. Just tell me where the money is, and I'll give you a quick end.' He stood up from the table and took a step toward me, leaning down close to my face. 'Painless and quick. I promise,' he whispered softly into my ear. 'Not like the others on the trails...'

It was classic Hobson's Choice. Tell Jade Tooth I had the money and die or deny any knowledge and die. Somewhere in the back of my mind a voice told me that if I was going to die anyway then SYO wouldn't get their money. Fuck them! I would say nothing.

'What money?' I groaned.

'*Jesus* man! The two and half million US. The money we *know* Zhou took from us when he ran. You were the last to see him alive... you have the money.'

I shook my head. 'Peter Toh was the last to see him alive. He shot Zhou and took the duffle bag. The money must have been in that...'

Jade Tooth squinted. 'Peter Toh? *He* took the money...?'

I nodded. 'He must have. After he shot me, he grabbed the bag and ran.'

Jade Tooth's mind was working furiously, I could almost hear the wheels in his twisted mind grinding away. I sucked in a deep breath and choked on a gobbet of blood. Jade Tooth turned and walked around in a tight circle, muttering quietly to himself. I prayed I had hooked him and that I might still get out of this.

Finally, Jade Tooth turned to face me. 'Toh, as we now know, was deep-plant SYO. Why would he steal from us?' He shook his head. 'No, he would not have. He wouldn't *dare*...'

I cackled insanely. 'You're *all* a bunch of thieving bastards. You'd steal from your own mothers if you felt the need. Don't imagine, for a moment, that Peter wouldn't take the chance to get away with a sack full of cash to whatever shithole he ran to ...'

Jade Tooth came in close and bent down, his face so close our noses touched. He shook his head. 'No. You're lying...'

'I'm not, you demented fool!' I shouted. This was it. Time up.

Jade Tooth stood, his hands on his hips and head cocked like a vulture eying a carcass. 'I'll look into this – maybe Toh *did* take the cash – but *your* time has come, Mr Jones. You have been a thorn in my side for years and now I shall pluck that nuisance sting from my flesh.' He looked at the soldier standing over my right shoulder.

'Finish it,' he said and, picking up his handgun, walked from the room. From the corner of my eye I saw the two old ladies scuttle out, their heads down and eyes averted.

The soldier moved around to face me and drew a knife from his belt. He grinned horribly, his twisted yellow teeth showing like fangs on a rabid dog. The six-inch blade glinted wickedly in the half-light of "The Lucky Dragon".

'I'm going to enjoy this, you bastard,' he said in Cantonese and dragged the blade across my right cheek, cutting it so deep I felt the rasp of steel against my jawbone.

I gritted my teeth and growled in agony. Smiling demonically, the gangster stuck the tip of the blade into my left shoulder and, after a brief pause, slowly pushed the knife home to the hilt. I roared in pain and fear, rocking helplessly in the chair. The knife was pulled out, a razor-sharp ripping sensation, and the soldier raised his arm to deliver another blow. I couldn't take it anymore and hoped desperately this one would end it. I closed my eyes and waited for death.

The shot came out of nowhere and my eyes struggled open in time to see the gangster stumble back, a red flower blossoming on his forehead, brain matter and blood spraying out behind him. The body hit the carpet with a thud and hot blood pumped onto the floor in a flood. I sobbed in disbelief and tried to turn my head as a voice sounded behind me at the back of the room.

'*Diu*, Galahad. When will you learn to do what you are told? I said: "stay home, don't go out." Did I not?'

My eyes widened in their puffed and beaten sockets as the bearded, squat shape of Tommy Ho stepped up to face me. The Panda threw the hem of his jacket aside and holstered his firearm, a SIG Sauer P226, then crossed his arms in mock annoyance. Despite what he had just done – or perhaps because of it – he smiled widely.

'Hello. It's been a while,' he said as he snapped out a knife and cut the ropes around my ankles then moved behind and cut my wrists free.

I tried to stand but fell to my knees, a trail of blood and snot hanging from my shattered lips and nose. The Panda's muscular arms pulled me up and held me steady.

'I think it's time we left, don't you?' he said quietly

I shook my head. 'Where...? How...?' I mumbled, blood still trickling from my mouth.

My cheek felt like it was split from my ear to the corner of my mouth. My shoulder was on fire, and I could feel the blood flowing down my side. I was losing a lot of it and I needed a doctor quickly.

'Later,' The Panda said. 'Right now, I want to get out of here... I hate SYO and I *detest* Mahjong.' With that Tommy Ho took me by the elbow, and under one arm, and guided me up the stairs of "The Lucky Dragon" to the sunlight of the street above.

I don't remember much of the rest of that day. A glimpse or two of a fast drive through Hong Kong, Tommy Ho at the wheel with one arm steadying me in the passenger seat. Sun shining brightly through the windscreen and exploding into a thousand rainbows that dazzled my puffed and squinted eyes. Snatches of conversation. Stairs. The stab of a needle into my arm. More conversation as someone cut the shirt and jeans off me. The sharp stab of a canula entering a vein. Pinpricks at my face and my shoulder then the tugging of sutures. My nose gripped painfully in a vice. Murmuring voices. Sleep.

22

IT WAS dark when I awoke. I couldn't see from my right eye and the left was slightly blurred. I glanced around without moving my head. The room was softly lit with a small bedside lamp, and it was warm. The one window was curtained, and a faint sound of traffic filtered into the room. On the left of the bed stood an IV pole, a bag of clear fluid slowly dripping through the giving set that ran into my left forearm. I couldn't breathe properly and realised my shattered nose was packed with cotton wadding. A ceiling fan turned slowly above me, stirring the warm air in the room. I turned my head slightly and looked at the figure seated on my right. I had seen him once before, two years ago. He removed his glasses and rubbed his eyes.

'Hello again, Mr Whoever You Are,' the doctor said smiling. 'Do you remember me?' I nodded. He leaned across and took my pulse. 'Good,' he said. 'Nice and strong. How do you feel?'

'Like shit,' I managed to croak, my voice sounding nasal and distorted. A second figure in the room moved into the light and brought a glass of water to my swollen lips. I drank it greedily and nodded at Tommy Ho as he put the glass down. 'Better,' I said. 'So, what's the damage...?'

'Well, yet again, you were lucky. You lost quite a lot of blood, but no serious damage done. I put one unit into you and that's a saline drip now to keep up your fluids. Mr Ho will change the bag during the night.'

He put his glasses back on to see me better. 'I gave you a shot of Butorphanol before I worked on you. I've stitched the wound on your shoulder and closed the gash on your face – you'll have a nice duelling scar there. The shoulder wound was deep, but it was clean. You were lucky the blade was so sharp. No nasty tearing.'

He pointed at my face. 'You have a blowout fracture of the right orbit. That will bruise badly and, most likely, you will always have some nerve damage there but nothing too serious, I think. The eye is safe. I can't see any serious damage. Your left eye is bruised slightly but I can't see any damage to it. Your nose is badly broken. I manually realigned it, and have splinted it, but I fear you will need surgery down the track to correct it. In the meantime, I must inform you that your rugged good looks are now somewhat less appealing.'

Across the room I heard The Panda snort. The doctor turned and fished around in his bag, coming up with two small bottles.

'Just like before, he said raising his right hand. 'This one is Amoxicillin. Good broad-spectrum antibiotic. Instructions on the bottle.' He gently placed the bottle on the bedside table. 'And this one,' he said rattling another bottle, 'is Panadeine Forte...it will take the edge off the pain, which I expect will be quite severe once the anaesthetic in your drip wears off.'

I raised my head. 'Tommy, any chance of a drink?' The Panda nodded and left the room. I could hear his footsteps clomping down a set of stairs.

The doctor harrumphed and collected his gear. He stood and looked down at me. 'I don't know who you are. I don't want to know. But you have a habit of getting into trouble and one of these days it will kill you. Do try and be more careful.' With that he turned and left the room, leaving me hoping I would never see him again.

Tommy Ho returned with a bottle of Chinese whisky and a glass. He poured a small measure and handed it to me. I gulped it down greedily, feeling the heat of it hit my throat and spread through me like steam. Tommy watched me closely.

'You don't take very good care of yourself, Mr Jones,' he said. 'I've noticed that about you.'

I shrugged, then winced as a stab of pain lanced through my left shoulder then again when the wince screwed up the broken right eye socket. 'Jesus,' I hissed.

'So, Tommy,' I said. 'Don't get me wrong but how in the hell did you find me at Jade Tooth's place?'

'You're welcome!'

'You know what I mean... I was a dead man when you, who I wasn't supposed to meet on the other side of Hong Kong until hours later, stride in, do the job on Jade Tooth's boy and carry me out. Thanks, by the way...' I added, a little sheepishly.

'I got a call right after you were snatched...'

'Who from?'

'One of my boys in your neighbourhood,' Tommy said, smiling.

'One of *your*...'

'Your sentries Galahad – oh, good idea by the way. They are all mine. They are all 14K runners. Some of them will soon be Blue Lanterns,' he said, referring to the triad's title for an uninitiated member.

My heart sank. I had hoped, somehow, to keep the boys out the reach of the triads but I should have known better. Even though they were still young, and far from initiation, they were in and would be for life. Until their life ended in a dirty alley, with a bullet in the brain.

Tommy frowned solicitously. 'Don't let it get you down, Mr Jones. It's the way of things...'

'Yeah,' I mumbled. 'Doesn't mean I have to like it though...'

Tommy shrugged, unconcerned at my moral gymnastics. I was in deep with a triad but didn't want any kids doing the same. Was that irony or hypocrisy?

'Anyway,' Tommy went on. 'I had no idea where you were headed. It really could have been anyone and anywhere. Luckily Ms Yeung told me last night about your "lottery win" ...' I groaned. The whole of Hong Kong would know in days at this rate. 'So,' Tommy said. 'I figured it *could* have been "The Lucky Dragon" you were headed for. I was already across the harbour when I got another call after one of my men saw you bundled in the back entrance of the club with a bag over your head.'

He shrugged. 'The rest, as westerners like to say, is history.'

I shook my head. 'You killed an SYO soldier, Tommy. In Jade Tooth's club! That sort of history has a way of repeating itself...' I clumsily poured another shot of the cheap whisky and swallowed it.

'Possibly,' Tommy conceded. 'But I don't think so. SYO won't declare war on that basis. What's one more dead soldier?'

'Jade Tooth isn't particularly forgiving, Tommy. He'll come out swinging after this.'

Tommy shrugged. 'Maybe, maybe not. If he does, then we shall "swing" back.'

'That's called "escalation".'

'No, that's called "life", Mr Jones.' He raised his hands. 'Anyway, there is no point in worrying about it now. What will be will be...'

'That's very Doris Day of you Tommy.'

'What?'

I shook my head. 'Never mind,' I said. 'Jesus, I'll have to have my head on a swivel now... I'm a marked man.'

'Not really,' Tommy said.

'Oh? How do you figure that?'

'Have I not made myself clear? You were about to be killed by an SYO soldier. I shot him. You're known now as 14K, as clearly as if we had tattooed you. Even Jade Tooth won't risk a street war by harming you.'

I frowned. 'Stupidly, I *had* been hoping to avoid being roped in completely...'

'Mr Jones, you were *in* from the moment you agreed to help our Mountain Master. Did not Mr Lee tell you in the car that day that no one is clean, and no one is ever out?'

I remembered back to that meeting in the back of Lee Pak-chun's

Mercedes. He had revealed the name of my father's killer in exchange for services I had rendered him. There was no doubt about it: 14K had owned me since that moment. I was just lucky they had not called in their marker. Yet.

I thought about that for a minute. 'I notice you haven't asked me about the money...'

'None of my business.'

'I guess not...'

'I will say this, however: With that amount of money in your account I am dismayed you still wear jeans and T-shirts at every opportunity. Can't you do better...?'

I grinned. It hurt to do that. 'I'm a man of simple tastes, Tommy.'

Tommy smiled back. 'Get some sleep, Mr Jones. You need it. Tomorrow I will drive you home and you can get on with your life. What's left of it...'

Tommy chuckled at his dark joke then left the room, closing the door softly behind him.

The Panda had a point: I needed to get on with my life, but I wasn't at all sure how long that life would be. I was unconvinced about Tommy's assessment of the day's events. With a groan I suddenly realised the next day was the long-planned meeting with Prudence and her new boyfriend. I couldn't go looking like this, but I decided that was a problem for the morrow so, switching off the bedside lamp, I closed my aching eyes and soon drifted off to sleep.

23

THE NEXT MORNING I woke in pain. I sat up in bed with a groan and reached for the bottle of Panadeine. Swallowing down two of the thick, white tablets with a mouthful of water I stood shaking and naked in the warm room.

I noticed a small bathroom off the bedroom and shuffled in, my feet slapping against the cold tiles. Leaning on the sink, I stared in the mirror. My right eye was closed and swollen, a dark green bruise spreading across the cheek. The socket ached. My left eye didn't look much better but at least I could see out of it despite the split across the eyebrow. My left shoulder throbbed, and surgical gauze covered the stitched wound. My right cheek, also covered in a piece of surgical gauze, stung as if I had glass embedded under the skin. My lips were puffed and fattened like over-ripe fruit and my nose, packed with wadding, and wrapped in a dressing, was bloated and misshapen.

I gripped the sink tightly as a wave of nausea swept over me and my legs threatened to give way. There was no doubt about it, I was a mess but I was lucky to be alive.

I staggered unsteadily back into the bedroom and sat on the edge of the bed as the dizziness subsided. By the bedside table, on the chair in which the doctor had sat, lay a pile of neatly folded clothes, some still in their wrappers. Jeans, a cheap brown leather belt, a black T-shirt, socks, underwear, and a navy puffer jacket. My desert boots were neatly aligned under the chair and my G-Shock was on the table beside the lamp. I smiled. The Panda had thought of everything.

After struggling into the clothes, I was pulling on my boots when the bedroom door opened and Tommy Ho stepped in, a delicate China cup and saucer in his hands.

'Green tea,' he said, holding up the cup. 'Good for pain and inflammation. Are you hungry? There's no kitchen to speak of in this place so I haven't prepared anything...'

I took the saucer and cup from Tommy and sipped gratefully at the hot, grass-scented brew. 'Thanks,' I said. 'That's good. No, I'm not hungry. I'm just ... confused. Not really sure what's going on...'

Tommy nodded. 'Yes, that will happen after a serious injury. Pain and shock can be a turbulent combination on one's state of mind.'

'Thank you, Dr Panda.' I said. 'I suppose I should get home.' I turned back to the bedside table. 'Where's my phone?'

Tommy shrugged. 'No idea. It wasn't on you yesterday. Jade Tooth must have taken it...'

I groaned. Jade Tooth would not be able to break into the phone, so I was not too concerned about that, but the inconvenience of purchasing and setting up a new phone was just another annoyance I really didn't need. 'There is a store for my provider near home, so can you drop me there?'

Tommy pulled out his own phone. 'I'll do you one better.' He flicked through his contacts and made a call while I sat back on the bed, holding my head in my hands. 'Done,' he said after a minute, ending the call. 'A new phone will be waiting at your place – one of the sentries will have it. It will have a sim fitted and your old number will already be ported across.'

I looked up. 'Jesus, thanks Tommy. I can't think straight and am feeling pretty sorry for myself. I really appreciate your help.'

Tommy bowed slightly, his right fist and left palm joined in the

Hold Fist salute. 'It is both my duty and pleasure, Mr Jones,' he said solemnly.

I believed him. Tommy Ho was a hardened criminal and an extremely dangerous man, but he was also a man with a deeply ingrained sense of honour – albeit of the kind seen among organised criminals. Despite who, and what, he was I felt a surge of warmth and respect for this triad soldier.

'Okay then,' I said. 'Let's get going.'

It wasn't until we were outside and in the black Mercedes heading south toward the Cross Harbour Tunnel that I realised I had been held in a safehouse on Kowloon-side. It made sense for The Panda to have taken me there. The district we drove out of was 14K heartland that bordered Sun Yee On turf. I settled back in the leather seat of the warm car and let the morning sun play across my face. I closed my eyes and was only half listening to the radio news when I heard Tommy grunt.

'What?' I asked, not really interested, keeping my eyes closed as I luxuriated in the gentle caress of the sun on my tortured face.

'Another hiking trail murder,' he said. 'Hong Kong Trail again, this time near Sheung Tam Stream.'

I snapped awake and reached to turn up the radio volume. The announcer's voice, in Cantonese, was breathlessly describing the events.

"*... another body, only this time an elderly gentleman. Police are declining to release details at this time although they confirmed the establishment of a Taskforce to track and capture the killer...*" "*The body was found by hikers yesterday afternoon in a remote section of Tai Tam Country Park, close to the waters of Sheung Tam. A brief Police statement describes the condition of the body as 'recent' and 'bearing similarities to the other murders on Hong Kong's hiking trails...'*" "*Two witnesses who found the body are assisting Police with their inquiries and have been held incommunicado at Arsenal House...*"

Tommy Ho shook his head. 'How many is that now?'

I thought for a moment. 'Three… that they know of.'

Tommy nodded, glancing out the side window as he steered the car around a bend onto tunnel on-ramp. 'If it's three then that's all … so far.'

'What do you mean?'

'He wants these bodies found. He's showing off. He doesn't want them to go unnoticed…'.

The radio commentary went on.

"Well, my friends, I think we can safely say we have a serial killer in Hong Kong. Don't you? Look, the cops are saying nothing, but it's well known these victims have all been brutally murdered, all on hiking trails and all in recent weeks. My source inside Arsenal House tells me the killings all show distinct similarities in the methods used and the violence inflicted on the poor victims...'

Tommy leaned across and stabbed a finger at the dash, silencing the morning jock. It was silent in the car, and I closed my eyes again.

'You know,' I said. 'Chief Inspector Wong seems to think there is a connection between me and these killings.'

Tommy made a sound of mild surprise. '*Is* there?'

I opened my eyes and turned my head to look at him. 'Of course not!'

'Why would Wong think that then? He's no man's fool.'

I shrugged. 'I can only guess because of the Thomas' two years back. He's fishing that maybe I know something… which I *don't*. Not only do I not know anything, Tommy, I have very few fucks to give about the killings. I mean, sure, they're brutal and it's all very shocking but they are nothing to do with me and are not something I want to bother myself with.' I indicated my face with the wave of a hand. 'As you can see, I have my own problems.'

Tommy Ho was silent for a long moment. 'These were innocent victims, Mr Jones,' he said, his voice calm. 'Brutally murdered for a reason they could not possibly have fathomed. I think your attitude is a little selfish…'

That shocked me, coming from a triad soldier. 'You kill people for a *living* Tommy!'

'I do not. Well, yes, sometimes, but only when ordered to do so and only for very good reason and those people are, most assuredly, *never* innocent...'

Here I was, all this time, thinking *my* moral compass was dubious. There was no point arguing so I decided to give a little ground. 'Yes, I guess I should have more sympathy for the victims, but it just doesn't affect me so I'm focussing on things that do...'

The car entered the Cross Harbour Tunnel, and our faces were lit the lurid tunnel neon orange as we sped down the left-hand lane, heading toward Causeway Bay.

'Every death, of every creature, affects each of us, Mr Jones,' Tommy Ho said. 'Whether we know it or not, each life ended is a ripple in the fabric of the universe in which we live for a fleeting instant. These deaths are as much about you, and me, as they are about the killer and the victims.'

Tommy Ho was like Confucius with a gun. We were entering murky waters best avoided and I hardly felt up to carrying on a discussion with a triad enforcer on the nature of life, death, the human condition, and the interconnectedness of all things.

24

*T*HE OLD MAN WAS*... a disappointment. I had already planned my next... Yes, planned. That one was to be special in every way. I have always relished the planned ones. It's such a tease; prolonging and intensifying my enjoyment. But more about that later. The old man just happened along, and I hadn't fed the beast in a while, so I decided "why not?" I quite literally stumbled on him. I came around a bend in the trail and there he was. His eyes nearly popped out of his head when he saw me, but I smiled as I passed him and he carried along on his way, shuffling in that disgusting old person shamble. I do hate the aged. They're so pathetic and weak. I passed him then turned around and grabbed him by his scrawny neck and forced him off the track into the bushes. He struggled like a frail old bird in my hands but that slowly stopped as I choked him, and he passed out. I quickly prepared him then I sat and watched him until he came to. We watched each other for ages and that was when I started to worry this was not going to be what I hoped for. He did not flinch. Not a sound – although the tape over his mouth would have muffled that – and he didn't struggle against the ropes. He just lay there, looking at me with his disgusting, rheumy old eyes. The filthy, wrinkled old creature. So, I went to work on him. Slowly at first. He made a few noises then but he bit down on them and just lay there, staring at me, while I cut him. I took off an ear and peeled back the skin of* *his skinny, liver-spotted chest. Barely a sound. Hardly a movement. Just those fucking eyes staring at me. Staring. When I took off his shrivelled old cock he screamed against the tape and his eyes bulged. No one can take that much pain, but I still couldn't find the feeling, the delicious stirring between my legs that told me I was getting what I wanted. His eyes never left mine and they showed... they showed* contempt. *The fucking piece of shit! Contempt... for me! I cut his throat. The blood was glorious, hot and dark, but it was a waste. His eyes were still fixed on me as he died. As I said, the old man was a disappointment. That's why I took his head off and stuck it in the tree. I put a photo in the pocket of his shorts. I didn't take anything. He wasn't worth it.*

25

THE DAYS after Tommy Ho dropped me home passed in a blur of pain and discomfort.

The varying levels of anger and annoyance from the three women in my life didn't make things any better. First there was Prudence. I had been due to meet her and her new boyfriend that evening in Central and that just wasn't an option. As soon as I had my hands on my new phone I had called her. To say she was angry is an understatement. She answered the call after two rings, her voice happy and light.

'Hey, big bro! Getting yourself all fancied up for this evening...?'

I sighed. 'Yes, about that Pru... I can't make it.'

There had been a long pause until Pru spoke, her voice cold. She was speaking through clenched teeth.

'What the *fuck* do you mean you can't *make* it? There are only two reasons you can't make this date Gal. You're dead – obviously you're not, although you are going to wish you were – or you're in hospital. *Are* you in hospital, Gal?'

'Not exactly... But I *have* had an accident. I'm not what you'd call "presentable" right now.'

'Fuck "presentable" Galahad!'

'I'm also in quite a bit of pain...'

'You'll be in a lot *more* pain when I get my hands on you!' She drew a deep breath and blew it out into the phone. 'What happened?'

So, I told her. Omitting Jade Tooth, the money, his soldier, the knife, the beating, the stabbing, Tommy Ho and the shooting. Another long pause.

Pru summed up. 'So, basically nothing happened,' she said 'but you're so beat up you can't come out this evening and meet Giles. Is that about it?'

'Pru,' I pleaded. 'Honestly, I'm sorry. Believe me I'd rather this hadn't happened. Please, don't be too mad. How about next week? I just need a few days to recover. When you see me you'll know what I mean.'

My kid sister had sworn then, long and hard in Cantonese. I had no idea she could swear like that – perhaps I just inspired her. I let her go until she was sworn out.

'Okay, Gal,' she said quietly. 'Next week... and you better be dead if you can't make it.'

If only she knew just how close to the mark she was. I agreed, told her I loved her, she didn't reply, and we hung up. I had barely made it into the kitchen to heat up the espresso machine when my phone rang. I looked at the contact and groaned. I knew what this was about.

'Hey Joey! What's up?'

'Don't you "what's up" me Galahad Jones! You know "what's up"! You've gone and got that triad hooker of yours to protect me...'

I sighed again. My face ached and now my head did.

'She's not a hooker, Joey...'

'Whatever! I don't *need* protection. I can damn well look after myself. *Diu*, protection from a *triad*? No fucking *way*, man!'

'Jo, please! Listen! I was snatched by Jade Tooth yesterday. You were right, we were being followed by his boys and it was about the money...'

'Shit! That *fucking* money! Are you okay? I mean, what happened, how did you...'

'I'm okay. A bit beat up, a couple of nicks here and there but okay. The Panda kicked in the door at exactly the right moment and got me out...'

Joey was silent while she took this all in. 'By that I'm guessing you got out leaving at least one body on the floor of Jade Tooth's place...? Actually, no. Don't tell me.'

'Let's just say Jade Tooth and SYO are pretty annoyed, so your protection *is* necessary. Just a few days until we get an idea of their reaction. Tommy seems to think they won't come at me but, as you said, they could try and get to me through you so, *please*, just take Angel's team and work with it. Will you?'

Joey hissed into the phone. 'Okay. *Dammit*! I'm not happy about this but, yeah, I'll do what you ask. *Diu*!'

'Great. Just a few...'

'On one condition,' Joey went on. 'I'm taking a week off. Paid. Your trollope's team can hang about but they had better *not* get in my way... Oh, and you'll pay my annual gym membership when it comes up next month.'

'That's two conditions...'

'Take it or leave it.'

I agreed to the extortionate deal and Joey hung up before I could say anything more. I was left holding the phone, wondering why both Angel and Joey thought of each other as trollopes. I really had to do something about that.

The espresso machine winked at me, so I rolled a cigarette, poured out a shot of rich, dark coffee and headed out to the terrace. Bors didn't lift his head as I passed him – someone else I would have to placate, I mused. At least I knew he'd come around with a strip of Biltong. Prudence and Joey wouldn't be so easy.

The next night I had paused outside a restaurant in Central and caught my reflection in a window. I looked terrible.

I had removed the gauze dressing on my cheek to let the stitches dry a little, but none of the swelling or bruising had gone down – if anything it was more pronounced. The split above my left eye was held together with a butterfly clip and the skin around it looked red and angry. My right eye still looked like I had gone three rounds with a gorilla and my nose was blackened and still swollen.

I had tried to dodge the dinner, but Angel wasn't going to be put off. I had promised her the date and one just doesn't back out on Angel Yeung. Besides, she knew what had happened without me having to say a word – Tommy Ho having given her a detailed brief the night I lay sleeping in the safe house. When I had called her to duck out of the dinner Angel had simply said I was to turn up, enjoy the meal and pay her a great deal of attention.

The Japanese and Peruvian fusion restaurant was magnificent and one of Angel's and my favourites. We went often. Even so, I caused quite a stir when I walked in. The staff and many of the diners watched with varying levels of concern and disapproval as I made my way across the room, the stitches on my face red and angry, my eyes swollen and bruised and my left arm hanging limply by my side. As I approached the table, Angel looked up from her phone and smiled.

I quickly forget my pain as I took in her long black hair that cascaded and waved down her back and over her left shoulder. I drank in her dark eyes, her blood red lips and slim figure wrapped in a pair of skinny jeans, a white cotton shirt, and dark woollen jacket. She stood and the heels of her black Louboutins brought her almost to my eye level. She draped an arm over my shoulder and leaned in to deliver a feather-light kiss on the stitches of my cheek.

'Welcome darling,' she whispered in my ear. 'You look dashing. Like an injured fighter pilot.'

I wondered just how many injured fighter pilots Angel had been with and kissed her lightly on the cheek.

'And you, Angel. Beautiful as usual. Not a woman in this room holds a candle to you...'

'Oh my God, Gal, I know *that*,' Angel said as she sat and sipped at the champagne she had already ordered. I took up my glass, gestured a cheers at her and took a long sip – I was sure the Bollinger's combination with my painkillers would ease the pain.

She reached across the table and took my hand.

'So, Tommy told me all about it. Are you okay?' She looked me over. 'My poor darling, they really went to town on you, didn't they!' She huffed loudly. 'If only The Panda had shot Jade Tooth! I *hate* that slippery little snake.'

'We haven't seen the last of Jade Tooth I think...'

'He won't dare come after you, Gal. You're ours and he knows it.'

I shifted uncomfortably in my chair and toyed with the champagne flute. I didn't like being referred to as "belonging" to a triad but, right now, I could see no way around it. It was a problem I would tackle as soon as I could work out a way to approach it. I had a deep and disturbing feeling I was standing in the middle of a patch of quicksand from which there was no escape.

'I see you've put a team on Joey,' I said.

Angel waved a hand, her bracelets tinkling like chimes. 'Pffft...' She polished off her champagne and reached for the bottle.

'Yes. I hear the little tramp isn't happy,' she said.

I smiled. 'I love it when you're jealous, Angel, but she's not a...'

'Whatever!'

Angel and Joey were more alike than they both knew, I thought picking up the menu and studying it.

26

FIVE DAYS later I walked into the bar in Central to meet Prudence and her boyfriend. My face was still a disaster and the stab wound in my left shoulder ached abominably despite the Panadeine Forte I had been swallowing like jubes. The bar was high-end and one of those places typical of the money market and banking types. Expensive suits were everywhere, wrapped around, mostly, less-than-fit expats who earned obscene salaries making a lot of money for other crooks. The place heaved with them, and I was on edge from the moment I walked in.

I had long harboured an irrational dislike of the money market boys; my life and experience nowhere approaching theirs. We were worlds apart. Perhaps it was jealousy, I admitted to myself, but I was set against the excess, hubris and arrogance that seemed to come with the territory of working for a stockbroker or private bank. With an effort, I swallowed it down, determined to be nice to Pru's boyfriend and give him a chance.

I glanced around the room and saw Prudence moving toward me, a man in tow. My heart skipped a beat to see her. My sister was one of the most beautiful women I knew, and she carried herself like an Imperial Concubine; confident, upright, slightly aloof, and mysterious. She was wearing a long, crimson cheongsam that slit up her left leg to above her knee. I could see the expat women in the room watching her jealously as she glided across the room, her long black hair swaying in time with her hips, the crowd parting before her like a receding tide.

She reached me and took both my hands in hers, her dark eyes sparking with an inner flame.

'Daaih lo, *big brother,*' she said. 'How good to *see* you, Gal! My *God*, look at you!' She gently touched my cheek. 'You weren't joking were you.'

I smiled and kissed her forehead – it was big brother thing and I had always done it. 'Sai mui, *sister*. How beautiful you are. Sorry I look a little frayed.

'Jesus, Gal. You look positively torn! What the hell happened?'

I glanced at the man standing behind her. 'Another time Pru,' I said quietly. 'But for now,' I said louder 'introduce me to this fellow at your shoulder.'

'Oh *God*! Of course...' Pru made the introductions. 'Gal, this is Giles. Giles this is my big brother, Galahad.'

We shook hands. His grip was firm and dry, and he regarded me with a slight grin curling his full lips. He was clean shaven and his aftershave was strong; an animal musky scent and he was immaculately dressed in a navy three-piece suit, crisp white shirt and dark tie. His shoes were highly polished. Oddly, he wasn't wearing a watch.

'Giles Tyler,' he said. 'It's a real pleasure. I've heard so much about you...'

'Good to meet you, Giles,' I said in return. 'I've heard nothing about you.'

The grin dropped for a moment before being replaced with a dazzling white smile.

'Ahh, Pru has been keeping me a dark secret. All the best things are "need to know", don't you think?'

I smiled back. 'Pru has always played her cards close,' I said. 'It's one of the many things I love about her.'

He turned to Prudence. 'God, *do* you, my love? I'd have not picked you for a poker player...'

My sister was frowning slightly, not really aware of what goes on when two men meet, and the subject of their meeting is the same woman. It's like stags butting heads.

'Well,' she said. 'I told Gal a *little* about you darling, but I thought I'd leave it to you two boys to get to know each other.' She looked over Giles's shoulder. 'Speaking of which, you must excuse me. I see someone I have been chasing to buy an exquisite piece I have, and she's just walked in...'

We both watched as Pru sailed back through the crowd and air-kissed an attractive middle-aged Chinese woman with a much younger man on her arm. I watched Giles's eyes follow her, a slow smile on his face. It seemed he was smitten by my sister. He turned back to me and gestured at two empty stools at the bar.

'Shall we?'

I nodded, we pulled up the stools and Giles called the barman over.

'What's your poison, Galahad?'

'Whisky Sour.'

He ordered that and a Tom Collins and turned to look at me. 'A summer drink really, but I do love them. Bloody refreshing, don't you think?

'I'll stick to my Sours,' I said. 'I don't branch out much, to be honest.'

He laughed, a genuine chuckle that showed his teeth and lit his startling light blue eyes. I did not know his age but guessed at late thirties. With his blonde hair, chiselled good looks and tall, strongly built frame, Pru's boyfriend reminded me of a Viking. I just hoped he didn't have a Viking's tastes...'

'Pru tells me you play for Valley,' I said to break the ice.

He nodded. 'Well, not quite yet. I've not been with the club that long and am on the training squad. Hopefully I'll get a run soon. You know, off the bench... You're Hong Kong Scottish, right?'

I nodded. 'Yes. Gave up playing years ago 'though. Age and knees. Never a good combination in a scrum.'

'You don't look that old. Good shape, if you ask me...'

I smiled. 'You can be my friend,' I said as the drinks arrived. We both sipped appreciatively at the cocktails, well mixed and served in cut crystal glasses.

We put our drinks down and sat in silence for a moment until Giles circled a finger in the direction of my face.

'Do you mind if I ask...?' he said

I shrugged. 'Business disagreement.'

'Business? It would seem your *business* is somewhat tougher than mine... Private Investigator, Pru tells me.'

'It has its moments,' I said. 'Nowhere as lucrative as yours, I'm sure. Private Banker, right?'

'Yes. Been in it for a few years now. I rather enjoy it...' he turned to look at me. 'If I'm honest, it's the thrill of the game I love. Wearing one face to bring a client along, while being another person entirely. Then another me for another person. Watching the market and knowing when to strike. I guess it's like hunting but, God knows, I'm not into blood sports!'

He gave a dramatic little shudder that was strangely at odds with his masculine size and physique. 'Clinching the deal on my terms – and to my great personal benefit, I might add – *that* keeps me at it.'

I thought that was an unusual thing to say at a first meeting, but I nodded politely and sipped my drink. I didn't much like the sound of that, but it accorded with what I thought of the money market boys, so I wasn't too surprised. Arrogance came with the territory. I supposed one had to be like that to survive and succeed in the dog pit that is the world of finance. At least he was honest about it, I thought.

Time for me, I thought, to deliver a message. 'I'd hope you'll present just the one, true, face to my sister,' I said with a grin that didn't quite reach my eyes.

He looked taken aback and his eyes flared but he quickly recovered, and that winsome smile lit his face.

'Oh, *Christ* yes!' he exclaimed and put his right hand on his heart.

'We're all shape-shifting, Janus-faced bastards in this game but one face only with Pru. I'll keep the darker side at bay, I swear.'

Something about his reference to Janus bothered me, but I couldn't resist but smile back. Giles was good looking, urbane and quick-witted. He was hard not to like. Besides, I trusted Prudence's judgement completely.

I was about to dive a little deeper into Giles's personal history when he finished off the cocktail and signalled to the barman for another round. 'So,' he said. 'Tell me about you. I confess to be being a little intrigued... a *Private Eye* of all things!'

I shrugged, uncomfortable that we were moving onto a subject I never liked to discuss: me. 'Nothing much to tell really. Ex copper, limited skills outside of that so when I left the force I just sort of fell into private investigation.'

He studied me, his chin in his hand like a school kid watching a lab frog.

'Somehow I doubt the "limited skills" bit,' he said. 'Pru has told me a little of your big case a couple of years back. Amazing! Trafficked girls! It sounds to me like someone with pretty advanced "skills" I would say... although God knows what those are! I'd have no idea really, but it all seems *way* too dangerous and physical for me.'

I doubted there was much that seemed *way* too physical for this man, and his efforts to ingratiate were starting to annoy me.

'True, that was a big one,' I said. 'A lot happening, and I got lucky. But it's not all like that. Mostly humdrum; long hours, boring routine.'

The drinks arrived and we both took a long pull. Talking about myself always put me on edge and I needed a cigarette. Glancing around, I made a mental note of the outside smoking area.

'Sure,' Giles went on. 'But you must be able to follow the clues, dig it all out, make the case, stay one step ahead. Fit all the pieces together... and I *bet* it can get dicey at times. You know, messing about with Hong Kong's criminal underbelly.' He waved a hand at my face again. 'I mean, look at *that*!'

'I have very little to do with what you call the "underbelly",' I said quickly but as casually as I could. This was not ground I wanted to cover with a total stranger. I wanted him to drop it.

'It's almost exclusively cheating husbands and cheating businessmen,' I said.

'Well,' he said in resignation. 'I'm not convinced. I just *bet* you're a formidable opponent and I *certainly* wouldn't want to be on the wrong side. Cheers!'

I smiled and we clinked glasses and drank our cocktails.

'My turn' I said genially, nodding over my shoulder toward Prudence who was deep in conversation with her potential buyer. 'It looks like we will be seeing a bit of each other so tell me a little about yourself. Where did you come from? Background… that sort of stuff.'

He blinked rapidly and I thought I had put my foot in it until he smiled broadly and wagged a finger at me.

'Oh, the Private Dick routine,' he said. I just shrugged and smiled into my drink.

'Why not,' he said, slapping the bar lightly. 'Where to start…? Well, born in UK. Surrey. Middle class. Nice town. Green, peaceful, and fucking boring… Dad was Navy, forty years. I didn't see him much as a kid and I haven't seen him much since. Mum drank and had boyfriends.' His eyes clouded over, and I could see his jaws working as he clenched his teeth. He took a long drink of his cocktail and studied the contents of the glass before he went on.

'I was an only child – probably just as well – and ran amok a bit as a kid. My grandparents finally took control and paid me through public boarding school where it turned out I was brilliant!' He smiled and lifted his glass to me.

'To brilliance' I said, and we drank.

'School days weren't great,' he went on. 'English public school you know. Rum, sodomy, and the lash…'

'I thought that was the Royal Navy.'

'The Royal Navy would be nowhere were it not for the English Public School system,' he said, his face serious. I had the distinct feeling we were stepping into very sensitive territory.

'Anyway…' he muttered, signalling to the barman for another round for himself. We sat in silence until his drink arrived.

'School was shit,' he said. 'It has always been…hard, being me,' he muttered, almost to himself. 'I was bullied quite a bit early on, but I soon realised I was surrounded by the inbred sons of country gentlemen, my intellectual inferiors, and that helped me through. Turns out I was also bloody good at rugby so that won me some reprieve.'

He was on a roll, so I sat silently, listening with interest, and nodding in all the right places as his story wound on.

'I took Blues for Rugby and Rowing and won an academic scholarship to Oxford in my final year to read Law but I only lasted a year before I was sent down. A small matter of a girl and an unseemly – and totally unfounded – allegation. Shame really. I always saw myself as a wigged barrister in the Old Bailey defending half-literate East End gangsters. Pity…'

Giles' eyes took on a faraway look and he looked bitter for a brief moment before he went on.

'Anyway, Grandad sorted me out with a cadetship in my first bank in The City when I was 19, and it turns out I had a knack for it. The bank put me though an economics and finance degree at LSE and by the time I was 22 I was kicking goals, making a mint, and living in a converted warehouse apartment on Canary Wharf.' He seemed to run out of steam and shrugged, a little deprecatingly.

'Well, that's pretty impressive,' I said.

He shook his head. 'Not at all. I've survived on my talents and hard work. It's just what I do. Nothing more.'

He was confident, I'd give him that. 'You certainly made good use of the opportunity given you by your family,' I said.

He turned and looked at me, his blue eyes cold and hard. 'Fuck them,' he said.

I kept my face expressionless and nodded, not really knowing what to say and not wanting to break his monologue. Get someone talking about themselves and you just have to sit back and wait for it all to come out. I had the feeling Giles Tyler had something that he needed to come out. After a moment he grimaced.

'That's a bit unfair,' he said. 'But I *don't* owe my benighted family anything. What you see before you is the product of me. No one else. I did this...'

Families are difficult things, but it seemed Giles had some serious issues with his. I decided to steer us into safer waters. 'How long have you been in Hong Kong?'

'About three years now.' He raised his drink, and I noticed his eyes were glassy. Whatever else Giles was, he was a heavy drinker. I was far from the person to judge another on that score. 'Here's to many years more,' he said happily and drank.

I was about to ask him about his time in Hong Kong when Pru arrived and threw an arm around each of our shoulders.

'How are my boys?' she asked, her voice bright. 'Just sold that piece to the Dragon Lady over there so I'm in the mood to party.'

Giles looked up and his eyes cleared. His face lit up at the sight of my sister. I had begun to form the opinion that he was a bit of a loose cannon, but I could clearly see his adoration for Pru and that was all I needed. As comforted by that as I was, I resolved to keep an eye on him – it's what big brothers, and ex cops, do.

Pru kissed him lightly but his face was turned from me so I could not see his reaction. I did see him raise his hand and gently stroke my sister's cheek. They both seemed very happy, and I felt mildly nauseated – and irrationally annoyed that he was pawing my sister. I bit it down with an effort and smiled widely when they both turned to face me.

I was about to suggest Prudence take my seat at the bar when the maître d' arrived and excused himself so, taking our drinks, we allowed him to escort us into the restaurant. Soon, amid the hubbub of the restaurant and its adjoining bar, we were lost in a rack of New Zealand lamb, bottles of Australian Shiraz, anecdotes and laughter. The hours slipped by and, by the time I stepped out onto Pedder Street to hail a taxi in the cold, late night, I was drunk and really quite happy with my sister's choice of boyfriend.

27

THATCHER ONCE SAID she was in politics because of the conflict between Good and Evil, and that she believed "Good" would triumph. She was an idiot. You know, don't you, that there is no binary choice between the two; no light and dark, good and evil. There is a hair-thin line between good and evil that cuts through the heart of every human being, you included. To deny the evil in you are you willing to destroy a piece of your own heart? So, you see, what I do and what I am is pure in its embrace of the evil in all of us. In my Evil I am Good. Or is that "God"?

28

THE PHONE RINGING INSISTENTLY by my head woke me, and I rolled over with a groan. I looked at the contact and groaned again, holding my head as I answered.

'Alastair,' I croaked, my tongue thick and mouth dry. Today's hangover would be epic.

'You're awake then?' said the voice at the other end. 'Time you dropped your cock and put on socks, my old darling.'

I shook my head and grinned, despite the headache that was rising to smash hammers against the back of my dehydrated brain.

I had last seen Alastair Chard only a few weeks before at the licentious and bohemian party held to celebrate his 65th birthday in his bungalow high up on Middle Gap Road. The evening had ended with Alastair punching a man in the mouth while he groped the man's wife with his free hand. It had taken me a week to recover from that little soirée. Hong Kong society was still reeling.

~

Alastair Xavier Chard had arrived in Hong Kong in the late seventies as a good-looking, long-haired junior reporter with The Times, initially covering the social rounds and odd jobs for that revered broadsheet. He soon moved across to the South China Herald – Hong Kong's newspaper of record – to cover the police beat and remained there to this day. In his day, Alastair had been a notorious lothario in Hong Kong, and had left a trail of broken hearts – on both sides of the fence – through Hong Kong's expat community. He had an extensive personal network of the high and the low right across Hong Kong; greater than anyone I had known – except perhaps my informant Fat Johnny Tong – and he had eyes everywhere and fingers in everything. Alastair Chard was the classic old-school foreign correspondent: hard drinking, overweight and florid, a chain smoker, brash and loud, with a swearing vocabulary that would make a docker blush, and sartorially inclined toward rumpled linen suits and stained ties of regiments of which he had never been a member. I liked him very much and for reasons that weren't clear to me, and that he never mentioned, he liked me. There were few people on the planet I trusted as I did Alastair.

'What time is it?' I mumbled.

'I don't know,' he replied. 'Fucking daylight! Get up, feed that mongrel hound of yours and come and have coffee. We need to talk.'

'We do? About what?'

'I'll tell you when you get here and I can look into those deep, green eyes of yours,' he said and hung up leaving me staring at my phone.

While we were friends, Alastair never called me socially. Something was up and I struggled against the hangover to work out what it might be. There was only one way to find out and I desperately needed coffee, so I stood and made my way shakily into the bathroom.

I climbed out of the taxi that had pulled into the kerb on Johnston Road. Behind me impatient Hong Kong drivers laid on the horns at the audacity of the cab's move. The sound ripped at my aching head.

I glanced up into the coffee shop as I paid the driver. There, sitting under a patio heater in shirt sleeves and tie, a copy of the South China Herald open in front of him, was Alastair. Some Christmas decorations were strung behind him and, from my angle, they appeared to be draped around his head. He looked like a fat and slightly seedy elf.

As I watched, he raised the newspaper, released one side of it and, in a practised move, reached with his hand to take up the coffee cup and a burning cigarette from an ashtray while continuing to read. I rubbed my eyes and flicked the still damp hair off my forehead. I needed that coffee.

'Good morning, Alastair,' I said, scraping a chair back across the tiles with a screech that set my teeth on edge. The patio heater was warm on my face, but I zipped my puffer to the throat and stuffed my hands in the pockets as I sat.

Alastair slowly lowered the newspaper and folded it neatly, before taking a furious drag of the cigarette crushed between his nicotine-stained fingers. He blew the smoke into the air and ashed the cigarette.

'Fuck me,' he said mildly. 'Look at you. And by "look at you" I mean what the *fuck* happened to your handsome face, old cock?'

Alastair knew a lot about me – more than most – but he did not know about the money I had stolen from SYO. I planned on keeping it that way.

'I slipped in the shower,' I said, waving my hand at the waiter and ordering a double Macchiato.

'Yes, those fucking showers can be dangerous places,' he deadpanned.

I nodded slowly as if that was the wisest thing Alastair had ever said. He sipped his coffee and slowly placed the cup back onto the saucer.

'It's hard to tell over your *shower* injuries,' he said. 'But I would also guess you have a massive hangover this fine Hong Kong morning.'

I rubbed my eyes again and sighed as the coffee was placed on the table in front of me. I rolled and lit a cigarette and sipped at the rich, dark brew. The caffeine and nicotine delivered a left-right combination to my brain, and I started to feel more human.

'I met Prudence's new boyfriend last night,' I said. 'Rather large night as it turns out...'

'I didn't even know she had a new beau. She's kept that fucking quiet ... not a sniff in the Social Pages. Who is he?'

'His name is Giles Tyler. Brit. Private Banker.'

'So, he's a complete cunt, then?' Alastair ventured.

I smiled and dragged on my cigarette, polishing off the Macchiato and signalling for another and one for Alastair.

'No, not really,' I said. 'He seems a little "loose". I don't know... pretty hefty sense of self-worth but he's pleasant and charismatic, I'll say that for him. Pru is obviously smitten, he seems to adore her.' I shrugged. 'I have to admit, I kind of like him.'

Alastair looked thoughtful for a moment. 'Never heard of him,' he pronounced. 'I'll ask around... By the way: how did you enjoy my birthday bash?'

I laughed out loud. 'It was everything I have come to expect from a do at your place. Boozy, loud, and mildly pornographic...'

Alastair grinned. 'Yes, it was fucking *brilliant*, was it not? I must admit, slipping my finger into that sweet thing's panties while punching her gormless husband in the mouth was probably the highlight of my year. Happy 65th Birthday *me*!'

I grimaced. Alastair was probably the most intelligent man I knew, and he was certainly the crudest.

'You'll pay for that one day, Alastair,' I said.

He shook his head, and puffed his cheeks out, rolling his eyes to the heavens. It was clear he had no fucks to give.

'I very much doubt that my old darling,' he said. 'I have the goods on Hubby and he knows I would be happy to reveal all at a time of my convenience. In the meantime, I shall do as I fucking please...'

Our coffees arrived and Alastair lit another cigarette.

'You said we needed to talk...' I prompted.

His face became suddenly serious, and he leaned in across the table. 'We do, Galahad, I fear something *very* nasty is coming your way...'

'When is it not?'

'I'm not trying to be fucking *funny*, you twat! Hear me out.'

I waved my hand for him to go on and sipped my coffee, taking a moment to collect my thoughts. I had no idea what was coming but I felt my pulse racing and it wasn't just the caffeine.

'What do you know about the Hiking Trail Murders?' Alastair asked, getting straight to the point.

My eyes widened. 'Why is everyone asking me that lately?'

'Who else is asking?'

'Michael Wong. He seems particularly interested but won't admit it. Gave me the usual bullshit about it being a general inquiry.'

Alastair sucked at his teeth. 'Well, yes,' he said quietly. 'I know he's interested which is why we are here...'

'What's going on, Alastair?'

'Hold on tight, Galahad, because this is going to curl your fucking hair...' He sighed. 'I should not even be telling you this, but we're friends – fucked if I know how *that* happened – and I can't just leave you to blunder around unknowing until Mr Wong decides to call you in.'

'Go on,' I said quietly, sitting stone still.

Alastair looked at me, his eyes heavy and sad. 'My contact in Arsenal House also happens to be on the murder taskforce and has revealed some very disturbing things to me. Before I go on, this is not conjecture... I've seen the evidence.'

'Get on with it, for Christ's sake!'

'Okay. Try this on for size...You're tied in, intimately, to these murders,' Alastair said and dragged on his cigarette.

I shook my head. 'What the hell do you mean "tied in"?' I flashed back to the conversation with Michael Wong in the back of the plain clothes car, speeding its way down Repulse Bay Road. I was still shocked when Alastair gave me the news.

'The murders. They would seem to be about you. Allow me to explain...'

'Oh fuck, please do...'

'The first – the young man – had, on top of his horrendous injuries, the letters "GJ" carved into his back and the female victim had the same carved across her belly. The third victim, the old man, did not but he *did* have a photo shoved in his back pocket.'

Alastair paused. My cigarette burned forgotten in my fingers.

'A photo of *you*,' he said and reached into his jacket to draw out an A4 sheet of paper that he unfolded and placed in front of me. 'The original of this photo, to be precise.'

I looked down. There, on the page, in crisp, high-resolution colour, was a photograph of me sitting at a street-side high table of the Italian bar on Staunton Street. I was frowning at something and staring into the distance while holding a beer. My face was uninjured, and a cigarette burned in an ashtray at my elbow. That meant the photo had been taken nearly two weeks before. I did a mental calculation – the photo must have been taken just before the third murder and certainly before my last chat with Jade Tooth. Was it the day I had met Prudence at the bar? Had the photographer seen her? I studied the photo in shocked silence, and I could feel Alastair's eyes on me. The photo had been stuffed into the pocket of the last hiking trail victim and my initials had been carved into the previous two victims. The enormity of what I was hearing and seeing crashed in on me. I felt sick and sipped at my coffee, spitting the cold brew back into the cup.

'What does this *mean*?' I said, stupidly. I didn't know what else to say.

'I would have thought that was fucking clear, even to brain-dead flatfoot like you,' Alastair said. 'The person merrily carving people up across Hong Kong's hiking trails has a particular *interest* in you. My theory – and I say "mine", but I know for a fact that Chief Inspector Wong also holds to this theory – is that this fucking *lunatic* is sending a message to you.'

'And that message would be...?'

'Fuck, I don't *know*... he loves you, hates you, wants to *be* you... I haven't a clue but he's sending you a *message* and he's using butchered corpses to do it.'

My mind was whirling, and I couldn't call it to order. Looking back now I should have connected the dots quicker, should have seen what it meant, but I didn't. I turned in my chair and gazed out across the busy morning traffic of Johnston Road.

An old lady pushed a flat-bed trolley loaded high with flattened cardboard out into the road, her back bent under the load, her head down. She ignored the traffic as she trudged along in a world of her own, the cardboard a trove for her to sell to local recycling plants, a supplement to her meagre, or non-existent, pension. Dodging the wheels of the trolley that surged forward like a battleship into the swell of the pedestrian traffic, a young woman with a Pug on a leash and her designer coat buttoned up to her neck, stepped unseeing around the old lady. Hong Kong can be a tough place. I dragged on the stub of my cigarette and stabbed it out into Alastair's ashtray.

'Why hasn't Michael Wong wheeled me in? He thinks I have something he needs – I *don't*, but he thinks it.'

Alastair nodded. 'Fucking good question, old cock,' he said. 'But I should think the answer, again, is obvious.'

'It isn't to me. Not right now...'

'You're his *bait*, my dear, stupid boy. He's staked you out like a fucking goat in the forest. He knows you have nothing to do with any of this, but he *also* knows it's *about* you, somehow. He's definitely not going to invite you into the investigation, but he *is* going to wait and watch for the killer to make himself known to you.'

I rubbed my eyes and ran my hands through my hair. 'But *why*? Why is the killer doing this to get to me...? Jesus Christ, Alastair, this it too much to take in...'

Alastair looked at me for a long moment as he fumbled for his pack and lit a cigarette.

'You know why, Galahad,' he said gently. And you know who... I just don't think you can bring yourself to admit it.'

I stared at him as my hangover fell away, the tumblers all fell into place and my mind unlocked. I ran a shaking hand across my mouth.

'Jesus,' I breathed. 'Peter Toh? It must be. It can't be anyone else... I thought I caught a glimpse of him a few nights back, but other things convinced me otherwise,' I said, fingering the stiches on my cheek. Alastair sat silently and I went on.

'Do you remember after I was released from hospital a couple of years back, and we had dinner?'

Alastair nodded. 'Yes I do. It was an expensive meal and I recall you had a spider in your pocket that night...I paid if memory serves. It was a mental health check on you. I was really quite concerned for your precarious state at the time.'

'Well,' I replied. 'That probably had something to do with my best friend turning out to be a deep triad plant and shooting me in the head... Anyway, I told you then that Peter had admitted his involvement in the Thomas murders and that he had "help". It must be the same person who is killing his way around Hong Kong. The M.O. is unmistakable. At least according to Michael Wong it is and, from what I've heard of these murders, and remember of the Thomas' bodies, I'd have to agree.'

Dragging on his cigarette, Alastair nodded slowly. 'I thought so too,' he said. 'It is the only answer I could come up with...The question now is "why?"'

'Who's the slow one now, Alastair?' I said, a faint grin cracking my face. 'Look at what I did to him. I wrecked his years long, carefully laid plans and sent him running to Christ knows where. I'd say ruining his shitty, treacherous life is motivation enough for him to come back at me... wouldn't you?'

'Yes...that could be,' Alastair said carefully. 'But you're not seeing the wood for the fucking trees. Why go to these lengths? We both agree it would not be him *committing* these murders. So why recruit whoever the fuck it *is* to do all this when Toh could just step up on you one dark night and shoot you in the back of the head?'

I had no answer for that.

'I don't know. Maybe I'm wrong...'I muttered.

'I don't think you are, but the problem remains: why and what happens next?'

Again, I drew a blank. 'I have no idea. Where would I even start to look and, more to the point, why? It doesn't look like I'm at any risk here. There's something else motivating them – if there is a *them*.'

Alastair slapped the top of table, hard, with the flat of his hand. The gunshot crack made me, and others around us, jump.

'Why? Fucking *why* Galahad? You selfish *prick*!' he hissed. 'They're doing this because of you, for some reason. *You*! How about stopping the vicious murder of innocent people? How's that for a fucking *why*?'

I swallowed hard and felt my face redden. He was right. Whatever it was, it *was* about me. Even if I was wrong about Peter Toh – and I had my doubts – I had to find out what the connection between me and the killings was and stop them before anyone else lost their life on a lonely forest track. Suddenly a thought broke through my deep embarrassment.

'Prudence,' I said. 'Joey. Adele. Angel... *Jesus*.'

'Ah, *now* you see a reason to act. Yes, you fucking *idiot*. Everyone you love, *everyone* close to you, is at risk. It is only a matter of time before the killer stops with strangers and attacks closer to home... I think he wants you to *hurt* Galahad, and that's how he'll do it!'

'I don't know what to *do*, Alastair,' I said.

I felt adrift on a strong current that was pulling me further and further from the safety of shore. I was flailing against a dark and remorseless ocean that I was sure would soon drag me under. Alastair stood and gathered his newspaper, tucking it primly under his arm.

'You'll think of something,' he said, looking down at me. 'You always do.'

With that he walked away without a backwards glance, leaving me to my turbulent thoughts and the bill for five coffees.

29

I PUT my phone down and heaved a sigh of relief.

Bors sat in the bar at my feet watching the passing parade in Soho on a Saturday morning, shifting now and then to sniff at the air as the small, fluffy apartment dogs skipped and toddled past. The day was cold but clear and streaks of cloud drifted slowly overhead like smears of white paint on a blue glass table. I checked my watch. 11:30. I had been on the phone for over an hour talking to the four women in my life and it had not been a pleasant experience.

Adele had been the first call. I had told her that "something was happening" and it wasn't safe for her to return to Hong Kong. After a steely silence, during which I was sure my a-yi was gritting her teeth in an effort not to lecture me, she had agreed to extend her visit with her cousin in Shantou. I wasn't sure that was long enough, but there was no way I could convince her otherwise, so I had meekly surrendered to her. Adele had whispered she loved me, told me to stay safe 'whatever madness you've got yourself mixed up in now' and hung up.

The call with Joey had been brief. She picked up after two rings and I had told her I was shutting the office for two weeks and that she was to take that time off as paid leave.

'I'm already on paid leave, if you recall,' Joey had said.

'Well, take longer,' I replied. 'Just stay away from the office and stay with Angel's protection team.' As an afterthought I added: 'I'll be speaking to her and extending the time the team is on you.'

I heard her draw a breath in readiness to explode down the phone, but I got in first. 'No, Joey. This is *not* negotiable. You will stay low, and you *will* cooperate with the protection team. Clear?'

'This isn't about Jade Tooth, and that damned money is it,' Joey said quietly. 'What's going on Gal?'

I told her about the initials carved into the brutalised bodies of a young man and woman, and about the photograph left on the body of the old man.

'My working theory right now is this is the work of Peter Toh somehow,' I said. 'The hiking trail killer is sending me a message but what that is, why and what's next neither Alistair nor I can work out. The fact is everyone close to me is unsafe until I can end this. Just how I do that and when it will be, I have not the slightest clue.'

I knew I wasn't exactly inspiring confidence, but I was so empty of ideas that I couldn't help but sound glum.

Joey had been quiet for a moment. In my mind's eye I could see her standing in her apartment, a frown on her face, biting her lower lip as she processed the news.

'Okay,' she had finally said, her voice calm and controlled. 'Just promise me you'll be careful *and* that you'll get me involved when you've worked out a way forward. You're not doing this alone. I won't let you. Will you do that?'

I knew I was going to need Joey's talents on this so I promised her I would, then had hung up after telling her one last time to keep her head down.

The call with Angel had gone exactly as I had expected it to. I had laid out the latest developments and her response had been clinically professional.

'I will speak with Mr Lee,' she said. 'We'll put our resources into finding who this is. If Toh is involved, it will be good to finally remove him from the picture...'

'"Remove", Angel? No, if he's behind this he must be brought in. Let Michael Wong and the Courts deal with him. No summary executions, please!'

Angel had responded in her usual manner. 'Pffft, why go to all that trouble? Think of the cost to the taxpayer! No, much better off with a bullet and a long swim off Lamma Island...'

'When did you start caring about Hong Kong taxpayers?'

'Galahad, *darling*!' she said in exasperation. 'You know very well we will *all* be much better off once Peter Toh is removed from the board. Permanently.' She sighed deeply. 'But, yes, I promise I will do what I can to see we deliver him up to OCTB in one piece. *If* we find him. Happy?'

'Deliriously. One more thing...'

Another dramatic sigh. 'You want me to extend the time my team is protecting that little biker slut of yours, yes?'

'Yes,' I said mildly. 'Angel, *please*, we've been over this...'

'And we shall continue to, Galahad my love. I do *not* like that girl.'

There was no point in trying to change Angel's mind so, rubbing my aching forehead, I had hung up after first extracting a promise of dinner that night and a 'stay over'. At least there was that, and my day had improved markedly for it.

Prudence had not answered her phone, but I wasn't unduly worried. I knew she was taking the weekend in a B&B on Cheung Chau with Giles. I had left her a message so there was nothing to do but wait. I caught the Nepali barman's eye.

'I'll take a pint, thanks Rama.'

He glanced down at his watch then back up at me as he reached for a glass and dropped it under the beer tap.

'You're open, aren't you?' I growled. 'Don't judge, pour,' I added as I rolled a cigarette.

The beer hit the bar top, the glass glistening with beads of condensation. 'There you go, Mr Jones,' the barman said. 'Enjoy.'

I smiled and raised the glass to him. 'I don't know about "enjoy" Ram, but it does fill a need right now.'

The barman shook his head and went back to polishing glasses. I dragged on my cigarette, and absently stroked Bors' ears while I stared unseeing out onto Staunton Street. The weekend crowds sauntered happily by, chatting, laughing and hand holding. Christmas was coming and all was right with the world; while I sat alone in an empty bar, feeling death's breath brushing my skin as a dark presence hovered unseen over the city.

30

THE NEXT DAY, I was sitting on a bench in Tsim Sha Tsui, gazing across Victoria Harbour to The Island.

My wounds till throbbed but my muscles ached pleasantly. Bors lay at my feet fast asleep, his black-pink tongue protruding slightly between his incisors and wolf-like canines.

Crowds of people meandered up and down the Avenue of Stars, enjoying the crisp, clear Sunday morning as they sauntered aimlessly along the waterfront to or from the Star Ferry Pier. Little kids on small three-wheeled scooters zipped around and past their parents, and fluffy apartment dogs yapped and pranced excitedly on their leashes, while young mothers set a course with their prams, hoping the kids and the dogs would see them in time.

Victoria Harbour sparkled blue and clean in the sun. Ferries cut their way from Wan Chai to Kowloon-side and back toward Central Pier. Small fishing sampans bobbed and tossed in the ferry wakes into which flocks of gulls, and the occasional Black Kite, dived in search of food. Across the water, on The Island beyond the tall urban sprawl of Wan Chai and Causeway Bay, Jardine's Lookout, Mount Cameron and The Peak stood as they had for aeons; immutable, green-clad guardians of the Fragrant Harbour, *heung gong*. The dragons who lived on the peaks had not been seen for months, and now a predator stalked their cloud-wrapped jungle dens. It was a bad omen and things were not looking good for the city. Our world had tilted slightly, and it seemed that everyone could feel it. I leaned back on the bench and closed my eyes, letting the weak winter sun stroke the wounds on my face that were now dry, scabbed and itching abominably. It was a peaceful scene and, letting my guard down in relief, I set my mind to wander.

Prudence had rung me the night before, slightly drunk from a big seafood meal and a few bottles of Tsing Tao. She had laughed when I said I was glad to hear her voice.

'Whatever is the matter, daaih lo, *big brother*?' she asked. 'You sound *super* serious.' I could hear Giles in the background saying I'd probably been punched in the face again.

I told her about the killings and the possible connection to me – although I left out many of the details. My kid sister didn't need to know the horrors of these murders – although everyone in Hong Kong, by now, had a very good idea.

'Somehow, Pru, and I really don't know how or why, I'm connected to these killings...'

'You're *connected*?' she said, her voice shrill in my ear. 'How *connected*?'

'It seems the killer is trying to send a message that, somehow, involves me...'

'How do you know, Gal? Actually, no. No, don't tell me. How you ever know anything of what's happening in this city, I shudder to think.' My sister sighed. 'So, why are you calling me?'

'I don't want you to worry but I want you to be alert. I don't know where this is leading, and I need to figure it out. In the meantime, I want you to be very watchful both at home and when you're out.'

'What am I being watchful *for*?' she asked.

'I don't know really. Just anything out of the ordinary. You being followed, watched. Anything unusual around you...'

'This is Hong Kong, Gal!' she said with a slight chuckle. 'Unusual shit happens all the time.'

I grunted. 'Pru, please. Take this seriously.' I paused for a moment to think through whether she needed a protection team or, indeed, whether my feisty sister would even accept one. I figured that she was as safe as she could be with Giles by her side.

'Stay close to Giles and don't go wandering on your own, especially at night. Will you promise me that?'

Pru was silent for a moment, and I could imagine her looking across the table at Giles, him looking back at her with an eyebrow cocked in inquiry.

'I'll be fine Gal,' she said finally. 'I'll be careful, but I have Giles with me almost all the time now...'

As a big brother I didn't like the sound of that, but I was pleased to hear it nonetheless.

'... and he looks after me. *Jesus*, I can't even cross the street without him looking left and right for me and taking my hand. Can I darling?' she said to the side, and I heard Giles mutter something and laugh as the neck of a beer bottle tinked against a glass.

Pru went on. 'The one I worry about is *you*. Galahad let's face it; you have a knack for finding trouble. You always have.' She sighed. '*Damn*! Do you remember those street kids who stole my bike when I was, what, 10 and you were 14? You spent three nights stalking Shek Kip Mei looking for them and didn't come home until you'd found them and my bike. Your shirt was torn, your nose was bloody, and you looked like a half-starved Pye-dog.' She chuckled again in warm reminiscence. 'Jesus,' Pru whispered. 'Mum was angry, wasn't she? I think Dad nearly exploded with pride...'

I felt my throat constrict a little at the memory of our parents. Both now long dead, their ghosts still haunted me; my mother lecturing me to be a good boy and my father exhorting me to push on and not give up. I sighed.

'Yeah,' I muttered. 'Good times, huh!' I cleared my throat and cuffed at the corner of my right eye. 'Look, I'll be fine. Just look after yourself Pru. Promise me. I love you, sai mui, *sister*,' I had said, and hung up.

My eyes snapped open, and I spun around on the bench as a shout rang out right behind me, followed by the thud of something heavy hitting the ground. Bors sprang to his feet, instantly alert. An elderly Chinese man was stooped over, picking up a small but heavy suitcase as passers-by rushed to help him.

My heart was thudding in my chest, and I realised my palms were sweating. I shook my head. I was wound way too tight. My skin tingled constantly, I had a strange tick in my right eye that came and went, and I had recently noticed my resting pulse rate was way over my usual. Joey had once told me that meditation, yoga and good sleep were essential in combatting nervous tension. My approach lately had been alcohol, and it wasn't working.

The sight of the old man, wrapped in a long, black coat, reminded me of my scrawny, drug-wrecked informant Fat Johnny Tong. I had called him the night before to get him on the case because no one I knew, not even Alastair Chard, was as connected as Fat Johnny. He knew everyone, every denizen of Hong Kong's underworld, and if there was some lone lunatic prowling the city, carving people up, Johnny would know where to find him, or at least where to start looking.

He hadn't picked up, nor had he that morning when I called again. Annoyed, I assumed that he was lying half-conscious somewhere with a fix of heroin coursing through his narrowed and needle-scarred veins. I made a mental note to slap him around the head when I next saw him – I was not happy that after everything I had done to get him off the street, he was back to his old ways. I closed my eyes again and sat back, my hands clasped loosely in my lap, and took a deep breath. My attempt to control my breathing and lower my heart rate lasted precisely two seconds.

'Nice day for it,' a familiar voice said at my side, and I felt the bench vibrate slightly as someone sat next to me. I kept my eyes closed, hoping he would go away.

'This isn't an accident, is it?' I muttered. 'You didn't just stumble across me while out strolling for an ice-cream...'

Caesar Li laughed. 'As a matter of fact, I live not far from here and my wife is in that ridiculously expensive tea shop just behind us as we speak. But, no, this isn't an accident.'

Resigned that my meditative morning was at an end, I turned with a scowl to face Station Sergeant Li. He smiled warmly back at me.

'How did you find me?' I said, scratching at the scar on my cheek.

'Easy. Remember, I'm a policeman! By the way, your phone is on silent...'

I nodded. 'Yes, I know. That was intentional...'

'So, I called Joey Loh and asked if she knew where you were... You do know she tracks your location on her phone, right?'

I nodded again, recalling the time two years ago when I had shared my live location with Joey during our tailing of triad human trafficking through Hong Kong. I had, thankfully, forgotten to end the live location and that had later saved my life on a rocky, wave-swept cliff near Shek O.

'Yes, I know. It's an arrangement we have...'

Caesar Li shrugged. 'None of my business, but that sounds like something a married couple would do.'

'You're right, it's none of your fucking business, Caesar.' I sighed. What do you want? It's Sunday ...'

Caesar looked about and stood up. 'Not here, Galahad,' he said as he checked his watch. 'How about a Bloody Mary?'

With that he turned and walked off in the direction of a pedestrian overpass that bridged busy Salisbury Road. Ten minutes later we were seated outside at a restaurant on the corner of Salisbury Road and Mody Lane. Tall Bloody Mary's stood invitingly on the table in front of us. Bors lapped happily at a bowl of fresh water before flopping onto the concrete. I rolled and lit a cigarette before biting the end off the celery stalk and raising the glass.

'Happy Sunday,' I said. 'Now, what's this all about?'

Caesar Li took a long sip of the drink and smacked his lips in appreciation. 'Perfect, he muttered as he lit a cigarette. He took a long drag and blew the smoke skywards before sipping again at the Bloody Mary and sitting back in his chair.

'Guo Yu-xuan appeared for Mention two days ago on a charge under Cap.212...'

'Offences against the Person Ordinance.'

Caesar nodded. 'Yeah, right. Section 14, Attempted Murder.'

I whistled lowly and shook my head. 'That's a life term if he's found guilty...'

Caesar sipped again at his Bloody Mary and dragged on his cigarette. 'No issues there,' he said. 'He pled guilty. The District Court Judge banged the gavel and sent him down for 25 years. At his age, that's "life".'

I used a pause while I rolled another cigarette to think that through.

'So, he's not giving anyone up,' I said. 'He's taken the fall for someone who ordered the hit.' I shook my head. 'We both know Guo isn't triad – I mean, just look at him. So he's been co-opted into the attack and driven by fear of repercussions to keep his mouth shut.'

Li shrugged. 'So it would seem.'

'So... who? Who is behind this and why? It has to be triads somewhere. Surely...'

Caesar shrugged again. 'I have no idea. Guo won't talk and he'll rot in Stanley. Case closed.' He rapped the table lightly with a knuckle to get my attention.

'There's a little more.'

I just stared at him and made a "gimme" gesture with my hand.

'Guo requests the pleasure of your company at Stanley Prison, on a date and time of your convenience,' Caesar said placidly.

I knew that Li popping up at my elbow on a Sunday morning would have something to do with Guo, but I was still surprised.

'He *does*? What for?'

Caesar shrugged. 'I'm not privy to that information. His lawyer called me and relayed the message. I am now relaying it to you. The message was he would talk to you only.'

He dragged again on his smoke and gazed out across the traffic of Salisbury Road. From where we sat, we could see a dozen multi-coloured spinnakers racing downwind to the finish line of Sunday Yachties at the Royal Hong Kong Yacht Club. I drew in a deep breath and exhaled slowly.

Caesar sucked his teeth. 'My guess is he wants to spill on the attack on Walter Chan.'

I nodded as I sipped at the spicy, red cocktail. 'Yeah, maybe. But why now? Why me?'

'Well, I sort of thought that would be for you to find out,' Caesar said, waving his right hand airily. 'I've been in touch with Billy Wong, and he'll get a pass from his cousin whenever you need it. As soon as this weekend if you want.' He laughed out loud. '*Diu*, Michael Wong is going to be *pissed*!' he said, his eyes sparkling.

I smiled back. 'I don't doubt it...' The thought of Michael Wong brought to mind the hiking trail killings and Wong's undeclared knowledge of their connection to me. As Alastair had said, C.I. Wong had staked me out in the jungle as surely as if he were on a hunt for a rogue tiger. I didn't like that.

I noticed Caesar was studying me closely. He leaned across the table and pointed at my face.

'Been meaning to ask. What happened here?'

'It's a long story...'

'It always is with you, Mr Jones,' he said. 'Slip in the shower?'

I nodded and drew on my cigarette. 'Something like that.'

He studied me for a moment longer before stubbing out his cigarette and swallowing down the last of the Bloody Mary.

'Rumour has it that Michael Wong is *very* interested in you?'

'Is he? Why would that be?'

Li shrugged. 'You tell me. Your triad girlfriend maybe...'

I must have looked surprised. Li clicked his tongue. '*Diu* man, it's not as if that's a mystery. The whole of Hong Kong knows...'

'I doubt that Caesar. Only nosey cops know that,' I said.

'Don't forget her boss,' he replied. 'Lee Pak-chun knows. No one gets to date his Straw Sandal without his sign-off.' He grinned, enjoying the game.

'I don't know any Lee Pak-chun.'

Li laughed out loud at that. 'Galahad, if you think your association with 14K is some sort of closely held secret you *really* need to think again.'

'What are you saying?' I growled, feeling the anger rise in me.

Li held up his hands. 'Peace, Mr Jones!' he said. 'I'm not suggesting you're a crook but, let's face it, your associations are, how should I put this...? P*roblematic*. Personally, I don't give a damn, I like you...'

'You're one of the few who does. Be careful who knows that.'

'... *and* I don't much care who you associate with. I'm just saying, that's why C.I. Wong is so keen to know more about you.'

Along with the fact I was his bait for a serial killer, I thought. I decided to chance a question.

'Caesar,' I said casually. 'Who is Hong Kong's authority on the criminal mind? I mean, who does HKPF go to for external advice on criminal profiling?'

Caser Li blinked twice but, otherwise, showed no emotion as he replied.

'That would be Professor Morris Ngan Fei-hung...'

I smiled. 'Fei-hung? As in Wong Fei-hung, the Hung Ga master?'

Li nodded. 'Same name but let's just say he's no martial artist – you will see that when you meet him... and I assume you *do* plan to meet him.'

I shrugged but Li wasn't fooled. He went on.

'Morris Ngan is more a sifu, *master*, of the mind. Psychiatry prof. Private practice but lectures now and then at HKU.'

I nodded. 'Yes, I've heard of him but never met him. He interviewed The Jars Murderer, didn't he?'

Lam Kor-wan was a serial killer who stalked Hong Kong in the 80s. As a taxi driver he had a ready supply of female victims who he murdered, butchered and, in at least one instance, ate. On his arrest in 1982, police found female body parts, preserved in Tupperware containers in his apartment, along with a gruesome hoard of photographs recording his heinous acts. There were certainly similarities between his modus and the Hiking Trails Killer, but Lam was still rotting in Shek Pik Prison on Lantau Island, his death sentence having been commuted to life in 1984.

Caesar nodded. 'Yes, Ngan was 27 at the time – same age as Lam, incidentally – and assisted the lead psych, William Green, in the interviews.' He shuddered. 'What a crazy fucker Lam is.... a lot like the one we've got now up on the hiking trails...' he suddenly stopped and stared at me.

'Wait. That's why you want to know who the Force's "go to" is for crazies? The Trails Killer?'

I decided to let him in, but not all the way. 'Professional interest, Caesar. That's it. I'm interested in what makes this monster tick...'

Caesar looked hard at me for a long moment. 'You know,' he said mildly. 'I think the reason Michael Wong has a hard-on for you is more than your very desirable and *very* dangerous girlfriend. I have the distinct feeling you are up to something, Galahad. Something else is going on.'

He lit another cigarette and dragged deeply as he gazed back across the harbour. 'But, hell, this is Hong Kong so you wouldn't be the only one with a dangerous secret...'

I scratched my cheek lightly. 'It's a very long story, Caesar,' I said. 'I'll tell you some day, but right now let's just leave it at "professional curiosity" shall we?'

'Well, just be careful. There are a lot of people who *really* do not like you in this town,' he replied.

I nodded. 'Yes, I'd got that impression lately.'

Li's phone rang and he rolled his eyes as he checked the contact screen. He tapped the phone and put it to his ear.

'Yes, my love,' he said. 'No, just bumped into a friend.... Yes, my angel I am running to your arms right now... See you soon my flower...' He pocketed the phone and stood, pushing in his chair.

'Must away, Galahad. Wouldn't do to keep my wife waiting; not when she's loaded down with expensive shopping that I must now carry home.' He turned and left, waving his right hand over his shoulder in goodbye.

'I'll get that pass to you as soon as I can,' he shouted as he ducked across Mody Lane against the traffic. 'Let me know how it goes.'

I finished my Bloody Mary and signalled for another while I rolled a cigarette. Bors growled faintly in his sleep, his back legs twitching. It occurred to me that that was the second time in as many days someone had walked off leaving me with the bill. I really needed to do something about that.

31

Later that afternoon, having caught the ferry from TST to Wan Chai and walked home, stopping only to pick up some steamed chicken and rice, we arrived home and I let us both in.

Bors surged across the tiny apartment to snap up his favourite toy while I pulled out my phone and called Johnny Tong. The call rang out again and, by now, I was beyond annoyed with my informant. He had obviously slipped back into his addiction and had, probably, by now also lost the job I had secured for him stacking shelves in a supermarket in Mong Kok. The next thing, he would be thrown out of the micro-apartment I had found for him and continued to finance. Johnny Tong was a useless druggie, and I swore viciously under my breath as I bent into the fridge and pulled out a cold beer.

The warmth of the day had gone as the sun began to set and I pulled on a puffer jacket as I stepped out onto the terrace. I flopped into one of the large outdoor sofas and popped the lid off the beer while I thumbed through the music app on my phone. I selected a playlist, and the sounds of heavy blues were soon drifting over the terrace and down into the alley below. I rolled and lit a cigarette and took a deep pull on the beer as I leaned back in the sofa.

Above me a Black Kite soared and wheeled in search of prey, his shrill, whinnying cry echoing between the glass apartment towers. The bird circled into a thermal, rising to height before he spotted something and tucked his wings in, rocketing to earth like a feathered Stuka. As I watched, he pulled out of his dive, banked away sharply and sped down the alley at eye level with me. Time seemed to slow as the bird flapped his metre-wide wingspan and turned his head to look at me as he passed. I seemed to stare into his glinting dark-brown eyes for seconds, but he passed me in flash, his mottled black and brown plumage ruffled in the wind as he sped away.

I sighed a deep breath and sipped at the beer, reaching down to scratch Bors' thick black and tan scruff. I tried to order my thoughts but there was so much going on I didn't know where to start.

With everything else happening in my life I hadn't given Guo Yu-xuan much thought lately. Caesar Li's revelation that Guo wanted to speak to me had re-fired my determination to run that case to ground.

Walter Chan was up to something, I was sure of it, and Guo was the key. The theory that Chan was tied into triad activity and Guo had been hired as a fall-guy assassin, or as a warning to Chan, seemed to hold water – despite what Michael Wong had said. It was possible Chan was a clean-skin and had not yet come to the attention of OCTB, just as it was possible Guo knew what Chan's criminal involvement was and had decided to tell me. I made a mental note to follow up on the visit pass from Billy Wong's cousin in Correctional Services and see Guo as early as possible the following week.

Sipping on the beer, I dragged on my cigarette as the playlist changed track. In the alley below me a motorcycle revved up and roared away, and I could hear the sound of kids' laughter coming from the heated public pool just across the small park behind my building. Somewhere out in Wan Chai a police siren wailed and in an apartment above me a man and woman argued while a baby cried. The thing about life is it goes on around you, no matter the troubles that press down on you, threatening to swamp you in a tidal wave of pain, regret, and sorrow. That cheery thought led me to Jade Tooth.

I was sure Jade Tooth would react to my escape and the death of one of his soldiers – despite Angel's and Tommy Ho's assurances he would not dare.

Men like Jade Tooth simply never walked away from a challenge or an insult and I had effectively done both; more than once. I was unfinished business for Jade Tooth, and if there was one thing nice I could say about Jade Tooth it was that he always attended to business.

The questions, then, were: when would he make his move, where and how? The only answers I could come up with, as I dragged on the cigarette and swigged again at the beer, was anytime, anywhere, and any number of ways. It wasn't a comforting thought.

Naturally, thinking about Jade Tooth led me to the money I had stolen from SYO. I was committed to keeping it, but I still did not know what I was going to do with it. I picked up my phone and tapped the banking app. There it was: 1.9 million US Dollars, staring me in the face, daring me to spend it. I had long ago come to terms with my shaky moral compass on which the needle rarely pointed true, but even *I* couldn't come around to spending SYO's ill-gotten gains on myself – as much as the idea appealed.

Hell, why not enjoy life? a tiny voice whispered in my head. *You deserve this. Go on! Live it up!* I shook my head and stubbed out the cigarette as I stood to fetch another beer. It *was* tempting and I had to agree with the little voice; I *did* deserve it. But I knew I wasn't going to do it, so what I needed to do was figure out how I was going to make the best use of the money, and without jeopardising anyone through any connection with the hoard. Again, I had no clue who that would be, or how I would do it.

I returned to the terrace with a beer and Bors looked up casually from his place on the tiles, where he lay licking his paws like a giant cat. I toed him gently with my boot as I slid past and lowered myself back into the sofa. I rolled and lit another cigarette and closed my eyes as I exhaled a plume of cherry-scented smoke, while I gulped greedily on the beer. I was smoking and drinking too much again, but that was the least of my worries. My biggest worry then rose up to hover over me like a foetid, black cloud.

I didn't bother re-examining the facts. My initials had been carved into the bodies of the victims, and a photo of me had been left with one of them. Facts. Besides that, there was nothing to go on.

Nothing, other than the possible fleeting glimpse, on the move, at night, of a figure who *might* have been Peter Toh, to give any clue as to what the killer's interest in me was. That interest, once I could discover that, would lead to a conclusion on what his next steps might be and how he might carry them out. *If* it was Peter Toh – and that was still a big if in my mind – Alastair's deduction was on the money: everyone close to me was at risk. So that was where I had to start. I had to protect everyone I loved. Fortunately, that was not a big list, and I was satisfied that was now covered.

But where to from there? Where did I even *begin* to look for a shadowy figure the brightest minds, and finest investigators, in HKPF could not find?

The obvious place to start was a visit to Morris Ngan. I needed a better understanding of what might be going on in the mind of this killer if I was to have any hope of tracking him. I was sure that Michael Wong's taskforce would have already spoken to Professor Ngan and would have shaped up a profile as a result, but I wasn't about to approach Michael Wong for that information. He wouldn't give it to me if I did. Ngan was the best lead I had at that point, so I decided to call the following day and make an appointment.

By now, the sun had set behind the tall apartment blocks to the west of my apartment and the early evening chill had settled around me. I zipped up my puffer and stood to turn on the patio heater. Bors stood and shook himself then sauntered inside to flop down onto his padded mat. I wandered inside for some beers, and a small woollen beanie I kept by the door for winter terrace drinking sessions.

I was still mulling over the presence of both Jade Tooth and an unknown murderer in my life, when the playlist changed track again. The hypnotic rhythm and soaring, aggressive blues riffs of Kenny Wayne Shepherd's "in 2 deep" sounded out into the night. The lyrics, warning me of a madman on the run, and that there was no place to hide, were like a Greek Chorus, giving commentary to me as the sole audience member in the tragic play that was my life.

The patio heater warmed the terrace around me, but I shivered involuntarily. Only a few short weeks ago I had relished the feeling that my life was on the up, that things were looking good. How could I have been so blind?

Now, I was somehow responsible for the horrific deaths of three innocents and the prospect of a violent death hovered over me and over those close to me. Notwithstanding the stolen triad cash, I did not know exactly how I had done it, but I had called this down on my head and now it was time to pay the piper. The night suddenly became colder and quieter around me.

It seemed the city was holding its breath, as I dropped the empty beer bottle to the tiles with a clank and, my food forgotten in the kitchen, reached for another.

32

Two days later, I had walked Bors and dropped him back home then decided to walk myself, to clear my head and try to make some sense of what was going on.

I had tried Fat Johnny Tong's number half a dozen times over the previous days and still nothing. Whatever gear the useless junkie had managed to get his hands on had certainly taken him out of circulation – and at a time when I needed his army of spies, informants and misfits dragging the depths of Hong Kong for the Trails Killer. I shook my head in annoyance and swore tightly between gritted teeth as I walked along Harbour Road toward the pedestrian overpass to the Wan Chai ferry. I did not really know where I was going and had no clear idea of where to start my search, but sensed Kowloon-side was as good a place as any to start.

I was thinking of nothing in particular, happy to let my mind wander and find its own path. The day had dawned bright and cold and the sky above the tall concrete canyons was a deep cerulean blue, smeared only here and there with a light brush-stroke of cloud, but I barely noticed it as I walked, my head down and hands stuffed deep into my puffer jacket. I was on Hung Hing Road, the harbour on my left, when I became aware of a black sedan pulling into the kerb and crawling along beside me. The car stopped and the back passenger door sprung open. I leaned down, looked in and shook my head with a sigh.

'Get in,' Michael Wong ordered from the other side of the back seat.

'You do know it's against procedure to drag innocent people off the street,' I said.

'You're one of the least innocent people I know, Jones,' Michael responded, his face tight. 'Just get in. You need to see this...'

'May I ask what it is I *need* to see?'

'Don't jerk me about, Jones,' Michael hissed. 'Get in the damn car before I throw the cuffs on you.'

Put like that I didn't see I had any choice, so I climbed into the car and closed the door. I was reaching for the seatbelt when the driver spun the wheel in a vicious U-turn and sped off into the traffic, heading west, oblivious to the hard braking and horns of protest of the cars behind him. I turned to face Michael who was staring out the widow as Wan Chai passed by.

'May I now ask where we are going and what this is all about, *Chief Inspector*?' I said, the sarcasm heavy in my tone.

Michael Wong was pissed off. That was clear. His body was rigid in the seat and his jaw clenched and unclenched. His hands, balled in fists, were resting one on each leg the knuckles white. His lips were tight and his eyes blinked repeatedly. I sighed and tried another approach.

'I apologise Michael, but I'm a little confused right now...'

'Jones, please.' he said. 'Just shut up until we reach our destination. Once you see what I have to show you I am sure you will have questions. I *know* I have many ...',

That didn't sound good. I shrugged and tried to look calm. I turned my head to watch the road, just as we sped through Sheung Wan and past Western Market with its Queen Anne Revival style red-brick façade. The car didn't slow and we accelerated along Connaught Road West, snaking in and out of traffic. Past Sun Yat Sen Park, under Route 4 the east-west road artery, and finally onto Shing

Sai Street, along the harbourfront in Kennedy Town. We were headed to the far west of The Island and Michael Wong could barely have taken me further from my intended ferry to Kowloon if he had tried. I knew something serious had happened and that, judging from Michael Wong's demeanour, I was in the shit. That seemed certain. The only questions were why and how deep?

I controlled my breathing, but I could feel my pulse racing as the car wound through Kennedy Town's side streets. I blinked as sunlight blazed through the windscreen and the driver expertly flicked the vehicle across lanes and through a series of left and right-hand turns. Michael Wong was a silent, stern and still figure next to me. As the car finally began to slow, I suddenly knew where we were headed.

I had been here many times during my career as a uniformed policeman, and later as a detective, and I had always hated it. It now seemed I had not seen the last of the place. We were headed to Victoria Public Mortuary.

Seconds later the driver slid the car into the carpark and Michael Wong unclipped his seatbelt.

'Get out,' he ordered as he opened his own door and stepped out. I followed suit and stood staring at the brutal, grey-white industrial facade of the mortuary. Whoever we were here to see hadn't died in a hospital – or we would now be walking into a hospital morgue. That meant the body we were about to view had probably died on the streets. Or on a hiking trail. I shuddered and pulled the collar of my puffer jacket up a little higher.

Without looking at me, Michael pushed through the door of the building and into the reception area where he spoke a few terse words to an attendant who had been waiting on his arrival. Stepping through a metal, rubber-sealed door, we pushed deeper into the building along a brightly lit and sterile tiled corridor. The rich, sickening stench of the morgue was instantly recognisable.

I had first been exposed to that smell nearly 20 years before and it had never changed. The stink of bleach, formaldehyde and, despite the chill of the facility, the odour of rotting flesh wrapped around me like a cloud. I opened my mouth to breathe against it. My heart thumped in rhythm with my steps as we approached a lone door at the end of the corridor. None of us spoke and the click of Michael's leather heels echoed in the clinical, dead space. The attendant swiped a RFID card over an electronic lock and pushed the door open.

In front of me, the post-mortem table stood stark and metallic in the centre of the room. It was shaped slightly down from both ends to a square hole that drained into a sink at the end of the table. A gurney stood off to the side, on which an array of sterile surgical tools, including a small angle grinder and reciprocating saw, were laid out ready for the next PM. The room was tiled brilliant white and was lit brightly by powerful downspots and overhead fluorescent lamps. I turned slightly to my left and the steel mortuary cabinets, arrayed in a bank three high and eight wide, stared back at me blind, soulless, and silent. The attendant paused and looked at Michael who nodded tersely. The attendant grasped the handle of a cabinet marked 12-VM in the middle row and tugged the drawer. It slid open silently and came to a soft stop as it reached the limit of its runner.

A body lay on the narrow, steel shelf and Michael Wong, pausing briefly to gaze at the corpse, motioned me forward with a finger. I stepped up to stand next to him and stared down onto the dead, naked body of Fat Johnny Tong. I took a deep breath and stepped closer.

Johnny's face was almost unrecognisable.

It was pale and bloated, with dark patches of purple bruising where the blood had settled during lividity. His lank, wet hair plastered his skull but could not hide the wounds where his ears had been. His eyes were missing and the ravaged, empty sockets stared back at me, partially filled with a mixture of sand and sea water. His lips were thickened, grey and spongey like a sea cucumber and had been partially eaten away by the fish and crabs to reveal his teeth that were locked in a rictus of pain and fear. His throat had been sliced open, revealing the white cartilage of the larynx and his tongue had been pulled out through the obscene gash.

Eyes, ears, tongue. He saw too much, heard too much and spoke too much. This was a triad killing and Johnny was doomed to wander hell for eternity blind, deaf and mute.

Letting my eyes wander further down, I took in the brutal wounds to the rest of Johnny Tong's tortured body.

His torso was covered in faint red and purple welts that had whitened slightly in the water, and his arms and chest were covered in slashes and stab wounds that had washed clean and were now puckered and grey. Four fingers from each hand had been hacked away, leaving only the thumbs which had both been snapped back to fold against his wrists. Both kneecaps and ankles had been drilled out. I swallowed hard at the bile that rose in my throat.

Michael Wong stepped up to stand beside me and handed me a small plastic evidence bag.

'He was fished out of the water off Telegraph Bay yesterday,' he said tersely. 'Probably there for about a week. That was found on the body, in a ziplock bag. You might want to read it.'

I unzipped the bag and drew out a small piece of paper. It was a note, written in Traditional Cantonese.

"Jones is this worth 2.5 million? Your sister is next"

My stomach dropped and I gasped slightly, but I tried to keep my face blank as I turned to Michael.

'I have no idea what this means,' I said.

'*Diu*! Don't fucking *lie* to me!' Michael hissed. 'Tong was your long-term informant; you have been using him recently, he was instrumental in your *exploits* two years ago... and the fucking note is addressed to *you*! Now, you tell me: what 2.5 million, what's your connection to it and why was Tong killed by a triad because of it?'

My mind was spinning as the realisation that my theft had now caused this. Johnny Tong, accepted on all sides of the track in Hong Kong's criminal underworld for years, had been tortured and murdered by Jade Tooth over the SYO cash I had stolen. The threat to Prudence was direct and real for the same reason.

I felt sick. I wondered, vaguely, if this was what guilt and conscience felt like. In the horror of the moment, I knew I couldn't tell Michael Wong why Johnny had been murdered. I wasn't about to admit to a Chief Inspector of the Organised Crime and Triad Bureau that I had stolen millions in triad Proceeds of Crime.

'Look,' I said. 'I owed SYO a lot of money a couple of years back but I paid them back through a loan from my sister. Ask her. It was a few hundred grand. A gambling debt. Shit, Michael, you *know* that about me.' I realised I was rambling and drew a breath.

'I have no idea why this note mentions my name, nor why it refers to a couple of million dollars,' I said, staring hard into Michael Wong's eyes. 'No idea, Period.'

Michael looked hard at me. 'You know nothing, this is all a massive shock and surprise to you. That's what you're telling me?'

'That's what I'm telling you.'

He shook his head. 'You're prepared to stake your sister's life on this? I know you're lying Jones, but I can't prove it. If it were up to me I'd drag you back to the station and beat the shit out of you until you told me the truth.'

'That would be both unnecessary and a breach of procedures, Michael.'

He poked me in the chest. 'Don't get fucking smart with me, Jones!' he shouted and was about to say more when he noticed the morgue attendant still standing in the room, his mouth agape.

'You! Get lost,' he said, thumbing over his shoulder to the door. The attendant got lost and Michael turned back to me.

'I've had my deep suspicions about you ever since I met you at the end of that trafficking case nearly three years ago,' he hissed. 'You're bent, Jones, and I can *smell* it...'

Something in me snapped then. 'So, pull me in!' I shouted. 'Interview me, charge me. Put me before the courts. But you fucking won't, will you! You won't because you have nothing on me *and* you *need* me to smoke out the Trails Killer. Don't you!'

It was Michael's turn to look me in the eye and lie. It seemed everyone was doing it these days. 'What are you talking about? Smoke out the Trails Killer? You have nothing to do with that case...'

I shook my head. 'I *know* what you're up to, Michael,' I said quietly. 'Don't ask how, but I know. You've got me laid out as bait so you can catch this maniac. But I've got news for you. I'm going to get him for you. Dead or alive.' I prodded him slightly on the chest. 'Now get me back home. I need a drink.'

Michael Wong stood stock still, his face immobile as he wrestled with his thoughts. He was so angry his breaths were coming in short pants – but, typically, he controlled it well. I was pushing it, I knew, but I also knew he wanted the Trails Killer more than he wanted me; he wouldn't to reel his bait in just yet. I was in the clear. For now.

Once we were in the car, I told Michael I had changed my mind and wanted to be dropped at Star Ferry Pier in Tsim Sha Tsui. He looked at me suspiciously but, as he was headed back into Kowloon, directed the driver to do as I asked. Thirty minutes later, I stepped from the car on Canton Road and stood on the footpath until Michael Wong had driven out of sight. As soon as he was gone, I turned on my heel and headed to West Kowloon where, I knew, I needed to see someone about Johnny Tong's murder.

Thinking about Johnny brought back memories of his long, slender fingers delicately feeding sparrows in the Yuen Po Street Bird Garden as his emaciated frame perched, birdlike, on the edge of a concrete bench.

The poor bastard never really stood a chance – either the heroin was going to get him or his lifetime of informing on Hong Kong's crims would. But there was another truth there, lurking, dark in my consciousness. I shook my head. I couldn't ignore the fact that my greed, dishonesty and general moral decay had brought on Johnny's untimely and brutal end, and now threatened Pru.

Again, my stomach clenched and I stopped in my tracks as I tried to control my breathing and prevent myself from vomiting onto the footpath of Hong Kong's ritziest street.

I hated myself at that moment. I shut my eyes tight and breathed deep. At least I was honest about that, I thought. At least I could agree that I was an immoral, thieving, coward whose avarice and lies had caused another human being to be carved up like pig on a block then thrown to the fish for good measure. There was no putting this right. No redemption, ever, for what I had done. Johnny Tong's ghost would haunt me for the rest of my days. I knew then that I would have to go to my grave carrying the burden of that secret.

I opened my eyes and started walking along Canton Road, my mind made up. I would deal at another time with the thin moral and ethical justifications I had conjured for myself from the moment I stole the triad cash. For now I was angry – a seething anger over what had been done to Johnny Tong, and the threat to my sister. I swore I would see Jade Tooth dead and I was heading to the one man who could make that happen.

33

THE HEADQUARTERS of YunCorp sits in the palatial surrounds of the 119th and 120th floors of the International Commerce Centre on reclaimed land in West Kowloon. ICC's towering glass façade is famous for the eye-burning reflections of the sun's rays it casts across Victoria Harbour to The Island. There was even a case on record of a high-end kit car melting down one side as it stood parked in the ICC's reflection. Without breaking step I stepped into the expansive and warm lobby and up to the specially designated lift tower that would rocket me to the 119th floor and the office of the man I was there to see.

After a silent ride during which I glanced twice at the floor lights to confirm the lift was actually moving – although I knew it by the popping in my ears – the lift door slid open with a quiet hiss.

I glanced to my left and right then walked straight past the reception desk and security point toward a grand, winding staircase that led to the top floor. I had never visited but knew where I was going from a previous description given by Angel. I heard the receptionist calling after me and the sound of footsteps behind me as security moved.

This was no ordinary building security in their poorly cut uniforms, half asleep with boredom. The footsteps I could hear behind me belonged to well-dressed, and very dangerous, young men who were all Red Poles; initiated triad enforcers. I increased my pace and was soon running up the stairs, taking them two at a time. I hit the top and took two paces before a hand clamped down on my shoulder, the fingers digging into my collarbone like steel pincers.

Without thinking, I reached up and grasped the hand, twisting the fingers up and away while I spun out of the grip and behind the triad soldier, twisting his arm behind him. He dropped to his knees with a grunt as his shoulder joint threatened to pop. I was wrenching his arm and about to drive my fist into his face when the patent leather toe of a shoe drove into the side of my left knee and I crumpled in a heap.

Both soldiers dived on me and pulled my arms behind my back, dragging me painfully to my feet. The gangster I had manhandled stepped around to face me and raised his right hand over his left shoulder. He was about to deliver a stinging back-hander when the oak double doors across the room were thrown open. The gangster dropped his hand and spun around. I looked over his shoulder and there stood Lee Pak-chun; the Chairman and CEO of YunCorp, and Mountain Master, leader, of 14K Triad.

He was, by now, nearing 70 but he carried it well and was still wiry and fit. Dressed in light grey, slim-fit pants with a crisp white shirt, French cuffed and pinned with discreet gold cufflinks, a Patek Philippe Calatrava at his left wrist, Lee looked every inch the multibillionaire tycoon (and criminal overlord) he was.

I had last seen him two years before and had sworn – as part of my failed attempt to distance myself from 14K – to never see him again. But he was the one man in Hong Kong who could order Jade Tooth's death so here I was.

With a barely discernible flick of his right hand, he ordered his soldiers to stand down and they instantly stood back. I tried not to put any weight on my left knee and that left me hopping slightly on my right foot like a school kid needing the toilet. Lee watched me with a look of mild amusement.

'Mr Jones,' he said, his accent English and refined. 'I had thought we were not on speaking terms. Yet here you are.'

I nodded. 'Yes, here I am. May I come in?'

Lee stood back and gestured into his inner domain. 'Please do.'

I winked at the two soldiers, who glared murderously back at me, and walked past Lee into his office.

I moved across the richly carpeted room to the floor-to-ceiling window that took in the entire southern side of the office. From this angle and height, the view over Hong Kong Island was truly breathtaking. I drank it in, knowing full well I would, in all likelihood, never stand in this room again. Far below me, Victoria Harbour glittered a deep blue-green in the bright winter's day and The Island sat crouched like a shimmering dragon, its dark green ridge back hunched as if ready to spring. Above me a Cathay flight soared off from HKIA, heading south into the clear, blue December sky.

'Impressive,' I said, turning to Lee who had crossed to a large, well-appointed bar and was holding up a fine cut crystal Old Fashioned.

'If I recall,' he said 'it's whisky, single malt. Will 'Aberlour' do?

'Well, it's almost Christmas so why not a sherry whisky at...,' I checked my G-Shock. '11.30. To be honest, I could use it.'

Lee poured two good measures and walked toward me; a glass held out. 'Yes, you'll forgive me if I say you *look* like you could use it.' He lowered himself into a dark brown leather chair behind his surprisingly small and utilitarian desk, took a sip of the whisky and gently placed the glass on the desktop.

'Now, Mr Jones. You could easily have made an appointment through Mei-ying...Angel, if you wished to see me. I am always happy to meet a friend.'

I sipped at the whisky, feeling the warmth of its spice and clove notes wash down my throat. I noticed my right hand was shaking slightly and I was sure Lee had also noticed. He missed nothing.

'I don't know that we *are* friends, Mr Lee,' I said.

Lee waved a hand in a something-nothing gesture. 'Semantics.

Friend...enemy Frenemy. Take your pick.' He sipped again at his whisky. 'Why are you here?'

I decided directness was my best strategy. 'I want Jade Tooth dead,' I said quietly, swirling my whisky around the glass before taking a big swallow.

'That is a sudden, and rather serious, request Mr Jones. May I ask why?'

'A friend of mine has been murdered. No...butchered. My sister has been threatened. Jade Tooth was behind it.'

'How do you know?' Lee asked politely, reaching for a small humidor, extracting a slim panatella and lighting it. He blew a cloud of smoke toward the ceiling. 'I mean, this is Hong Kong, people die. Are killed. How do you know it was Jade Tooth?'

'I know. It was him.'

Lee studied me silently then pointed at the yellowing and crusted wounds on my face. 'I assume this was Jade Tooth's handiwork...?'

I nodded. 'One of his goons. Yes.'

Lee suddenly smiled and nodded. 'Oh yes,' he said. 'I recall now. The Panda arrived just in time to prevent your untimely, but probably richly deserved, demise. Mei-ying has briefed me on that little fracas.'

I kept my face blank but my mind was racing. What else had Angel briefed Lee on? Did he know about the missing SYO cash?

'I believe,' Lee went on 'It was a question of a sum of missing SYO money. Jade Tooth thinks you have it. But you don't ...Do you?'

He didn't know! Angel, bless her heart, had kept quiet on that – at great risk to herself – so I wasn't about to drop her in it with a confession. Besides, what did he care what happened to 2.5 million in his competitor's cash? Nonetheless, I was playing with fire. Lee Pak-chun was not someone you lied to without being prepared to back it up with your life. What the hell, I thought, I was a dead man walking anyway.

'No. I don't have it.'

Lee studied the tip of his cigar as he spoke. 'That's good enough for me, Mr Jones. I know you would never lie to me...'

"I would, Mr Lee. Don't kid yourself. It's just that I'm not on this occasion.'

'*And*,' he went on, mildly annoyed at being interrupted. 'It really is a matter of supernatural indifference to me what happens to SYO's money. The more they lose the better. *Unless* of course it was a member, or affiliate, of 14K who took it without disclosing it. *That* would be a *very* different matter. I hasten to add that, since The Panda's shooting of Jade Tooth's man, to your very great benefit, you are now, most assuredly, an affiliate member of 14K. Congratulations.'

He smiled at me then but there was not a scintilla of warmth in it. It was a warning. I groaned inwardly. I now had both of the major Hong Kong triads after my blood – at least I would if Lee ever found out I had just lied to him – as well as a knife-wielding psychopath who enjoyed carving my initials into his victims. A sudden thought occurred to me, but I parked it and took a took pull of the whisky.

'Jade Tooth. Will you help me on this? He has murdered a friend, and no one close to me is safe – *I* will never be safe – as long as he lives.'

Lee shook his head. 'I am sorry, Mr Jones, but no. Jade Tooth may be a truly dreadful creature, but he is a *very* senior member of SYO and I am not about to start a war with another society – with all the cost in blood and treasure that would entail – because you can't keep yourself out of trouble. You will just have to work out your own way out of this.'

I was about to speak when Lee held up a finger. '*And*,' he said. 'Apropos my earlier point, I also forbid *you*, as an affiliate of my society, to take direct action against Jade Tooth personally.'

I clenched my jaw and put the empty glass on desk. 'Well,' I said. 'I guess that's my business here done.'

Lee held up both hands. 'Please, Mr Jones. Don't be so hasty. I haven't quite finished.' He glanced over at the bar. 'Would you care for another?'

I considered telling him to stick his world-leading single malt whisky that I could never afford myself, but decided why be a bore? I shrugged. 'Sure'.

Lee pressed a button discreetly set in the desktop.

'Miss Chu, would you be so kind to come in?' A woman's voice answered politely and Lee turned in his chair to gaze out of the window over the territory he commanded.

I suddenly remembered the conclusion to the human trafficking case two years before, when I had last seen Lee, and the uncomfortable secret I shared with him about his true dominion over Hong Kong. I would have given almost anything – perhaps even 2.5 million USD – to know what he was thinking at that moment. The door clicking open broke my thoughts, and I turned my head over my shoulder.

A beautiful young woman, dressed in a dark grey, figure-hugging skirt and jacket, white shirt and black heels stood at the entrance to the office. Lee's office was probably full of young women like this. In my experience, men with Lee's money and power collected bright and ambitious women like porcelain dolls to be trotted out and gazed upon with delight whenever the whim took them.

'Yes, Mr Lee?' she asked, stepping into the office. Her voice was soft, alluring.

Lee indicated the bar. 'Two 'Aberlours' please, Miss Chu. Make them a good pour please, my dear.'

'Certainly, Mr Lee,' the girl said, moving seductively across the carpet, her hips swaying.

Moments later I had another drink in my hand and I had to admit, I was feeling more relaxed with every sip. I was enjoying the time to just sit, if not exactly relax. Lee Pak-chun was both a very dangerous and extremely engaging man, and I could never decide which it was about him I preferred.

Lee politely thanked the woman as she left, barely looking in her direction then lit another cigar and offered me the humidor. I selected a panatella and lit up, making a mental note to get some food in to me just as soon as I left Lee's office. I had a habit of not eating when I drank and it was catching up with me the older I got

Lee exhaled a cloud of smoke and sighed in contentment. 'Allow me to continue,' he said.

'Please do.'

'While I forbid any action against Jade Tooth, I do give you this: we will put every effort into locating the man, or men, who executed your friend. You may then take whatever action you wish to avenge your friend and clear your conscience...'

I blinked. Clear my conscience? What did he mean by that? Lee knew more than he was making out, I was sure of it. The cagey old bastard always did.

'Do you find that arrangement suitable?' he asked, sipping at the whisky in his hand.

I nodded. 'I do. What now?'

'I will leave it to you to organise details with Mei-ying and you have my approval to utilise Tommy Ho should you wish.'

I nodded again. 'I wish.'

Lee dragged on his cigar. 'Good,' he said. 'So, I think we're done here.'

I was being dismissed so I threw back the 'Aberlour' and stood. I politely nodded to Lee and turned to walk to the door. I had grasped the handle when Lee spoke behind me.

'Please remember what I have said, Mr Jones. And ... I don't think we should meet again. Goodbye.'

34

OUT ON THE street I headed east into Tsim She Tsui.

The footpath was heaving with shoppers, tourists and office workers all doing their thing in Kowloon's retail and business district where expensive watch shops competed for space with Chinese herbalists, Indian tailors, noodle joints, high-end sneakers, craft beer taprooms and foot massage parlours. The roar of traffic and din of nearby construction work beat at my senses, throwing up a challenge to the mic'd-up store touts and their blaring Canto-Pop.

I ducked across Canton Road, dodging the traffic and wound my way to Ichang Street, where I entered a noodle bar and greeted the woman who ran the place. She smiled distractedly and waved a hand at me as the fingers of her other hand danced across a calculator, toting up the bill for a customer. Her mother sat in the doorway hand-rolling fresh wantons. Roast duck and joints of Char Siu hung in the window. I took a seat at a small, steel-framed formica table and ordered wanton noodle soup and a glass of lemon tea. I needed a clear head after the whisky, so my usual bottle of Tsing Tao was off the menu.

A plastic jug of boiling red tea and a small bowl were brought to my table, so I filled the bowl with tea and washed and sterilised a set of plastic chopsticks and a curved *tong chi* spoon. The thought I had parked in Lee's office bounced back suddenly to front of mind and I drew a breath.

The injuries inflicted on Johnny Tong were eerily similar to those I had seen on James Thomas two years previously and, from what little I knew to that point, bore distinct similarities to the trails murders. Was Jade Tooth the Trails Killer or, more to the point, one of his hatchet-men? Why would I think that...? It seemed too improbable. I rubbed my eyes and forced myself to concentrate.

Suddenly, I had it. Jade Tooth had whispered something to me as I sat bound and bleeding in that chair... What had it been? Did I really remember him making a reference to the victims on "the trails"? I shook my head. It was just too crazy to seriously consider Jade Tooth would go these lengths to discredit me over a paltry 2.5 million. Still, Jade Tooth was a dyed-in-the-wool psycho so one never really knew.

I drummed my fingers on the tabletop for a moment considering my next move. I had to focus on the matter more immediately to hand, also featuring Jade Tooth. My first call was to Prudence. She answered quickly but sounded distracted, busy.

'Gal, hi, what's up?' she said, a little out of breath.

'Pru. Listen. I can't go into detail now but I have evidence of a direct threat against you. It goes back to my dealings with Jade Tooth.' I had still not told her about the money and I did not intend to. 'He's coming after me and has threatened you.'

Prudence was quiet for a long moment then: 'Okay. That's not good. What do I do?'

'Like I said last week, stay close to Giles. Don't go out alone. Stay aware... Look, I can get some protection for you...'

'*No*!'

'No? Why the fuck not, Pru? This is serious.'

'I do not want any of your less-than-reputable friends handing around me. I have Giles. That's all I need...'

I sighed. I knew she wouldn't agree to a team following her

around, and that I would never win that argument. I heard Giles' voice in the background, asking what was going on.

'Is Giles there?' I said. 'Put him on.'

There was shuffling of the phone and Giles' voice sounded in my ear, concerned but controlled.

'Galahad, how are you? What's happening? Pru has gone as white as a ghost...'

I needed Giles to protect my sister, but I wasn't going to tell him everything. 'An old case has surfaced,' I said. 'And I've just come from the police. There is a direct threat against Pru. Some triad shitheads...'

'Jesus Christ! Do you really think so?'

'Yes. I think it's legitimate and while I deal with it I need you to look after her. Stay close to her.' I paused. 'I'm also worried about the killer we've got on the loose in Hong Kong...'

'The Trails Killer? Why?' Giles asked, his voice low, barely a whisper.

'No particular reason,' I lied. 'It's just so damn frightening, what's going on... I worry about Pru.'

He was silent and I could hear his breathing over the phone.

'Galahad,' he said. 'I will give my life for hers, of that you can be certain. No one will touch Prudence while she is with me...'

I heaved a sigh. 'Thanks Giles,' I said. 'That's reassuring. Look, I have to go but I'll keep you posted.'

'Do that,' he replied. 'I want to know everything you know when you know it. I need that if I'm to do this properly.'

'Deal,' I said and hung up. I still didn't like the fact my kid sister had a new boyfriend but I was pleased it was Giles. I knew Pru was safe with him.

Given Michael Wong's interest in me and his, justified, deep suspicion of my activities, I decided calling The Panda was not a good idea, so I drew out my phone, opened a secure messaging app and pulled up Tommy's contact. Squinting at the small screen I tapped in:

No calls. This app only. Meet at the usual place. 3 hrs

Next, I tapped on Joey's name. We hadn't spoken in a few days, and I wanted to check in with her and tell her what had happened. The phone rang for longer than usual before she answered. She sounded tired, distracted.

'Gal. Hi.'

'Hi yourself,' I said. 'You okay? You don't sound your usual.'

There was a long pause and I heard her heave a sigh. 'I'm okay,' she replied. 'Just a bit going on now. Sorry I haven't been in the office for a while...'

'No apologies necessary, Joey,' I said. 'We agreed you needed to lay low for a while.' I paused. 'Is Angel's team still with you?'

'Yes. Yes, they are. I'm sick of being surrounded by gangsters. I can't move an inch without them crowding me...'

'It's a necessary evil, Jo. Just for a little while longer and especially considering what I have to tell you.'

She seemed to gather herself and her voice became firmer. 'What's happened?'

I told her about Johnny Tong – keeping a description of his injuries to 'it was horrendous' – and the link to Jade Tooth and the stolen triad cash.

'The cash,' she said. 'I told you that would come back to haunt you.' She drew in a breath. 'How do you feel? Are you okay?'

I blinked a few times and stared across the crowded restaurant. On the footpath an old man, bent over a walking stick, was arguing with a bicycle courier in a grubby white singlet, and two young women hurried by, covering their smiles with their hands.

'I blame myself, Jo,' I said quietly. 'No doubt about it: Johnny's death is down to me and I hate myself for it. But beside that, I'm bloody angry. I'm going to get Jade Tooth for this. Somehow, I'm going to make him pay.'

Joey was quiet for a few seconds. 'Nothing good is ever going to come out of what you did taking that cash, Gal. *Nothing*,' she said angrily, her voice shrill. 'Yes, I know it's triad cash and, yes, *fuck* them but your life – *our* lives – have been turned upside down by it, and not in a good way. We're slinking and hiding like cowed dogs, living our lives looking over our shoulders... Johnny Tong is dead, and all because you thought it was a good idea to take a bag belonging to people who would never forget it and never stop looking for it... *Fuck*!'

It was an unusually emotional outburst from Joey. She was normally buttoned up much tighter than that, but she was right and I couldn't blame her. Acknowledging my stupidity didn't change anything: I had the cash, SYO wanted it back, they suspected I had it, I wasn't going to admit it nor was I returning it. Still, I had the feeling something else was happening with Joey but if she wasn't going to tell me, I wasn't going to push.

'You're right Jo, I said. 'Absolutely. I'm going to make this right. I promise...'

'*Fuck*, Gal...Whatever!'

I looked at my phone in mild shock. This *really* wasn't Joey Loh. She had never bitten back at me like that, no matter the situation or the provocation. Something was very wrong.

'Joey, are you okay?' I asked quietly. 'I mean *really* okay... Is something happening?'

A pause and a deep sigh. 'I'm fine. Nothing I can't handle. Look, I have to go.'

'Sure,' I said. 'Call me if you need me. I'm always...'

Joey ended the call and I was left holding the phone to my ear with a stunned expression on my face. I shrugged. I would get to the bottom of whatever that was all about at another time.

Next was Angel. Michael Wong knew all about Angel and me – at least the romantic connection bit – so I decided a call to her was safe, provided I used veiled speech. We both knew OCTB were monitoring her phone. Angel would know what was going on and would play along. The phone answered after three rings.

'*Galahad*, my *love*!' Angel said, she sounded busy. 'What's up?'

'We need to talk,' I said without preamble. 'Do you have time now?'

'Mmm, not really. I'm *super* busy,' she replied. I could hear hair dryers and women-chatter in the background.

'Angel, this is serious. Johnny Tong has been murdered...'

'Oh, my poor love,' she breathed into the phone. She was trying hard, but failing, to sound solicitous. 'I know you were weirdly attached to that awful little man...'

'That "awful little man" was, well... a friend.'

'You don't have any friends, Galahad.'

'Angel. *Fuck*. This is serious! Jade Tooth killed him... No, "killed" is the wrong word. He massacred him. The poor bastard *suffered*...'

Angel was quiet for a moment. The snip of scissors was clear in the background, just above her phone. I rolled my eyes.

'Sorry Gal. Really. *Are* you okay?'

'I'm fucking angry.'

'I can guess why Jade Tooth killed your little snitch. Sorry! Your *friend*.'

'You guess right,' I said. 'Look, we need to meet, and we need to do it now. I know where you are, so I'll head to Central after I've finished my lunch. I'll be there in an hour. You should be finished by then.'

'It takes a lot of hard work to look as beautiful as I do, Galahad.' Angel said, sounding a little miffed. 'I do it for you, you know.'

'Angel, I wish that were true...'

'Oh, you wound me my love. My heart is *paining*.'

I was about to answer when my noodle soup and tea hit the table. I nodded my thanks and picked up the chopsticks, stirring in some chilli oil and pushing the wantons around.

'The big park,' I said around a mouthful of noodles. 'You know the place. One hour. See you there.'

I hung up and sipped thoughtfully at the lemon tea, considering my next moves. I had filed away my own shame at Johnny's death – for the moment at least – to replace it with a cold determination to track down his killer and take revenge. The least I could do was give the shade of Fat Johnny Tong some peace; I owed him that much, but I already knew that would come at a cost.

The question was: would I be prepared to pay?

35

Fountain Terrace Garden was busy. Dozens of office workers sat on the lawns taking their lunch and chatting in small groups, while still more meandered peacefully along the footpaths for a brief moment of respite from whatever grind they were facing in the tall glass towers of Central.

Large trees spread their shade but were ignored by most as the weak winter sunlight was sought out and soaked up. The fountain was operating and shot its many water jets skywards to curve glittering back to earth in millions of droplets each throwing out tiny rainbows of light.

I came in along the northernmost path and stopped just as it emerged into the gardens, quickly scanning the area through my Wayfarers for any tails. Nothing stood out to me – but you can never be certain – so I gazed over at the park bench we used. Angel was there, her back to me, sitting with her legs crossed one over the other at the knees, and arm thrown casually across the back of the bench.

Her head was tilted back to allow the early-afternoon sun to caress her face. With one last visual pass of the gardens, I walked in and sat on the bench next to her. She turned to face me and lowered her oversized, tortoiseshell Ray-Bans and gave me her best Holly

Golightly glance; part ingénue, part callgirl. I turned my face from her, stretched out my legs and leaned back with both elbows on the back of the bench.

'Are you okay?' Angel asked.

'Not really. No.'

'What are you going to do?

'With your help I'm going to find whoever murdered Johnny Tong and I'm going to kill him. Them... whatever.'

'You're going to *kill* him...?

I sighed. 'I don't know. That's what I *want* to do. I want him dead. But... that's not me really, is it. Maybe I'll write him a stern letter and take away his Octopus Card.'

'They'll be Jade Tooth's men. *If* you kill them, he won't like that,' Angel said, pulling a slim cigarette from a gold case in her handbag and snapping a flame to it.

I glanced at her. 'I thought you gave that up...'

She snorted and ashed the cigarette. 'Yeah. Like you... Don't lecture me, Daddy.'

I smiled. She had a point.

'So,' Angel said. 'As I was saying ... Jade Tooth will be pissed when you start popping off his soldiers. He's still unlikely to come after you now – but he could. No one knows what's going on in that twisted little mind of his.' She suddenly stopped and looked at me. 'Mr Lee knows about this, right? He *has* cleared it?'

I nodded. 'Yes. I expect you'll get a call from him very soon. He was ... surprised, to see me.'

Angel stared at me. 'Wait,' she said, a frown on her face. 'How did you get to see him? I mean, no one just barges in on Lee Pak-chun.'

'I did...'

Angel blew out her cheeks. '*Diu*, Gal. You do love to play it loose and dangerous, don't you!'

I shrugged. 'It seemed like a good idea at the time. Anyway, you and Tommy Ho can help me he said, so I'm assuming that means anyone inside your networks. Get your network on it, get everyone out on the street. Anyone inside Jade Tooth's circle. You've got someone in there, right?' I glanced over at Angel. 'You listening...?'

She had turned away to watch a young woman pushing a pram, stop and adjust the infant within and stand back gazing down at the child with a warm and loving smile. I couldn't see her eyes, but Angel's shoulders were slightly slumped and her head was tilted to one side. She looked wistful to me.

I shuddered. The last thing I wanted was for Angel's biological clock to begin gonging. I had never liked children – they were a noisy, expensive, inconvenience. I would rather wrestle a tiger than be left alone in a room with a child. Angel turned back to me.

'What? Yes... sure. "Jade Tooth's circle." No, we don't. We *do* have someone just outside the inner circle but still quite close. He may be able to dig something up...'

I looked over at the pram then squinted at Angel. 'Are you okay?'

She dragged on her cigarette and ashed it casually, tapping her perfectly manicured index finger on the smoke. Her smile was radiant as she answered. It looked a little forced to me.

'Of *course*! Why would I not be? It's a beautiful day, you are beside me, we are about to reach out and tweak Jade Tooth's nose... what could be more perfect?'

I nodded unsmiling. 'I need a name and a location. That's all I want then leave the rest to me.'

'Don't be ridiculous, Gal. If you think you're doing this without Tommy Ho, you have another thing coming. This isn't a John Woo movie. You're not charging alone into a den of thieves, guns blazing, to win the day and the girl...'

'I've already won the girl,' I said.

Angel snorted again. 'Don't be so fucking sure of yourself, buddy...'

'Look, Angel, I'm well aware I can't do this on my own. I plan on The Panda being along for the ride every step.'

Angel nodded. 'Good,' she snapped. 'Make sure you do.'

I glanced at her again. She was still sitting casually but her body was tense. Was she worried about me?

'Are you worried about me? That's sweet...'

'Fuck off, Galahad, she sighed. 'You're being childish.'

'Sorry...'

Angel hissed, a sound like a kettle coming to boil. 'Before you ask: I've had everyone out looking for clues on the identity and whereabouts of this Trails Killer...'

'And...?'

'Niente. Nothing. A big, fat fucking zero. The guy is a ghost...'

I nodded and scratched my chin. 'That nut will be a lot tougher to crack but keep at it. I'm screwed now I've lost Johnny Tong's network. I'm sure if anyone could find this guy they could.' I suddenly had a thought. 'Aren't most of them in your network of informants anyway...?

Angel shrugged. 'Some are, most aren't. Johnny ran a tight ship and his people were super loyal. He was like some kinda fucking Hong Kong Bowery King, you know, like that guy in that movie...?

'Yeah well, he's gone now.' I shook my head. 'I don't think there'll be another like him,' I said, my voice low. 'Poor little bastard. I'll miss him.'

Angel reached across and put a hand on my leg. She squeezed slightly. 'Don't worry, Gal. We'll find this guy then you, me and The Panda will make things right.'

I stood and checked my watch. 'I've got a little under 90 minutes before I meet up with The Panda back over in Mong Kok, so I best get moving.'

Angel looked up at me, the Ray-Bans covering her beautiful eyes. 'Tonight? Dinner. A drink, freaky monkey sex...?'

I was sorely tempted. I really was. I shook my head. 'I'm sorry. I'm not up for it. I just need some time alone. Me and a bottle of booze... you know my critical incident procedure. It never fails me.'

Angel studied me. 'I think it's slowly killing you,' she said, her voice quiet.

I had no response to that, so I left her sitting on the bench and walked off out of the park without looking back.

36

Anyone can kill. *It's not that hard. Any idiot can do it. A rock, a knife, a pistol. A blow to the head; a sudden, savage thrust; a gentle caress of the trigger and a life is snuffed out. Gone. One moment the other is a walking, breathing being with thoughts, feelings, hopes and dreams, and the next they are a crumpled sack of flesh, bone and organs. Decomposing. It's sudden and it is easy. I have never killed like that. It's cheap. Lazy. The real art is in taking time to snuff out the light in another's eyes. It takes skill to prolong life even after the other prays for release, struggling against the pain, desperate to give up and die. One tiny nick after another, a small incision here and there. A slash, cut and stab. Take off an ear or a nose or lips. The flesh warm and soft in my hands. Pull back on the skin to peel it like a sheet of paper coming off a gift. They want to die but they can't. And while they struggle and writhe and scream their blood pulses. So much blood, hot and dark. So much I can bathe in it. Pain itself won't kill but it's what makes the exercise so worth it. So very worth it. And so it was with the next woman. The jogger.*

37

THE RECEPTION of Professor Morris Ngan Fei-hung's private rooms was warm and welcoming, if a little old and worn. I sat with my hands clasped in my lap, staring at a cheap and faded print of Sampans somewhere in a pre-industrial Pearl River Delta. I wasn't in Professor Ngan's rooms as a patient – perhaps I should have been – but I was nervous, and I found the old print oddly calming.

Rows of old books lined the wall and gave off a musty library smell. The Prof's secretary – a tiny, elderly Chinese woman who glared at me over the top of her pince-nez glasses – could have been Adele Chung's twin. The disapproving stare was certainly familiar. A tall mahogany hall clock stood guard across the room and ticked away patiently, its gears making an occasional whir and a clank as the hands clicked to a new minute. The relentless march of time.

I was lucky to be sitting there, I thought. I had called only two days before after meeting Tommy Ho in the back room of a watch shop in Mong Kok, part of a network of such shops that 14K used to launder their cash. Professor Ngan, unsurprisingly, was extremely busy but he had a one-hour gap in his diary on Thursday if Mr Jones would like to take it. Mr Jones did, so here I sat counting the ticks of the hall clock, waiting for it to chime the hour.

The silenced phone vibrated in my jacket pocket. I drew it out and frowned at the contact my finger poised over the 'answer' button. Alastair Chard. I would call him later. I was about to drop the phone back in my pocket when an SMS pinged through with another vibration.

Answer your fucking phone!!! There's been another killing. Tai Mo Shan Country Park again. If you thought the others were brutal this is fucking dreadful. Call me. A

I drew a breath and shakingly slipped the phone back into my jacket pocket. The hall clock ticked on. Other than that, all was silence.

The killer had claimed a fourth victim – that we knew of – so my faint hope that he was done and would just fade away had vanished like a morning mist. He was never going to stop. He would keep coming, and keep killing, until he had me or I stopped him. I sighed and shook my head. Michael Wong and his taskforce were looking. Alastair Chard was looking. Angel and the immense manpower of 14K triad were looking. *I* was looking but I was a blind man in a darkened room reaching hesitantly for something solid. There was nothing. Angel was right: the killer was a ghost...

'Professor Ngan will see you now, Mr Jones.'

I started in my chair and looked across at the professor's secretary. She gestured to the only other door in the room, her eyebrows raised over her pince nez in a "yes you, idiot" look.

'Thank you,' I mumbled as I stood and adjusted my belt and shirt before knocking on the door and walking in.

Caesar Li was right. Professor Morris Ngan was no martial artist – perhaps he was, I didn't know, but he was certainly no Bruce Lee. He would have been in his late sixties but, apart from this balding, monkish pate, a few wrinkles around the eyes and a slightly stooped posture, he didn't look it. I smiled slightly as I sized him up, covering it by moving toward him with my hand out in greeting.

If I could have painted a picture of a stereotypical professor of psychiatry, I would have painted Morris Ngan as I saw him then. He was dressed in a brown three-piece herringbone tweed suit, complete with suede patches at the elbows and a gold pocket watch attached to the waistcoat by a sturdy, gold fob. A large, white handkerchief flopped boldly from the front breast pocket of the jacket and the tie over the rumpled white shirt was regimental in style, dark navy with evenly spaced diagonal red and white stripes. He wore small round glasses that were perched low on his nose, and he squinted at me over their top as he shook my hand.

'Mr Jones,' he said. 'Do come in, do come in.... Please sit. Make yourself comfortable.'

I expected to see a couch but there wasn't one. In front of his enormous desk stood a large, leather chair, and I noticed a small ottoman in the same leather tucked away in a corner of the room. I took a seat and glanced about the room as Professor Ngan stepped spryly around his desk and took a seat.

A series of degrees and diplomas were framed and hung on one wall, and the window behind the professor's desk had a view over Central toward Victoria Harbour. Sun streamed into the room and dust motes danced in their rays. It gave the otherwise Dickensian office a bright and airy feel.

The desk was in a dark hardwood and the size of an average dining table. It was littered with piles of papers and books, some opened at pencil-inscribed marginal notations. Three small, framed photographs stood in a corner of the desk, facing the professor, and a tea pot sat steaming dangerously close to his right elbow where an empty cup and saucer perched near the edge of the desk.

The wall to my right was a floor to ceiling bookcase, jammed with books the vast majority of which were psychiatry tomes, many obviously old and well-thumbed. My eyes lit on the spine of a small, battered book wedged between "Sociology of Deviant Behaviour" and "The Diagnostic and Statistical Manual of Mental Disorders". It was a thin paperback by Raymond Chandler. "The Big Sleep". Professor Ngan tracked my eyes and smiled warmly.

'You have discovered my interest in detective novels, I see. I find that one, in particular, quite illuminating as a study in betrayal, lust, murder, and greed. All very human traits.'

'I haven't read it,' I said. 'But my father was a fan.'

'Oh, I *am* surprised, Mr Jones...You being a private detective I would have thought you would be an avid reader of detective fiction.'

I smiled. 'Do you read a lot of novels about psychiatrists?'

'Are there any...?'

'I really have no idea – to be honest, I'm not much of a reader. I used to be, but I find now I have too much going on in life to be able to find the time to sit and clear my mind enough to read. It's ...' I snapped my mouth shut. I had been in Ngan's office, in his comfortable leather chair, for under three minutes and I was already unloading like a Californian after a moderately hard day.

Ngan gazed at me, elbows on the table, his chin resting on a hand-wrapped fist. I had the uncomfortable feeling he was psychoanalysing me, and I was sure he wouldn't like what he saw.

'I'm not psychoanalysing you, Mr Jones,' he said merrily. 'Just surprised you don't like detective fiction. I thought everyone did...'

'I didn't say I did not like it, Professor. Only that I didn't read it. I can do one without being the other.'

Ngan picked up the teapot and held it up toward me. 'Tea?'

'No. Thank you. I'm more a coffee man.'

He poured out a cup of black tea, added a splash of milk then sipped at it, his eyes briefly closed in enjoyment. I waited patiently.

'So,' the professor said, dabbing his lips with a napkin. 'You would like to talk to me about the Trails Killer.'

'First, thank you for seeing me at such short notice,' I said

'It's my pleasure. After being told who you were and what you did, I could not resist meeting my very own Phillip Marlowe. Besides, I am happy to help in any way to catch the Trails Killer.'

'Professor. I'm *not* Phillip Marlowe , *and* I'm not involved in the official search for the killer. This is more by way of professional interest. I want to try and understand what makes a person like this tick. Get inside his head if I can.'

'Why?'

'I beg your pardon?'

'I asked "why". Why do you want to get inside the head of this killer? What is he to you?'

I shifted my weight in my chair and blinked. Unless Ngan was blind, he could not have missed my lie.

'No particular reason. As I say, professional interest. Perhaps I might be able to assist the police. Besides, isn't everyone in Hong Kong talking about the killer and swapping theories? Everyone wants to know why this monster does what he does...'

Ngan considered me again for a long moment. He was making it a habit and it made me twitch.

'Oh, he's not a "monster" Mr Jones... but more on that shortly,' he said finally. 'I think you have a very personal interest in this case. I don't have to be a psychiatry professor to see that: it's washing off you and, to be honest, you are a very poor liar.' He paused for a moment while he sipped again at his tea.

'I thought I was quite good.'

Ngan chuckled slightly, a warm fatherly sound. 'I am fully aware,' he said, 'of the linkages back to you by way of references to your name and a photograph of you taken, probably, by the killer himself.'

I sat quietly, there was no point in protesting or lying. I was an idiot. Of course, the professor would be assisting Taskforce Bai Xi – that name being a reference to a creature in Chinese Mythology who defeated evil monsters to protect humans.

'To be perfectly frank, I have known of you and your connection to this case for quite some time and I am surprised it took you so long to seek me out,' Professor Ngan said with a slight smile.

I drew a breath. 'Forgive me for the obfuscation... the lie, Professor. I am still trying to work out what is going on, why I seem to be, in some way, a motive for this person. C.I. Wong is not being any help as he has flatly denied any link between me and the case...'

The professor sat up straighter. 'He has?' he said, surprised.

'Yes. Instead of enlisting my help, the Chief Inspector – who has, with some justification, a very low opinion of me – has decided I am to be his bait. I doubt C.I. Wong is going to call on me any time soon.'

Ngan sighed. 'We must fix that,' he said. 'Anyway, to business. The trick is to find the killer before he loses patience with his game and escalates things toward a speedier resolution for him. Whatever *that* is.'

'"Escalates"? Can it really escalate more than it currently is? He is taking a victim every week...'

'Oh, it most certainly can. I think we have only seen a glimpse of the real him. He's toying with us at this point. Although, yesterday's body reveals he is certainly feeling untouchable and his savagery has gone to another level. He is shaming us to act faster. Even though we do not know why he is doing this and what the link to you is. So, let's talk about this person,' he said. 'A little earlier you called him a monster and I said that he was not. Let me see...where should I start?'

I pulled out my notebook and clicked the top of my pen. 'Tell me about serial murderers generally. Is there a typology? Does what we know so far fit a type?'

'Were you not a detective, Mr Jones?'

How would he know that? Wong, obviously. 'I was Drugs, not Homicide...'

Ngan shrugged as if my career choice was meaningless. It probably was.

'I'll start by saying that serial murder is not new,' he said. 'However, what it does represent is the emergence of a form of murder different from that of most murders perpetrated in earlier times. There are always exceptions, but as a rule, serial murder tends to reflect nonrational motives or goals, and its victims stand in depersonalised relation to the perpetrator. The distinguishing feature with serial murder appears to be the extent to which offenders believe that violence against humans – often extreme violence – is a normal and acceptable way of achieving their goals.'

'So, what are his goals?' I asked.

'We'll come to that,' Professor Ngan said and began to pace about his office.

'Where was I?' he said, as he pushed his glasses up with an index finger. 'Oh yes, as you quickly discerned, understanding the type of serial murderer - goes a long way to understanding motives, thus to understanding target identification and, from there, hopefully, to identifying behaviour and movement patterns from which an arrest might then be made.'

The professor paused and turned to look out the window.

'But it's not quite that simple of course,' said. 'We are dealing with the non-rational and irrational so there is no truly definitive answer to all of this. The best we can do is make an educated guess based on the mountains of evidence that have emerged over recent decades. Sometimes we get it right and sometimes we get it wrong. It's illustrative to note that clearance rates on serial murders globally are much lower than those for "conventional" murders. Many cases go for years before there is a breakthrough. Many are simply never solved.'

Ngan stepped back to his desk and fished about in a drawer before pulling out a small Tupperware box. He opened the lid, thrust his hand into the box and pulled out a red jelly snake and stuffed it into his mouth.

'Low blood sugar. I can feel it,' he said and offered me the box. 'Snake?'

I shrugged. I could have used a drink but a sugar hit would have to do. 'Sure, why not. Thank you.' I selected an orange snake and stuck its head in my mouth, devouring it slowly as I wrote.

Professor Ngan pointed at me. 'That's interesting,' he said. 'The way you are eating that. Tells me a lot about you...'

I pulled the snake out of my mouth and was about to say something when he burst out laughing and slapped his knees.

'Oh! I got you! Look at your face...! I am so sorry. It's psychiatrist humour.'

'I didn't know Shrinks had a sense of humour.'

'Oh, my Lord. It's an essential part of the skill set. Can you imagine doing what I do, day in day out, without being able to have a laugh at it?' he shook his head vigorously. 'No. Not possible.'

'I guess that's a refreshing way to look at things,' I said. 'Perhaps I should adopt a little of that...'

Ngan looked at me seriously for a moment. 'Mr Jones, you don't look much like a laughing man, to be honest.'

'Can we please just move on?' I asked. 'You were leading to typology? At least I hope you were...'

'Ah yes. Right. Well, in very simple terms, typology of the serial murderer starts at geography. Spatial mobility is a critical factor. Is the killer a transient – does he move around a lot – or is he geographically stable?'

'He's killed four here in Hong Kong, so I'd say he's killing his victims within a specific area,' I ventured.

'True. But has he killed before? If so, where?

'The first place to consider would be the Mainland,' I said. 'I assume Taskforce Bai Xi has made inquiries with the Ministry of Public Security. Does MPS have unsolved murders that fit this M.O.?'

Ngan shook his head. 'No. They do not. It was one of the first things the Taskforce checked, although work with the MPS goes on.'

'Doesn't it always these days,' I muttered as I made a note in my book.

Ngan looked sideways at me. 'I didn't take you for political, Mr Jones.'

'I'm not,' I said mildly. 'I couldn't care less. Move on.'

The professor continued. 'Just because we can rule out like killings on the Mainland, doesn't mean this person hasn't killed before, often, somewhere else. He could be an international.'

'Do you mean he's a Gweilo?' I asked quickly. 'An expat?'

'I'm not saying that, but he could be. Just as he could be local, African, Arab or from the Subcontinent. Ethnicity is almost impossible to profile in cases like this.'

'But, as far as what we are working with, we agree he's geographically stable. Killed only in Hong Kong.'

Ngan nodded. 'I suppose that's fair, but I caution you – as I have the Taskforce – not to take a blinkered view of that. I have the distinct feeling – backed with no evidence, I might add – that this person is not from Hong Kong and has most probably killed elsewhere.'

I scribbled "not from HKG??" in the notebook and looked up.

'So, if that's in question what's next?' I asked, tapping my pen to my lip. 'How do we fit what he is doing into a type? *Does* it fit?'

Ngan checked his watch. 'Mr Jones, I am afraid we are running out of time so I will keep this as short as I can – as you can imagine this is an immensely complicated subject area.'

I nodded silently and sat poised while the professor gathered his thoughts.

'In essence,' he began 'there are four main types of serial murderers. It is apparent in each type that the motives inherent in the type provide the serial killer a personal justification for his crimes.' Ngan stopped pacing and faced me.

'First there is the Mission-oriented type. He has as a mission, a conscious goal to rid the world of a particular group of people who are "undesirable" or "unworthy" to exist along other humans. Generally speaking, he is not psychotic in that he doesn't hear voices or see visions calling him to action. He lives in the real world and interacts rationally with it on a daily basis. No, this isn't our man. Just look at the victims thus far. No discernible pattern, other than the fact they were all Hongkongers.'

'And that's not a pattern...?'

'No. Not of any significance anyway. It's hard to avoid killing Hong Kongers when Hong Kong is your killing ground.'

'And next...?'

'Next is the Visionary Type. This one murders because he is impelled to do so. He has heard voices or seen visons that drive him to it. God or a demon tells him to go forth and kill. There is little doubt about the mental state of this killer. He is often completely out of touch with reality, especially in the immediate lead up to, and the act of, the kill. In psychiatric terms, this killer would be considered psychotic. Again, not our man.'

'Why?'

'The deliberate carving of your initials into each victim, and the taking of a photograph of you *before* a murder all point to a person who inhabits the real world. He is calculating; planning his next move. He's not coerced or impelled by an inner voice and acting on that impulse.

I lowered my pen to the notepad. 'That leaves two more. Can we just skip to your choice...?'

'Patience, Mr Jones. No, we cannot. You must know the second last option because there is a degree of relationship between that and the type I consider most likely. Allow me to explain...'

Ngan recommenced his pacing. I noticed, for the first time, a well-worn path in the thick carpet of the office.

'This brings us to the Power-oriented Type,' he said. 'The gratification for the killer here is not strictly sexual – although there is an element of that. This type of serial killer receives gratification in the complete power he exerts over another human. Utter domination, total control. The power of life or death over a helpless victim. There is an aspect of that in our killer...'

'How so?' I interrupted.

'I shouldn't be telling you this, but the Trails Killer is using cord to bind his victims, trussing them up like an animal for slaughter.'

'What sort of cord?'

'Pardon?'

'What sort of cord is he using?'

Ngan shrugged. 'I don't know. I haven't been told.'

'Okay.' I said. 'Go on, please.'

Ngan gathered his thoughts briefly. 'He is taping the mouths of his victims – although he likes to look into their eyes. Crime scene evidence seems to show he sits with them for some time before he kills them. He does this to reinforce his domination and their helplessness. But that's the extent of it. It's in the *killing* that our man is clearly of the final type.'

'And that would be ...?'

'Our killer is a hedonist. Murders of this type are the most striking, and often the most bizarre. These killers reflect a truly perverted, utterly deviant, means of thrill-seeking. They derive a rush of excitement, and visceral sexual pleasure, in the act of the kill. The bloodier the better. Those that have been caught – and they number few – have often used the same word during interview. "Pure". For them the purity of enjoyment they derive from the kill is the only enjoyment they have and, most often, also the only sexual release they can achieve. Our killer kills because he enjoys it. He kills because the thrill becomes an end in itself.'

I stopped writing and lowered my pen. Outside the sun was setting. The last golden glow of the day burst through the office window and crowned the diminutive professor in a diffused halo.

The room was warm and still and, through the door, I could hear the hall clock ticking relentlessly away. Ngan was standing stock still, his eyes distant and I was sure he was conjuring mental images of the Trails Killer's victims. I know I was. It was a scene I didn't want in my head. The thought of such horrors being visited on anyone close to me turned my stomach and sent an icy chill up my spine. I shuddered in the chair.

'There's more, isn't there?' I said, dreading what I was would hear next.

Ngan nodded and slowly removed his glasses. He chewed on the end of one of the arms, his eyes blinking rapidly.

'There is, I am afraid. Much more...'

'Go on.'

'As I have said, this killer experiences sexual enjoyment – *release* – in the homicidal act but the sexual act for him is not what we think of it as. Our man is inflicting truly deviant forms of sexual aberration on his victims. There appears to be no penetrative sex associated with any victim but there is dismemberment and, most disturbing, clear signs of anthropophagy. That's...'

'I know what it is. He's a cannibal?'

'Not in the Hollywood sense of the word, but he has viciously bitten all of his victims and it is clear he has eaten sections of their flesh.'

'Jesus Christ,' I breathed. 'And you said earlier he wasn't a monster.'

'He's not. At least not in a psychiatric sense. Yes, he is a deeply disturbed and perverted individual but, unlike monsters of mythology that acted with no consciousness, not possessing what we'd now call a "bicameral mind", our killer is a free-thinking, rational being who acts with free will.'

'Doesn't that make him worse?' I challenged. 'Is he not worse, then, than the Minotaur or Grendel? He thinks about what he's doing, he plans it out, he executes it with cold and brutal efficiency, conscious of what he's doing...'

'Oh, he's worse than poor, twisted Grendel. Make no mistake,' the professor retorted. Then held up a finger. 'The question is, are *you* to be our Beowulf in this saga?'

I rubbed my eyes and checked my watch.

'Professor, I have taken up a lot of your time,' I said. 'And to be honest, I need to walk this all off. You have been immensely helpful but let's end shortly. The big question I have is: What is the Taskforce looking for? What am *I* looking for? Tell me about him...'

Ngan started pacing again, his hands clasped behind his back as he summed up for me.

'Mr Jones, I am a psychiatrist, not a criminal profiler. Profiling is an imprecise science,' he said. 'If, indeed, it's a science at all,' he muttered. 'It is impossible to speak in absolute terms when one is dealing with an aberrant personality. Still, I will give you what I have given the Taskforce.' He stopped pacing and turned to face me, ticking off on his fingers as he spoke.

'He's smart. Very. Probably a genius IQ. He's strong and probably big – bruises on the victims show a larger than average hand span. He's probably highly mobile given the distances across Hong Kong between the kill sites.'

'So, he drives?'

'Probably. It's unlikely he could depart a crime scene, covered as he would be in blood, without the privacy of a vehicle.'

I nodded and jotted a note. If we could prove the same vehicle had been seen close to more than one of the kill sites we would have a breakthrough. I was sure the Taskforce would be running that down and it was troubling nothing had come up.

Professor Ngan continued. 'He's probably charming, quite charismatic and he's probably a psychopath – impaired remorse and empathy, bold, disinhibited, and egotistical. He kills with "hands on" weapons such as a knife and his hands and teeth. His kills are elaborately planned although the victims are probably random. Wrong place at the wrong time.'

I suddenly remembered my hazy sighting of a figure I thought to be Peter Toh and my conversations with Michael Wong and Alastair Chard.

'Could he be doing this on someone else's orders?' I asked. 'Might he just be the tool...?'

A shake of the head. 'Possible but unlikely. This sort of person is simply not going to do anyone else's bidding. Psychopaths are selfish, they could not care less for the feelings, or wishes, of anyone else. No, I don't *think* our man is following orders.'

That ruled out the major theory that had been troubling me. So, no, it wasn't Peter Toh. 'Okay,' I said. 'What about his earlier life? His upbringing, early experiences?'

'Ah, that is often a key factor,' Ngan said. 'He was probably physically, sexually, or emotionally abused as a child, most likely by a family member or close family friend. He tends to abuse alcohol or drugs and he probably has an interest in sadistic pornography or other depictions of violence. He's probably heterosexual and there is every possibility he is involved in a stable relationship with a partner who has no idea of his darker side, although sexual relationships with his partner are often characterised by binding, choking and other forms of sadistic behaviour.'

I hurriedly scribbled notes and saw I had written *Girlfriend??* If he had one, who was she, where did she live, did she know what was going on?

My eyes ached and I my mind was whirling. I felt we had gone as far as we could for one session, so I looked up from my notebook and started to rise from the chair. 'Thank you, Professor. This has been ...'

'Before you go Mr Jones, allow me to give you a parting thought. One I haven't shared with the Taskforce.'

I sat back down and dropped the notebook into my jacket pocket. 'Go on,' I said.

'There is an added complexity to this case, and I think it has to do with you. There is little doubt our killer is of the hedonistic type – remember I said they are enormously difficult to track and bring to justice – but aside from the deviant sexual objective of his kills there appears to be a second motivation. To do with you. I think it is revenge, or challenge. Or perhaps both.'

'What do you mean?'

'If it is revenge that is motivating this spree, why and to what degree? Are you his ultimate target? If it's challenge; why? Does he want to challenge your investigative talents? Prove he is smarter than you, that you can't fit all the pieces together?'

"Fit all the Pieces." Where had I heard that before? A half-formed thought blew out of my consciousness before I could even identify it. I nodded as I stood up. '

'I've been thinking the same lately,' I said. 'I have no answers. I did think it might be revenge, a person from my recent past, but... I was seeing things, imagining things. And you have just ruled it out yourself. I'm quite sure that's not it.'

I stood again, and pulled at my ear, wincing as it tightened the skin over my wounded cheek. 'Still there are any number of people in this city who could be a contender for the revenge angle – it's just that none of them are homicidal maniacs.' I shrugged. 'Maybe it is a challenge, but why? What's the point?'

'He's very intelligent *and* immensely egotistical,' the professor offered. 'Perhaps he has heard of you and wants to prove he is better than you...If it *is* a challenge, we will know when he starts sending you clues, defying you to solve the riddle and catch him. He will have to deliberately leave you a clue. *You* won't find clues – not with this killer...'

'Serial murderers are still criminals, professor,' I said. 'Like all criminals, they eventually make a mistake, a slip up that draws attention to them. He will slip up, I guarantee it.'

'I admire your confidence, but I think you are wrong. Anyway, if it *is* revenge, he will make himself known to you when it suits him, to pull you to a time and place of his choosing. The final act, as it were.'

With the words "final act" ringing in my head, I thanked the professor for his time, promised to stay in touch and left him standing silently in his warm, safe office.

I felt hot and dizzy. My eyes were blurred and my heart hammered against my ribs. Outside in reception, the professor's secretary was a gargoyle, perched malevolently on the edge of the desk, eyeing me greedily as I passed. The room tilted and the hall clock gonged the hour. The sound was laden with horror and impending doom, echoing after me as I fled down the corridor.

38

'I THOUGHT I'd find you here,' Alastair Chard said as I lowered the beer glass to the bar and watched him order a Gin and Tonic. The pub was quiet, with only a few patrons scattered about its warm room in ones and twos.

'You were supposed to call me,' he said then studied me a little closer. 'You don't look well, old cock.'

'Are you stalking me?' I asked moodily.

'You fucking wish,' Alastair said, a slight grimace on his face. It looked like he had gas. 'You're way too old for me now...'

'I feel it,' I said as I swigged at the beer.

Alastair's gin arrived and he twirled the swizzle stick, studying the clear, effervescent contents of the glass.

'Did you get my text?' he asked.

I nodded. 'I did. As it happens, I was meeting with an expert on serial killers...'

'Morris Ngan.'

'How did you know?'

'If you are even *half* as good as you think you are, Professor Ngan is the *one* man you would speak to in Hong Kong if you want to get to know this monster that's slaughtering people on our hiking trails...'

'He's not a monster...'

'Fucking *what*?'

I shook my head. 'Long story. Something about consciousness and a unicameral mind...'

Alastair stared at me incredulously. 'Fuck me, that's a dizzying theory for your tiny brain to grasp. I can see why you look ill.'

I rolled and lit a cigarette, huffing out the fragrant cherry smoke. 'Tell me about the latest victim,' I said.

Alastair grimaced. 'Jesus Christ, Galahad. This one was bad. *Very* bad. A woman out jogging. My contact on the Taskforce shared some of the crime scene photos with me, and I truly wish I hadn't seen them.'

'I don't suppose you have them on you, do you?'

Alastair patted his jacket, over his left breast. 'As a matter of fact, I do.' He glanced around the bar. 'Not here. Let's move into a booth,' he said.

We picked up our drinks and crossed the bar to a booth in the corner of the room. No one was close and I sat facing the door. Alastair drew out a sheaf of A4 pages and dropped them on the table.

'Submitted with no comment,' he said. 'You'll see for yourself.' He took a long, shaky pull of his gin while I studied the first colour photocopy of the crime scene.

A young woman lay on a patch of bare earth, the close foliage of the jungle pressing in on her, her arms and legs spread and staked out. A pair of trainers, stuffed with socks, had been neatly arranged off to the side. The dirt was scuffed at her feet where her heels had drummed and scraped in her agony.

She was naked except for a shredded jogging singlet that looked black, soaked deep with blood. Her feet were bare and were covered in mud as she had struggled and fought against the ties that bound her. I turned over the next sheet. A close-up of the victim's face. I looked up at Alastair who was studying me closely.

'See what I mean?' he said quietly and lit a cigarette, his hands shaking slightly.

The girl's face was a study in horror, a sight I knew then I would never forget. Her eyes were wide open and bulging sightlessly from their sockets. Professor Ngan had said the killer liked to look into his victim's eyes. In the late 19th century, forensics in the United Kingdom had given rise to the pseudoscience of optography, that had claimed the image of a killer was printed on the victim's retina at the time of death. If only, I thought. I dragged hard on my cigarette as I studied her face.

Her mouth was gaffer taped, the tape wrapped around her head and hair, and her nose was gone. Entirely. I could see into the blood-filled gash to the nasal cavity. I leaned in closer. The nose had not been taken off with a sharp implement. The tissue around the wound was ragged and torn and, on the left cheek, a bite mark showed purple and deep. I swallowed.

'He bit her nose off.' I said unsteadily, remembering Professor Ngan's observation that the killer was eating his victims.

Alastair nodded. 'I'm told it hasn't been found at the scene,' he said quietly. 'The fucker ate it... The "cannibal" angle hasn't hit the press...yet,' Alastair added. 'The cops have slapped a No Publish order on that juicy morsel.'

I winced at Alastair's deliberate use of "juicy", turned back to the pile of papers and flipped over a page. Close-up of the victim's torso.

The singlet was blue and had been ripped ferociously from her body, leaving only the right strap and a piece at the shoulder intact. Fragments of material clung stickily to the wound over what had been her left breast that had been sliced clean off, exposing the muscle beneath and the faint whiteness of the ribcage. Four savage, long gashes ran diagonally along each side of her torso from her breasts and around the ribs.

It looked like she had been raked by the claws of a wild beast. Again, bite marks were clear on her neck, clavicle, shoulder and one on the outside of her left breast had been halved by the knife. I shook my head slowly.

'Jesus Christ,' I muttered.

'Keep going,' Alastair said, his voice shaking.

I turned the last page and drew in a shuddering breath.

A stake, similar to the one that anchored her limbs, had been driven deep between her legs and the blood had pooled on the dirt in a congealed, black mess. I looked up at Alastair who was studying the contents of his drink, both hands gripping the glass tremulously. I couldn't go on. I flipped the sheet face down and sat back in the booth, my head back as I studied the ceiling, breathing deeply.

Something rang a bell in my head, and I shuffled back through the papers, returning to the wide shot of the victim. I peered closer at the photo. Her wrists and ankles were bound to the four stakes with red cord. The cord was thick, not rope or twine. It looked good quality. Each length that bound the girl seemed to be misshapen, twisted. I was sure I had seen cord like this before, but I couldn't recall where or when.

I rubbed at my eyes, willing my memory to conjure up the answer but got nothing. I pushed the photo across to Alastair and pointed at the cord.

'Have you seen this before? Ring any bells?'

Alastair looked me in the eyes before he glanced down again at the photo, swallowing hard. He studied the photo for long seconds, leaning in closer to squint at it. Finally, he looked up and nodded, slowly.

'I've seen cord like that often – and so have you. I could be wrong, but it looks like the draw cord on a barrister's gown bag. You know, those posh fucking things made from weaved brocade or damask...'

I grabbed at the photo and studied it again. He was right. That's exactly what it looked like and the twists in the lengths were where the draw cord of the gown bag had been carefully unwoven. I scratched my head.

'A gown bag...What does this mean? Is he a barrister... or used to be?' I muttered. 'What does the Taskforce make of this?'

Alastair shrugged. 'I have no fucking idea, dear boy. To be honest, that cord could be anything...Take it up with Michael Wong.'

'We're not talking,' I observed quietly, as I shuffled through the A4 pages again. Alastair coughed slightly and shifted in his seat. I looked up.

'What?' I demanded. 'What now?'

He reached into his coat pocket and drew out a single piece of folded paper. With great care, he unfolded it and smoothed out the creases before dropping it on the table in front of me.

'The original of this was impaled on a tree branch hanging over the victim's corpse,' he said.

He swallowed the last of his gin and lit another cigarette, eyeing me closely. I picked up the photocopy. Typed, Times New Roman 10. No punctuation. A hissing, rambling voice read the note in my head.

death is coming and he rides a pale horse named despair you think youre smart but youre not you wont find me until I want to be found Im coming for you Jones and you cant stop me vengeance is mine and retribution in due time their foot will slip for the day of their calamity is near

I dropped the note to the table. 'Well, that answers one question,' I said.

Alastair cocked an eyebrow in inquiry. 'Oh..?'

'Deuteronomy 32:35,' I said quietly. 'Professor Ngan opined that the killer's interest in me was either a challenge – I'm smarter than you and I'll prove it – or revenge.' I tapped a finger on the photocopy of the note. 'This would appear to support the "revenge" theory.'

Alastair grinned lopsidedly. 'Fuck, *really*. By any fair estimate, about half of Hong Kong wants to exact revenge on you Galahad. It may have escaped your attention, but you're not very popular in these parts of late.'

'Right. So, all I have to do is narrow it down. I've tackled harder riddles before.'

'Jesus Christ, Galahad,' Alastair said, shaking his head. 'You're a dear, dear boy and I love you like a drunken uncle, but you're *insane* if you think you are going to get near this maniac before he slips a knife into your slender throat...'

I smiled but my eyes were hard. 'You like the horses don't you, Alastair? Wednesday evenings at Happy Valley?'

'You know I do, you patronising little prick. Why?'

'I've seen you bet. You love a long shot. The bigger the odds the better for you.'

'Yes, and they *always* fucking lose Galahad!'

I shook my head. 'Not this time Alastair. Not this time. I'm going to track him down and I'm going to stop him. You can bet on that.'

39

I STEPPED THROUGH THE ROPES, pushed in my mouthguard, and adjusted my head gear.

My sparring partner stood quietly in the opposite corner of the ring eyeing me with an amused grin. He was shorter than me and about my age. He was a Scot who, thirty years before, had signed on as a teenage crewman on a freighter to flee Glaswegian poverty for the allure of the Far East. He had been in Hong Kong ever since and proudly told anyone who listened that he had not journeyed further than Macau in those 30 years. He was built like an armoured vehicle, low to the ground, squat and tough, and was utterly fearless.

My heart hammered. I rolled my shoulders and cricked my neck, wondering what the hell I was doing. It was two days since I had met Alastair and the images of the killer's latest victim still burned in my mind. I had barely slept and what little I had grabbed had been plagued with feverish nightmares of a hooded creature, emerging out of a mist-shrouded jungle, a woman's head tucked under its arms, to stand silently pointing at me. I wasn't ready to spar, and I was certain this would hurt, but I needed to clear my head, so I had called on the Scot to do his worst.

'You look like shite, laddie,' he said with a chuckle. He pointed at the raw scar on my face. 'Ye sure you wanna do this...?'

I eyed him and beat my gloves together. 'Angus, I'm ready to give you a bashing.' I didn't sound convincing.

He laughed at that. 'Och, Galahad there's nae danger ye'll lay a glove to me. I'm no worried. Let's dance shall we, ye big git.'

With that, Angus surged into the centre of the ring, his body balanced and low, hands up in a classic Peek-a-Boo stance. It was the perfect stance for pressure, close-in fighting and I felt a surge of concern as I moved in, my feet step-dragging as I advanced and felt my partner out, looking for an entry. I threw out left jabs with each forward step, my right hand up and guarding the side of my face that still ached from my last dealings with Jade Tooth. My left shoulder still ached and my punches from that side were weak. Angus saw that.

He met me low, feet square on, crouching and weaving as he blocked my jabs and threw some of his own while looking for a chance to throw a hook. I bladed my body and dropped into my favoured Philly Shell guard and rolled my left shoulder to deflect Angus' jabs, right hand up on alert for the hook I knew was coming. I threw out a jab with my right hand and Angus was caught momentarily off guard, so I swung out a left hook, perfectly balanced, eyes on the target. The punch met clear air.

Angus was suddenly on my exposed right and I pivoted, but too slowly. The stinging hook to my right ear jarred my head and I saw stars for a second before pivoting again to complete the turn and face Angus.

Boxing is all about keeping a clear head, maintaining posture, and working your combinations. I was angry at the easy hit Angus had put in on me, but I managed to swallow it down and focused on the dangerous little Scot in front of me. He came in fast with a jab-right cross-left hook combination that I rolled and deflected, throwing out my own combination to his body, ending with a right cross. That worked, and the last punch snaked in to rock the little Glaswegian's head.

He stepped back and grinned. 'Och, Galahad, let's nae kiss. Come and play like a man...'

I knew he was trying to needle me into anger and a slip-up. Then he would step in and hammer me. He came in fast again and drove me up against the ropes with a jab-right cross-jab combination. I tucked up and let him batter away at my body. Images of Ali and Foreman in Zaire danced in my head. I was bigger than Angus but probably not as fit. I had to take the hammering in the hope he would tire. He didn't.

He came at me again, but I didn't wait for him to arrive. I moved into him, fast and hard. My punches were landing, and I was advancing on Angus as he stepped back across the ring, shaking his head, his guard down. I had him now and I stepped forward after him to finish it when out of nowhere my head was rocked by a vicious left hook and I staggered.

The following cross to my body and the right uppercut that caught me squarely under the chin jolted me back across the ring and onto the ropes. As soon as my back hit the ropes the murderous little Scot was on me, throwing punch after punch into my body and head.

Suddenly the blows stopped, and I peered over my raised gloves to see Angus pull off his headgear and spit out his mouthguard. I lowered my hands, panting like an old dog.

'Ye ken, Galahad, there was time I'd have a lad agin a wall and I'd punch the life out o' the wee bugger...I would nae stop.'

I lowered my hands to my knees and bent over to suck in big breaths. 'Yes, Angus, I can well imagine that...'

'But, because ye're a gud lad and I've a soft spot for ye, I've decided nae to kill ye today...'

I held up a gloved hand. 'I appreciate that, Angus, I really do,' I wheezed.

I pulled off my headgear and rubbed the sweat from my eyes. I was still managing to hold my own, but it was getting harder. I was a 47-year-old smoker and drinker. You can't keep doing that and not expect it to catch up with you in the ring and laugh in your face. Stepping slowly through the ropes, I walked to the showers. I felt old.

40

Twenty minutes later, showered and changed, I walked from the gym and was waiting for an elevator to take me back down to Jaffe Road when my phone buzzed in the hip pocket of my jeans. The call was coming through on the secure messaging app. It was Tommy Ho. I glanced around the lift lobby and answered.

'Tommy. What's up?'

'We've found Johnny Tong's killer,' The Panda replied. 'You were right: one of Jade Tooth's boys.'

I drew a breath. 'Where is he?'

There was a moment's silence before Tommy answered. 'That's the problem. He's not in Hong Kong. He boarded CX907 for Manila at 7:00 this morning. We got word of a positive sighting of him at the departure gate.'

I checked my watch. 'Jesus, Tommy. That was nearly four hours ago...'

The Panda paused. 'Yes,' he said patiently. 'And we waited until we had a positive of him coming out of arrivals at Ninoy Aquino. I wanted to be certain before I called you. I'm certain.'

'I'm sorry Tommy,' I said. 'That's great. Where is he now?'

Another pause. 'We don't know. He gave our guy the slip in the taxi line. We're looking for him now.'

I closed my eyes. There are 12 million people in the Manila Metro area and one man, on the run with an eye to his survival, can disappear in that city for months. Still, it was a lead and more than I had five minutes ago.

'Okay,' I said, my exasperation clear. 'Keep your people on the hunt. Have you got a name and a photo?'

'I just messaged it to you,' Tommy replied, my phone pinging as he did. I paused to open the app and view the picture.

The face staring back at me was narrow and pinched, clean-shaven with a buzz cut hairstyle. A tattoo of a dragon curled out from the collar of the man's white shirt and up his neck to just below his right ear. His eyes were cold and dark, and his left eye drooped slightly, either from an old injury or an illness. I didn't care which. I read the text. Fung Yi-chen aka Fast Danny Fung. The little fucker is going to need to be fast, I thought.

'Got it,' I said. 'I am going to head to Manila, but I will need Angel to set some things up to cover my tracks.' I paused while I quickly thought a few things through. 'I'll be going alone but I'll need your support from here with your people in Manila.'

'No, you won't,' The Panda said calmly.

'What?'

'You won't be going alone. I've spoken to Miss Yeung, and she was *very* clear on that point. I am to accompany you and, as I have said many times before, I am scared of Miss Yeung. I do as she tells me.'

'That makes two of us, Tommy,' I replied. 'Let me sort things out with her and I'll get back to you. Okay?'

Tommy agreed and I hung up the call as the elevator arrived and the doors swished open. Minutes later I was out on Jaffe Road, heading west toward my apartment, my phone pressed to my ear while I sipped a bottle of water.

Angel answered quickly, her voice clipped and business-like.

'I was waiting for you to call. You're using the app so this must be about Danny Fung. I take it The Panda has spoken to you...'

'He has,' I said, as I sidestepped a delivery boy, his arms loaded down with cardboard boxes. I crossed the lights on Lockhart Road and took the Percival Street overpass toward Times Square.

'I'm heading to Manila, but I need your help for cover. Get on to a legitimate business associate in Manila and have them email me within the hour to invite me to visit and discuss a possible investigations job for their company. I'll reply that I will be delighted to assist. I'll then make my flight booking 15 minutes after I send the reply email.' I checked my watch as I jogged down the steps of the overpass onto Percival Street and across the lights at Russell Street, still heading west toward Wan Chai Road Wet Markets.

'I hope to be going out about 4:30 this afternoon, if I can get a seat, which will get me into Manila about 6:45. I don't want any meet and greet, no overt contact with any of your people in Manila. This has to look every inch the business trip. Clear so far?'

'Clear. But Tommy Ho is to ...'

I cut in over the top of her. '*No*. Tommy can't come along. It's just too risky to have him exiting Hong Kong the same day I do, to the same city. As I said, this is a business trip. It has to be Persil white.'

I sipped at the water bottle and Angel sat silently on the other end of the phone. I could hear the barely controlled anger in her breathing. Angel did not like to be interrupted, or corrected, by anyone, ever.

'I need to have two legitimate meetings with your contact,' I continued. 'We don't have to actually say anything, but I have to be seen entering his office a couple of times. Just make sure your guy is solid – I can't have him collapsing in a heap if PNP start nosing around once I'm gone.'

I did not think the Philippines National Police would rumble to either my presence or any involvement in a body turning up in a Manila alleyway, but I had to cover the bases as best I could.

'Anything *else*, my love?' Angel said sarcastically, the annoyance clear in her voice.

'Nope,' I said cheerily, knowing it would needle her further. I also knew I'd pay for this sometime soon.

'Thank you Angel, I mean it. This will probably end up as we discussed earlier so all tracks covered is the best approach. Softly, softly, catchee monkey...'

'What's that?' she asked, surprise in her voice. 'Fast Danny Fung *is* an ape, but that sounds racist...'

'Old English saying. Kipling, I think... Anyway, it means approach a target without startling it.'

'Mmm,' Angel replied. 'I expect Fast Danny will be startled when you put a bullet in his head.'

'Let's hope it doesn't come to that...'

'If it does not, Galahad, I have to ask what is the point?'

I didn't want to get into the pros and cons of the various methods at hand to deal with Jade Tooth's boy – mostly because I didn't know myself what I planned to do if I finally found him. Also, I was trying to convince myself I would not end up with blood on my hands. I was fairly sure I would, but it helped to deny it.

'There's something else, Angel,' I said. Images of the latest Trails victim played through my mind in a rapid, horror slideshow. Angel needed to know.

'There always is with you...'

'I haven't got time now but it's the Trails Killer. It's clear now he's on a crusade to avenge himself for something I've done to him. He's after me. But that's not what keeps me awake at night... It's Prudence, Joey, you. Everyone I know and love is at risk. You're all a target and he won't stop...'

'I'm fine, Galahad,' Angel said quietly. 'He can't get to me. We have a team on your little biker moll, and Pru has her boyfriend, so I can't see how he could possibly get to them. Don't fret, my love. They will be safe. I promise.'

'Don't underestimate this animal, Angel. He's smart and has no fear. He won't bat an eye at what would deter the average gangster.'

Angel paused for a moment. 'He should not underestimate *us*, Galahad. We have an army out hunting him with kill orders. He won't get close...'

I sighed deeply and rubbed my eyes. There was no doubt about it:

the Trails Killer had put the wind up me. I had no idea who he was, where he was or when he would try a strike closer to home. All I knew was I was in his sights. Angel broke into my thoughts.

'Also, Chaya is back from Indonesia. She arrived this morning.'

'How is that supposed to make me feel better?'

Angel huffed. 'Galahad don't be a child. It's unbecoming. You don't need to know – at least not now – but Chaya is more than she appears. Much more.'

I shook my head. Chaya was not yet 20 years old. She was a kid, an orphan, who had been sex-trafficked out of Cambodia and who Joey had saved, at risk to her own life, on a storm ravaged night in Cha Liu Au two years previously. I had no idea what Angel was getting at.

Then suddenly it dawned on me. Angel had told me on her return from Indonesia that she had left Chaya in Megamendung for "business training". It had bothered me at the time, and I remembered now where I had heard the name before.

Megamendung is a small town in the hills, 50 kilometres south of Jakarta. It wasn't known for much. But it was known for one thing. It was the home of Special Detachment 88, better known as Densus 88 – the Indonesian National Police counter-terrorism unit formed after the 2012 Bali Bombings and trained by the CIA, FBI, US Secret Service and Australian Federal Police. I had no idea what sort of "business training" Chaya had been doing in Megamendung, but I was sure it wasn't balance sheets and workplace counselling.

I had a feeling Angel was trying to tell me something without actually telling me. I decided I would leave that for later – if there was one.

'I have to go, Angel. Keep safe and look after Pru and Joey. I promise I'll stay in touch with The Panda and I'll see you soon.'

There was a long pause before Angel replied. 'Just be careful, Gal,' she whispered. 'I want you back in one piece.'

41

Later that afternoon, I had arranged for Bors' favourite dog sitter to live in for a few days and I was standing in the queue to board a Cathay Pacific flight to Manila.

Bored businessmen leaned on the handles of their carry-on luggage, and mothers chased their rebellious children around the terminal trying to line them up like ducklings.

I flipped on my Wayfarers and looked out of the giant window across the taxi apron and runway. The green hills on Lantau Island were wreathed in wisps of cloud against an opal blue sky. It was nearly five days since I had viewed Johnny Tong's body and, while the shock had abated, the anger only seemed to grow inside me like a tumour. I was in a murderous rage over the death of a junkie; someone I had not really considered a friend. It was puzzling.

I was contemplating this when I felt my phone vibrate in my back pocket. I shook my head to clear the woolly thoughts, drew the phone out and looked at the screen. Joey. I tapped the screen and held the phone to my ear.

'Penny has gone, Gal!' she said immediately, her voice tense with an edge of panic.

I froze in place and the hairs prickled at the back my neck. 'What do you mean "gone"?' I asked.

'She wasn't there when the guy from the protection team arrived to pick her up from school. He waited an hour after school but she didn't show. She hasn't come home this afternoon. *Hours* ago… It's not like her!'

Joey was sounding frantic and I tried to calm her. 'Jo,' I said. 'She's probably playing hooky. She's a street kid. They're like stray cats… they come and they go. It's only been a few hours. She'll come back when she's bored or hungry.'

'You're not listening to me, Gal' Penny hissed. 'I said it's not like her and I *meant* it. She doesn't dodge school and has *never*, not once, run off since she has been with me. I'm the only one she trusts and she stays close…'

I was about to speak again when the boarding announcement for my flight cut across me.

'You're at the airport?' Joey demanded. 'Where are you going?'

'Long story,' I replied I didn't want to tell her the real reason for my flight over an open line. 'Possible job. I'll message you later… Look, I'm about to board so get on to Angel through her team and get a search underway for Penny. Try not to worry Jo. I'm sure she will turn up before dark.'

'I've done that! They're out there now looking for her…'

'Wait…!' I interrupted. 'Have you got anyone covering you now?'

'No I don't and *fuck* that! Those criminal jerkoffs are better used out there looking for my girl…'

I noted Joey's use of the possessive, So the street kid was *her* girl now. This was serious – but, I admitted to myself, it always had been.

'I'm heading out now to look for her, Gal. Nothing you say and no risk to me will change that.'

'Okay,' I said. 'But for Christ's sake be careful, Joey. Stay in touch.'

Joey tersely said she would and hung up. I was staring through the window, my thoughts spinning crazily when a female voice at my side gently reminded me to board. I shouldered my overnight bag, scanned my boarding pass, and stepped into the airbridge. Seconds later I was welcomed aboard and ushered to my single seat in Business Class.

I was travelling light and stowed my carry-on in the overhead locker while the cabin crew busied themselves with seating the other passengers and running through their pre-flight routine. Idly, I picked up the menu and flicked through it. I wasn't hungry so I dropped the menu before taking out my phone and flicking open the secure messaging app. I brought up The Panda's contact, thought for a moment then tapped out in Cantonese:

Onboard CX903. ETA 1830. Staying in Makati on the down low. Stay clear but stay in touch. Find this guy!! Also Joey's street kid has gone missing – probably just run off but find her!

Tommy Ho replied in moments.

We'll find the kid, don't worry. Have a lead on Fung. He may have gone to ground in Tondo. He has help. Enjoy your flight.

That was not surprising. Tondo is a poverty-stricken district, on the port in Manila, made up of some of the city's roughest barangays, neighbourhoods. It was one of the most notorious slums in the country, populated by squatters and the unemployed, many of them excons. If Fast Danny wanted to disappear in Manila, then Tondo was the place to do it.

The problem I had was twofold: finding Fast Danny in the first place, then stalking him without him being alerted by an army of informers, gang members and street lookouts. I sighed, closed my eyes, and leaned back in the spacious Business seat of the Airbus A350-900.

A gentle tap on the arm woke me. I looked around, momentarily confused until my eyes lit on the flight attendant who crouched down at my seat, a radiant smile on her face.

'I am sorry to disturb you, Mr Jones, but we are at cruising altitude. Would you care to order dinner?'

I knew I should eat but I shook my head and ordered a Betsy Pale Ale instead. The beer arrived in minutes and I sipped at it while I ran through what faced me in the coming days. First of all, Penny was missing. While I still thought she had simply done a runner, an uncomfortable feeling was growing in me that she had been taken – either by Jade Tooth or, worse, by the Trails Killer. But did I really think that was likely? Even if Jade Tooth and the killer knew about Penny, what was she to me? What possible pressure could her disappearance exert? I shook my head. Who was I kidding?

Obviously Penny's abduction would mean something to me – if only indirectly through Joey – and both Jade Tooth and the killer would guess that. They would be right. I didn't want to, but I cared about the little brat – if only for Joey's sake. I desperately hoped I'd hear she had been found when I landed in Manila and switched my phone back on.

Manila. Where to from here? I wondered. There was no doubt I would need help to locate Fung and, possibly, to deal with him. If he had disappeared down a hole in Tondo, he had to have help to do that and that help had to be SYO soldiers in the bustling Binondo Chinatown district that bordered Tondo. I was on my own, in a city I hadn't visited for over five years, tracking a man I had never seen, through a maze of alleyways and shanties covered by a million eyes. I sighed. It seemed impossible.

On the upside, neither Jade Tooth nor Fung himself knew he had been identified nor tracked to Manila.

Fung would be complacent, his guard down, enjoying the pleasures of Tondo while he waited for the smoke to clear in Hong Kong before he returned. He didn't know I was coming. And I was coming with The Panda and his soldiers across the city behind me.

I sipped at the cold beer and gazed out of the window at the brilliant blue sky and thick cumulus clouds, the sun dazzling bright at

35,000 feet. The aircraft wing bounced slightly as we hit a small thermal and I thought, not for the first time, how insane strapping into a metal tube and taking to the skies actually was.

Once I got to Manila and checked into the low-profile hotel in Makati, on the edge of the red light district, I would need transportation and I needed a firearm. The Panda would provide there. I also needed to buy some cheap, local clothing to try and mask my frame that was taller and broader than the average Filipino. I had to do something about my face. Not only did I not want it to be remembered should anyone start poking about into Fung's disappearance, but I also knew my fairish skin, green eyes and freckles would stand out in Tondo, alerting every street crim and watcher to my presence.

I sipped again at the beer.

A nylon face and neck gaiter would do the trick – they were worn everywhere in Manila, pulled up over the nose, as protection against both the sun and pollution, especially when on a scooter in the notorious Manila traffic. I finished the beer and the sun warmed my face through the aircraft window. My eyes grew heavy so I closed them briefly, willing my mind to calm down and my thoughts to order.

Without being aware of it, I soon drifted off into a deep sleep that ended only with the thud of the aircraft's wheels on the runway at Ninoy Aquino International Airport.

42

I STOOD up from the narrow bed in my hotel room and parted the curtains to gaze out at the street below me. I had been holed up in the room for two days after attending the first of two planned sham meetings at the offices of Angel's contact. The morning after my arrival in Manila, I had been ushered into his office, high above Makati and a few blocks from my hotel. He had studiously ignored me, tapping away at his laptop, while I sat quietly passing the time. After 30 minutes, he checked his watch and stood, passing me to open the door to his office. Half a dozen heads popped up in cubicles around the open plan office outside.

'Thank you for coming, Mr Jones,' he said brightly, holding out his hand. 'It has been a most constructive meeting and I look forward to our next.'

I grasped his hand and smiled broadly. 'And thank *you*, Mr Espanilla. I look forward to seeing you again and to working with you and your team. I'm sure we can assist.'

He grinned tightly back at me. He wanted me gone. I wondered what motivation Angel had given him to set up the meeting and the alibi. Knowing her as I did, I assumed it would have been a sweet and very attractive delicacy wrapped in barbed wire. I almost felt sorry for Espanilla.

'Yes, indeed. Goodbye,' he said quickly, giving me a light shove and closing his office door behind me. I had smiled widely and nodded at a number of curious faces as I walked slowly out of the office.

My thoughts turned to Joey. She had called the previous evening, frantic with worry. Penny had still not shown up and had been missing, by that time, for almost 72 hours. Joey's search of Penny's usual haunts had failed to turn up a single sighting. She had contacted a former colleague of hers still working at Mong Kok Police Station and logged a Missing Person's Report but had been told, given Penny's background, it was unlikely the report would receive much attention.

I had told her Tommy Ho was working on it and she replied that she had met him and, together, they had coordinated their search which had turned up nothing. Joey was serious. There were no circumstances I could see that would force her to work alongside a triad enforcer unless someone was in mortal danger – as I had been two years previously when, together, they had found and rescued me.

I still thought the kid had bolted – probably fed up with being forced to attend school, keep herself clean and not run with her pack of feral mates through the streets of Kowloon. But a creeping feeling of doom had grown in me and now I was more and more concerned that she had been taken. If that was the case, I thought, it would not be long before her brutalised body turned up somewhere on one of Hong Kong's hiking trails. The whole issue had helped harden my resolve to confront Michael Wong and demand access to the case, which I was committed to do on my return from Manila. But first there was the matter of Fast Danny Fung.

Below me now, the street bustled with a sea of cars, vans, scooters and pedestrians that rolled and swelled up and down the wide asphalt channel.

Neon lights were coming on against the early evening gloom and the early-shift hookers had emerged to gaze expectantly about. A tangle of powerlines danced crazily over the street like a thick, black spider's web and kids skipped in and out of the traffic begging or selling bottles of water.

Cops leaned bored against their motorbikes, smoking and messaging on their phones while security guards, turned out in resplendent police-style uniforms, directed traffic and checked people in and out of the high-end shopping mall across the road. A Philippines Airlines Airbus A330 roared in overhead, its engines backing off to a whine as it powered down on its finals into NAIA.

Over it all, the roar of traffic and the blare of car horns rose in the air, giving cacophonous life to the blue-grey cloud of exhaust that wrapped the street in a noxious blanket.

I turned back to the tiny room and kicked out at the small rubbish bin by the bed, frustrated that I had heard nothing in three days. Oddly, that afternoon I had received two silenced calls from unknown numbers that had gone straight to voicemail, although the callers had left no messages. I had dismissed them as common spam calls so I had blocked the numbers but had not deleted the notifications. The secure message app thread from Tommy Ho remained stubbornly silent.

I had another meeting booked with Espanilla the following morning then time was up. The back-story would give me no reason to hang around after that meeting, and my flight was booked for that afternoon. I needed to find Fast Danny Fung in the next 18 hours. I swore loudly and snapped back the curtain to gaze again into the street. I stood like that for perhaps half an hour, not really seeing or hearing anything, staring blankly at a moving picture, when suddenly my phone pinged loudly into the quiet room. I turned and grabbed it up, flicking open the secure messaging app. Tommy Ho.

Got a positive. Been seen twice now in the same location. Address to follow. Your tools are at corner of Mercado / Calderon. On your own, can't get my guys in there without starting a war. Good luck.

. . .

Two more messages pinged in, giving me further details, then the room was silent. I heaved a deep breath and looked up at the ceiling. This was it. There was no going back now. With the help of one triad I was deliberately setting out to track a member of another and... what then? What would I do when I found him? I knew the answer to that but I still couldn't bring myself to say it out loud. There really was only one way this would end. Either I walked away or Fast Danny Fung would; it couldn't be both.

43

It was warm outside, the humidity climbing as thick, dark clouds rolled in overhead closing in the dull evening light. Somewhere out to sea, thunder rumbled menacingly and the first fat drops of rain started to fall as I crossed the road outside the hotel, dodging the jam of slow-moving scooters and cars.

I was wearing a pair of jeans, a dark t-shirt and a lightweight nylon tracksuit top, all of which I had bought from a street market stand two days before. A black neck gaiter wrapped around my throat, scrunched down low and a battered, second-hand cap was pulled down low over my eyes.

I walked slowly and deliberately along Kalayaan Avenue, past the convenience stores, bars, fried chicken joints and small restaurants, stepping around and over upturned boxes, broken footpath slabs and skinny stray dogs. Checking the map app on my phone, I paused at the ATM on the corner of Kalayaan and Mercado before turning right and walking casually up the street.

It was dark and the street was poorly lit but, up ahead, the lights from the foyer of a cheap hotel shone out into the street, illuminating the corner I was heading to. I stopped short of the corner and leaned against a wall, pretending to check my phone while I quickly scanned the intersection and the front of the hotel. It was busy with people coming and going. Dozens of parked scooters clogged the narrow street. I had to quickly find the scooter Tommy Ho's team had positioned for me without attracting attention – if I looked like I was looking for it, people would notice.

I checked my phone again and noted the registration number and description along with the grainy photo The Panda had sent me. He had wanted to set me up with a faster, more powerful motorbike but I had rejected that for two reasons. First, I couldn't ride a motorbike – at least not well – and second, I did not want to be connected to a flashy, powerful bike should questions be asked later. I needed a clapped-out old scooter of the kind that plied the roads of Manila in their tens of thousands. I needed to be invisible.

With a last glance at the photo, I pushed myself off the wall and sauntered to the corner of Mercado and Calderon, my eyes flicking around from scooter to scooter, feverishly trying to pick out mine in the crowd.

I was nearly at the jam of parked scooters and hadn't spotted the bike. People were starting to glance casually in my direction. I felt the sweat prickle under my arms and start to run down my spine. My heart was hammering as I slowly drew up the neck gaiter to cover my lower face and bent to fiddle with my shoelaces. Where was it? I stood and pretended to wave to someone in the crowd and as my head turned slowly to my left I finally saw the bike. A quick check of the registration plate confirmed it and I heaved a sigh of relief as I walked purposefully toward it.

Tommy Ho had outdone himself. The scooter was a battered and dirty Yamaha and, at 300cc, was a good size so I would not look too big on it and the engine was powerful enough to move fast when I needed to. I knew Joey – an accomplished rider – would laugh at me but the scooter's automatic transmission was exactly what I needed. Reaching into my back pocket I pulled out, and snapped on, a pair of disposable black gloves. I got to the bike and, without looking around, casually leaned down and extracted the key secured under the rear fender with Blu Tack. I unlocked the seat and flipped it up. In the tool well sat a small, rolled oilskin package. A screwdriver poked out of one end.

Using the seat as a screen, I carefully unwrapped the cloth and looked down at the automatic sitting nestled inside.

It was clean and well-oiled but obviously old. A 32 calibre Walther. The Panda had chosen well. The Walther was small and compact, easy to conceal and light to carry. Importantly its recoil was soft and the snap of the shot was relatively quiet.

I glanced up and, seeing no one looking in my direction, slipped out the magazine and rolled my thumb over the top round, depressing the spring. It checked out, so I quietly clicked the magazine home. I waited a moment for a bike to start up and used the noise to cover the sound as I racked the slide of the handgun and chambered a round. I snicked on the safety and wrapped the Walther back up, dropping the bike seat back into place.

I tapped my destination into the map app, silenced the phone, and clipped it home on the small holder on the handlebars. Throwing a leg over the scooter, I rocked it off the centre stand and lifted the grimy and dented helmet from the rear vision mirror and slipped it on, pushing the scratched visor up. The helmet smelled feral, a sort of dank, animal musk and I turned up my nose in distaste.

Beggars can't be choosers so, again, I silently thanked Tommy Ho for his selection of gear – I looked like any one of a hundred thousand people on a scooter in Manila that night. The bike started with the first press of the starter button and I crept it back slightly before rolling out onto General Luna then Makati Avenue, heading northwest toward Tondo.

I was quickly surrounded by dense traffic, my scooter joining the flow of hundreds of others that jostled for space on the wide road, clogged with cars, delivery vans and large trucks. Headlights danced and swayed ahead, and thousands of bright, red taillights winked and glowed like fireflies in the night.

I swung the bike in and out of the traffic, at first hesitantly then more confidently as I got the feel of the scooter beneath me. Clumps of banana palms lined the road, planted in patches of dirt between the roadway and concrete barriers that separated the two directions of traffic. An old man wearing a wide-brimmed straw hat was quietly picking a hand of bananas as if back on his farm.

The tide moved under a large overpass and past squatter camps perched precariously on the concrete verges, just off the traffic's tide-line. Poly tarp lean-tos propped up by hastily erected plywood structures, plastic buckets and striped poly storage bags littered the side of the road.

Dark-faced, sullen men, women and children sat silently over open cooking stoves, preparing whatever meagre rations they had. Small, raggedly clad children skipped and danced through traffic stopped at lights to sell bottles of water and bags of peanuts while women holding babies tapped on car windows, their hands held out in supplication. Above all this, a beautiful woman on a giant billboard, incongruously selling high-end cosmetics, smiled down benignly and blindly on the grinding poverty below her.

I swerved to miss a stray dog, his hide covered in mange, only to see it go under the wheels of the truck beside me in an explosion of blood and fur. The girl on the back of the scooter to my right, her jacket reversed and neck gaiter pulled up to her nose, flipped me the middle finger as her boyfriend accelerated away.

I throttled back a little, letting the loud and noxious swarm buzz by me, and checked the map app as I passed Fort Santiago and crossed the Pasig River, it's waters sluggish and black beneath the bridge. Minutes later I turned left onto Asuncion Street and I was in Tondo, heading north and deep into the Barangays.

Glancing down at the map, I crossed Moriones Street and swung the bike into a series of right and left turns, negotiating the tight streets and laneways of the inner Tondo barangays. It was dark and rain was falling steadily, but lightly.

The streets were jammed with pedestrians winding their way through the night to food stalls and grocery stands. Long lines of bare lights were strung across the street, washing away the grime and poverty with a bright, festive glow, and music from a dozen street-side stereos blared over the crowds. I had slowed the bike to a crawl and, with a final glace at the map, pulled over beside a stall selling Pinoy Barbecue.

I swung off the bike and adjusted the gaiter to make sure it was up over the bridge of my nose.

Covering the view of the bike with my body, I opened and lifted up the bike seat. With a quick glance around, I quickly unwrapped the Walther and slipped it into the waistline of my jeans, pulling the cheap tracksuit top over it. Last, I pulled out my phone and dimmed the backlight on its screen – I had seen too many people give themselves away with a bright phone screen not to have learned that lesson.

I turned back to face the street and my stomach cramped at the smell of the charcoal-grilled pork, served on bamboo skewers. I realised I had not eaten since breakfast, and looked longingly at the food sizzling on the open grill. It was a risk but I was hungry so I pointed at the grill and held up two fingers.

I grabbed the proffered pork skewers, wrapped in a flimsy white napkin, and tossed down 300 Pesos before moving off slowly into the crowd weaving its way up the street. I made my way a short distance up the street then casually leaned against a doorway, lowered the face gaiter and munched on the pork, quickly stripping it off the skewers and devouring it hungrily. I felt my stomach settle as the food hit home so, leaning back into the darkened doorway, I rolled and lit a cigarette. My heart raced as I drew deeply on the cherry-scented smoke and studied my phone.

The maps app had me one corner and about 200 metres away from the location Tommy Ho had sent. Fast Danny Fung had last been seen sitting outside a small street bar over an hour ago by one of The Panda's men, and there was no guarantee he would still be there. I shook my head. It was impossible. Fung would be long gone. We had no one tailing him and Tondo was a seething mass of humanity, despite the dark and the rain. I would never find him, I told myself.

What would I do *if* I found him? I couldn't just walk up to him in a crowded street, produce the handgun and shoot him in the face.

Even if I could bring myself to do that, I'd be tackled and beaten to a pulp by the crowd seconds after pulling the trigger.

I dragged on the cigarette and rubbed my eyes. I *had* thought this through but had always skipped over the obvious conclusion that I was going to have to kill Jade Tooth's boy. There were no half measures here and I knew that – I had known that from the moment I boarded the flight in Hong Kong. I had never killed someone in cold blood and that line, once crossed, was a line that could never be erased.

I had once been told that I was on my own personal Road to Perdition but that the final destination on that journey to damnation was unknown. It wasn't now.

'Fuck it,' I muttered as I flicked the butt of the cigarette into the rain. Jade Tooth had been a dangerous presence in my life for over three years, he had brutally murdered Fat Johnny Tong and had now openly threatened my sister. A message needed sending. If Lee Pak-chun had forbidden me from acting against Jade Tooth – on pain of my own death – he *had* given the nod to finding, and dealing with, Danny Fung. I drew a deep breath, pulled the gaiter back over my face, stepped out into the street and turned the corner.

The side street was dark.

Rain dripped from the corrugated iron eaves of the shanties. I walked slowly on.

The sound of a man and woman arguing over the screams of their baby echoed up the street, and somewhere near a dog barked frantically. A police chopper passed low overhead, its powerful spotlight swivelling and searching like an eye.

Up ahead a single, bare bulb lit the entrance to a small street bar and the three men seated on cheap plastic seats in the shelter of its tin awning. They were hunched over a table littered with empty beer bottles, each holding a hand of cards, smoking and talking quietly as they played. A small radio sat on a wooden shelf, playing a tinny Filipino pop song and a cat sat in the doorway grooming itself.

I watched as one of the men laughed out loud and threw down a card, punching the air in victory while the others slammed their cards onto the table in disgust. Fast Danny Fung had just won a game and he looked very pleased with himself as he scooped up the fistful of dirty and rumpled Peso notes.

I ambled slowly past the men, feeling their eyes on me. Fung turned his head to watch as I walked past, then returned to shoving his winnings into the pocket of his jeans.

I was sweating freely as I frantically searched out a place into which I could disappear, close enough to watch Fung but far enough down the street to not give myself away. The dark of the street helped and I soon found the doorway of a deserted shack that was partly obscured by a large stack of wooden shipping pallets. The doorway was on a small left-hand bend in the street so I slipped to my left and disappeared into the gloom where I stood and looked back down the street.

Fung and his mates were clear to see, about 75 metres away, in the bright light of the bulb hanging over them. With their night vision destroyed, and me standing still in the dark of the doorway, I was invisible.

One of the men called out into the bar and a tiny woman soon appeared carrying three beers that she sat down on the table. Fung took a deep drink, then another. That was good. He had probably been drinking for hours and I needed him slow and foggy. I was eyeing him intently when my phone vibrated in my back pocket. I drew it out slowly and cupped my hand around the dimly lit screen. Another spam call from an unknown number had gone straight through to my voicemail. I shook my head and dropped the phone back into my pocket.

I stood in the dark for nearly an hour, watching as Fung and his pals drank more and more and became rowdier and more unsteady. I craved a cigarette and my feet were numb from standing still. My back ached. The rain was falling heavier and the street was deserted and silent except for Fung and the two drunks who were, by now, in intoxicated embraces and declarations of love for each other.

As I watched, one of the men drew out a small glass pipe. He packed and lit the pipe, drew on it then passed it to Fung who dragged deeply on it. The sweet, chemical smell of Shabu wafted up the dark street. I wasn't surprised they were smoking ice but I was concerned. The last thing I needed was for Fast Danny Fung to be fired up and pain tolerant as the methamphetamine coursed through his system. The laughter of the three men died down as the drug hit home and they surrendered to its warm and menacing grasp.

The police chopper swung back low overhead, the roar of its turbine engines and the beat of its downwash pounding my senses as it swept down the street and banked away.

I looked back to the bar just as Fung stood and patted the man closest to him on the shoulder. I tensed. He was leaving; the only question was which direction he would take. I held my breath as Fung swayed slightly and looked around before walking away from the bar. He was coming in my direction, away from the crowded main street a block back. I edged back further into the darkened doorway and pressed myself against the wall.

Fung padded slowly past me and I held my breath. He swayed slightly as he walked and he was muttering to himself.

I watched as he passed and gave him a slow count of twenty before I stepped out of the doorway and followed after him. My trainers made no sound on the wet pavement and I was a shadow in the dark. I hugged the wall as I stalked slowly after Fung, my head turned slightly to the side to enhance my peripheral night vision.

Suddenly, Fung disappeared and I realised he must have turned a corner. I sped up, running my hand along a wet concrete wall until I reached a small alley that branched off to the right. I peered intently ahead, seeking out Fung's shape in the dark. The alley was quiet and I could hear soft footsteps so I stepped around the corner. As I did so, Fung passed a dimly light window. I increased my pace.

Somewhere ahead, the noise of raised voices and music was becoming louder as we moved down the alley. The drumming sound of rain on the tin roofs of the shanties was loud. I couldn't see anything but we must soon be emerging into a busier side street where there would be light and people. Witnesses. I had to make my move and I had to do it now.

I drew the Walther from my jeans and ran forward lightly, my trainers making only a faint hissing sound through the puddled rain-water. Fung's shape loomed up clearly and I realised with a shock I had been much closer to him than I thought. Sensing something, Fung stopped suddenly and began to turn. I raised the handgun.

'Danny Fung?' I said quietly in Cantonese. 'It's time to pay the bill.'

Fung squinted at me and his body tensed. He no longer looked unsteady on his feet and I could see his shoulders bunch as he coiled, ready for action.

'Dude, who the fuck are you?' he said slowly, his voice clear. 'Diu lei lo mo, caat tau! *Fuck your mother, dickhead*!'

I didn't have time to stand in the street chatting with him. The job had to be done and done quickly.

'Fat Johnny Tong,' I said. 'This is for him,' and I pulled the trigger.

Instead of the sharp crack of the Walther firing a .32 calibre round, my stomach sank at the metallic click of the hammer striking home onto a faulty firing pin. I stood frozen for a split second then Fung spun on his heels to sprint off down the alley.

It turned out Danny Fung *was* fast and he soon opened a gap between us as he darted down the alley. Stuffing the Walther into my jeans, I ran after him, my dodgy right knee grinding painfully.

We had not gone 50 metres when Fung jinked left and I followed him into a laneway, brightly lit by overhead strings of bulbs and congested with boxes, pallets, cheap furniture, rusting metal trolleys, piles of rubbish in split black plastic bags and wandering stray mongrel dogs. Worse, the alley was jammed with shouting, excited men clutching Pesos in their fists as they leaned in close over a tupada, illegal cockfight.

Fung didn't pause and he surged through the crowd, directly over the top of the two maddened birds that stabbed and slashed at each other with the sharpened double-edged blades attached to their left legs.

People, roosters and dogs scattered in a shower of bodies, wicker baskets, feathers and rotting rubbish as Fung and I bolted through the game. A large blue poly tarp, that had been sheltering the fight and its fans, collapsed in a flood of pooled rainwater. A hand grabbed my tracksuit top and I was nearly pulled off my feet before I chopped down with my left forearm and broke the grip to sprint away after Fung. Three men chased after me, shouting and waving their fists. Everything was going to hell in a handbasket. Fung was getting away, and I had attracted the attention of 20 or 30 witnesses – the angrier and bolder of whom were now chasing me.

Fung darted away, opening the gap further, and we ran on through the back alleys of Tondo, some lit, some dark but all narrow and congested with rubbish and junk.

The good news was Fung seemed to be heading away from the main streets and we were largely on our own except for the occasional curious face peering from a tin shack and the men chasing me. I risked a glance over my shoulder and saw my pursuers had dropped off to one man who was falling further and further behind.

I rounded a corner, slamming noisily into the corrugated tin of a shanty wall and nearly tripping over a small kid's tricycle. My lungs were burning and my right knee screamed at me to stop. Fung darted around the next corner and out of sight. The rain was falling heavily now, thunder grumbling overhead and further out to sea. We ran on.

The alley seemed to lighten slightly and I could see Fung's silhouette against a bank of spotlights that shone toward us from across a darkened strip that was lined with the winking lights of another barangay. I did a quick calculation in my head and realised we must have reached the canal that ran north from the Pasig River through Tondo to the port. Fung turned left again and out of sight. I picked up the pace for the last few metres and burst out onto a service road that paralleled the sluggish, thick waters of the canal.

I stopped, panting like a dog, my eyes straining in the half-light for a sign of Fung. I looked frantically up and down the road but he had disappeared.

The road was lined on the left by shipping pallets and steel shipping containers. The canal bordered it on the right. Glancing around at my feet, I bent and picked up a lightweight metal pole. It wasn't much but it was something so I gripped it tightly in my right hand as I moved cautiously forward, scanning for Fung among the stacks of pallets and rows of containers.

My heart was hammering and I could hear the pulse thudding in my ears. Just ahead, the sound of a slight scratching. I opened my mouth to quieten my breathing and listened intently. The scratch came again, so faint I almost missed it.

I had moved only two paces toward the sound when a stack of timber pallets suddenly toppled over. I leapt to my right but not fast enough to dodge the edge of one pallet that struck me painfully on the left shoulder. I gasped in pain and had barely collected my thoughts when the dull metallic gleam of a knife snaked out at my face.

Reacting instinctively, I leaned back slightly and felt the blade, that would have embedded itself in my mouth, swish over my left shoulder. Fung was overbalanced as he missed the strike. I dropped my shoulder while pivoting to my left foot and swung the pole around in a downward blow. I caught him across the back of the neck and he grunted once before spinning to face me, the knife held in his right hand, low down. Fung didn't look disoriented and he didn't look tired. His eyes gleamed maniacally and he licked his lips as he circled me, looking for an opening.

'I don't know who you are,' he hissed in Cantonese. 'But I'm going to gut you like a fish, you bastard.'

I watched him as if I were watching a cobra, weaving and swaying in front of me.

Street fighting isn't a choreographed, blow-for-blow dance. It is messy and ugly and brutally quick. I figured I would have only once chance at this.

Fung was watching my eyes, so I darted a glance fractionally left, then feinted the same way. He fell for it and lunged to where my stomach would have been, but I had spun on my left foot, shifted my weight over my right and was suddenly behind him. I kicked Fung hard behind the left knee and heard the patella pop with a loud crack, then I slammed the pole down in a full-blooded blow to the back of his head. He groaned, dropped the knife and sank to his knees.

I hit him again over the back of the head.

The pole bent and the scalp over his fractured skull split. Blood gushed hot and dark over his shoulders and face, and onto the road. I had raised the pole to finish him off when Fung suddenly grabbed up the knife, leapt to his feet, dashed the blood from his eyes. Roaring dementedly, he rushed into me.

The shabu was running through his veins like dragon's smoke and Fung was an enraged animal, feeling no pain and stronger than any man I had ever tackled. He stabbed out at me, slashing, cutting and hooking with the wicked blade. I did my best to cover up and parry with the pole while I stumbled backwards. Before I knew it, my back was against another stack of pallets and I had nowhere to go and no room to swing the pole. There was only one thing I could do.

With a roar I charged into Fung, taking him momentarily off guard, and swung the pole down on his right arm. The wrist shattered with a loud crack and the knife dropped but Fung, without a sound, punched me in the mouth and swept out with his left leg to whip me off my feet. I hit the ground hard, winded, and dropped the pole with a clatter.

I could taste blood in my mouth and I was sure the not-yet-healed gash on my cheek had re-opened. Fung was instantly on me, the knife in his left hand, snarling like a rabid dog. His knees on my shoulders, he had hooked my left arm behind his right leg and I grabbed desperately with my right hand at the knife that he drove down toward my face.

My hand gripped his left wrist as I tried to slow the descent of the blade but Fung had dropped his right forearm over the top of his left and the knife came down. Fung's strength was incredible. The rain belted into my face, half blinding me, and my grip on his wrist was slipping. I started to panic. Any second now the tip of the knife would enter my left eye then push its way through the vitreous and fine muscle into my brain.

I scrabbled with my left hand, straining against the lock of Fung's right knee, and bucked my body hard but Fung didn't move. The knife was millimetres from my eye, my right hand straining, when I suddenly felt the leather of Fung's belt with the fingertips of my left hand. With a last desperate effort, I grabbed onto his belt. As soon as I had a grip I pulled back with all my might, feeling the muscle in my rotator cuff tear, while bucking up with my hips.

Fung tipped backwards and to his right only slightly, but it was enough to release my left arm and allow me to slither out from under him. My right hand was still gripping his left wrist. Against the pain of my shoulder, I grabbed my own right wrist with my left hand, twisted Fung's knife hand down and pushed down with all the strength I had left.

The knife slid effortlessly between Fung's ribs and he gasped. I pushed again. Slowly, inexorably, the blade sank into Fung. His eyes widened and he started to say something but he choked as blood flowed from his mouth. I shoved the knife hilt home, feeling the blade tip scrape on the concrete beneath him. Fast Danny Fung snarled, once, then slumped. It was done.

My shoulder ached and my face stung. Still on my knees, I pulled down the face gaiter to suck in deep breaths, sweat and rain stinging my eyes and dripping from my hair and the tip of my nose. I hung my head and closed my eyes. I was suddenly bone weary, as the adrenaline of the clash began to wear off. If I just closed my eyes for a moment...

I snapped my eyes open and looked up and down the deserted canal-side road.

Fung's body and I were hidden in a deep patch of shadow and I could see no one that might have witnessed our struggle. I rolled Fung's body over and rifled through his jeans, taking out the wad of cash he had won that evening along with his wallet. I rolled the cheap watch off his wrist then rummaged around under his shirt. My fingers touched on what I was looking for so I drew it out from under his shirt and broke it from around his neck with a vicious tug. A finely cut jade dragon pendant, that all of Jade Tooth's hoods wore, glinted in the soft light of the moon that had broken through the rainclouds and now faintly lit the scene. I stuffed it into my pocket and jammed Fung's wallet and cash into another.

Standing, I took his hands and, with a final look up and down the road, dragged the corpse to the canal edge. With a push of my foot, I rolled the body over the edge. Fung's corpse hit the black water with a splash and instantly disappeared beneath floating garbage, tangled weed and the bloated carcass of a yellow dog. The useless Walther followed seconds later.

44

Two hours hour later, showered and changed, I was sitting in a Makati bar, in the corner booth, nursing a whisky and enjoying the sting of the liquor as I rolled it around my injured mouth. After dumping Danny Fung's body, I had dropped Fung's empty wallet in a rubbish bin on the way back to the scooter. Passing a homeless man, I had walked back and pressed Fung's wad of Pesos into his hands. The watch and the dragon pendant had been tossed into the river as I had ridden back over the bridge. It would look like a robbery if his body ever surfaced. Even if CCTV footage emerged – which I doubted given that area – the whole mugging and robbery theory would only be bolstered.

Getting back into the hotel via the back stairs was easy and, once again, I was pleased the place had no CCTV – the hookers didn't like cameras and the girls were worth too much to the night manager for him to change anything. I had showered, treated my cut mouth and split cheek with my small travel med kit, and swallowed two 100mg tablets of anti-inflammatory with painkiller against my throbbing shoulder. I had bagged up the clothes in separate rubbish bags and dropped them out a rear window into the carpark where one of Tommy Ho's boys had been waiting to pick them up. The clothes would be scattered around Manila after they had been splashed liberally with bleach. The scooter had disappeared and, by now, was probably sitting on the bottom of the river or was a roaring bonfire on the side of Highway 26. I sipped at the whisky and dragged on my cigarette, ashing it lightly into the small bowl at my elbow. That bloody Walther! I thought. I reminded myself to talk to The Panda about whoever his armourer was in Manila and their need to stock and provide firearms that worked as advertised.

Danny Fung was dead. I had killed him. Admittedly not in cold blood but in a hot him-or-me fight, but I had killed him regardless. How did I feel about that?

I sipped at the whisky and sat back in the booth as I contemplated the question. It didn't take me long to realise I felt nothing about it. I was completely devoid of any feelings for Fung, or his family for that matter - assuming the rat bastard even had one. I felt pleased that I had avenged Fat Johnny Tong. I snorted at that. I was at least honest enough with myself to admit *that* feeling was more relief that I had done something that would excuse my having been responsible for Johnny's death in the first place. Deep down, I knew it wouldn't excuse anything but it did help me to think that.

Fung was dead but the problem was Jade Tooth would still be above ground and an ever-present threat to me and my family for as long as that continued. He had to be put under, and I resolved to work out a way that would both get the job done and leave Lee Pak-chun none the wiser. What that was, I had no idea.

A girl across the bar caught my eye as I glanced up and signalled for another whisky, but I shook my head and turned away. The last thing I wanted that night was company. I needed to be alone with my thoughts to start the process of rationalising what I had done and why it wasn't, necessarily, a bad thing. I drank deeply and rolled another cigarette.

45

THE NEXT AFTERNOON, after another meeting with the harried Mr Espanilla to reinforce my cover, I walked into Ninoy Aquino International Airport, my carry-on slung over my right shoulder.

I pushed my Wayfarers up onto my head and strolled across to Cathay's check-in, apparently without a care in the world. I was sweating heavily and my heart was thumping as I glanced around me, taking in the pairs of heavily armed police patrolling the terminal.

Minutes later, checked in and through security, I was standing before a stern-faced immigration officer at passport control. Sliding my passport across to him I kept my face blank as he flicked through the pages, glancing up at me now and then. The officer dropped my passport onto his desk, turned to his computer keyboard and began tapping away.

My pulse raced as the seconds ticked away into a minute, then two. His fingers tapped the keyboard and his eyes darted from back and forth from his screen to me. Over his shoulder an armed policeman began to move slowly toward us. Scratching my ear casually, I quietly let out the breath I was holding as the cop sauntered past without a glance. The immigration officer finally picked up my passport, stamped it with a thud and handed it back to me.

Feeling a trickle of sweat run down my side, I grabbed my passport and nodded my thanks, passing through into the departures terminal. I could feel my hands shaking so I gripped my shouldered carry-on tighter and shoved my other hand deep into my jeans pocket. My heart was fluttering as I wandered into the terminal and I was sweating freely despite the chill of the air conditioning.

I made my way toward the airline lounge, craving a drink to settle my nerves. My pulse stared to slow and my breathing calmed as I realised I was through. I shook my head. I had nothing to worry about.

I had covered my tracks well, was sure I had not been seen the night before, and the odds I had already been connected to a body that had probably not yet resurfaced from the polluted waters of the canal, let alone been identified, were almost zero. Espanilla was a possible loose thread but I was sure Angel had both incentivised and terrified him enough to guarantee his silence.

I took a deep breath, willing myself to calm down. I smiled slowly as I strolled toward the lounge. Then, out of nowhere, a light tap on my left shoulder. I turned slowly and the floor seemed to tilt as I stared at two cops standing in front of me, one cradling a Chinese Type CQ assault rifle and eyeing me balefully.

'Can I help you, officers?' I asked politely, conscious of my swollen lip and split cheek. My mind raced. I was done. There was nowhere to run. If I did run I was likely to get two 5.56 mm rounds in the back. If they took me in I would just have to stick to my cover and act bewildered and indignant. I held my breath.

'Your bag is unzipped sir,' the cop said sternly, pointing at my carry-on. 'There are many pickpockets here in the terminal watching for unwary travellers such as you. I recommend to zip it up?'

I blinked and rolled my eyes. 'What an idiot!' I exclaimed with a stupid grin that hurt my mouth. 'Thank you very much officer...'

The cops nodded and moved off as I dropped my bag, bent over and zipped it closed. I was breathing heavily. A drop of sweat, then another, splashed onto the worn leather of my bag. I was a wreck and badly needed that drink.

The airline lounge bustled with businessmen carrying plates piled high with lukewarm noodles, soggy spring rolls and a flavourless chicken curry.

I had calmed down, bringing my heart flutters and racing pulse back to their usual steady beat. I swirled the remnants of the whisky around in my mouth, swallowed it and checked my watch. A little over 15 minutes before boarding, so I unplugged my phone charger, rolled it up and dropped it into my bag. I stood and was sliding my phone into the back pocket of my jeans when it vibrated, once, in my hand. I turned it over and read the message on the screen.

I will call in 5 minutes. Answer it

Puzzled, I looked at the sender's number. It was a Hong Kong number but not in my contacts. I didn't recognise it. Then, suddenly, I recalled the three silenced calls I had received, all from different numbers, over the past two days. Someone was trying to reach me, and they were using different numbers every time. Who would be doing that and why? I quickly changed the settings on my phone, allowing calls from unknown numbers to come through, then grabbed my bag to head out into the crowded anonymity of the terminal.

I was on the escalators going down from the lounge when my phone rang. I glanced at the screen – another unknown number – and quickly started call recording on my phone. I answered the call, raising the phone to my ear. The voice at the other end was robotic and distorted. The caller was using a voice modifying app. With a sudden chill I realised who it was.

'Are you there?' the mechanical voice said, disembodied and emotionless.

'I'm here. Who is this?'

A low, metallic chuckle sounded in my ear. 'Yes you would love to know that, wouldn't you Galahad.'

'How did you get my number?' I asked. I had a feeling I already knew the answer to that one.

'Let's see...I'll give you three guesses,' the voice said.

I didn't answer.

After a long pause the voice continued. 'I have the girl,' it said.

'What girl?'

'Don't toy with me Galahad. The little girl who belongs to your offsider – Ms Loh, isn't it?'

I drew a breath. 'What's that to me?' I said as casually as I could muster. 'Why would you think I give a shit about some street kid...?'

'Oh, you care Galahad. Of course you do. As I said, do not play with me. Our relationship will go so much better if we show each other mutual respect. Don't you think?'

'Okay,' I replied. 'Respect. Let's do that. Look, it's me you want. *Isn't* it? Let the girl go, she's nothing to you...'

'Oh, but she is. She's everything to me, Galahad. So fresh, and sweet. I think I will keep her. At least for now.'

I shut my eyes tight against the images in my mind of what Penny faced at the hands of this maniac. I tried to calm my voice. The caller wanted me angry and emotional, so being dispassionate and calm might prod it into a mistake I could use.

'I want proof you have the girl,' I said. 'Send me a photo. Do it now.'

'Don't order me around Galahad. I don't like to be ordered around...' A pause. 'No photos. I'll do one better: you can talk to her. Wait.'

There was a rustling, a faint click that I assumed was the voice masking app disabling, and a muffled exchange on the other end. I heard a sob, then...

'Hello?' a young girls voice, frightened and shaking.

'Hello sweetheart,' I said quietly. 'I'm a friend. Can you tell me your name?'

There was sniff then a single, whispered word. 'Penny.'

I went on, pressing gently. 'Penny, can you tell me the name of your auntie who is looking after you?'

'Josephine...Joey... Loh.'

'And Joey lives where, Penny?'

Another sniff. 'I... I don't remember the address. Soho.'

I closed my eyes and drew a deep breath. 'You're doing very well, sweetheart. You're *very* brave. Can you tell me what big thing Joey has in her apartment, in the corner of her bedroom?

'Yes' the girl said softly. 'It's her Wing Chun dummy. It's dark, very old...'

That confirmed it. I shuddered. The poor kid probably only had hours to live. There was nothing we could do.'

'Penny,' I said. 'Has the bad person hurt...'

The phone was snatched away, a moment of rustling, another click and the monstrous robotic voice was back on the line.

'Ah ah, Galahad. No leading questions. Naughty.'

'Why are you calling me?' I demanded. 'We both know you want us to meet, want to bring this to a head, so why not just do that? Let's just get this done.'

'Don't you want to know why I'm doing all of this? Don't you want to "get into his head"?'

There was mistake number one: of course it was always a solid assumption but I now had confirmation the killer was a man. He went on.

'Aren't you interested to know why I kill and what the connection is to you?'

'Would you tell me if I was?'

That chuckle again. 'Frankly, no.'

'Then I'm not interested. I just want it to end. I want whatever it is to finish and I want you to stop slaughtering people.'

'Oh, I expect that will happen at some stage but we have a long way to go before then Galahad. I have plans for you.'

'Which are..?'

'I am going to destroy you but I am going to take my time doing it. I am going to take you apart, piece by piece. I am going to torture you as if I were using a knife on you, except it will be your mind I will be ripping at.'

I stayed silent.

'Have I shocked you?'

'No,' I replied. 'To be honest you seem exactly as I had imagined. Unhinged, not very smart, calculating yet not rational...'

'Oh. You have been speaking to a psychiatrist. Well done you. And what did he tell you? That I like to utterly dominate my partners? That I only truly derive pleasure in the final act of the kill?'

'Something like that?'

'Well then he probably also told you I'm a genius level IQ...'

'Not really. No.'

That got to him. There was a long pause while he collected himself. 'Well... it's naff to proclaim oneself a genius...'

"Naff", another mistake. This guy was a Brit, probably English.

'But I will say,' he continued 'that you don't seem to be rising to my challenge. It would seem you're having trouble putting the pieces together.'

I came to a sudden stop, and someone ran into my back shooting me an angry look as they moved off down the crowded concourse.

Something about what he had just said rang bells in my head. I had heard that before, from different people, but I couldn't remember who and when. It was a fairly common turn of phrase so I was probably overreacting but I couldn't shake the feeling of having pried the killer open just a little.

'Oh? There are clues?' I asked. 'I would have said you've been fastidious in cleaning up your kill sites. You haven't been in contact, sent us nothing. It's not as if you're playing a game of "Cluedo" with us. I mean, there's nothing pointing to Colonel Mustard, in the library, with the candlestick.'

The voice cackled. It sounded like a small motor monotonously winding up. 'That's funny. Oh, Galahad, there are always clues,' it droned. 'You should know that. Look harder, I beg you. Make this a challenge for me...'

'So this isn't about revenge then?'

'Why do you say that?'

'The psych. "Challenge" or "revenge". That was the dichotomy he presented.'

'Galahad, in a dichotomy everything must belong to one part or the other, and the parts are mutually exclusive. Nothing can belong simultaneously to both parts. So that's not what you are looking at here.'

'I'm not?'

'No, Galahad. Do try and keep up. What you are facing is a bit of both: it's a challenge *and* its revenge... You just have to figure out which is which, why and how that stops me.'

'Why don't we just acknowledge you've won the challenge,' I said quietly. I mean I have no idea what is going on, nor how to stop you. Let's move to the revenge piece. Let's meet and you can exact your revenge for whatever it was I did to you.'

Another pause while he chewed on that for a moment. 'That is tempting, Galahad, I must say. But I can hear you are busy... airport is it? I'll call you again soon. You can send the voice recording to your friends in the Police now.'

With that the call was terminated and I was left, frozen in place, staring at the phone in my hand while my boarding call sounded overhead.

46

THE NEXT DAY I sat in the warm morning sun on a park bench off Wong Nai Chung Road, at the southern end of Happy Valley Racecourse.

The park trees spread their branches overhead, whispering in a gentle breeze, and the sun spotted my face and danced across the brick paving. Bors sat quietly at my feet, watching the kids on the playground equipment. Christmas was just around the corner and the children romped excitedly, quizzing each other about Santa and what he would bring, while their parents chatted sociably over take-away coffees.

I had called Joey the evening before, the moment I had disembarked at HKIA. The call had been difficult. She admitted she had thought Penny had been taken by the killer for some days but was obviously heartbroken to hear me confirm the shocking news. Typically of her, she had quickly pulled herself together and switched into action mode.

'So what are our next steps?' she had asked. 'What have we got?'

I had been thinking about that during the three-hour flight from Manila to Hong Kong; wrestling with what I knew, what I could deduce and the vast number of things I didn't know.

'The killer is male, almost certainly, and he sounds like a Brit... uses English colloquialisms. He's arrogant. Confident. Hard to push any of his buttons but he didn't like it when I suggested he was only moderately bright. Told me he was a genius...'

'Fucking *genius*?' Joey cut in. 'I'll tear his IQ from his brain and choke him to death on it...' I smiled grimly. That was the Joey I knew and loved. She was back. I really had missed her and I was glad we were working together again.

'He's obviously using a burner phone with a collection of pre-paid sims,' I went on. 'I demanded a photo of Penny but he dodged the question, so I think the device he's using is fairly basic. Can't send MMS. It's probably a simple old-school flip phone. That means he'll be very hard to track. Not impossible but very hard.' I gathered my thoughts briefly. 'If they're not already, the Taskforce needs to trawl local telcos for purchases.'

Joey exhaled into the phone. '*Diu*, boss! How many little phone and sim sellers are there in Hong Kong? Thousands...'

'Yeah I know, but it's *something*. It's a place to start.'

'Yes,' Joey said. 'A place to start...'

'There are one or two other things,' I said. 'There's something about the cord he's using to bind his victims. I can't be sure yet but I think it points to his professional background. I also get the feeling he hasn't been in Hong Kong long... maybe a couple of years. I spoke to a psychiatrist about the killer and he agrees he's probably "geographically mobile" and has probably killed elsewhere. That means he likely doesn't have a support network here so he's on his own. That might start to tell on him at some point and the pressure of holding it all together might make him careless.'

'That has to be something the Taskforce is looking into,' Joey said. 'Killings with a similar M.O. in the UK – now we believe him to be a Brit.'

I nodded. 'Yeah, but the difficulty here is I'm hearing he's spotless when he kills. There doesn't seem to be a shred of DNA left at any of the sites. Not sure really, so we need to quiz Michael Wong on that.' I paused again as I remembered another small, but possibly vital, detail.

'He drives. He can't do what he does while using public transport so the same car turning up in the vicinity of the kills could be an angle.' Joey was quiet and I could tell she wasn't convinced.

'Yeah,' she finally said. 'Maybe. Long shot, but maybe.'

I drew a breath before going on. 'Look, Jo, this is hard for you to hear but I don't think he's going to kill her... at least not right away. He said he wanted to "keep her" so we need to hang on to that. It would seem we have some time. Christ knows how much, but time we can use to find her.'

Joey was silent for a long minute. I waited for her to wrestle with the demons in her head.

'I know,' she said finally, her voice shaking. She sucked in a breath. 'The Taskforce,' she said. 'We need to get onto them.'

'I'm calling Michael Wong next and setting up a meeting. I want you there.'

'Try and keep me away!'

'That's my girl,' I said gently. 'I'll get back to you later with time and place tomorrow for a meet with C.I. Wong.' With that I had hung up.

Now, sitting in the park, the sunlight warming my face in the cool December morning, I briefly closed my eyes to await the arrival of Michael Wong. I didn't have long to wait. I felt movement beside me and I opened one eye and glanced sideways before closing my eyes again. I waited for him to speak first.

'I'm not going to apologise,' C.I. Wong said without any introduction.

I opened my eyes and turned to him. 'I wouldn't expect you to, Michael,' I said.

He nodded. 'Look, we have our issues – and I *still* don't trust you – but I think I may have been wrong. I probably should have brought you in – at least at the edges – as soon as we saw the killings were connected to you in some way.'

'That sounds like an apology...'

'It isn't.'

'As it happens, I agree with you,' I said mildly. 'I knew early on you were using me as bait. I resented that. But I'll concede, I probably would not have been of much help to you at the start. That all changed yesterday...'

The sound of a motorcycle shifting down gears interrupted me. I glanced over my shoulder to see the bike pull into the kerb, the rider kick down the stand, swing off the bike and pull off a full-face helmet. Joey shook out her bob-cut hair and slipped on a pair of Aviators before walking into the park and taking a seat on the bench on the other side of Michael Wong.

Joey leaned back into the bench, her right arm cocked over the back and gave Michael Wong a nod.

'Good morning, Chief Inspector,' she said, her face grim.

'Jou-san, *good morning*, Miss Loh,' he said, looking distinctly uncomfortable at being sandwiched between the two of us.

'Now that Joey's here we can start,' I said. 'Where was I...?'

'"That all changed yesterday" ...' Michael prompted.

I nodded, 'Right. That all changed yesterday when I took the killer's call.

'Where were you when he called?' Michael asked, watching me carefully.

'Business trip.'

Michael nodded. 'And how *is* Manila these days? It's been years since I have been there...'

I wasn't surprised but I acted it. It wasn't hard – my heart was hammering so hard I thought the cagey detective could see it. 'Are you having me followed?' I growled.

'Of course I am,' Michael said, matter-of factly. 'As you say, you were my bait for the Trails Killer *and* I still want to get to the bottom of your connection to Fat Johnny Tong's murder and a certain sum of money...' I caught Joey's quick glance over his shoulder. He shrugged. 'I mean, what would you do?'

Joey had tensed in her seat and I looked blankly back at Michael. He went on.

'The fact the killer has contacted you validates my decision on this...It was clear from early in the investigation that you were, somehow, a focus for him.'

I nodded. 'I've spoken to Morris Ngan...'

'I know. He was most insistent I pull you into the case...'

'Ngan is convinced the killer is out to destroy me,' I said. 'It's revenge for something I've done to him. It also seems he likes the challenge of pitting himself against me... and the resources of HKPF for that matter.'

Michael nodded thoughtfully. 'That fits. It may have escaped your attention, but you're not very popular.'

'Yes. I've been told that ... I don't really care,' I said. I heard Joey snort and saw her shake her head.

'And the other killings...? If it's about you, why them?' Michael asked.

'He enjoys it. They're a way to attract attention to himself while satisfying his perversions.'

Michael drew a deep breath and sighed. 'Yes, that's what I think. Okay, so let's talk,' he said and, with that, launched into a rundown of the Taskforce's investigations to that point.

As I had thought, the Taskforce had been busy and the avenues of inquiry were many. The killer was adept in keeping his kill sites – and victims – clean of physical evidence. No fingerprints had been found, and no strands of hair. The victims had no defensive wounds – their hands having been bound – so none of the killer's skin had been found under their nails. Shoe imprints had been meticulously brushed or scuffed away, and no viable DNA samples had been found on the bodies.

'Hang on,' I interrupted. 'He bites his victims – we both know he does *more* than that! What about saliva?'

Michael shook his head. 'No good. Saliva can yield high quality DNA and doesn't quickly break down if stored correctly, but you need at least 2 mils for a viable sample. We're not getting *any* saliva, let alone 2 mils, *and* tests have shown our guy is swabbing down his bite sites with alcohol wipes.'

I shook my head and Michael went on. The geographic angle was being actively investigated. The Thomas killings, that bore all the hallmarks of the latest murders, had occurred a little over two years previously so the Taskforce had made inquiries of the Mainland's Ministry of Public Security, Taiwan, South Korea, Japan and a variety of Southeast Asian nations. All had turned up a fat zero. Michael stopped and watched me as I rolled and lit a cigarette. It seemed a dead-end.

'We have, however, had one hit,' he said. 'And a good one.'

I snapped my head around to look at him and saw Joey shift forward on the bench.

'A few days ago we receive a collated response from the UK,' Michael went on. 'Both The Met and North Yorkshire Police have been investigating a string of murders that had occurred on and around the North York Moors. Eleven victims in all, going back nearly a decade. The M.O is identical to our killer... in *every* way.'

'Jesus,' I breathed.

Michael nodded. 'There's more. The killings suddenly stopped three years ago. Nothing since. Not a clue, not a sign...'

'So he relocated to Hong Kong? Ran quiet for a while then committed the Thomas Murders...?'

'That's my working theory right now, yes,' Michael said.

I sat perfectly still and gazed out across Happy Valley Racecourse public sports grounds. A team of expats were training for a game I had never really understood, Australian Rules Football. I watched them kick, handpass, and catch the strange ovoid ball as my thoughts whirled.

'If that's true,' I said, turning back to Michael 'then it's also true that Peter Toh is involved in this. Remember: he admitted to at least facilitating the Thomas murders.'

Michael shrugged. 'Yes, maybe...'

'So I *did* see him that night in Wan Chai...' I muttered.

'You *saw* Peter Toh?' Michael asked quickly. 'I didn't know that!'

I scratched my chin and winced. 'I've had various reasons to discount it was him. I never got a clear look and I couldn't figure why he would suddenly re-appear...'

'Except to take you down for throwing a spanner in his well-planned works a couple of years back. Revenge.'

'Exactly,' I nodded. Peter Toh was an angle I needed to think a lot more on. I had been his friend for many years, right up until the time he tried to put a bullet in my brain two years before, so I knew his hangouts across the city. Perhaps I could flush him out, and if I did that...

Michael pulled out a notebook and jotted down Peter Toh's Chinese name. He nodded and folded away the notebook. I suddenly remembered my conversation with Joey following the killer's call.

'What about the phone angle?' I asked. 'He's either using burner phones or throw-away sims, or both. Surely that's...'

'A lead worth running down? Thank you, Mr Jones. Yes, that had occurred to us idiot flatfoots...'

'You know I didn't mean it like that,' I said mildly.

'You thought it... Anyway, we drew a blank on the numbers you sent through. They are local sims, bought anonymously in some small phone stall. I have our tech wizards working on cleaning up the voice mask on the voice recording, and we've got teams out all over Hong Kong right now speaking to telcos and every little phone stall we can find...'

Joey snorted. 'Good luck with *that*,' she said.

'*And*...' Michael went on, ignoring her, 'we've locked down all phone and sim sales across the city. All purchases now require positive ID and must be reported directly to a taskforce hotline number.'

Joey snorted again and Michael turned to her. 'Miss Loh, I have known you for quite a while now. I respect your narrow professional skills in the protection field, but this is *detective* work. It's long, it's tedious, methodical, detailed and, often mind-numbingly boring. But we're good at it, we know what we are doing. If the killer has bought these phones and sims in Hong Kong – and there's almost a 100% probability he has – we will find them.'

Chastened, Joey sat back, her arms crossed and a scowl on her face. I gave her a wink over Michael's shoulder and she glared at me.

Michael turned back to me. 'I also have RF engineers monitoring your phone's signal in the hope he calls again and we can triangulate his position.' I opened my mouth to speak but Michael held up a finger.

'*Before* you point it out to me, it's a long shot we will triangulate his signal, but we have one thing going for us, or so I'm told by the wizards. Distance from cell tower required for a Measurement Report is smaller in 4G than years past so triangulation will be easier.' He shrugged. 'I live in hope...'

We sat in silence for a while, each caught up in their own thoughts, then Joey spoke.

'Is he going to kill Penny?' she asked quietly.

Michael Wong shifted on the park bench and looked heavenward, as if seeking guidance. Finally he sighed.

'I don't know, Joey,' he said. 'Maybe. Probably... I don't know how to soften this for you but it is not likely she will be released and, even if she is, she will be broken by the experience.'

'Maybe he's using her to draw Galahad in...?' Joey said desperately. 'Maybe he'll agree to an exchange: her for him.'

Michael shook his head and I felt sick watching Joey's agony. 'Maybe. But if he were going to do that he would have agreed to the swap demand Galahad made yesterday.' He reached out and gently squeezed Joey's shoulder. 'We're doing our best, Joey,' he said gently.'

It was the most human gesture I'd seen from this hard, taciturn cop in the two years I had known him. Joey angrily cuffed away a tear and stood up to watch the last of the kids and their parents as they filed out of the park.

'How about a vehicle?' I asked. 'He can't be using public transport or walking... he has to be using a car or a van.'

Michael nodded. 'Agree. We are working through government

CCTV and private camera footage in a five kilometre radius from each kill site. So far nothing.'

I wasn't surprised the Taskforce had drawn a blank on that. With tens of thousands of government CCTV, and almost as many more private cameras across the SAR, taken across the five weeks since the first victim had been found, that represented hundreds of thousands of hours of footage that needed to be trawled through to try and link one car from over 900,000 on the roads across the city. Even with licence plate recognition software it was a long shot.

'Tell me about the cord,' I said. 'It looks like the draw cord on a barrister's gown bag.'

Michael's head snapped around and he frowned deeply. 'How do you know about that?' he demanded.

I shrugged. 'Professor Ngan told me...'

Michael Wong pointed a finger at me, and his eyes narrowed accusingly. 'The prof has no *idea* what the cord looks like. No one does outside of the Taskforce. It's about the only significant piece of physical evidence we have – except maybe for the tape used to gag the victims; and you can get *that* in any one of thousands of stores across the city.'

'Look, Michael, I know about the cord. Let's just leave it at that for now...'

The cop's eyes suddenly widened in realisation. 'Your fat, obnoxious journalist friend. Chard... He's got a source inside my Taskforce? *Diu...*'

I tilted my head and raised my eyebrows. 'Come on, Michael. What did you expect...?'

'A little loyalty would be nice!' Michael sputtered. He shook his head. 'I bet you it's Kwan,' he muttered. 'That oily little shit...'

I almost laughed but knew it would infuriate him, so I bit my lip. 'I really don't know,' I said. 'Let's talk about the cord, can we?'

So we talked about the cord. Joey continued to stare out into the distance, the dark green hills of Sha Tin Pass and the colossus of Lion Rock were faint on the northern horizon in a hazy sky.

The Taskforce, assisted by the government Forensic Science Division, were conducting an examination of the cord to ascertain its origins in the hope that would help to identify its owner. This was being done by deconstructing the cord and dissecting its constituent elements. Such aspects as the cord's diameter, number and direction of twists, number of strands, colour, coatings and much more were being microscopically analysed and tested.

'Once the results are in,' Michael said, 'we should be able to identify where the cord was manufactured and when. Then, with the assistance of UK authorities, to which shop it was supplied, what use it was put to originally and to whom it was finally sold.'

'But,' I interrupted. 'We *are* working on the assumption it *is* from a barrister's gown bag so are also looking for a connection of such an item to any suspect...'

'If we ever come up with any,' Michael said gloomily. 'We might be chasing this guy for years and not come up with a single suspect we can take past initial elimination.'

That was a pessimistic prediction, and I could tell it angered Joey, but Michael was probably right. What was it Professor Ngan had said about the difficulty in tracking and apprehending serial killers? Unless, of course, our killer started making mistakes. It was our job to apply the pressure where we could, force his hand and, hopefully, the error.

Chief Inspector Wong and I talked for another 15 minutes before he walked off in the direction of Blue Pool Road and his waiting car. Joey and I agreed to meet the next morning in the office, and I promised to contact Angel and The Panda again to light a fire under their search for Penny and her captor.

As I hailed a red taxi and jumped into the back seat, giving the driver an address in Central, I could not shake a glum feeling of defeat.

I had had it out with Michael Wong and was now, effectively, part of his investigation. That was positive, but we had nothing to go on. The killer held all the tiles in this deadly game of Mahjong. We were completely at his mercy, able only to respond to his provocations and his inhuman brutality. I felt like I was treading water and that the tide was fast rushing out under me. I was going backwards and Penny didn't have the luxury of time on her side.

I looked out of the taxi window as the city passed by along Wan Chai Road, heading west. Pedestrian crowds surged up and down the footpaths on either side of the road like a stream in flood, washing over and around any obstacle in their path. Traffic crawled horn-blaringly, exhaust-chokingly toward the intersection with Johnson Road and its wider thoroughfare.

Everything, including the traffic, was moving glacially to its final destination and I could not shake the feeling the killer was watching over it all, content to play it out slowly and painfully. Little did I know that, only hours later, the pace of events would accelerate and time would pass like the spinning hands on a cartoon clock while Joey and I ran Pell-mell around the city in ever more frantic circles.

47

THE BAR OF THE FOREIGN CORRESPONDENTS' Club on Lower Albert Road was quiet.

The FCC was an institution in Hong Kong and had been since its relocation from the Mainland in 1949. It was a club for women with a past and men with no future. While the club had seen a lot, the Vietnam War era was still regarded as its heyday. Back then the bar would heave with battle-weary war correspondents, Hue mud still on their boots or Nui Dat dust in their hair, loudly necking gallons of beer, while neatly dressed American and Australian spies nursed their Bourbons and G&Ts through hushed conversations.

The Club was a hub of information, some honestly obtained, much of it not and both journalistic exposés and the overthrow of governments had been plotted in its booths and around the mahogany-topped bar. These days there were fewer journalists – the younger generation preferring to grab snippets online than work contacts and slog their beat – and even fewer spies, but a few diehards still clung tenaciously to the past and the glories of their youth. Alastair Chard was one of those.

'Hello, my old darling,' he said genially, as I pulled up a stool next to him and signalled the barman. 'How did you know I'd be here?'

I checked my G-Shock. 'It's 11:00 a.m.,' I said. 'It's Wednesday...'

'Very clever,' Alastair growled. 'Now tell me why you are disturbing my fucking brunch...'

'Brunch? I don't see any food,' I said.

'Gin *is* food...'

I sipped the cold local pale ale that had been slipped in front of me and smacked my lips. 'You might be interested to know; I was contacted by the Trails Killer yesterday...'

Alastair shovelled a handful of peanuts into his mouth and crunched them loudly. 'I know,' he mumbled, spraying small pieces of nut onto the bar top. 'You forget: I have a contact inside the Taskforce.'

'No,' I said. 'I haven't forgotten that. Is it Kwan...?'

Alastair stared at me. 'How the *fuck* would you know that?'

I shrugged. 'Michael Wong's onto him. "Oily little shit" I believe he called him... Anyway, want to hear about it?'

Alastair nodded and sipped his Gin. 'I would very much like to hear about it,' he said. 'My chap has told me bugger all about the call other than it was masked with some tech app thingamajig. *And* that it confirms he has that street kid... Penny?'

I nodded. 'Yes, Joey's apprentice. Protégé. Niece... I'm not sure what to call her, but Jo is destroyed and I'm lost because I don't know what I can do to help.'

Alastair grimaced. 'The kid is as good as dead,' he said. 'Nothing you *can* do.'

He was right, we both knew it. But I couldn't just let it go at that. I had to try. I sipped again at the beer. 'Our guy is a Brit. Probably English.' Alastair didn't move or make a sound so I went on. 'The Taskforce has had a breakthrough on overseas inquiries. The UK has come back and it looks like our man has relocated from England following a near decade of identical murders. The murders there stopped three years ago and ours started the year after – if you include the Thomas' murder.'

'So he moved out East, laid low for a few months then started up again,' Alastair commented. Then: 'Fuck *me*! Peter Toh has got onto him somehow and stashed him away for a rainy day – and the Thomas' were that. Do you think Toh is behind the latest lot?'

I nodded slowly. 'I do,' I said. 'I really have nothing solid to go on but I believe Peter is behind this somehow. It certainly fits the revenge theory. It's not his *own* revenge the killer wants to exact, but Peter's...'

'While getting his jollies along the way...' Alastair observed grimly.

'Which means...' I went on before Alastair turned to look at me.

'Find Toh and you find the killer,' he said. 'Find *him* and you've found the kid...'

I nodded. 'Exactly. I know everywhere Peter used to hang out for many years – at least I think I do. Certainly most of them. He'll be laying low in one of those joints, I'm sure of it.'

Alastair appeared to not be listening. He was looking at a space in the air, above the top shelf of the bar. The fingers of his right hand drummed lightly on the bar top. I had known him too long to interrupt him when he was in thought mode, so I sat and quietly sipped at my beer. After a while he turned to me and spoke.

'Didn't your Pru's boyfriend arrive from Blighty three years ago?' he asked, toying with a drink coaster.

'Yes but...'

'Enough time to cool his heels,' Alastair went on. 'Maybe get found out by your angry ex-friend, Toh, and recruited – or, probably, blackmailed – into the Thomas job.'

I could see my jaw drop in the reflection of the bar mirror. I stared incredulously at the rumpled old journalist.

'You're out of your mind, Alastair,' I said. I wound a finger around my right temple. 'Fucking nuts...'

'Remember when I said I'd look into this white knight of Prudence's?' Alastair said. "Well I did. He was very, *very* hard to find and that, in itself, is unusual. Turns out I was working with only half of the necessary information...'

'What do you mean?' I asked, frowning.

'It's his *second* name that is Giles, His first name is Richard. Also, the surname is Tyler-Browne.'

I sighed. 'So what, Alastair? So he goes my Giles Tyler. I've lost count of how many times I have thought of changing my first name?'

'I like Galahad,' Alastair quipped. 'But he doesn't "go by" Giles. Everyone knows him as "Dickie". So why bullshit Prudence and you?'

I shook my head. This was a mad discussion. 'The fuck do I know, Alastair? It means nothing. *Is* nothing...'

Alastair ploughed on regardless. 'He's a loner. No one really knows him. No one has ever been to his apartment, no one has ever seen the car he drives...'

'Maybe he doesn't drive, Alastair,' I observed. '*I* don't for Christ's sake! *I* don't have any friends, Alastair, in case you'd not noticed. *I'm* a loner. Honestly mate...' I rubbed my face. 'Do you know how many Brit expats took up residency in Hong Kong the year before the Thomas' were killed? Three years ago?'

Alastair looked hurt. 'I thought *I* was your friend,' he said quietly. 'And no, I don't know how many Brit residents we had three years ago ... or any other fucking year, for that matter.'

'Well I do,' I said. 'That year 31,293 Brits arrived in Hong Kong and over 11,000 took up residency...'

Alastair sighed, nodded then shook himself like a fat, wet Labrador. 'Sorry,' he said. 'Madcap theory, too much Gin, innate dislike for banking types...'

I could tell he wasn't really letting it go. 'It's okay, old man,' I said. 'This whole thing is a shadow puppet show. It's hard to know what's real and what is not.' I was sipping at the beer when I suddenly had a thought.

'Shit,' I said. 'Speaking of "banking types" I've been seeing that crazy bastard Toby whatsisname around a bit lately...'

'Sanderson,' Alastair said. 'Known deviant and coke head. You want to talk about a loner ... now *he's* fucking nuts that one. How he's survived in this town without being deported – or jailed – is beyond me. What's eating you about him?' Alastair asked.

I ticked the points off on the fingers of left hand. 'One: he has an unhealthy fascination with me. It's like he has some sort of man-crush on me...'

Alastair chuckled and I went on. 'Two: his known appetites both for drugs and the darker side of sex. He was arrested briefly for a serious assault on a working girl in Wan Chai a couple of years ago but was cut loose when she withdrew the complaint – Peter told me he probably paid her to back out. Three: he knows Peter Toh, or at least, I know Peter knew of him. Four: he was hanging about outside that Italian bar the day that photo of me was taken by the killer. I caught him just standing there, eyeballing me. Finally, Five – and this circles back to One: He has tried to talk to me a few times over the years and I've shut him down every time. I've been a bit of a shit to him, to be honest...'

Alastair finished his Gin and ordered another.

'Okay,' he said. 'I can see how he's different to your Prudence's Dickie...' He grinned at his play on words. 'Sanderson certainly seems to fit aspects of the profile.' He paused. '*But*, we just finished saying it's *Toh's* revenge we could be looking at, not the killer's. You being a nasty bitch to young Toby doesn't fit that *and* Toby's not likely to be running around Hong Kong murdering people because you were snippy.'

I sighed. 'True,' I said. 'There's just *nothing* to go on. It's *all* speculation – except the phone call. Even the connection to Peter Toh is smoke and mirrors. Am I just squeezing it in to make it fit?'

We both sat there for a while, lost in our own thoughts, drinking silently and disconsolately. I swallowed down the last of the beer and put down my glass.

'The more I think about it,' I said, standing from the bar 'the more I'm convinced Peter Toh is at the heart of this somehow. I can't just sit on my arse waiting for Penny's body to turn up. If he's here I'll find him. But, first, there's something I need to do.' I turned to leave.

Alastair threw another handful of peanuts into his mouth and swivelled on the bar stool. He looked up at me, his round face creased in lines of concern, his eyes rheumy.

'I seem to be saying this a lot to you, Galahad, but be *very* careful with this one. I feel it in my bones. None of this is going to turn out well.'

I nodded, patting the old journalist on the shoulder, and left the club.

48

LATER THAT AFTERNOON, as the sun was sinking below Lantau Island in a golden blaze, the high, grey walls of Stanley Prison rose above me, casting a gloomy and forbidding shadow.

I closed the door of the taxi and quickly crossed to the security checkpoint. With the fallout over the murder of Johnny Tong and the disturbing closeness of the Trails Killer case, I had pushed aside any involvement with Guo Yu-xuan and his predicament. But I had not forgotten it. Guo's attack on Walter Chan and the reasons behind it had continued to itch at me like a rash.

Somewhere in the back of my mind, when I had been pacing the small hotel room in Manila, I had decided to visit Guo and I was determined to get him to reveal the reason for the attack. In the taxi on the way to the Foreign Correspondents' Club I had called Billy Wong who had agreed to contact his cousin, a Senior Superintendent in Hong Kong Correctional Services Department, and arrange for a meeting pass that day. Typically of Billy Wong he had delivered.

The moment I entered the secure reception office, the smell of the prison wafted over me. It was a stink of despair and hopelessness – a pungent scent that the worst of society put out when crowded together in row upon row of green-painted cages. The Corrections officer in reception looked up at me when I approached the counter. I handed over my Hong Kong ID.

'Galahad Jones,' I said. 'There should be a pass for me to visit Prisoner Guo Yu-xuan. Unescorted.'

I stood quietly while the officer shuffled through a pile of papers. Finding the one he was looking for, he pulled it from the pile and examined it closely, looking up at me and back to my ID as he read. Finally he stamped the pass, handed it to me and made a short call on his radio before buzzing me through into the main prison.

I was met by a silent, armed guard and minutes later was sitting again on a spartan metal chair in a sterile, vomit green interview room. The guard scowled at me then reluctantly left the room. It was quiet with only a faint hum of the human ant colony seeping in under the door. I sat back in the chair and gazed disinterestedly into the CCTV that scanned the room from a ceiling corner near the door. Recalling my last visit, I took out my tobacco pouch and rolled two cigarettes, placing them neatly on the metal table beside the tin ashtray. I took my lighter out and laid it on the table in front of me. I didn't have long to wait before Guo was escorted into the room.

Guo stopped when he saw me, surprise clear for a moment on his otherwise impassive, care-worn face. The guard connected Guo's handcuffs to the manacle chain secured to the table and left without a word or backward glance. The room was silent and I could hear the faint tick of water through a pipe in the wall behind me. With some difficulty, Guo moved his cuffed hands along the chain and picked a cigarette up from the table, leaning down to put it in his mouth. Still he said nothing.

I took up the lighter and leaned across the table to fire up his smoke. He awkwardly took the cigarette between his shackled fingers and dragged deeply, blowing the smoke slowly back into my face.

'So,' Guo finally said in Cantonese. 'The footballer returns... It's nice to see you again Mr Jones.'

'I apologise for not...' I began in Cantonese but Guo cut me off with a wave of his hands and rattle of the manacles.

'Think nothing of it, Mr Jones,' he said calmly. 'I expect you are a very busy man and I... well, I am going nowhere.'

I nodded. 'Let's get right to it, shall we? You sent a message a while ago that you wanted to see me. Alone. Here I am... What do you have to say to me Mr Guo?'

He shrugged. 'Perhaps I just want a visitor. I know you can get in to see me and you seem like a good person...'

'I'm not.'

Guo dragged again on the cigarette. I could see that, despite his calm outward appearance, his hands shook. 'Do you have children?' he asked.

I shook my head. 'I don't. I have a dog.'

'I feel sorry for you,' he said. 'Children can be difficult but they are the greatest blessing in life.' I sat quietly and Guo continued. 'The last time you were here you told me to think of my daughter... reveal the reason behind the attack, free myself and return to her. Do you remember that?'

I nodded.

'I think of her every minute of every day,' he said quietly. 'I think of nothing else really. There is nothing I would not do for her. But, you see, I am locked in a puzzle. If I don't talk I stay here, probably for the rest of my life, but my daughter is safe. If I *do* talk, I might get out but that would only bring further shame to my daughter and my wife. Shame that I cannot allow them to suffer.'

'If you're involved in criminality you can cut a deal,' I said. 'Freedom or a reduction in sentence in exchange for information that convicts the others. There is no shame in that. Don't you want to see justice done?'

Guo chuckled, but there was no humour in it. 'Mr Jones, I am a simple man with no education but even I know justice is a myth. It is for the rich and powerful. Not for people like me.' He paused for a moment. 'The dragons have left our city, you see, and there is no longer any power that protects common folk. No luck, no courage, no wisdom.'

I shook my head, exasperated. 'What's Walter Chan involved in?

Tell me and I'll help you... No one will get to your daughter. I promise'

Guo Yu-xuan smiled faintly, his face sad. He leaned forward and butted out he cigarette, then loudly called for the guard. I remained seated while the guard entered and unshackled the skinny little man in front of me. As he was escorted to the door, Guo turned back to me.

'It's too late for that now, Mr Jones,' he said, blinking at the tears that welled in his eyes. With a clang, the interview room door slammed shut and I was left alone, the stink and depression of the prison pushing down on me.

49

THE TAXI SPED up the winding Tai Tam Road, through the hills to Tai Tam Reservoir, Shek O Country Park and Tai Tam Gap. Left and right of the road the jungle closed in, thick and dense and green and to my right I could see Dragon's Back, the sharp ridgeline running south from the hights of Mount Collinson.

Two years before, Peter Toh had tried to kill me in a small, moonlit clearing not far from where I now gazed out of the cab window. The red taxi sped on, heading to Shau Kei Wan on the north of the Island.

Peter Toh. He had frequented a small bar and noodle joint in SKW and I knew the owner was indebted, in some way, to him. On leaving Stanley Prison I had decided to start my hunt for Peter there. Shortly after hailing the taxi I had called Joey and given her the address of the joint. If what I knew about this place was true, I was going to need backup.

Settled in the back seat of the cab, my thoughts turned back to Guo Yu-xuan. His daughter was the key – I was sure of it. Someone, somehow, had threatened to get at her to guarantee Guo's silence...

Suddenly a thought hit me and I rubbed my chin.

'*Diu*,' I muttered out loud and the taxi driver's eyes flicked to me in the rear vision mirror.

Had I been looking at this from the wrong angle? Maybe it wasn't about what someone would do to Guo's daughter if he talked... maybe someone had already got to her. Was that it? I pulled out my phone and tapped on Caesar Li's contact.

'Galahad,' Caesar said, his voice suspicious. 'Where have you been?'

'What, now or just generally?'

'Well, I know where you have been just now – Billy Wong told me and I got a call from Corrections before your pass was okayed. How did it go?'

I paused for a moment. 'Nothing new,' I said. 'He still won't talk. But I get the feeling he really is trying to tell me something. I'm sure it's about his daughter. Can you get me the address of their apartment?'

'Sure. That's easy. I remember a reference to it in the report. They live in an old low rise in Kwun Tong. It's not far from the Sau Mau Ping public housing estate... I'll get the address for you and text it through.' He stopped and I heard him draw a breath. 'Wait! What are you going to do?'

'I'm going to pay the wife and daughter a visit...'

'*Damn*, Galahad! Is that wise?'

'Probably not,' I admitted. 'But I'm sure the answer to all of this is there, somehow.'

Caesar Li muttered an oath under his breath and hung up. I dropped the phone into my jacket pocket, nestled back into the loosely stuffed and sagging taxi seat to watch as we wound our way out of the hills and down into Chai Wan.

Fifteen minutes later the taxi pulled up in a small side street off Mong Lung Street in Shau Kei Wan. I passed the driver a hundred and told him to keep the change, then stepped out onto the street.

A powerful sports motorbike was parked across the road and Joey was sitting propped casually on the seat, her helmet hooked over the right wing mirror. She was wearing jeans and a pair of solid ankle-high boots. A black leather jacket was unzipped to reveal a white T-shirt. Squinting, I could see the shape of an ASP expandable baton in its pouch, snugged against the small of her back. She had come prepared. That was good. I nodded at her and crossed the road.

The bar was more of a small alcove, with three or four stools along one wall, and a commercial refrigerator stocked with bottles of Tsingtao and Blue Girl beer along the other. The front corner of the small room had a gas stove on which a large pot boiled, and the window was festooned with hanging joints of roast duck, steamed chicken and Char Siu barbecued pork. All fairly common and straightforward so far. What wasn't, was the group of hard-faced, T-shirted men gathered around the front door of the joint. They all held a beer and were smoking.

Conversation stopped as they saw me approach, and one of them slipped inside and out the back door. Two others put down their beers and two picked up solid lengths of bamboo, the third hefting a wooden pick handle. Without a word, they started to fan out across the footpath toward Joey and me. A fourth man, overweight in a grimy white singlet, his hair lank and plastered to his fat skull, stayed seated and sipped quietly on his beer as he watched his boys move into position. I stopped short of the three thugs. Joey stopped next to me, on my right. I ignored the thugs and addressed myself to the fat man in the chair.

'I'm looking for Toh Luo-yang,' I said in Cantonese. 'Peter Toh.' The fat man didn't blink, he didn't move other than to sip again at his beer. 'I know this was one of his joints,' I said, 'and I know he's back in town…' I knew nothing of the sort but it was worth a try. 'Have you seen him?'

The fat man put down the beer bottle and took a long time to light a cigarette.

'Never heard of him,' he said from the chair.

'My name is Jones,' I said. 'Luo-yang and I worked together for many years. We… were friends.'

'You're boring me. I don't give a fuck who you are,' Fat Man said. 'So turn and walk away before something nasty happens to you and your slutty little biker chick there.'

I grinned faintly. That was a mistake Fat Boy, I thought. As if in agreement, I felt Joey bristle at my side.

'I just want to talk,' I said. 'Tell me where I can find Peter Toh and I'll leave you alone.'

The fat man stood up and sighed. '*Diu*, man,' he said, shaking his head. 'You're not listening to me. I tried to warn you. Just remember: you asked for this...'

He made a chopping signal with his right hand then turned and walked away through the small room and out the back door. As soon as he made the hand signal the three thugs moved in, fanning out a little more to take us from the front and sides. I slipped sideways to my left a couple of paces, giving Joey more room to move and to ready myself to go for the thug on the right of their assault line. He was closest to me and carried the pick handle.

From the corner of my eye I saw Joey throw off her leather jacket and reach around her back to draw out the ASP. With a snap of her wrist the baton extended and Joey took up a classic baton stance. These clowns would never see it coming, I thought. And they didn't. It was all over in less than a minute.

Pick Handle Guy came at me with a shout, swinging his weapon in a wide arc. As soon as he moved I sensed the other two surging in on Joey.

I easily stepped inside the thug's swing and grabbed his right arm, twisting it out and away. I spun and wrenched his arm savagely up behind his back. He screamed in pain and I punched him hard on the side of the head. He dropped the pick handle and collapsed to the ground like a marionette with its strings cut. To make sure, I bent down, grabbed a fistful of his T-shirt, raised him from the ground and punched him again, flush on the nose, driving the blow through as hard as I could.

His nose exploded and his upper lip smashed. I let him go and his head hit the ground with a dull thud. I stood and turned to help Joey.

One thug was already on the ground, motionless and the other flailed at her with his bamboo pole. Joey weaved to her right, blocked the blow with her left forearm and swung the ASP. The baton, true to its name, lashed out like a cobra and the black, high carbon steel cracked into the side of the thug's head with a sound like breaking tile. The thug's eyes rolled back in his head and he sagged to his knees then face first into the hard concrete.

'You okay?' I asked, panting hard.

Joey collapsed the baton and slipped it back into its pouch in a practiced motion. She took one look at the man at her feet, then snorted hard through the back of her sinuses and spat a gobbet of phlegm onto the prone figure.

'Fucking triads,' she said. 'I *do* hate them.'

'Stay here,' I said and walked into the small bar. The cook was standing there open-mouthed, a ladle in his hand dripping soup and noodles. I moved past him and flung open the back door. It lead into a small alley, congested with rubbish. There was no one in sight so I turned and walked back to Joey.

'We have to get out of here,' I said. 'Fat Boy has probably gone for the cavalry and they won't be far off. I can't hang around here waiting to flag down a taxi.' I pointed at Joey's bike. 'I know I'll regret this, but can you give me a lift to the MTR? I've got another visit I need to make this afternoon.'

Joey grinned and rolled her shoulders, pointing at the three injured and unconscious men on the footpath. 'I needed that! I'll take you where you're going. Where to?'

'Prudence's place up in Mid-Levels,' I replied. I looked dubiously at the sleek and powerful bike. 'Are you sure I'll fit on that?'

Joey crossed the road and pulled on her helmet. 'I've had bigger,' she said. 'Just sit still, hang on to me and don't scream in my ears like a bitch.'

She threw a leg over the bike and fired the ignition, gunning the engine in an aggressive snarl that echoed up the narrow street. I gingerly climbed on, fumbled for the rear foot pegs with my feet and gripped Joey tight around the waist.

'Are you comfortable, princess?' Joey shouted. I squeezed her once and we roared off, my head tucked against her shoulder and my eyes shut tight against the bike's speed and the blur of lights as Joey weaved the beast in and out of the manic Hong Kong evening traffic.

50

I STRAIGHTENED my shirt and ran a hand through my hair before ringing the doorbell. I felt that my face was locked in a serious frown so I consciously relaxed it and smiled lightly as the door opened.

Prudence's dark eyes widened as she saw me standing in the corridor and her face lit into a wide grin. She reached out and wrapped me in a warm hug. Her perfume was soft, discreet and faintly spiced. She was dressed in a pair of high-waisted denims that flared down the legs and a loose fitting T-shirt that slipped off her left shoulder and told the world to "Relax".

'Daaih loh, *big brother*,' she said with genuine delight. 'What a lovely surprise... what brings you here at...' she checked her slim Cartier watch, '...6:30 in the evening?'

She stepped back and ushered me in, still holding my hand.

I had been struggling with how I would approach this during the hair-raising run through Hong Kong on the back of Joey's bike and I still didn't know. I decided to play it very low key.

'Hi Pru,' I said, collapsing into her expensive and lush white Italian sofa. 'Just passing, thought I'd say hi. Any chance of a drink?'

She smiled knowingly and turned to a small, dimly lit bar across the room. I sat quietly and took in the magnificence of her apartment

– a place I had visited only a few times over the years. I had always thought I brought a grubby presence into the place that Pru – and certainly her friends – could have done without so I figured it was best to stay away.

The apartment was huge. With the size of the place, and the cost of Hong Kong real estate, it had to be worth in the tens of millions. But it wasn't just the scale of the place. The apartment was decorated in high-end Italian furniture, rugs, cushions and throws, and the eclectic mix of art – some Chinese, some Western – that hung on the walls was all gallery quality, each piece probably being worth more than my annual salary.

Looking past Pru and through a large floor-to-ceiling window, I could see the glow of Central and Admiralty, blinking red and green channel markers in Victoria Harbour and the lights of ferries that criss-crossed its dark waters, then the glittering Xanadu of lights in Tsim Sha Tsui and out northwards across Kowloon. The apartment smelled of fresh lemongrass and a soft swing tune played through artfully hidden speakers. Billie Holiday. My kid sister had really come a long way.

She turned back to me, holding two cut-crystal Old Fashioned glasses with what I hoped was a very expensive whisky in a least one. She passed me a glass and sat elegantly down on the sofa, her left leg tucking effortlessly under her. She moved with the grace of a swan and, for a moment, I couldn't speak.

'Mum and Dad would be so very proud of you, Pru,' I said as we clinked glasses.

She sipped at her drink then frowned. 'Are you okay Galahad?' she asked. 'Have you been drinking?'

I sampled the whisky in my hand and rolled it pleasurably around my mouth before swallowing it. I sighed. 'I'm fine sai mui, *younger sister*,' I said. 'Maybe a little tired. I was just thinking how beautiful you are and how clever and strong and successful...'

She laughed. 'My *God*! You have been drinking Gal! Knock it off...'

I chuckled along with her but my heart felt heavy. A feeling of deep dread smothered me as I sat looking at her.

I drank again at the whisky, deeper this time. 'I don't suppose I can smoke,' I said hopefully.

'No you bloody well cannot.'

I shrugged. 'Thought so...' I realised I was fidgeting. I affected to look around. 'Hey, where's Giles?' I asked.

Pru waved a hand in the air. 'Oh he's at work. He doesn't finish most evenings until quite late.' She looked sideways at me. 'Is this about him?'

'No,' I lied. She knew it.

'Darling, she said. 'You have a nasty, suspicious mind. It's in your DNA. You're just like Dad. You see ghosts and bad guys around every corner.' She was right, of course. It's who I am and that was my job. It always had been. I sat silently and let her go on.

'If this is about Giles,' she said 'why not just ask him? Call him. Go for a beer together. I really want you to get along with him...'

I squirmed a little. 'I haven't got his number...'

'I'll give it to you, Galahad,' she said. 'Anyway,' she continued 'you *do* know he doesn't live here. Right? He hasn't moved in. He doesn't even have a key but has a few things here. He lives at his own place... *Diu*, I need my own space Gal. Don't want another man traipsing all over my calm.'

'Where is it?' I asked as disinterestedly as I could.

'His apartment? Oh, in Sai Ying Pun.' She gave me the address. 'Renovated loft with a little terrace. Very... Spartan. Very *male*.'

'I like SYP,' I said. 'Dad lived there as a kid after the war.'

Pausing, I scratched my chin. 'Tough place to find a park, though. He must have a carpark in the building.' I felt dirty leading Pru on like that.

'Oh, he doesn't have a car,' she said. 'As far as I know he doesn't even have a Hong Kong licence. He says he can't cope with our crazy traffic... Gweilos hey?' she observed with a smile.

I nodded and took a breath. 'So tell me, I heard around the traps that "Giles" isn't his first name. Is that right...?' I watched my sister's reaction closely.

'See?' she laughed. 'There it is again! Galahad the copper. Seeing as you ask, no "Giles" is not his first name,' she said. 'It's "Richard" but everyone calls him "*Dickie*". He hates it! *And* he has one of those posh English double-barrelled surnames, but he prefers a shortened version.' She smiled. 'I think "Dickie" is cute...'

There it was. I knew there had to have been a straightforward answer to Alastair's brooding conspiracy. Giles had not lied to Prudence or, technically, to me. He simply had "name issues" like most of us. Nor did he drive and couldn't possibly have a vehicle such as the Trails Killer obviously used. I felt a fool for having even momentarily contemplated Alastair's wild theory. I promised myself I'd slap the old reprobate over the back of his bald head next time I saw him.

'Ha!' I said, amused. 'Dickie Wheel-Barrow... that doesn't surprise me!'

Prudence joined in, chucking throatily. 'Oh behave yourself, *Galahad*. You can't talk...' She checked her watch again. 'Look, Giles will be here soon I think... want to stay for another drink and dinner? I'm doing Singapore Noodles.'

I did want to stay. I wanted time with Pru and I had nothing to do. I had only Bors' company and a polystyrene box of roast duck and rice to look forward to, but I hated the whole "third wheel" thing.

'No, I can't Pru,' I said. 'Got lots on. Gotta go...' I swallowed down the last of the whisky and stood up. Pru walked me to the door. Standing in the corridor I turned to her.

'He *is* looking after you, right?' I said. 'Things are not good out there right now and I need to know you're safe. *Promise* me you'll stay safe. Don't take any risks. Don't go out alone...'

Pru leaned in and kissed me lightly on the cheek. 'I'll be fine, big brother,' she said. 'Really. And, yes, Giles is on the job. I would only be safer if I had you next to me every day.'

'Well, I'm not and that's what's worries me.'

She sighed. 'Don't worry, my love,' she said softly. 'Everything is going to be okay.'

I nodded and gave my sister a wink and walked off down the corridor, her door closing quietly behind me.

Life is full of those moments you wish you could take back and relive. Make better. I wish I had kissed Prudence on the forehead and stroked her long dark hair like I did when we were kids and she came to me with a scraped knee or a lost dolly. I wish I had told her I loved her and would always be there for her.

51

LEAVING my sister's apartment I wandered down the hill through Mid-Levels into Soho and, without thinking, found myself at the little Italian bar on Staunton Street. It was busy.

Expats crowded into the small space, drinking and talking and laughing. Lynyrd Skynyrd was playing, loud, over the top of it all and the place glowed yellow and warm into the cold December evening. I caught the barman's eye from the footpath and pointed at the beer tap, making a "large" sign with my hands. He knew me, nodded and smiled.

I knew I should have been thinking through the puzzle of hunting down Peter Toh and flushing out the Trails Killer but I was tired and I just wanted to switch off. I needed to clear my head, have a beer or two and just let the thought process work itself out. It always did. I grabbed my Peroni and moved out onto the footpath to get away from the crowd. I rolled and lit a cigarette and was taking the first pull on the beer when my phone pinged. I pulled it from my pocket and looked at the message. It was from Senior Sergeant Caesar Li.

Thought you should know. Guo Yu-xuan tried to kill himself this morning.

He didn't succeed and now in prison hospital. They're investigating

I replied.

How the hell does a prisoner in maximum security obtain the means to kill himself? Or did someone get to him?

Caesar replied.

I have no idea. Too many conspiracies! Calm down. Who would want to off him?

Me.

Chan for one...

Caesar.

You're an idiot! Come on man!

I thought the possibility of Walter Chan trying to get at Guo was a real possibility – I was sure Chan was up to something and silencing Guo would be a good option for him. I ignored Caesar's last message and dropped the phone back in my jeans.

A few minutes later I was halfway through the pint, and not paying attention to anything, when I felt a light tap on the shoulder. I turned.

'Are you avoiding me, Mr Jones,' Angel said, half seriously, her head tilted and an eyebrow cocked. 'I think you are...'

I smiled and reached an arm around her waist. She felt good. Slim and warm, and she leaned into me. 'Jesus, I'm sorry Angel. Things have been... busy the last few days. I meant to call but ...'

She laughed. 'I'm just teasing you.' She glanced swiftly over my shoulder then said 'I'm told your business trip to Manila was successful. Were there any difficulties in getting the job done?'

I shook my head. 'Not really. One or two minor things. That laptop Tommy Ho gave me didn't work,' I said using veiled speech for the useless Walther that had jammed on me. 'So I had to improvise...'

'So I heard. Apparently your client hasn't resurfaced, or if he has his company is keeping it quiet.'

I sipped at my beer. 'Drink?' I said. She nodded and I signalled the barman. 'Well,' I said quietly, 'I'm sure he'll pop up soon...'

'And then...?'

'And then his company will put his absence down to local issues. I'm satisfied I did everything I could for the client.'

Angel frowned slightly. 'You do know Jade Tooth is *never* going to leave you alone, right? He wants you dead. He's *not* going away...'

'I know,' I said. Jade Tooth had been an itch under my skin for years. I had thought, for a while, that it had gone but it kept coming back. I needed to do something about that, and it was going to take more than a cream from the pharmacy.

It was then, looking over Angel's shoulder that I spotted Chaya.

The young woman had certainly changed in the two years since I had last seen her. Gone was the terrified, wide-eyed girl who had been sex-trafficked out of Cambodia and in her place stood a lean, stern-faced woman. She was dressed from head to toe in black and watching the street around Angel like a hawk. I noticed she had a small, ornate tattoo on her right forearm; a Javanese design with the inscription "D-88" as the centrepiece. Densus 88. So I had been right about her trip to Jakarta and Megamendung. I looked back at Angel.

I already knew the answer but I asked anyway. 'Where's your protection team?'

Angel smiled and fluttered her eyelashes. 'You are looking at her.'

I nodded to Chaya. She didn't move, didn't blink. She looked at me for a second then resumed her scanning of Staunton Street and the crowds around her boss. I didn't know what skills she had picked up in recent months but I knew I didn't want to be in position where I found out.

Angel's drink arrived, along with another beer for me, and we clinked glasses and drank in silence. Angel spoke first.

'We haven't had any leads on the Trails Killer,' she said quietly 'I've thrown a lot of manpower at it and we have come up empty. It's like this guy doesn't exist. He's some kind of evil spirit...'

I rolled and lit a cigarette. 'Someone said to me today that the dragons had left Hong Kong. It feels like that. It feels like we are on our own while evil stalks our city... But he's not a spirit. He's very real.'

I dragged on my cigarette and blew the cherry-scented smoke skyward. 'He called me yesterday.'

Angels' eyes widened. '*Diu*! He did? What did he say?'

So I told her everything that had been said during the call, my subsequent call with Joey and our meeting with Michael Wong earlier that day. I told her of my theory about Peter Toh, and about Joey's and my clash with the triad thugs in Shau Kei Wan. Angel was silent for a long moment then she nodded.

'Okay,' she said. 'So we find Toh and we find the killer. Yes?'

'That's about the size of it.'

'Toh will be easier to find...if he *is* here. We know most of the holes that rat would run to. It has to be a Sun Yee On safe house or establishment,' she said, referring to the rival triad to her own 14K.

I butted out the cigarette.

'Maybe, but I have a feeling he'll be hiding out in a place even SYO don't know about. Remember, no one knew he was a triad plant for years. Not even someone with Jade Tooth's seniority.' I paused while I finished off the beer and belched lightly. 'But you're right. We have to beat the bushes and see if we can flush him out. It's the only thing we have to go on right now.'

Angel didn't reply. Instead, she rummaged into her Ferragamo bag and drew out a gold cigarette case, extracted a smoke and lit it.

She held her right elbow with her left hand and the smoke dangled between the fingers of her right. She tilted her head and studied me, a faint smile on her full, red-glossed lips. Not for the first time under her stare I felt like a goat facing down a tigress. I could tell what was on her mind. I glanced nervously at Chaya but she was studying two men talking on the corner of Staunton and Aberdeen. I looked back at Angel and held her stare. Finally, she spoke.

'You know,' she said. 'Either one of us could be dead tomorrow... although the smart money is on you going first. Lord knows how you've stayed alive this long...'

'Thank you. That's a cheery thought.'

'Well... what are we going to do?'

'About what?'

'About *us*, you idiot!'

I had been thinking the same thing for months but I played it dumb. I suddenly remembered her longing looks in Fountain Terrace Garden while she was pram and baby-watching. '*Us*?' I said. 'What do you mean...?'

She made that hissing-snorting sound Hong Kong women use as an exclamation when they're annoyed. In fact, they use it to express a range of emotions, but usually it's annoyance.

'Where are we going with *this*!' she said, waving her hand in the air to take in the two of us. '*Us*. What are we going to do? I'm not getting any younger – nor are you although at least *I* still hold my looks. We've been dancing around this subject for over two years and every time it looks like coming up you sidestep like a cow fighter swinging his cape...'

'Bullfighter...'

'Cow. Bull. Whatever...' She dragged furiously on the stub end of the cigarette and turned away. I stepped forward and wrapped my arms around her.

'I asked you,' I said 'to marry me two years ago, if you remember...'

'You were joking you imbecile!'

'I shrugged. 'Maybe I wasn't...'. Angel looked up into my face, her dark eyes were deep pools and I fell into them. 'I love you, Angel,' I said. 'I always have. You know that, but there are... complications in our lives that keep getting in the way. We need to work through those...'

'What complications?' she breathed.

'Well for a start, you are a senior member of 14K triad. I am an ex copper trying to stay straight – well, as straight as I can. *And*, as you said, right now it looks like I could be found floating face down in the Harbour at any time having been bumped off by any number of nasty means.' I sighed. 'It's not a great time to be talking domestic bliss...'

Angel pushed me away. Her face was flushed and her eyes narrowed. 'I can't walk away from the Society. You know that. It's an oath for life. *But*, I *have* stepped back a lot the past year and I've done that for *you*.' She sighed deeply. 'What I am, what I do, none of that matters, Galahad. None of it matters if we matter to each other...'

I was starting to panic. I could see her walking out of my life if I messed this up and I knew I couldn't live with that. She was right. We mattered to each other and to hell with convention and what others thought about an ex-copper and a triad girl. I gently pulled her back into me, our bodies melding warm and comforting.

'Angel,' I said again. 'I love you. Let's just get through this thing with the Trails Killer, Jade Tooth, Peter Toh and Michael Wong all chasing me. I need to find Joey's kid and I have to stop the killer before he hits closer to home. I promise when that's done we'll talk and we'll make plans...'

Angel pouted and punched me lightly on the chest. 'Okay. You go and do that, superhero, and when you're done I'll be waiting for you – just don't take too long!' She gave me a little shove. 'I hate you,' she said moodily. 'And I love you...'

She had never said that before and I swallowed hard.

She stood on tiptoes and brought her face close to mine. I could feel her warm breath in my ear and smell the intoxicating scent of her. I was defenceless.

'Now... shall we go to your place?' she murmured.

I nodded dumbly. Angel dismissed Chaya with a word and the young woman stalked away done Aberdeen street after first shooting me a scowl that would strip paint. I paid the bill by throwing a few hundred on the bar, then Angel took me by the hand and led me off into the night.

52

THE NEXT MORNING, I rose early and left Angel snoring lightly in bed, her hair fanned out across the pillows and one long, brown leg wrapped around the rumpled duvet. Bors cannoned into me as I shuffled into the kitchen to make a coffee so, sipping at the hot espresso, I dressed quickly, clipped Bors to his leash and set off to walk him around Happy Valley Racecourse.

It was another typical Hong Kong December morning. It was cool and the air had a fresh, crisp feel to it – the sort of air you love to suck down deep into your lungs. Helpers strolled up Wong Nai Chung Road, chatting quietly while they walked pampered little dogs and here and there an expat mother pushed a pram through the kaleidoscope of shade and light along the footpath.

They were mowing the racetrack at Happy Valley and the smell of fresh-cut grass wafted sweet and pleasant up the road, while birds called raucously as they flitted from tree to tree in their hectic early morning routine. A jogger passed me at pace, puffing loudly but rhythmically, his arms pumping in sync with strong, tanned legs. I felt a twinge of guilt but was happy at the sedate pace that Bors set us both as he sniffed and snuffled his way along. It gave me time to think, and I needed that.

The killer held all the cards and our search for him was a desperate race against time that would be unlikely to yield any result unless we got lucky. Real lucky. Michael Wong and Alastair Chard were both right – Penny was as good as dead. The only hope we had was that the killer would keep her alive long enough to suit his purpose.

Which was what exactly?

Revenge still seemed to be the motivator and it was beginning to look like it was Peter Toh's revenge, so the questions were what revenge exactly, and how long would it take to play out? Why hadn't the killer agreed to a meet and a swap; me for Penny.

The disembodied voice rang loud again in my head: *I am going to destroy you but I am going to take my time doing it. I am going to take you apart, piece by piece.* He wanted me to suffer so a quick ending to it wasn't part of the game plan.

Was Jade Tooth the killer? When I pulled at the threads of *that* question it seemed to me more and more likely he was. He had motive, he was an associate of Peter Toh, and was certainly capable of the disgusting acts of violence the killer was inflicting on his victims. But what of Toby Sanderson? He seemed a fit too – and where was he right now? Why had he dropped out of sight?

Bors stopped to sniff at a tree then pee against its sturdy trunk, his wide mouth grinning in delight. I gazed down at him. Peter Toh. It had to be him. It was the only sense I could make of any of this. We had to find him but searching for an individual who wants to stay hidden in a city of 7.4 million souls seemed an impossible task.

And what of Guo Yu-xuan and his daughter? I still had to follow that up. I had a strong sense of a deeper wrong at the heart of Guo's rushed and emotional attack on Walter Chan; and I knew I couldn't rest until I had discovered what it was.

I sighed and tugged gently at Bors' leash, heading down the road and past Hong Kong Football Club. With Guo, the Trails Killer, Jade Tooth, and Michael Wong, my dance card was full and I felt I had no control over the direction or timing of events. I had never liked not being in control – it was an unpleasant feeling.

53

I LOOKED up from my desk as the door was flung open and Joey stepped in, balancing two takeaway coffees and Danishes in a cardboard tray. She kicked the door closed with her heel, crossed the office and placed a coffee and pastry on my desk. She wrinkled her nose.

'You've been smoking in here!' she accused.

'It's my office and I'll do as I please,' I said.

'Adele will murder you when she finds out.'

'Adele's not here and won't be until the New Year. By then the place will have aired out and she'll never know...'

'Oh, she'll know,' Joey said with a faint grin. 'The old battleaxe *always* knows about everything...'

I took the lid off the coffee and sipped at it, the earthy aroma of the Robusta wafting headily around me. I picked up a piece of paper from the desk and waved it at Joey who was slouched on the old Chesterfield across the room.

'While I was waiting, I made some notes,' I said. 'It's every place I can remember Peter Toh having mentioned, or that I knew, was a hangout of his. There are 37 on the list, and they're scattered all over

The Island and across Kowloon-side. Some are known SYO joints but many are not – they're just small bars, restaurants and a shop or two.'

'How many each side of the harbour?' Joey asked.

I glanced at the sheet. 'About half each,' I said.

Joey nodded. 'Okay,' she said. 'We're obviously going to have to split up to get this done as fast as possible.' She pulled out a coin and balanced it between thumb and forefinger of her right hand. 'Call.' She flipped the coin, spinning it into the air, and caught it deftly onto the back of her left hand.

'Heads,' I said.

Joey peeked under the handed cupping the coin and looked up at me. 'Tails. I win. I'll take Kowloon...'

'Would you have told me if it was heads?' I asked.

'That's for me to know and you to ponder...,' Joey said and took the sheet of paper out of my hand, snapping off a picture of it on her phone. Next, she crossed to the safe and, crouching down, spun the lock dial. I munched on the Danish, watching with interest. With a click the locks disengaged and she pulled the heavy door open. She held up the two Glocks in their Fobus paddle holsters.

'I know what you are going to say,' she said, as if daring me to challenge her. 'You've never carried on a non-approved task and you don't propose to start now. Right?'

I swallowed the mouthful of pastry and wiped my mouth. 'Right.'

'And I'm telling you put that out of your head. This is *serious*. By my last count at least three very dangerous men want you dead, probably along with me, your sister and...' Joey's voice stumbled a little, her throat tightening. '...and Penny,' she finally whispered.

She threw a holstered weapon across the room followed quickly by two loaded 15-round magazines. I snatched them out of the air like I was juggling hot rocks, the remains of the Danish clamped between my teeth, and placed them on the desk in front of me.

I nodded. 'You're right,' I mumbled around the pastry, loading a magazine into the handgun. 'It's a serious offence to go armed in public in this city but I've got an excuse even Michael Wong couldn't argue with...' I stood up and fitted the holster to my right hip and pulled my T-shirt and puffer jacket over it. I eyed Joey for a moment.

'Why are you so keen to do Kowloon-side?' I said.

She didn't look up while she loaded her Glock and dropped it into its holster that she fitted home under her leather jacket. Finally, she shrugged.

'I've got a sense that Penny is over there somewhere. This fucking animal has my girl hidden away deep in Kowloon, maybe even New Territories. Toh's also over there – I'm sure of it. I want to find him and when I do I'll make him talk...'

I didn't tell her of my fears that we would find neither Peter Toh nor the killer and that Penny's tortured little body would soon turn up on the side of a hiking trail.

'Well,' I said grimly. 'Let's get out there and do just that.'

Joey and I left the office, its door slamming locked behind us and jogged smoothly down the stairs and out onto Ko Shing Street. Joey pulled on her helmet and flipped up its visor as she straddled her bike.

'Don't get dead, boss,' she shouted from inside the helmet's protective case and gunned the bike's engine into life.

I nodded and crossed Ko Shing Street, dodging deliverymen and their trolleys piled high with boxes. I was headed to Queen's Road West and the first of Peter Toh's bolt holes on my list – a small trinket seller, and former con, a few blocks west near Tung Wah Hospital.

54

FIVE HOURS later I had criss-crossed The Island from Causeway Bay to Pok Fu Lam, and Aberdeen to Chai Wan. Every step of the way I felt the prickle of unease that told me I was being followed.

I had seen nothing unusual but I always listened to my instincts and they rarely let me down. Someone was tailing me. They were doing it well and staying their distance. I doubted they were waiting for an opportunity to pounce – there had been many and nothing had happened – so I figured they were just watching me, wanting to know where I was going and what I was doing. It could have been one of Michael Wong's men and it could have been the killer. There was nothing for it but to carry on with the checklist in the hope of flushing out Peter Toh.

I had checked tobacconists, bars, jewellery sellers, a hardware store, a bakery, a cardboard recycling plant and even a foot massage joint. I had knocked on the doors of seven tiny apartments and had spoken to five wet market grocers, two butchers and a fishmonger. The reaction of everyone I spoke to was the same. Every time.

As soon as I mentioned Peter Toh's name, faces went from open and smiling to closed and inscrutable, and I would be dismissed with an angry wave of the hand or, in the case of the butcher, a cleaver being raised into my face.

I had called Joey and she had the same result. On the upside, Joey had tailed a kid who had been sent as a runner shortly after Joey left a market stall in Yau Ma Tei. She had lost him in the nearby maze of alleys and side streets but it was a positive sign.

It was clear to us Peter was back in the city – his network knew it and they were zealously covering his back. We had drawn a blank but I had the feeling that, like a line of beaters in the jungle, we were moving in on the tiger and driving him out of the thicket. When he broke out, the army of informants we had on the streets would notice and we would throw the net over him.

I was back in Sheung Wan and heading to the last address on the list, a small courier business with its office in Soho. It was cold, the sun having given way to a grey, cloudy afternoon. A chill wind blew down the tunnel formed by the tall buildings on Queen's Road West and streetlights were coming on against the early gloom of late afternoon.

My hands were stuffed deep into the pockets of my puffer jacket and my feet felt cold and leaden in my lightweight desert boots. I could feel the reassuring bulk of the holstered Glock, nestled cold and deadly in the small of my back. I had just crossed Possession Street, by a fruit shop and small roast joint, heading east when my phone rang.

My heart lurched briefly as I snatched the phone from inside my jacket. Was the killer calling me? I checked the phone screen and this time my heart didn't lurch, it seemed to stop for a beat or two. The contact details of the caller stood out large and bright on the phone screen and my breath was taken away as if I had been punched hard in the gut. Peter Toh.

I took a deep breath and answered the call. 'Peter,' I said. 'It's been a long time...'

The voice on the phone cackled, a dry rasping sound. It sounded only faintly like Peter but it *did* sound like the figure Bors and I had chased in Wan Chai weeks before. So it had been him I had seen after all. I had stopped on the footpath and was staring into the oncoming traffic as I spoke, headlights shining in my eyes.

'Yes, Galahad,' Peter said. 'A long time...'

'What happened to your voice?'

A brief pause. 'Oh, a small incident with a knife in Taipei not long after I saw you last. It damaged my throat...'

'It's a shame it didn't take your fucking head off, Peter,' I said.

He had run to Taiwan after being exposed as a Sun Yee On triad deep plant within HKPF. I had done the exposing and it had very nearly cost me my life. It made sense that Peter had fled to Taiwan – a lot of Hong Kong criminals did. With no extradition treaty between Taiwan and Hong Kong, it was next to impossible for Hong Kong authorities to get their hands on fugitives who had made it to the island state.

'Where are you?' I said.

'Turn around and walk back to the corner of Lok Ku Road...'

I did as I was ordered, the phone held to my ear. I could hear him breathing as I walked. It sounded like someone gargling river sand. At the corner of Kok Lu Road I stopped.

'What now?' I said.

'Look up the stairs Galahad,' Peter said, his voice cold.

I looked up Ladder Street. It is a long staircase of hand-chiselled granite steps leading up to Hollywood Road and Man Mo Temple. The stairs reach even further up the hill to Caine Road, almost at the very top of the hill on which Mid-Levels squats overlooking Tai Ping Shan and Victoria Harbour. I could see him clearly in the early evening, although dusk was settling. He was standing under a light on Upper Lascar Row, looking down at me and, as I watched, he raised a hand slowly in greeting.

'Hello Galahad,' he said, lowering his arm. 'I know what you're thinking: can I get up the stairs to him before he reaches his car and disappears? You can't, so don't bother trying...'

I had been thinking just that. I knew exactly how many of the steep steps there were to where he stood then a short burst further uphill to Hollywood Road where he, doubtless, had parked his car. I knew because I ran those stairs often and I knew I would not get to him in time.

'Why are you here, Peter?' I asked. I knew the answer but I wanted to hear it from him.

'I'm sure that's obvious to you by now, Galahad,' he said. 'I'm here for revenge. You owe me for everything you ruined: my plans, my career, my life, the millions of dollars I have lost. I'm back to claim what's mine. I'm back for *you*.'

'So you *are* behind the Trails killer,' I said. '*You* gave him my number. He's your man...'

'He's *no one's* man, Galahad. Yes, I've used him as a tool – first with the Thomas' and now to destroy you – but I've unleashed the beast. I can't control him so don't bother asking me to call him off. Even if I wanted to do that – and I don't – I couldn't. He's unstoppable now, a remorseless, implacable killing machine.'

'Tell me where he is, Peter,' I said. 'It's not too late to do something good. Tell me *who* he is.'

'No, Galahad. I can't do that. I'm enjoying myself too much watching you run around the city like a madman. You will *never* find him – nor will that idiot Michael Wong.' He shifted the phone to his other hand. 'But rest assured, Gan-Li, he said using the Cantonese abbreviation of my name 'he will reveal himself to you when he is ready to do so. When it suits his purpose and maximises his... excitement.'

'Peter,' I said. 'This is between you and me. Call him off and we'll settle this, just the two of us. No one else needs to die for this...'

'Oh but they do, Galahad,' he said. 'Others *have* to die before you do – or maybe you won't die and I'll just leave you to live with the agony of their deaths. I haven't decided yet.'

I knew who he was talking about. 'If you come near my sister I'll kill you, you bastard, and I promise you I'll make it slow.' I took a breath to control myself. 'Just let Penny go... Please. She's just a kid, this has nothing to do with her.'

'Your whore sister and that little brat of Joey Loh's are bonus tiles in this game,' Peter said, his voice icy. 'One of them is Spring and the other is Autumn. One may yet live and start afresh while the other will surely die like the falling leaves. Like any good player, I will set these aside and keep them near my other tiles to add to my score when I win the hand. And I *will* win.'

By now I was judging the distance between me and Peter. 62 stairs, probably less than 50 metres. He had another 33 stairs to Hollywood Road. Could I reach him in time? I tensed myself and shifted my left foot slightly forward ready to launch.

Peter stopped talking and lowered his phone.

We stood staring at each other like two old dogs, battle-scarred and hackles raised. We had been friends for many years. Close friends. But that had ended years ago and now he was back to close the book. There was only one way for this to end: one of us had to die, and I was determined it would be him. I took a deep breath and sprang forward, taking the stairs two at a time, my eyes locked on his.

He seemed to take a five count then turned calmly and walked swiftly up the stairs behind him. He was on Hollywood Road and turning the corner before I had even reached where he had been standing. I surged upwards, my chest aching as my lungs struggled to draw in enough air to drive my muscles on. 70 stairs. 74, 78, 83... 95.

I hit Hollywood Road and sprinted around the corner just as a black Tesla with Macau plates whirred past me, Peter behind the wheel and grinning widely. I considered drawing the Glock and putting rounds into the back of the car, but pedestrians up and down the road prevented that. I stopped, my hands on my knees, dragging in deep, ragged breaths as Peter Toh disappeared around the bend and out of sight.

I had lost him but, while he held what looked like a winning hand, I had never been one to throw a game of Mahjong. I would play this through to the bitter end.

55

THE TAILLIGHTS on Peter Toh's car had barely disappeared from view when I pulled out my phone and called Prudence. I checked my G-Shock. 1830. 'Pick up. Pick up,' I muttered.

'Hi, Gal,' Prudence's voice. I heaved a sigh of relief.

'Pru, listen to me. Don't interrupt,' I said hurriedly. 'Pack a bag. Make it light enough to carry but you'll need at least a week of gear. Keep it simple. Grab your passport. You're going away. I'm going to call a friend and have a car sent over. I'll have a flight booked for you and will message you the details. You're to stay in the apartment and open the door to no one until the driver arrives. He'll identify himself with the name 'Sparrow.' When you get to the airport he will escort you through check-in and see you into security. You'll then go straight to the Cathay First Lounge, take a seat facing the door and wait for the second boarding call before you move to your gate.' I paused. 'Have you got all that?'

'Gal,' she said quietly. 'What's happening?'

'There's no time to go into detail, sis, but it's the Trails Killer – he's coming for you. You have to get away.'

Prudence sucked in a breath. 'Oh my God, Galahad! What? *Why*...?'

'No time, Pru. Just do as I say. Do it now.'

'Okay,' she said. 'Look, Giles will be here at 9:00 – we were going to dinner. He can come with me to the airport and see me off. I'd be happier knowing he was with me.'

I thought about that for a moment. 'I hear you, but no. The driver won't want to be seen by anyone else and you'll be safer with him than anyone I know. Call Giles, tell him what I've just told you. He can join you later if he wants but right now it's critical you move fast.' Pru was silent. 'Do you read me, Pru? Promise me you'll do as I say...'

'Yes, daaih lo, *big brother*,' she said. 'Reading you loud and clear. Make my flight somewhere nice, will you? Love you. I'll be in touch. Pru out'

I began to say I loved her too but she had already hung up.

Next I called Tommy Ho. I told The Panda about my encounter with Peter Toh and gave him a description of the Tesla then ran through the requirements for a First Class flight for Prudence to anywhere his people could secure a ticket within five hours flying. I told him I wanted him to pick my sister up, gave him the nickname and instructions to see her through to security at HKIA. He told me he would do one better and escort her to the First Class Lounge, sit with her until the boarding call then escort her to the gate.

I didn't ask how he could do that but wasn't surprised The Panda could seemingly wander at will in and out of the international airport. Tommy told me it would take an hour to set everything up and that he would message me the flight details before he picked Pru up around 1945.

'Look after her, Tommy,' I said.

'With my life, Mr Jones,' the burly gangster said quietly and hung up.

A minute later I called Michael Wong. There was never any chitchat with Wong, he was always "on" and this was no different. The phone answered after two rings and the cop's voice sounded clear and calm down the line.

'What have you got?' he said

'I've just seen Peter Toh... in Central.' I described the conversation, what I had observed and the fact that I had made a try for Peter but that he had evaded me easily.

'So this confirms our theory,' Michael said. 'It's Toh behind all of this, and we know he's back in town. Give me a description of the car – if he hasn't dumped it we'll be able to run him down.'

'Tesla, Model 3. Black. Light coloured interior. A dent and scrape above the left front wheel. Macau plates...' I recited the vehicle registration from memory.. I could hear Michael tapping at a keyboard, running a vehicle check. He responded in seconds.

'Macau registration, owner is Macanese. The vehicle was reported stolen in Repulse Bay yesterday. I'll pass it to Traffic Branch and Information Systems Wing to run a scan through the city's traffic monitoring CCTV and alert all mobile patrols. If he is still with the car we'll have a location on him in under an hour.

'Michael,' I said. 'He admitted the killer is working for him, that he set him on this path. He's coming after my sister. I've called some friends to get her out of the city. I don't give a damn about me, but we have to protect her...'

He was silent for a minute and I could tell he was wrestling with the difficult choice of coming after me and my triad links or keeping me on side and going after the Trails Killer. He made the right choice – as I knew he would.

'Okay,' he said finally. 'This is all a bigger issue between you and me that we'll deal with *after* we nail the killer. For now, we do whatever it takes to get this asshole. Agreed?'

I didn't answer but hung up and slipped the device into my jacket. I walked quickly along Hollywood Road to the Aberdeen Street hill and up to a quiet little bar on Elgin Street. I needed to gather my thoughts and I badly needed a drink. Seeing Peter Toh again, although unsurprising, had shaken me and there was no denying it: this was all going to end in blood. It was 6:45 p.m. Exactly an hour later my world fell apart.

56

I WAS RUNNING. Running as fast as I could up the steep hill that led deep into Mid-Levels. My chest hurt and I was sucking in deep breaths as I drove my legs on. Prudence's apartment was further up the hill and I glanced at my watch as I ran. Four minutes. Four minutes since I had hung up the phone from Tommy Ho and sprinted out of the bar, ignoring the broken glass at my feet and the cries of the barman.

~

At 7:45 p.m. The Panda had called on the secure messaging app and I had nodded as I picked up my phone, thinking everything was going to plan.

'She's not here,' he said without introduction. 'I've been ringing the bell and no answer. There are no sounds from inside.'

My blood had chilled and my stomach lurched. 'What the fuck do you mean she's not there?' I demanded, unable to think of anything to say that would make sense.

'She's not here. She is *not* in the apartment,' Tommy said. 'What now?'

I thought for a moment, trying to push down on the wave of panic that was threatening to choke me. 'Okay. Get down to the parking basement. Check if her car is there. She might have gone to pick up some last minute things… It's a green Mini Cooper S.' I gave him the registration plate number.

Tommy acknowledged, said he would call me back and the line went dead. I stood up and started pacing in circles, rubbing my hands through my hair in frustration. My pulse was racing and I kept telling myself it was going to be okay. Tommy would find her in the garage, retrieving something from her car. It was going to be okay … The phone rang again.

'I found the car,' Tommy Ho said. 'It was unlocked and the driver's door is open. I found her phone under the car.' He paused and drew breath. 'There's something else,' he said ominously. 'I found a hypodermic needle cap in the car. She's been drugged, Galahad. She's gone.'

I clenched my eyes tight and thumped a fist into the table top. My beer bottle jumped and tumbled to the ground, shattering in a spray of amber liquid and slivers of glass. My mouth was dry and I could barely get the words out.

'Stay right there,' I said. 'I'll be there in seven minutes.' With that I had hung up and raced from the bar.

I checked my watch again. Five minutes. Prudence's apartment was on the corner of the next block. The hill steepened and I leaned into it, pushing myself the last 100 metres. My heart felt as if it were about to leap from my chest and my right knee was on fire. I ran on.

Suddenly, I was at the corner and without pausing burst through the doors of the apartment building and into the lobby. I waved away the concierge and stabbed at the lift button. In what seemed like an age, the lift arrived. It was lit brightly and warm. I stabbed again at the lift buttons, sending it to the parking basement, and seconds later ran out into the dimly lit garage. Controlling my breathing, I looked left and right but could see neither Prudence's car nor Tommy Ho. I was about to call his name when I heard his voice off to my right, two rows of cars down.

'Over here,' he said, raising a hand.

'What have we got?' I said, as I reached him. He pointed silently at the green Mini Cooper S and stepped back.

Beside the car, preserved in a small patch of engine oil on the garage floor, I saw the imprint of the toe and part of the heel of a running shoe. It was large, a men's size 44 or 45. The print had been twisted slightly as the offender had stepped out of the oil and to his right. In front of the oil patch, closer to the car, were clear signs of a smaller shoe being dragged first backwards then to the left. The oily footprint moved away from Prudence's car, its shape becoming fainter and less distinct until it disappeared altogether about six metres away, just short of a now empty parking space.

I looked up to the garage ceiling and scanned around. As expected a CCTV camera was only metres away but it was angled mostly away from Pru's car. I looked to the right and there, 20 metres away, was another camera pointing right at me. That was good; we were bound to get some solid evidence from both cam's footage as well as the camera that was aimed at the exit ramp to the carpark. I turned my attention back to the car. The driver's door was ajar so, grabbing a corner of my T-shirt, I gently pushed the door open and leaned inside.

The orange plastic hypodermic cap lay on the floor of the driver's footwell, just beside the brake pedal. Pru wasn't a drug user nor was she using syringes for any medical reason. It was clear the cap was from a needle, probably a 1ml syringe, that had been used to sedate her.

I ran my hands between the driver's seat and centre console, stopping as my fingers brushed against a sharp metallic object. I grasped it with my fingertips, drew it out and held it up to the light. It was Prudence's car and apartment keys on a small, decorative key ring. From their position between the seats, she must have had them in her left hand and dropped them as she was grabbed from behind.

I pulled a tissue from the box in the centre console and opened the glove compartment. There was nothing in there besides the usual rubbish most people keep in the glove box: registration papers, tissues, a nail file, a spare phone charging cable, two lipsticks and the parking stub from a mall in Causeway Bay. Turning my head, I checked the back seat. It was clear, as were the rear footwells.

I shuffled backwards out of the car and glanced at Tommy Ho. He was standing silently, watching me, waiting for me to speak. I moved around to the rear of the car and, using the keys, opened the boot. Empty reusable shopping bags, a yoga mat, a small umbrella, and a gym bag with a towel and half empty drink bottle, a pair of running shoes and a sports bra.

I walked back around the car to Tommy Ho and held out my hand. Without a word, he passed me Prudence's phone. The screen was cracked and I noticed the phone was unlocked – unsurprising for Pru who had always complained about the inconvenience of unlocking a phone whenever she wanted to use it. I had argued endlessly with her about that but had never won the point.

I opened her Phone app and checked the recents list. The last call had been outbound to "Giles T". I tapped on the information icon beside the call and saw that it had lasted 15 seconds – long enough for Prudence to have left a voicemail. The call below that was an incoming call from me. Other calls to and from Giles littered the recents list, along with calls to and from names I did not know, presumably Pru's friends and clients. Nothing stood out to me there.

Next I tapped on the green Messages icon and brought up her list of recents. Her last message had been to Giles, telling him she tried to call but could not get through and of our plans to fly her out. There was no reply. There were a few earlier messages to girlfriends – all innocent looking enough – and one to her hairdresser then the list got too long for a quick scan. There didn't appear to be anything of note on the phone and I was about to pocket it when I decided to tap on the photo of me in Pru's message favourites. As soon as I opened the contact I could see an unsent message in the text box.

Big brother just to tell you I love you. I'll miss you, see you soon. XXX. P

I pressed send and my phone pinged instantly as her message landed. I had no idea when she had tapped out the message but it had to have been shortly after we last spoke. For some reason she had decided not to, or had been unable to, send it. My throat constricted and my eyes blurred. But it wasn't sadness or grief; it was a red murderous rage that had descended over me, and I clung tight to it.

I felt as if every muscle in my body was flexing, growing, and I was morphing. I felt stronger than I had in years, my mind cleared and my senses seemed sharper. I was ready and I longed for what was to come. I would find Peter Toh and his pet lunatic and there would be no arrests, no rights, no trial. There would be only vengeance, violence and death.

Fifteen minutes later, having checked through Prudence's apartment, The Panda and I were standing on the road in front of the apartment building. I had called Michael Wong and he and a team were on their way. Tommy did not want to hang around for that. I was smoking and pacing – it helped me to think. Pru's apartment had been clean. There had been no signs of any forced entry, no signs of a struggle. Her bag had been packed and was sitting at the end of her bed but, for some reason, she had gone down to the parking garage, to her car, and it was there she had been taken. Tommy Ho coughed politely.

'We *will* find this guy, Mr Jones,' he said. 'I know we will. Toh can't stay hidden for much longer and when we find him, he won't be able to withstand the questioning. He *will* reveal the killer's name and location.'

I nodded. 'Sure, Tommy,' I said absently. It was hard to order my thoughts. 'We have to find Peter Toh and we have to find him quickly. Neither Pru nor young Penny have time we can waste.'

I kept telling myself I would find my sister. I had to hang on to the thought that I would get to Prudence in time – anything else was too horrible to consider.

Tommy and I were talking in low tones, working out our next steps involving all the 14K assets at his disposal, when a red taxi pulled abruptly into the kerb. The door swung open and Giles stepped out, looking up and grinning widely to see me. The grin was instantly replaced by a frown. Tommy Ho nodded to me and turned his back on Giles to walk away down Castle Road.

Giles watched Tommy's back for a second or two then turned back to me. 'Galahad! Hi,' he said. 'Why so serious? What's up?'

'You better come inside, Giles,' I said. 'We'll talk in there.'

Giles checked his watch. 'I got here quicker than I thought,' he said. 'Pru's still here, right? I couldn't let her go on this crazy jaunt without saying goodbye...'

I turned and walked back into the building with Giles following me silently, a puzzled look on his face.

57

IT WAS quiet on my terrace. A lot had happened in the past two days and I was sitting in the lowering sun of the late afternoon trying to make sense of it all.

I was still shaking and was nursing a large whisky. Bors sat in his usual place at my feet, listening to the evening birdsong in the trees of the primary school across the laneway. It was peaceful, bucolic. A far cry from the events of recent days. It would have been easy to forget, just for a moment, that a vicious killer, a stone-hearted murderer, still stalked the streets of Hong Kong and had, as events had proven, taken my sister. I shuddered and drank deep at the whisky, but I could still taste the vomit in my mouth.

The conversation two days before with Giles had been difficult. We had gone up to Prudence's apartment, sat across the dining table from each other and I had told him that Pru had, almost certainly, been taken. He had blinked rapidly and his face flushed. Both his hands were clenched into fists on the top of the table. He was shaking his head in denial, saying 'No' over and over. Finally he rubbed his eyes and lowered arms to the table, one hand wrapping the other.

'How could this have happened?' he had demanded, his voice brittle with anger.

I said, 'It looks like she was grabbed in the garage when she went to her car to get something while she was packing...'

He pointed at me. 'This is *your* fucking fault!' he hissed. 'If you hadn't come up with the crazy plan to fly Pru out of the city she wouldn't have even been in the garage – she'd be with me, right now, at dinner.' He paused, thinking.

'Wait,' he said. 'How did this maniac know Pru would *be* in the garage? How did he even get in there in the first place?

'I'll answer your second question first,' I said. 'The garage has public access for visitors to the building. As to how he knew she would be there, he didn't. He probably sat in there for hours, hoping to have a chance at her – I mean it's a fair assumption she would have gone to her car at some time.'

Giles nodded. He was calming down and I could see he was thinking hard. 'Okay,' he said finally. 'I assume you've been working with the cops for a while on this...' He shook his head again. 'Jesus, you should have *told* me. I could have protected her better.'

He had a point but I wasn't going to take a lecture from him. 'Maybe,' I said. 'Maybe not. It's not as if we have much to go on. This guy is a ghost. He's smart. He's done this before and he knows how to stay under the radar. What little we knew was all speculation.' I paused. 'Until today, that is.'

'What do you mean? Giles asked.

'I found the man who has unleashed this maniac – or, more to the point, he found me. It's the first confirmation we have on who is behind this and why...'

'So who is it and *why* is he doing this?'

I shook my head. 'That's something you do *not* need to know. You can get as pissed off as you like but I'm not going to tell you. What's important is that we may yet get our first breakthrough on the killer.'

'How so?'

'He had been sitting in a vehicle, waiting for Pru. A car or a small van. We've always assumed he had to use a van. The Taskforce will be here soon and they will run through the building CCTV. We should get a clear look at the attacker and his vehicle. He's made a big mistake and it could be his undoing...'

Giles had been quiet for a moment. 'Maybe he didn't have a choice,' he said. 'Maybe this other guy stepped up the schedule... maybe the killer himself did that and took a chance, knowing you'd probably still be unable to find him.'

I looked at him. 'Why do you say that?'

Giles shrugged. 'I don't know... just maybe that's what's happened. Less he made a mistake and more he wanted to up the ante. Apply the pressure. You said he was smart. Maybe he's defying you and the cops to put the pieces together...'

That was a perceptive comment. I had never said Giles was stupid, just arrogant. I sat silently and let him talk.

'I mean, let's look at this thing so far,' he said. 'He's killed, what, six people around Hong Kong and the cops have nothing to go on. It looks to me like he's outwitted all of you...'

'I'll remind you, Giles,' I said, my teeth clenched. 'he has taken my sister, *your* girlfriend, so rooting for him isn't an approach I want to hear from you right now.'

That hit home, and Giles looked shocked. 'What? No! That's not what I meant... I was just saying...'

'The best thing you can do, Giles,' I said 'is keep your theories to yourself and let the professionals deal with this. We will find him and we will take him down. You can be certain of that.'

Giles' face reddened and I could see his jaw working. He was angry but I didn't care. He swallowed and seemed to bring himself under control. Looking chastened he said:

'Sorry, I didn't mean it that way.' He paused and pulled at an ear lobe. 'So has the killer contacted the police? You?'

I wasn't sure how much I should tell Giles so I answered but kept it vague.

'Yes, he has. He has called me. Once.'

Giles leaned forward. 'So trace the call. You must have a number.'

I shook my head. 'It doesn't work like that. He's using what are called burner phones or a different sim card every time he makes a call. It makes it nearly impossible to get a lock on the call location.'

Giles' eyes widened. 'Jesus! You've *spoken* to him. What did he say? What did he sound like...?

'That's another thing you don't need to know, Giles. What I can tell you is the police have now locked down the sale of phones and sim cards across Hong Kong. Every seller must register and report the full details of the buyer to the Taskforce. Anyone buying burner phones, more than one phone or a number of sim cards will be flagged and pulled in.'

Giles nodded. 'Yes, that makes sense,' he said. 'Good move. That will make things difficult for him *if* he wants to continue communicating – and I get the feeling he does.'

Again I asked, 'What makes you say that?'

He shrugged. 'I guess just because he's doing this for some sort of recognition. It's maybe a contest for him. My guess would be he wants to keep talking to rub it in, keep you running in circles.' He sighed. 'You're right. You're the expert on this. What do I know? Look, I just want to help so let me know what you need me to do.'

There wasn't much he *could* do and I certainly didn't want him blundering around the investigation, but I decided to go easy on him. He was just as upset and shocked at Pru's abduction as I was.

'Look, Giles,' I said. 'Sorry. I didn't mean to dump on you earlier. I'm sure you can help in places. Maybe we can get you out looking in some areas of interest we identify. I mean Hong Kong is a big city...' I had no intention at all of doing that.

He sighed and smiled hesitantly. 'Thanks Galahad. I appreciate it. I'll do my best, I promise...'

'We'll stay in touch by phone,' I said. 'I don't have your number...'

'My old phone is broken,' he cut in. 'No idea what's wrong. I've bought a new one today and only gave Pru the number this afternoon – just before ... before..' He broke off and hung his head. His big frame seemed to shake with a silent sob and I looked away, embarrassed. He gathered himself and pulled a phone out of his pocket.

'What's your number?' he asked. 'I'll send you a text.'

We had swapped numbers and I was tucking my phone away when the doorbell rang.

Crossing the room, I let Michael Wong and a team of three investigators into the apartment and made the introductions. Michael shook Giles' hand, studying him closely.

'It's a pleasure to meet you, Mr Tyler,' he said, gripping Giles' hand for an uncomfortably long moment. 'So you are Ms Jones' boyfriend?'

Giles gingerly pulled his hand away and rubbed it hesitantly on his pants leg. 'Yes. That's me,' he said with a handsome smile. 'I have that great honour...'

Michael nodded, unsmiling. 'Well, I am sure you won't mind answering a few questions then. Just procedure, you understand...'

Giles blinked. 'No, not at all Chief Inspector. I would be happy to help in any way. What sort of questions?'

Michael winked at him then. I had never seen Michel Wong wink. What was he up to?

'Oh, that would be telling, Mr Tyler,' he said. 'I will leave you in Sergeant Kwan's capable hands. Good evening.'

Giles nodded and smiled. Michael and I had then walked down to the carpark with one of his team while Kwan stayed behind to interview Giles and eliminate him as a suspect – just procedure as Michael had said – and the other cop remained in the apartment to give it the once over. By the time I returned to lock up Prudence's apartment, the cops and Giles had gone.

The following morning I had taken a call from C.I. Wong as I was drinking a coffee and preparing to hit the streets for the day. There was good news and bad news.

'Give me the bad news first,' I had said.

'The Tesla was found burnt out last night in the back of Quarry Bay. Toh has disappeared and we've got nothing. No sighting, no intel. Nothing.' I heard Michael sigh into the phone. 'All those years on the Force and I never knew he was this good...'

Quarry Bay, I thought. That made sense and explained why Fatty and his band of men in Shau Kei Wan were so jumpy. 'Oh, he's good,' I replied. 'Don't underestimate him. I did once and it nearly killed me. Anyway, he can't just disappear – he's good but he's not Kuei-Shen, some nature spirit. We'll find him Michael, I'm sure of it.'

Michael grunted and I continued. 'So, what's the good news?'

'We hit the jackpot on the CCTV from Prudence's apartment,' Michael said. 'Well, almost jackpot. First the vehicle: It's a white Hyundai commercial van with Hong Kong plates. There are probably 20,000 of them on the roads out there. Unfortunately the plates were both partially obscured with mud but we can make out the two letters and two of the four numbers. The techies are spitting out a list now of all the possible combinations currently registered. We'll get a match very soon.'

'And the attacker?' I said. 'Any luck?'

I could hear Michael flipping pages in his notebook. 'Male, big. About your size. Has to be a gweilo...'

'I'm not,' I interrupted.

Michael sighed. 'You're not what?'

'Not a gweilo. And *I'm* big... you just said so yourself.'

'You're only quarter Chinese Galahad – at best,' Michael said patiently, as if speaking to a five year old. 'That makes you three quarters gweilo. Anyway not only the size but he moves like a gweilo... you know, kind of lumbering? Our guy is big and powerful. That fits with jaw size from the victim bite marks and hand size from victim bruising.'

'So, did you get a look at him?' I asked.

'No,' Michael said. 'He was wearing a long, black coat, gloves, a beanie of some sort pulled down over his forehead and ears, and one of those damn face masks...?'

'A surgical mask?'

'No, one of those Buff things. Pulled up over his nose. His eyes are visible – he's definitely *not* Chinese – but being black and white footage we can't tell the colour.'

'Anything else?' I asked quietly. I sensed Michael was holding something back.

He was silent for a long moment. 'You were right about Prudence being drugged. She could walk, but barely. He half carried her to the back of the van. And… something else.'

'Go on,' I said, a cold edge creeping into my voice.

'He assaulted her pretty bad. Slapped her around to quieten her down while the sedation took effect, then four punches – that we can see. Three in the face and one… one between the legs.'

I had gripped the phone then as if I were strangling the life out of it. A red mist lowered again over my eyes and my heart rate soared. My G-Shock beeped out a pulse alert. I ignored it, embracing the rage that consumed me. Relishing it. I stabbed at the phone and hung up the call.

That day, and most of the next, had been spent in a fruitless search across Hong Kong for a sign of the girls and Peter Toh. Joey and I were looking for anyone who might have seen something, anything, but we came up empty.

The match on the Hyundai van had come through the afternoon of my call with Michael Wong and licence plate analysis had revealed the presence of the van close to all four kill sites at the time of the murders. The breakthrough gave us renewed energy. The Taskforce, and the rest of HKPF, now had a description of the van used by the killer although the owner had been discounted as a suspect, the van having been stolen shortly before the first killing. Every cop in Hong Kong knew about the van and they were turning the city upside down in a race against the clock to find it.

At one point, Joey had tried to talk to me about Pru's abduction but I had shut her down. I knew Joey was suffering the loss of Penny and maybe she just wanted to talk. *I* didn't want to talk to anyone about it and the last thing I wanted was an exploration of my "feelings". I knew what I felt and I didn't want to share that rage and hate with anyone. I wanted it all to myself.

Early in the afternoon of the second day I had taken a brief call from Tommy Ho. The Panda didn't say much – they were still checking things out – but he seemed confident they would narrow down the search for Peter Toh in the next day or two. I had no idea how they would do that and didn't ask. I only wanted the result. It had given me hope to think we could be close to bringing down the man behind this nightmare. I clung to that hope like a drowning man clutching at a plank of water-logged timber. And then the box had arrived.

I had returned home shortly before and was feeding Bors when my doorbell rang. It was the apartment building manager and he passed me a small package, telling me it had been left on the doorstep at the secure front entrance. I thanked the manager and closed the door.

The package was small, about the size of a smartphone, and was wrapped in plain, brown paper on which my name and apartment number were written in black marker pen. It was tied with thin, white kitchen string that had been wrapped neatly across and lengthways and was finished off in a bow. I put the package down on the kitchen bench and studied it for a moment before tugging at one end of the string bow. It came undone and I ran a thumbnail into the neatly folded and taped end of the brown paper, pulling it aside and tearing the wrapping away.

Inside was a brown cardboard box.

It was thick, good quality, the sort of box you gave your girlfriend a necklace in. I lifted off the lid and there, sitting inside the box, nestled in cotton wool, was a human finger. It was a woman's finger. The nail polish still glowed bright red but the butt end, where the finger had been cut away with a pair of secateurs or a heavy knife, was discoloured purple and green. It gave off a faint odour of rotting meat. A small bead of blood sat in the cotton wool like a precious stone and matched the small ruby inlay of the slim gold ring that still circled the pale and wrinkled finger. The ring had been our mother's and Pru never, ever took it off.

I had gently placed the lid back on the small box and took a deep breath. My stomach suddenly clenched and I had bent over the kitchen sink and threw up, the vomit hot and bitter in the back of my throat.

After throwing up in the kitchen, I spat out the last of the vomit from the back of my throat, wiped my mouth then grabbed a bottle and a glass and walked unsteadily out onto the terrace. I was pouring a long glass of whisky when my phone vibrated inside my puffer jacket. Holding the glass with my right hand, I clumsily reached into the left pocket of the jacket and pulled out the phone. I drew a breath when I saw it was a Hong Kong mobile phone number, not in my contacts. I started call recording. It was him.

'Hello,' I said, my voice firmer than I felt.

The strange robotic voice, cold and empty, clicked onto the line. 'You got the box,' it said.

'Yes. You delivered it. Didn't you.'

'Of course, Galahad. Personal service. Check the CCTV... but you won't see anything.'

'You fucking animal,' I growled. 'I'm going to find you and I'm going to kill you...'

'Oh, I doubt that. You're not in my league *Mr* Detective. Besides, the lovely Prudence will be long dead, even if you do. So why bother?'

'I will make it my life's work to find you. You will never be able to rest knowing I'm out there, hunting you.'

The voice chuckled. 'Admirable sentiment. Brave. I do admire persistence...'

'Peter Toh. I know he's your master. I'll find him then I'll find you...

'No one is my *master*,' the voice said, its volume raising and distorting. '*I* am the master of my own destiny and *I* am the master of this game...'. The line was silent but I was sure I could hear a faint whimpering in the background. The voice spoke again.

'There will be further special deliveries, Galahad' it said. 'I'm going to return your sister to you after all. Piece by piece.'

The anger rose in me and my pulse raced, my eyes clouding over. 'You're a pathetic, grovelling creature, you fucker! You're going to scream when I have my hands around your throat...'

There was a pause. 'Oh. Scream? Do you mean like this...?'

There was a shuffling and the phone clicked once, then the sound of the phone being put down. Then a scream, long and agonised; a primal, animal shriek that tore at my insides and chilled my blood. A moment's silence then another long shriek and I caught the sound of Prudence's voice calling my name.

The phone clicked again and the voice said, 'Now *that's* a scream,' and the line went dead.

I dropped the phone with a clatter and collapsed onto a chair, holding my head in my hands. I reached for the bottle and poured and swallowed a glass, then another. Tears ran hot down my face while rage and grief battled each other for dominance deep in my soul. I pushed Grief aside and grabbed Rage into a close, hot embrace vowing I'd never let it go. I reached down to the small table beside me and snatched up the bottle again, pouring another long shot into the glass that I threw back in one big, desperate gulp.

58

My tongue stuck to the roof of a dry mouth and my head pounded.

Behind my Wayfarers my eyes blurred and teared, and my chest felt hot and congested. I had woken that morning on the cold, hard tiles of the terrace where I had collapsed, drunk, after a bottle of whisky that had taken me deep into the night. At some time during the night I had opened up the fresh scar on my right cheek and a line of bloody scab now crossed my face. The fingers on my left hand still felt numb but were starting to ache as I warmed up in the weak December sun. I wondered if I had frostnip.

My phone was ringing and I fumbled for it in my puffer jacket, the pedestrian crowds on Canton Road moving smoothly around me, avoiding eye contact, as I stood there dishevelled and angry. It was Michael Wong and he sounded excited.

'We've got the van,' he said.

I shook my head to clear the fog. 'Where is it?'

'A beat cop was asking around and found it after a local resident mentioned seeing something unusual. It's in an old garage on an abandoned industrial lot in Kwai Chung...'

I checked my watch. 'I can be there in about 20 minutes,' I said. 'Can I take a look before forensic start work?'

Michael paused, thinking. 'I shouldn't,' he said. 'But we're talking about your sister and we *are* working together on this. So yes. Get here quick and I'll give you 5 minutes with the van.'

Michael gave me the address and I hung up, throwing an arm into the air just as a red taxi approached up Canton from the Star Ferry Pier.

Sixteen minutes later I stepped from the taxi onto a dirt road, leading into the former factory allotment. The building was ramshackle and coming apart at the seams. Rusted corrugated iron sheets hung from the roof, exposing the concrete floor and stripped-out walls to the elements.

As I crunched across the gravel of the weed-choked driveway, pigeons clattered up from their roost, scattering feathers and dried bird shit everywhere through the abandoned building and across the broken-down machinery. The sun glinted off steel and through what were left of the windows, blinding me momentarily despite my dark sunglasses. I blinked and rubbed my temples. I needed a cold Coke but that had to wait. Michael Wong waved to me from the other side of a line of police tape stretched across the doorway of a small garage.

Stepping under the tape I nodded at Michael who handed me a pair of disposable overshoes and white surgical gloves.

'He called me again last night,' I said. 'I'll send you the recording.'

Michael nodded. 'Yes I know. We picked up the incoming number but couldn't get a fix on it. I really thought we could break through with his calls to you, but my tech geniuses tell me it's not that simple.' He shrugged. 'We'll keep at it... Anyway, what did he say?'

'I recorded it,' I said, my throat constricting. 'The usual stuff. He was torturing Pru and he wanted me to hear. I don't want to talk about it.'

Michael stood silently. There was nothing he could say that would make any difference. I turned my attention to the overshoes and gloves. As I was slipping them on, Michael spoke.

'Your boy, Mr Tyler...'

I looked up from trying to pull a disposable overshoe onto my boot. 'He's not my boy...'

Michael shrugged. 'He doesn't like police, it seems.'

That caught my attention, I slipped on the second overshoe and stood up. 'What makes you say that?' I said as I snapped on the surgical gloves.

'Just something Sergeant Kwan said. Mr Tyler was ever-so pleasant and cooperative but under that perfect smile of his he was jumpy, nervous. His answers to Kwan's questions were terse and dismissive. Evasive.'

'Giles thinks he's the smartest man in the room so I'm not surprised he was dismissive of Sergeant Kwan. And not everyone, Michael, has experience with being interviewed by police in the disappearance of their girlfriend. I would have been nervous too.'

Michael nodded. 'Yes, perhaps.'

I stared at the taciturn detective; my face creased in a deep frown. 'Is there something you're not telling me Chief Inspector?'

'No...I just don't think I like the guy. I felt it when we shook hands.' He tugged at an ear lobe. 'I'm sure it's nothing... but we're looking at him.'

I looked sceptically at Michael as he gestured me into the garage with a sweep of his hand. 'You know the drill,' he said. 'Don't pick anything up and don't get into the van.'

The garage wasn't a garage after all, but more a large, concrete storage room with a roller door. The van was parked at the rear of the space. It had been driven straight in and the back doors of the van were open to me as I approached.

My shoes crunched through broken glass as I walked carefully forward, observing my foot placement in relation to the obvious large footprints in the dust and grime on the floor. I stopped at the open doors, flipped my Wayfarers to the top of my head and peered into the rear of the van.

The rear windows were covered in black plastic, and a large roll of gaffer tape sat against a clear plastic bag that was filled with rag cut-offs. Next to the rags lay a 3 litre plastic bottle of bleach. Two boxes of disposable surgical gloves, one box opened and a glove sticking out from where the killer had last snatched a pair. A half-drunk 1 litre bottle of water and a roll of thin-gauge tie wire. In the centre of the van lay a discarded length of quality red cord, its smooth strands expertly twisted, a piece of the barrister robe bag still attached to one end where it had been hacked away with scissors or a knife.

At the rear of the van two overstuffed black garbage bags, one of which was knotted at the top, the other open and leaning over to expose bundled up clothes. A length of dirty carpet lay along one side of the van with a grimy, yellowed pillow at one end. Hanging from the van roof on a piece of fishing line, a small toy clown, its eyes plucked out, slowly spun in the light breeze blowing into the garage.

There was blood everywhere. It was as if someone had taken a bucket from the abattoir and sluiced down the inside of the van with it. It was on the floor, sprayed up the walls and spattered across the roof. I leaned in a little and peered closer at the right hand side of the van, just above the wheel arch. Turning to Michael Wong I held out my hand.

'Pass me a torch please,' I said.

He nodded to a uniformed cop who unclipped his duty torch and handed it to me.

Switching it on I played the beam of light over the wheel arch. There, in the dried blood on the lower part of the van wall, someone had scratched two letters. "PJ". I took a deep breath. Prudence Jones. Despite her pain, despite being bound and drugged, my sister had managed to scratch her initials in the dried blood as a desperate message to us she had been there. I snapped off the torch and turned around.

'She was in here,' I said, pointing at the initials.

Michael peered in then nodded. 'Your sister, and probably young Penny, aren't the only ones to have been in this van. I mean, look at it. He has killed in there. That means there are more victims out there – we just haven't found them yet. I'm afraid,' he said pointing into the van 'something terrible has happened to the girls and it happened in there.'

I looked at Michael without answering.

He sighed then said, 'I know this asshole is careful, but there just has to be something in here for forensic to find.'

'Maybe some hair?' I suggested.

Michael shook his head. 'No. Well maybe, but we won't be able to extract nuclear DNA from it. We'd need hair with roots, in the growth stage, and it would need to be very recent. Much over a few days and it's useless. I'm hoping for a good old-fashioned fingerprint. Surely there has to be at least a partial in there somewhere...'

I gestured over my shoulder with my head. 'What's in the front?'

'Nothing.' Michael said. 'At least nothing I can see... I'm pinning my hopes on the boys and girls from Forensic.'

I nodded. 'Okay,' I said. 'What about the location? What does it tell us?' I paused to gather my thoughts. While I did so, I gazed into the dark green hills that rose above where we stood. I thought a minute or two more then pointed east.

'This place is bloody close to both Kam Shan and Lion Rock Country Parks. An easy walk up into the forest. It would have to be close for him to stumble-carry Prudence. The jungle is remote, quiet. An ideal place for a bolt hole.' I stopped and rubbed my eyes. My blood was coursing and I was thinking more clearly but I still felt like death warmed up – it was hard to concentrate.

Michael passed me a bottle of water. 'You look like shit. More than usual...' I thanked him and drank deeply.

'There's just no way,' Michael said looking up at the hills. 'No way he could stash two wounded, unwilling people in an apartment without being noticed. No way he could wander about covered in blood without someone saying something. It has to be the jungle.'

I told him then about the finger in the box. 'He probably took it off in the back of the van, then boxed and delivered it after he hid Prudence away – probably the same place he's holding Penny. All of that in such a short time frame means his hole *has* to be close'

Michael sucked in a breath through clenched teeth. 'I am very sorry, Galahad. But we have to expect more of this. He is mocking you... us. I'll need that box.'

I nodded absently. 'Yes, of course. It's in the fridge at home. Send a car around for it later today.' I leaned against the wall of the garage and rolled and lit a cigarette. 'Close,' I mumbled. 'What's close to here once you get into the jungle?'

Michael shrugged. 'Hiking trails...?'

'Yeah, and what else? What is scattered around many of the trails, in particular in Kam Shan?'

Michael looked blankly at me for a moment then his eyes widened. 'Fortifications! World War Two fortifications. Bunkers, tunnels.... Gin Drinkers Line and Shing Mun!'

The Shing Mun Redoubt, a 12-acre citadel situated underground on the northern part of Smuggler's Ridge, formed a critical part of the Gin Drinkers Line, a badly built defensive line of trenches, fighting pits, pillboxes and bunkers constructed in the mid-1930s to defend against an expected Japanese attack from the north. The decisive action during the Japanese invasion of Kowloon had been fought at the Shing Mun Redoubt.

After several hours of fierce close-quarter fighting on the night of 9 December 1941, the Redoubt was taken by the Japanese. The Japanese invasion of Kowloon and Hong Kong was another story, but Michael and I stared at each other as the pieces started to fall together.

It made sense. The killer was using a remote hole in the jungle, probably part of the old Line, in which to hide and from which, like a spider, he would emerge to entrap and kill his prey. He had Penny and my sister in that hole.

Michael grabbed out his phone. 'I have to make a call,' he said. 'I need to get onto GFS and get a chopper allocated immediately. We'll need FLIR. With that, and a team from SDU. We will find him and soon!'

I nodded and dragged on my cigarette. A helicopter, flying a low-pass grid search over the area, reaching out with its Forward Looking Infrared, would pick up any human movement above ground. Then it would be a simple matter to drop in a team from HKPF's Special Duties Unit to corner the killer and take him down. I had no doubt C.I. Wong could get the assets – the hunt for the Trails Killer was the highest priority mission for HKPF in years. For all that, I still felt powerless.

Time was against us. The killer, if he *was* holed up underground somewhere on Gin Drinkers Line, would be taking my sister apart, piece by piece, while we flew blind and unknowing overhead. We had been lucky in the days since Prudence was taken but we needed more than luck now if we were to track down and capture this beast in time. We needed a miracle.

59

THE SEAFOOD RESTAURANT opened up onto Nanking Street in Jordan.

After Michael Wong and I had examined the van I had prowled Kowloon looking for clues to Peter Toh's whereabouts. Joey had done the same and we had met once or twice to compare notes during which I told her about the van, and we discussed the Shing Mun theory. She had agreed it made sense and I could see her eyes light up at the thought we might be getting close. But, again, we had come up with nothing in the search for Peter Toh. Then, late in the afternoon, as the sun was beginning to set and cold shadows were being cast by the tower blocks on Nathan Road, I had taken a secure call from Tommy Ho.

'Our man is seeing a girl in Jordan,' he said in Cantonese. 'He's been each evening the past three days at around 6:30. He goes in for about an hour then comes out, grabs a cab and disappears.'

I couldn't believe it. After all this time and effort, all the dead ends, it was this easy. 'Who's the girl?' I asked

'We don't know exactly. A working girl. She's a hooker for SYO. Young.'

'Any chance we can track down the taxi drivers?'

'Cannot, Mr Jones. That's like finding a grain of rice in the harvest.'

'So it has to be the girl's place.' I checked my G-Shock. 5:15. 'Message me the address and apartment number.'

'Will do. You don't want me to deal with this...?'

I shook my head, although The Panda couldn't see it. 'No. This is all me. I want this bastard and I don't need help.'

'Suit yourself,' the gangster had said. 'We will stand by and do the clean-up.'

I had moved quickly to get from Shek Kip Mei to Jordan and now I was seated at an outdoor table, my cap pulled down low over my eyes, drinking quietly from a bottle of Tsing Tao. A plate of razor clams sat in front of me, but I only picked at it. My focus was on the steel security door across the street that led up into a small apartment block, just off the corner of Temple Street.

The Night Markets were open, and trade was brisk. Crowds wandered up and down Temple Street, browsing the goods on offer, now and then picking a piece and haggling with the stall owners. The restaurants up and down the street were full and early evening diners were enthusiastically tackling their meals. Laughter rang up and down the street and the shouts of the restaurant ladies calling out the orders was a comfortable din. I sipped at the beer and checked my watch. 6:20.

I rolled and lit a cigarette, slowly trickling the cherry-scented smoke from my mouth as I stared fixedly at the door.

The heavy frame of the Glock prodded the small of my back, nestled in its holster, and I discreetly touched the hem of my puffer jacket to make sure it was covered. My mind was blank. I was thinking nothing, focussed only on the street and the door like a gundog on a grouse. I took up the bottle and drank the last of the beer. The neck of the bottle was still raised to my mouth when I froze.

Peter Toh walked quickly down Nanking and paused at the door, his eyes roaming the street. I lowered my head, my cap covering my face, and peered at him from under the brim as I pretended to read the menu on the table. He turned, pressed the intercom button and spoke briefly. The door clicked open, and he disappeared inside. The door began to swing closed behind him so I leapt up and sprinted across the narrow street, getting a foot in it before it clanged shut.

I eased the door closed behind me and stood in the tiny entrance, looking up a flight of steep stairs. I could hear Peter's footsteps treading heavily up them. I held my breath and finally, faintly, I heard a knock on a door, Peter's voice then a woman's as a door opened. The door closed. I ran lightly up the stairs to the second floor and stopped outside the apartment, breathing rapidly, my mouth open.

The landing was dark, and I stood there straining to hear the voices inside. In less than two minutes I could hear the woman groaning and deep, masculine grunts. I moved in front of the door and, taking a deep breath, kicked out hard, planting the sole of my boot square on the cheap door handle. The door exploded open with a crash, and I stepped inside, drawing the Glock in a single, smooth movement.

The woman was bent over the back of a small sofa, her panties around her ankles and Peter Toh, his shirt off and pants down, was thrusting away vigorously behind her. He froze as the door crashed open and the woman screamed, grabbing up her dress to cover herself. Slowly he turned around. He looked ridiculous. His cock was shrivelling in surprise and fright, and his fat belly jingled under his flaccid chest. I pointed the handgun at him.

'You got fat, Peter,' I said quietly. I waved the Glock at a chair in the corner of the room. 'Over there. Sit.'

He bent to pull up his underwear and pants.

'*No!*' I barked. 'Leave them,' and he shuffled comically across the room to sit clumsily in the chair. His eyes were alight with hate and his face was tightened in a scowl. I glanced at the woman.

'Get out,' I said in Cantonese. 'If you know what's good for you, you saw nothing. Heard nothing.'

With a quick look at Peter, she slipped into her dress, stepped into her flop flops, and ran out of the broken door and down the stairs. I turned back to the man in the chair, the flab of his belly covering his cock, his hands gripping the armrest of the chair.

'What happened to you Peter?' I said. 'All your skill, all the work to stay invisible for two years, all the tradecraft over so many years.... Gone, so you could dip your wick.' I shook my head. 'Fucking pathetic.'

He said nothing and glared at me balefully.

'Nothing to say for yourself?' I said. 'That's unusual. Where's the Bond-villain monologue you're so fond of?'

Still silence. I stepped forward and raised the handgun. 'Okay,' I said. 'Let's keep this simple. Where is my sister?'

He snarled at me, his lips pulled back to reveal a mouthful of yellowed teeth. 'Go fuck yourself, Jones,' he rasped.

I shrugged. 'So you want it to play like that. Suits me. In fact, I'd prefer it that you did.' I stepped into him and whipped out the handgun, crashing the barrel against his temple. His skin split and blood flowed quickly down his face and into this eyes.

'I'll ask you again: where is my sister? I can keep this up all night, Peter.'

He spat on the floor at his feet. 'You think I'm going to just *tell* you? Just give up because you're *hitting* me? You're as stupid as I always thought you were. Look at you! The brilliant Galahad Jones, shitting his pants because he can't find his sister who is, as we speak, being carved into thin slices...'

I hit him again, harder, the butt of the handgun smashing into his mouth. His head rocked back, and he groaned. He leaned forward and spat a gobbet of blood, and two teeth, onto the threadbare carpet of the room.

'We found the van, Peter,' I said. 'It's just a matter of time now. We *will* find him.'

He looked surprised at that but quickly gathered himself. 'You won't find him – no one *ever* finds him. Haven't you figured that out yet?' he shouted. 'And it doesn't matter if you *do*! Your sister and the kid will be long dead by then.'

I hit him again with the Glock. Once, twice. The skin on his cheeks split like an overripe Pomegranate and blood flowed from a deep gash on his scalp.

'You can kill me, Jones,' he mumbled through his torn lips. 'But I'll never tell you. Your slut sister is going to die and there's nothing you can do about it, except know I did it! *Me*!' He started to laugh, the blood bubbling from his mouth and over his chin.

I looked down at him, the man who had been my close friend for so many years, and sighed. He wouldn't tell me. It was all part of his revenge.

Raising the Glock I fired a single shot into his face. The round took him on the bridge of the nose and the back of his skull blew out, spraying his brains grotesquely over the grimy wall at the back of the room. Peter Toh was dead.

Bending down, I picked up and pocketed the expended casing then left the room, closing the broken door gently behind me. Back out on the street I rolled and lit a cigarette, dragging the smoke deep into my lungs. Tommy Ho and two other men were standing idly by on the other side of the street. They had large duffle bags slung over their shoulders and were wearing black disposable gloves. The big gangster crossed to me; an eyebrow cocked in inquiry.

I nodded. 'It's done,' I said. 'He's upstairs. Clean it up.'

'Consider it done,' he said. 'He'll never be found.' The Panda looked closely at me in the weak streetlight. 'Are you okay Mr Jones?'

I dragged again on the cigarette. 'I'm fine, Tommy,' I said as I crossed the street without a backwards glance. I dropped a few hundred dollars on the restaurant table and, weaving my way through the crowds on Temple Street, walked off toward the MTR and home.

60

THE NEXT DAY, the fourth day following Prudence's abduction, I awoke at 4:00 a.m. after a largely sleepless night, my bedsheets sticky with sweat. What little sleep I had stolen had been tortured by dreams of blood and death. Prudence had appeared to me, dressed in a long, white gown that I instinctively knew to be a sacrificial vestment. She was standing on a large, marble alter her left arm held out, pleading with me. The gore from the missing ring finger of her right hand dripped thick. A fly gorged itself on the boned, bloody stub. I tried to reach her but I couldn't move. I was mired in a thick jelly I couldn't see but that anchored my legs in place. When I tried to call out to her I was mute. All I could do was stand and watch as piece after piece was cut from her by a figure in a black cassock with a deep cowl covering his head and face. Prudence didn't scream but her beautiful dark eyes, wide with fear and pain, called to me to stop the agony, to save her. All the while the cowled figure cut and sliced and laughed...

I swung my feet to the floor, groaning, and shuffled into the kitchen to make a coffee. Switching on the espresso machine, I turned the apartment lights on and stumbled into the bathroom. Bors didn't move from his bed as I shuffled past. I glanced briefly into the mirror and winced at what I saw. A haggard, desperate man with wide, crazy eyes stared back at me so I broke eye contact and stepped into the shower, bowing my head to let the needles of hot water massage me back to life.

Showered and with a pair of jeans and a parka thrown on against the cold, I stood on the terrace sipping the espresso and smoking my first cigarette of the day.

The dark of the pre-dawn, and the silence that wrapped my neighbourhood, cloaked me in a protective blanket. It was peaceful and I felt my mind begin to ease, just a little. I dragged in deep, long breaths feeling the chill night air refresh me and fire my blood. Bors padded out to stand beside me, the nails on his paws tick-ticking across the terrace tiles. He looked up at me and I scratched his ear and rubbed his powerful snout.

Above me, a car was speeding silently down Peak Road, its headlights blinking in and out of the forest as it negotiated the bends and curves, the driver revelling in the early morning freedom of the notorious Boy Racer strip. Drawing another deep breath, I pondered what the day would hold and made my plans.

Peter Toh was no longer a tile on the board so that was one less thing to deal with, although I knew I'd have to continue to play Michael Wong – and everyone else – that I was still searching for him. That was another secret I would have to take to my grave. They were starting to pile up. But Toh's death brought us no closer to finding the killer – hopefully a Eurocopter EC155 with FLIR and a good pilot would do that but I had my doubts.

My mind suddenly went blank and I found I was staring into the dark, a voice in my head telling me to concentrate, listen. I walked inside and made another coffee, rolling and lighting another cigarette once back on the terrace. I sipped at the strong black brew and dragged deeply on the smoke, absently stroking the ruff around Bors' powerful neck and shoulders.

I froze , the coffee glass midway to my mouth, as the words "fit all the pieces" suddenly echoed in my head. Only two people – both associated with the case – had used that phrase in my hearing in recent weeks. One was Morris Ngan. The other was Giles Tyler.

Giles had said that to me when I had first met him nearly six weeks previously. He had been gushingly admiring of my investigative skills and it had embarrassed me at the time. Then Professor Ngan had said it – the killer wanted to prove he was smarter than me, that I couldn't "fit all the pieces together." Then Giles again, only four days previously, had said it. I suddenly remembered a third person had used the phrase. During the call in Manila the killer had mocked me for "having trouble putting the pieces together."

I dragged on the cigarette and shook my head. Could it really be possible? I could see Alastair's faraway look at the FCC and hear him giving voice to his crackpot theory that Giles could be the killer. Was it so mad? Now that I thought about it, standing there in the predawn silence of Wan Chai, it seemed to me it wasn't.

There was something about Giles that had pinged my antenna when we had first met. He was loose and seemed consumed by a deep anger going back to his childhood. He was a loner, highly intelligent and supremely arrogant – like the killer – and he was a Brit who had arrived in Hong Kong shortly before the Thomas murders. He seemed to come from nowhere... and, unlike anyone else in this case, he had had close and immediate access to Prudence for weeks, having met her just before the first killing.

The last time I had spoken to Giles he had seemed to be applauding the killer's ingenuity and the fact he was always a step ahead of us. Lastly, Prudence had disappeared less than two hours after telling Giles she was flying out of the city to parts unknown and, the last I heard, he didn't have a convincing alibi for his whereabouts at that time. I dragged at the tail-end of the cigarette.

'Jesus Christ,' I muttered. I flicked the butt away into the dark and shook my head again, this time slapping myself lightly on the face. It *was* mad. Everything I had just ticked off in my mind was, at best, circumstantial. Even Michael Wong and the Taskforce, while "looking at him" weren't that hot on Giles as a suspect.

I had not a single shred of evidence to point to Giles as a key suspect in any of this and I was doing the worst thing an investigator could do – shoehorning in a suspect to fit the narrative. I had seen the way Giles looked at my sister, the way he doted on her. He was obviously deeply in love with her. The guy had been utterly broken when I had told him Prudence had been taken and had almost wept while pleading for me to let him help in the search. No, I was still half asleep and conjuring up fantasy. I shook my head and finished the coffee.

The back streets of my neighbourhood were starting to come alive. Hundreds of birds called to each other, singing the rising of the sun over Mount Butler and Jardine's Lookout, and a faint pink twinge ran through the sky like a stroke from a painter's brush.

I pulled the parka tighter around me as the temperature suddenly dropped, heralding dawn, and stood watching the light start to wash across the shadowed, dark green hills above me. Soon, the first rays of sunlight blazed into the windows of the tall hotel tower a block away, dazzling me so that I raised my hand to cover my eyes. With one last look around, I picked up my coffee glass and moved inside.

I had no idea then of what was to come during the day I had just seen born. After months of effort and the frustrations of the hunt, the case would be blown wide open – and all because of two simple mistakes.

61

I FINISHED a late breakfast at the small restaurant on the corner of Wan Chai and Morrison Hill Roads, then jumped a tram heading west and took a seat on the wooden bench beside an old lady clutching a string shopping bag. Michael Wong had called while I had been eating, with news the air assets had been allocated and they had done their first pass the night before. There had been no sign but another mission was scheduled for the early afternoon and again that night.

'I want in if you spot him,' I had said.

'With the SDU team?' Michael replied. 'No way. I can't authorise that. It will be a specialist mission and I can't have you blundering around in it. You're not trained...'

'Listen, Michael. I can look after myself and I won't get in the way. It's my fucking sister. What would *you* do?'

He had sighed and I waited, idly watching the buzz of the restaurant around me. 'Okay,' he said finally. You can ride along...'

'And Joey Loh...'

'*Diu* man! Anything else?'

I spooned a dumpling into my mouth. 'No, that's about it.'

'You better be ready to get to the helipad in under 20 minutes from when I call. SDU have a team on standby and they won't wait.'

I had thanked Michael and hung up. It was interesting, I thought, how his attitude to me seemed to be warming. I didn't for a moment think he wouldn't still pursue me over the triad cash the moment he had a chance. The Chief Inspector was a determined investigator and he was like a dog with a bone when it came to me and my links to 14K.

I shuffled along the bench a little to give the old lady some room and she smiled at me. I nodded and pulled out my phone. Tapping Joey's contact I waited while the call connected. The tram clanked its way down Johnston Road past Southorn Playground.

'Any news?' Joey asked without introduction.

'You and I are riding along with SDU if the FLIR sweeps pick anything up in Kam Shan. I'm heading to the office now to prep our gear. Can you meet me there?

'I'll be there in half an hour,' Joey said and hung up.

I dropped the phone into my pocket and caught the old lady staring at me. I smiled at her. 'We're going for a picnic,' I said. 'Lovely day for it.'

62

THE OFFICE WAS cold and I had turned on the two ancient steam heaters. They burbled and groaned but, after a while, I could feel some warmth seeping into the frigid room. I sat in the old Chesterfield and scanned over the equipment I had laid out on the dark wooden floor.

A black tactical vest lay at my feet. Attached to its Molle was a utility pouch for a torch, two 9mm magazine pouches, a pouch for a First Aid Kit, a black SOF Tactical Tourniquet, and a hydration pack. A radio and GPS pouch completed the rig. Laid out neatly beside the vest was my Glock, a Fobus paddle holster, two loaded magazines, a Surefire G2X torch, a 3 litre hydration bag, a Motorola VHF two-way radio with a push to talk headset, a Garmin GPS, a first aid kit and a Smith & Wesson folding rescue knife.

I looked across the room and Joey, dressed all in black in a pair of close-fitting jeans, boots, T-shirt and a softshell jacket was doing the same, her kit laid out on the floor in front of her desk. As I watched her, she took up her Glock, checked it was clear, then broke it down and got to work with the cleaning kit.

We had not spoken much since Joey's arrival, each caught up in our own thoughts as we prepared our gear. Joey was wiping down the inside of her weapon's slide with a piece of lightly oiled cloth when she cleared her throat.

'You know,' she said, holding the slide up to the light, 'you won't get near him...'

I looked up. 'What do you mean?'

'You won't get near the killer once SDU get onto him. We'll be right at the back of the team – if they even let us follow them in – and they'll take him down without batting an eye. This will be a kill mission. The best you'll get is to stand over his body once they're done.'

I thought about that for a minute. 'Suits me,' I said. 'I just want him dead and the girls back. I don't care who does that...'

Joey shook her head, a sad smile on her face. 'Yes you do. You want to be the one to do it.'

She was right, of course. 'That's unfair, Joey,' I said. 'This isn't about me.'

She shrugged and returned to cleaning her weapon. I was still mulling over what she had said when my phone rang. I looked down at the screen. It was Giles on his new phone. I picked it up and answered.

'Hi, Gal,' he said. 'Any news? What can I do? I'm sitting here useless and worried. I need to be helping...'

I remembered my feverish thoughts earlier that morning but pushed them down. I could hear the fear and concern in his voice.

'There's nothing for you to do right now, Giles,' I said. 'But we do have some developments. The police found his van.'

'What? That's great. How did they find it? I mean, he must have had it well hidden.'

'It was. Just good old-fashioned police work. A beat cop put two and two together and stumbled on it.'

'So where was it?' Giles asked, his voice tense.

'In an abandoned factory in the New Territories. The police are focussing their search on the area now.'

'Was... was there any sign of Pru?'

'There was. But she wasn't in there. He's moved her after he...'

'He what?'

'After he hurt her, Giles,' I said, my voice grim.

'What the fuck did he do, Galahad?' Giles shouted. 'What did he *do* to her?'

'Giles, it's best you don't know,' I said softly. 'It was bad and, to be honest, it is probably getting worse...'

I heard Giles groan. He sounded like a wounded animal. 'Worse?' he said. 'What "worse"? Do you mean he's *eating* her...?' He stopped suddenly.

The room, quiet before, seemed to go deathly still. I looked at Joey who was looking back at me, an eyebrow raised in question. I swallowed hard and drew a breath. The fact the killer was devouring parts of his victims had not been released by the press, the police having successfully applied a No Publish order two weeks previously. And yet Giles knew.

'How did you know that Giles?'

A pause. 'Know what?'

'How do you know the killer was eating parts of his victims?'

'I... I don't know,' he said hesitantly. 'Not the papers... social media! Yes, that must be it. Social media. It's all over the place.'

That was the right answer. It certainly wasn't in the press and was probably plastered all over social media – although I had not checked. It was plausible, it made sense, but my heart still hammered in my chest. I needed to call the Taskforce.

'Giles, I'm busy right now,' I said. 'I have to go. Don't drop off the grid. Stay in touch with me, Okay? I might have news at any time.'

He heaved a sigh of relief. 'Sure, Gal. Whatever you say. I'll stay in touch. I'll call back later this afternoon, okay?'

I hung up and looked across at Joey and shook my head. She frowned but didn't push it. I need time to think so I grabbed up my tobacco pouch and headed to the door. 'Stepping out for a bit, Jo,' I said over my shoulder.

'Okay,' she said. 'And when you get back you can tell me what the *fuck* that was all about...'

I had not reached the door when my phone rang again. It was Michael Wong.

'Who was that who just called you?' he demanded. 'I'm running the number now but it's quicker to call and ask.'

'I was about to call *you*,' I said. 'It was Giles...'

'Did he say where he was calling from?'

'No, not exactly but he implied he was sitting in his apartment.'

I heard Michael flicking through sheets of paper. 'Which is,' he said, 'in Sai Ying Pun, right?'

'Right.'

He was clicking the top of a pen as he answered. 'We easily triangulated that call. New generation device, screaming out to the cell towers all over town. That call was made from Shek Yam. Corner of Lei Muk and Wo Yi Hop Roads, to be precise.'

I stopped and looked back at Joey. 'Jesus Christ,' I said. 'That's even closer to the Redoubt than where the killer dumped the van!'

'Slow down, Mr Jones,' Michael said. 'There could be any number of reasons he's out there. Shopping at the mall – it's a good one – or he could be visiting the Jockey Club with friends. He could just as easily be out hunting for Prudence himself...'

'Michael...'

'Before you go on, we have sent a blue and red out,' he said, referring to the colour of HKPF patrol cars. 'We'll try and locate him and pull him in for a chat. If he isn't there we will be waiting for him outside his apartment.'

'You could be right,' I said. 'There could be a perfectly reasonable explanation for all this, but I've been thinking. There is a lot of about this guy that just doesn't stack up. I mean, just before you called he let slip he knew about the killer's cannibalism...'

'Social media...'

'Jesus, Michael...'

'I'm just saying what a good lawyer will say. Evidence, Mr Jones. That's how we work. Physical evidence. The old methods – *your* methods – are a thing of the past.'

'And "intuition"?' I said. 'That's a thing of the past too?'

'No,' Michael said patiently. 'It is not. Intuition may get us the arrest but *evidence* gets us the prosecution. We will apply both to this case.'

'Okay, Michael,' I said. 'Do it your way. Us dinosaurs will watch and learn.'

He paused briefly then said: 'Speaking of "learning", the overflight for this afternoon has been cancelled but we're good to go this evening. I'd like you here at Arsenal House to watch the feed. Your opinion could be useful. I'll arrange passes for both you and Miss Loh. Be here at 18:30.'

I thanked him and agreed Joey and I would be there. I heard Michael clicking his pen top again.

'One last thing,' he said. 'I know what you are thinking but don't. Stay away from Mr Tyler's apartment. Unless he invites us in, we will need a warrant and that *annoying* Police Force Ordinance requires me to provide at least reasonable grounds to suspect he has committed an offence – which I don't yet have. There's that pesky evidence thing again. Do you remember all that, Galahad? *Please*, just leave this to the professionals.'

With that, he ended the call and I moved back to the Chesterfield and sat, looking at Joey.

'You might as well go home once you're done here,' I said. 'We're summoned to Arsenal House this evening to observe the FLIR overflight and it's not for…' I checked my watch. 12:30. 'Another six hours.'

'The hell with that,' she said. 'I'm not sitting on my ass for six hours when we could be doing something. Come on! Let's *do* something.'

Michael Wong had specifically warned me off Giles' apartment and that was probably the worst thing he could do if he really wanted me to keep clear. I grinned at Joey and moved to my desk and rummaged around in the drawers. Deep in the third drawer, underneath a pile of bills and a rumpled advertisement for dog food, I found what I was looking for. I pulled the small canvas roll out and stuffed it into my back pocket.

'Joey,' I said. 'Lock up the weapons. We're going to Sai Ying Pung. I'll fill you in along the way.'

Scooping up the Glocks and magazines she smiled at me. 'That's better,' she said. 'See: co-op-er-ation. Most effective partnerships have it.'

I shook my head and headed for the door with my sassy offsider in tow.

63

JOEY and I stood on High Street at the corner of the path leading to the Old Lunatic Asylum. Ironic, Joey had observed. It was nearly 12:30 and Sai Ying Pun was humming.

Delivery vans crawled up the narrow street and double-parked to offload their wares and people moved purposefully in and out of the fruit and vegetable stalls, the butcher shops, bakers and convenience stores. The office lunch crowd had walked up from Queen's Road West and were packed tight into the small noodle joints and roast restaurants. Bicycle couriers weaved their way in and out of the traffic, their bikes laden with food delivery, office supplies and bunches of flowers. Two uniformed police officers stood in front of the small, renovated apartment block diagonally across the street from us. They stood like all cops who had been given a crime scene duty – stern and bored at the same time. Joey looked at me.

'What now?' she said.

I dragged on the cigarette in my hand and shrugged. 'They beat us to it,' I said. 'It doesn't look like they've been in yet. We'll come back later tonight and try again.

Joey looked back across the road. 'No, I've got an idea.' She grabbed my hand. 'Follow my lead.'

With that she dragged me out into the street and walked toward the two cops. She was babbling away in Cantonese about her friends and shoes and lunches, looking up at me and giggling ridiculously. I didn't like this Joey. She sounded like a true Gong Nui, a materialistic, daddy's princess "Hong Kong Girl", obsessed with foreign culture and wealthy boyfriends. That, of course, was her plan. I slipped an arm around her waist and chuckled along with her in appalling Cantonese, leaning down now and then to peck her lightly on the cheek.

'Easy tiger,' she whispered from the corner of her mouth.

I glanced up and the cops were watching us, disapproval stamped all over their faces. The younger cop stepped forward as we approached the door.

'Sorry, Miss,' he said. 'There is no entry. Residents only.'

Joey let go of my hand and planted her hands on her hips. 'Officer, I *am* a resident. Aren't I darling,' she added looking up at me

I smiled widely at the two cops. 'She sure is...' I said in Cantonese. Both cops winced at my barbarous pronunciation.

Joey went on, her voice soft and alluring. 'Officer, I just need to go upstairs and pick up some fresh... *things*, then we will leave. I mean, goodness me, what is this all about anyway?'

The cop who had spoken shuffled nervously. You don't mess with Gong Nui. 'It's a police matter, Miss. But I suppose, as it's your home, you can proceed. Please be quick or do stay indoors.'

Joey fluttered her eyelashes again. 'Oh we may be a few minutes at least...' she grabbed my arse and gave it a squeeze. 'We have *business* to attend to.'

The older cop's lip curled in distaste and the younger one blushed and stepped aside, opening the door for us. We were in.

'That was very convincing Joey,' I said over my shoulder.

I heard a snort behind me. 'Don't get any ideas. Remember: you're not my type,' she said as she slapped my backside.

The apartment directory at the front door gave the names of seven of the eight occupants. Only one nameplate was blank. I checked my notebook. 'Third floor, apartment B,' I said and we moved up the stairs.

The stairs were narrow and each landing was short so we arrived at the third floor quickly. I glanced around and pointed at the apartment with "B" lit up next to the door by a soft downlight. I knocked, loudly, three times.

'Giles,' I said. 'It's me Galahad. Open up, I've got some news.'

We both listened intently. Not a sound came from the apartment. I knocked again. Still nothing, so I snapped on a pair of disposable gloves and passed a pair to Joey, then pulled the small canvas roll out of my back pocket. I opened the roll and selected two of the tools from their compartments. Joey leaned over my shoulder.

'A lock pick kit?' she said. 'I didn't know you could do that.'

I leaned down, concentrating on slipping the picks into the lock, listening for their engagement with the lock's tumblers. 'I'm full of surprises,' I whispered. 'My father taught me.'

'Your father the Royal Hong Kong Police Superintendent, 2IC of the Organised and Serious Crime Group. *He* taught you how to pick a lock?

I ignored her and kept working away at the picks. I was beginning to sweat when, suddenly the second pick engaged and the lock opened with a satisfying click.

'Jesus,' Joey said. 'I'm impressed.'

I opened the door and we walked in, closing the door softly behind us. The apartment was what they now call "minimalist". It was stark white. The walls, floors and ceilings were white. The fittings, lights, lamps and the single, small bookcase were white. The furnishings, sleek and modern, were all dark grey and looked harsh and uninviting. There wasn't a single artwork on the walls or a photograph anywhere.

I noticed the strong smell of bleach as we stepped into the small living room, our shoes rapping against the bare faux-timber floor. A 42" TV and cable unit sat on a low cabinet across the room and, in front of me, two glass French doors opened up onto a small balcony looking north over Central and Victoria Harbour. I looked around.

The bookcase held four books only, perfectly aligned in the centre of the centre shelf. There was nothing anyone would expect to see in a lived-in space. No odds and ends, not a single ornament, knick knack or piece of junk most people have in their homes, regardless of how fastidious they were. There was nothing there that gave any sign anyone actually lived in the place. It reminded me of a morgue, right down to the tang of bleach in the air.

I crossed to the fridge and opened it. It was empty except for a bottle of cheap Vodka and a single snack pack of cheese and biscuits. The freezer, however, was stocked with cuts of beef and pork, each meticulously wrapped in cling wrap and labelled with dates. The rubbish bin was empty, but freshly lined.

'What are we looking for?' Joey said.

I shrugged. 'I don't know. We'll know when we see it I suppose.'

There were only three rooms to the apartment: the living room with galley kitchen, the bedroom and the bathroom. I signalled to Joey to check the living room and I moved into the bedroom. Again, the room was cold and utilitarian. There was nothing in there but a Queen bed and a single bedside table on which sat a small lamp. No clock, no book, no phone charger. Nothing. A small open-sided robe took up one corner of the room, in which were hung three, starched white shirts, a dark navy suit, a single yellow tie, a pair of black shoes, a pair of jeans, a black overcoat and a denim jacket. A drawer in the robe held three pair of men's underwear and two pair of dark socks. The other two drawers were empty.

The bathroom cabinet was similarly bare. A toothbrush, half used tube of toothpaste, a razor, comb, shaving cream and brush, and a small bottle of aftershave. I pushed the mirrored cabinet door closed and it bounced back, slightly out of place. I pushed it again and it closed with an odd thudding sound that seemed to echo behind the wall.

I stepped around the sink and peered at the cabinetry. The right hand cabinet had a deeper recess than that on the left, it seemed to stand out further from the wall, but seen from the front the two married up. I ran my hand up the side of the right hand cabinet, feeling the smooth joinery and was about to move away when my fingers brushed a small, metallic clasp. I pushed at it and the cabinet sprung open, carrying with it the outer compartment and revealing an inner recess with three shelves. I peered inside.

'Joey,' I called. 'You'll want to see this.'

I pulled the notebook from my jacket, took out the pencil and lifted the first object with it.

It was a cheap woman's necklace, the small links clogged with dried blood. I held it up to the light and could see strands of dark hair snared in the clasp where the necklace had been pulled violently away. I gently placed the necklace back on the shelf and lifted out a man's watch, a Seiko. It, too, was smeared in blood, the steel link bracelet was jammed with it, a small flap of dried skin hung from the fogged and broken face. I caught Joey's reflection in the mirror as she entered the bathroom. She peered over my shoulder.

'Holy shit,' she whispered. 'Are they what I think they are?'

I nodded. 'Victim trophies. Souvenirs,' I said, placing the watch carefully back on the shelf. 'Look at them all.' I pointed with the pencil.

The shelves were lined with a bowerbird's collection of personal possessions from who knew how many victims. The necklace and watch, a gold bangle, two hoop earrings, another men's watch with a snapped leather strap, a thick lock of black hair wrapped in a red ribbon, a pair of glasses, a small silver ring, a cigarette lighter and, finally, a withered ear that looked like a dried apricot and three teeth. Michael Wong was right: the killer had clearly taken more than the four victims we knew of.

On the top shelf stood a large notebook bound in aged leather and secured with a strap and buckle. I took down the book and undid the strap.

The notebook was A5 in size. It was thick, perhaps 120 rough-textured unlined pages, hand bound into the cover in five sections. I flicked through the pages. Each was covered in tight, handwritten text, the handwriting spidery and erratic. It was a journal. A number of pages had hand-drawn maps and I paused on a rough sketch of what looked like a young woman, lying on her side, her mouth open in a silent scream. I opened the notebook, held it by the spine and gently shook it. Out fell a collection of polaroid photographs, each one depicting a gruesome scene in their trademark washed colours inside a white border.

I quickly thumbed through the photos, feeling my heart race and saliva and bile rise in the back of my throat. They were graphic, disgusting, and taken from every angle, during every stage, of the victims' horrific murders.

I passed three to Joey and she stared silently at them, her face grim at the thought of Penny in the killer's hands. I was thinking the same thing about Prudence and couldn't speak for fear of choking. It had been Giles Tyler all along and I hadn't seen it.

Peter Toh had set him at Prudence as part of the master plan to destroy me – he *knew* my sister's life meant more to me than my own. He didn't want me dead, that was why he hadn't just stepped up behind me on put a bullet in my brain. He wanted my suffering long and agonising, a living death. I shook my head, dizzy with the implications. *I* had run my eye – and my famed intuition – over Giles and had cleared him. *I* hadn't added up all he had said and the many inconsistencies. *I* had missed flag after flag. *I* had handed Prudence into his care. *I* was responsible for my sister's abduction and torture at the hands of a maniacal serial killer. I was a complete failure both as an investigator and as a brother, and now Prudence was going to die. I couldn't stop it.

My stomach clenched painfully and I leaned over and hawked acidic yellow bile into the bathroom sink, turning on the tap to wash it away. Joey touched me on the shoulder and I waved her away. Wiping my mouth with the back of my gloved hand I picked up the notebook, flicked back to the very first page and read the opening lines:

I'm a bad person.

But you know that by now.

I secured the strap and placed the book back on the shelf and closed the cabinet carefully, hearing the concealed lock mechanism click shut. Looking at my reflection in the mirror I saw the horror in my eyes and the moment they widened as the realisation hit me. The freezer. Those weren't cuts of beef and pork. I turned to Joey.

'We have to move fast,' I said. 'Get into the kitchen and grab the bin liner from the garbage bin. Take a video of you opening the freezer, removing two different packages and placing them in the bin liner. Video your watch over the bag while you're doing that.'

Joey knew instantly what I was driving at and moved into the kitchen without a word. In moments I heard her at the fridge so I took out my phone and, filming my actions, unlocked the hidden cabinet and scanned slowly through the souvenirs, and over the notebook. I took a number of photos of various pages of the notebook, all with my watch date and time visible in each shot, then replaced the notebook and closed the cabinet again. I joined Joey in the living room.

'Let's go,' I said. 'We have to get to Arsenal House right now and get that bag, and the videos, to Michael Wong. We'll go via the office and pick up our kit for this evening's mission. We're going in ...'

Joey's face was tense and she just nodded and opened the apartment door, clutching the bin liner in her right hand. We moved quickly down the stairs and out the front door, nodding to the two cops, and headed down High Street and around the corner where we hailed a taxi.

64

JOEY and I stood at the reception desk in Arsenal House, as police officers in groups of two or three, moved in and out of the building. We had our kit bags slung over our shoulders and Joey gripped the bin liner with its grisly contents. Chief Inspector Michael Wong checked his watch.

'You're early,' he said.

'We need to talk,' I said. 'Right now.'

With a nod to the front desk Constable, Michael led us through the security doors, and into the elevator. Minutes later we stepped from the lift and walked along a bright corridor to an office with Michael's nameplate on the wall by the door. The office had been Peter Toh's and memories of our last meeting there, two years previously during the height of the human trafficking case, washed over me. Michael opened the door and gestured us in.

'So,' he said, reclining in his office chair, hands behind his head. 'What's so important that you are barging in on me four hours early.'

I pointed to the bag at Joey's feet. 'First thing, we need to get the contents of that into a freezer right now...'

Michael leaned over his desk and peered down. 'What is it?'

'If I'm right, it's flesh from the killer's victims.'

He stared at me for a long moment. I held his gaze. 'I'm going to regret asking this,' he said, 'but why do you say that and *where* did you get it?'

So I told him about entering Giles's apartment, our search and what we had found. Michel stared, unblinking at me, his hands clasped on the desk in front of him. When I had finished he sat silently for a long minute then made a quick phone call, telling the person on the other end to drop everything and get to his office immediately. His eyes swivelled back to me.

'*Diu*, Jones!' he said, his jaw clenched. 'You have broken into an apartment, conducted an illegal search, removed evidence from a crime scene... wait! Weren't there uniforms in front of the building?'

'Yes, two.'

'Those imbeciles will be handing out parking tickets at Disneyland Park for the rest of their careers.' He pointed at the bag. 'Just what the hell do you expect me to do with *that*?'

'Get it tested,' I said. 'It's human flesh. I'd stake my reputation on it...'

'Your *reputation*?' he exploded. 'Jesus Christ! Your reputation for breaking the rules, for working fast and loose with the truth, for violence? *That* reputation? We haven't picked Tyler up yet – there are uniforms out hunting for him now – so I have nothing, zero, on which to base a warrant application...'

'Michael, you've got reasonable grounds to suspect an offence is being committed,' I said. 'If I recall you don't need a warrant for that. Get the two uniforms to kick the door in and conduct a quick search then call it in...'

'What offence? There *is* no offence! Tyler made a call from Shek Yam... That's it! How am I expected to convince a magistrate I miraculously connected the dots between that call and a fridge full of human body parts?' He shook his head and calmed himself with a visible effort. I could see he was thinking fast. There was a knock at the door and a plain-clothes officer entered. Michael pointed again at the bag.

'Get that in a freezer pack and to Forensic right away,' he said. 'I want to know what it is, and I want to know inside the hour.

The officer nodded, grabbed up the bag and exited the room. We could hear his footsteps racing away up the corridor.

'Okay... what's done is done,' Michael said quietly, rubbing his hands through his thick, black hair. 'I'll work out a way to tidy up this mess later.' He shook his head again. 'Jesus, Galahad! You really make things difficult for me...' He pointed at Joey. 'And *you*! You should know better Miss Loh.' He rubbed his eyes and sat back in his chair, staring at the ceiling.

'Forget the fishing gear when the fish is caught,' he said, finally using the Chinese proverb for the ends justify the means. 'We'll play it this way: uniforms will continue the search in Shek Yam and if we get lucky we'll pick him up. Meanwhile I'll get those two clowns in Sai Ying Pun to think they heard something from inside the apartment and "kick the door in", as you so elegantly put it. They'll find the cabinet mechanism with a hint or two from me and call it in – although I'm not sure they could find their own asses. We'll then declare a crime scene. No warrant needed. The air mission goes ahead but I'll bring it forward and get extra air hours. We need that chopper on station as long as we can get it. It's a long shot, but we could get lucky and catch him moving about outside his lair – *and* we still don't know for sure we are right on *that* one.'

'We *are* right,' I said. 'He's somewhere in the Shing Mun.'

Michael pointed at me. 'I am *so* tempted to run you in,' he said. 'But, and this is hard to say, your old school methods worked – I should have been more aggressive.'

I shook my head. 'No Michael,' I said. 'It's not any failing on your part. I'm just not bound by police procedure as you are. You're a good copper and Christ knows we need those in this town.'

He nodded. 'That's gracious of you. Thank you.'

Joey cleared her throat. "When you two have finished your man hugs, can Galahad and I get a lift to the GFS Helipad?

'Of course,' Michael said. 'I'll have a patrol car drive you down now. But you don't want to be in the CommCen to watch the feed from the overflight?'

Joey shook her head. 'No point in us being in the Command Centre that I can see.' She looked at me and I nodded. 'Better,' she said 'we join the SDU team, get briefed and be ready to go. If the overflight finds this animal we need to get in the air as quickly as possible. Us being here will only delay that.'

Michael nodded his acceptance, so Joey and I stood, grabbed up our kit bags and moved to the door. Joey was in the corridor and I was stepping out when Michael Wong called my name. I turned back to the room.

'If we are right,' he said '*and* we find him, this will end in blood. You know that. It will be a miracle if we get the girls back alive, but we *will* get him. Just stay out of the way and let the assault team do what it does best.'

I didn't answer him, but nodded and left the room.

65

I DROPPED the cigarette end onto the concrete and crushed it out under my boot.

My tactical vest was on the ground at my feet and the Glock was in its holster on my right hip. Joey lay on the ground, her head resting against her rig, eyes closed. The six-man assault team from SDU were lounging about in the way special operators always do before a mission. Dressed in their Crye Precision G3 multicam uniforms, their ballistic helmets laid on their body armour, and their SIG516 assault rifles close at hand, the men sat quietly talking, listening to music through their headphones, or reading.

Giles Tyler had not been located in Shek Yam, nor had he returned to his apartment – probably alerted to the police presence by a heightened, beast-like sense of danger. Now it all hinged on spotting him from the air, the FLIR of the Government Flying Service EC155 ranging its all-seeing eyes across the dark of Kam Shan Country Park.

The overflight had been in the air for hours and would soon be approaching its range. When it did, it would be offline for 45 minutes while it re-fuelled. When that happened we would be blind, GFS having been unable to allocate two aircraft to the mission. I was sure

Michael Wong, hunkered down in the CommCen, would be chewing his nails, praying for a sighting before our eyes were taken away.

I checked my G-Shock. 21:00. The helipad was brightly lit and a single AS332 Super Puma sat squat and powerful on the pad like a giant insect, the four blades of its main rotor drooping at rest, waiting to be thrust into action by the beast's two Turbomeca Makila turboshaft engines.

The waiting is always the hardest. It's a time when all the worst outcomes roll through your head, when your confidence is shaky and self-doubt threatens to run amok. It's when you shine a light on your assessments and plans and see they are full of holes, just waiting to tumble like a house of sticks built on shifting sands. I rolled and lit another cigarette, noting the six butts already on the ground at my feet.

'They are going to kill you one of these days,' Joey said without opening her eyes.

I dragged deeply on the smoke and was about to reply when the silence of the helipad was shattered. The Team Leader's radio burst into life with a tinny voice tense with excitement. The team all looked up as he responded. We all heard the transmission, and everyone shot to their feet, grabbing up their kit and throwing it on, checking fit, securing weapons on the single point slings already draped around necks and shoulders. Helmets on and secured, night-vision devices powered up flicked upright and out of the way until we hit the jungle dark. Actions were racked on the assault rifles, safeties applied.

Joey checked the back of my gear and slapped me on the shoulder, then turned around so I could do hers. As we did so, the Super Puma started up, its turboshaft engines emitting a deep whine as they fired into life and began to drive power to the main rotor. As the revs built the chopper began to bounce lightly in place, eager to be off. The assault team were on their knees now, in a single file on the edge of the helipad, awaiting the signal from the Loadmaster to board. I felt the phone vibrate in the inner pocket of my vest and I pulled it out.

'Michael,' I shouted. 'What have we got?'

His voice was barely audible above the roar of the Super Puma. 'We got a spot! Five minutes ago. Two figures seen moving south along Wilson Trail down Smugglers' Ridge. One small, one large. The vision showed the small one to be a kid, probably a girl, and the larger figure was our guy almost certainly. I gave orders to the aircraft to buzz them and drive him off which they did.'

'And...?'

'They pushed him north back along the trail and he disappeared – probably underground. The crew circled back and picked up the girl. We've got Penny! She's inbound to Eastern now,' he said referring to the Pamela Youde Eastern Hospital in Chai Wan, the only hospital in Hong Kong with a helipad. I looked across at Joey. Michael went on. 'We won't be able to interview her for a few hours yet, but you're on your way, Mr Jones. Good hunting!'

I ended the call and tucked the phone away, careful to ensure it was silenced. The assault team in front of us stood and started moving toward the chopper. As Joey moved, I grabbed the drag handle on the back of her vest. She turned around.

'They've got Penny, Jo!' I shouted above the din of the chopper's engines. 'She's alive! She's on the way to Eastern right now.'

Joey looked shocked for a moment. She closed her eyes and drew a deep breath, her head hung. I thought she was about to crumple. She didn't.

She gripped my right arm. 'Right,' she shouted into my ear. 'Now let's go get Pru!' Then she turned and strode across the helipad, racking back on the action of her Glock and reholstering it.

Let's go get Prudence, I thought. I felt a deep sense of dread at what we would find that night and, as events were to prove, I was right to.

66

THE JUNGLE ALONG SMUGGLERS' Ridge was pitch black, the vegetation a dark tangle beside the track, lit a lurid green by our NVDs. I had Joey behind me, and the assault team in front of me were slowly patrolling the narrow track, eyes and weapons in sync as they covered their arcs, left and right, always moving forward, ready to respond.

It was still and warm under the canopy, the smell of rotting vegetation rich in the air, and the night was alive with life. Frogs croaked and burped in a nearby creek and the sound of crickets filled the air, while somewhere off to the left a Nightjar called longingly into the dark. To our right the forest exploded in sound. An excited clan of Macaques had detected our presence and sent out their scouts to assess the threat. I could hear the monkeys scampering through the trees, keeping pace with us, watching and chattering as they decided whether or not we were a risk to the rest of the troop.

We had been moving for about 20 minutes since the chopper had hovered low over a small clearing high on Wilson Trail and we had jumped the two metres to the ground. The jungle and the dark confused the senses and it seemed we had been patrolling for hours and kilometres but, in reality, we had made good time to cover the 450 metres from the LZ at a wary patrol pace.

We were new to this game so Joey and I took our cues from the men in front, their watchfulness and stealthy movement readying them for action at a moment's notice. The monkeys left us, deciding we posed no threat, and all was quiet when the Team Leader held up a fist and dropped to one knee. He keyed the throat mic on his headset.

'Romeo Bravo this is Tango One,' the Team Leader's voice quiet but clear in my ear. I winced at the callsign I had been given when one of the team had first spotted me and called out 'here comes Rugby Boy!'

I keyed my mic 'Go ahead.'

'We are 50 metres out from the entrance to the Redoubt. It's a big area so I'm splitting the team, but we'll be able to cover each other – one on a western axis and the other on the east. Go with who you want but do not get in the way. Clear?'

'That's clear,' I said. 'We'll go east.' The transmission ended and we moved off, the Team Leader using a hand signal to indicate a staggered file. On reaching a small fork in the track the team split into two, with the Team Leader and two others heading off slightly to the left and Joey and I following the three that went right.

Before long we came to a large sign, lit bright in our NVDs that, in Cantonese and English, said "Danger. Desolate Trench. Do Not Enter." I scanned up and could see, at the entrance to the system, the reinforced concrete roof of the large bunker had been blown in. It was overgrown with jungle vine and coated with leaf mulch. The Japanese artillery decades before had been devastatingly effective against the Redoubt and the under-strength allied force defending it.

The three men in front of us didn't pause and entered the trench, their weapons pointed steadily forward as we crunched our way over the broken glass, shattered concrete and gravel that littered the floor. It was eerily quiet as we stepped into the tunnel system. As silent as the grave, and the place smelled of jungle rot and damp concrete.

Somewhere ahead I could hear the steady, patting drip of water. The tunnel was narrow, a little under two metres wide, and the roof closed in on us, scraping the tops of our helmets. We hunched lower as we moved slowly forward, deeper into the blackness.

We had gone perhaps 30 metres when we passed a tunnel branching off to the right. The lead officer stopped and inspected it before discounting it and moving on. As I passed I saw it was barely half a metre wide and a metre and half high. It was blocked by another large warning sign that was fitted to a steel frame, fixed to the concrete of the tunnel wall, and covering the entire entrance. I had taken two steps on when I felt a tap on my shoulder. Joey was holding up a hand for me to stop.

'Take a look at this,' she whispered, pointing to the tunnel entrance where the sign frame was anchored into the concrete. I leaned down and peered closer, difficult to do under the green, distorted light of an NVD.

There, where Joey was indicating, I could see the concrete had been chiselled neatly away exposing fresh grey marks, and both steel pickets on the right hand side of the sign were loose. The sign had been deliberately cut away by someone wanting to enter but keep the tunnel entrance looking impassable. I turned my head and looked up the main tunnel. The SDU team had disappeared from view and, holding my breath, I couldn't hear their footsteps. I made my decision quickly.

'Good work, Jo,' I said. 'We're going in here. If it's nothing we'll double back and join the team.'

Joey nodded and we both gripped the sign, swinging it away to the left as quietly as we could. The screeching of the steel on concrete sounded like an angle grinder in the silence of the tunnel, but we got the sign open enough to squeeze through. As soon as we were in, we had to remove our helmets just to get low enough to move. Without the NVDs we took out our Surefire torches and switched them on, the powerful 600 lumen LED brightly lighting the narrow crevasse.

The floor was littered with decades of rubbish, dried animal carcasses and bits of timber with faded military markings on them – the remains of ammunition boxes broken open during the desperate battle for the Redoubt. I sniffed the air and could smell a faint odour of decay. There was a dead animal somewhere ahead. Probably a Macaque, I thought, that had somehow been separated from his troop and died alone in the dark.

Joey and I moved on, hunched low under the claustrophobic press of the ceiling, and scraping our shoulders and hips against the walls. Holding the torch in my left hand, my thumb against the butt of the torch, I drew my Glock and raised it, placing the back of my master hand against the back of my left hand. With both the light I needed ahead and a stable platform from which to shoot, I crept forward.

The light from Joey's torch danced overhead and I knew she was doing the same thing, her weapon pointed over my right shoulder.

The smell of decay was becoming stronger, a sweet green stench of putrefaction that filled the tunnel like a fog, and I heard Joey gag quietly behind me. The radio headset blocked my right ear, and I could hear nothing from my left except the subdued crunching of our carefully placed steps on the litter of the tunnel floor.

I had no idea how far we had come when, out of the dark, a fork in the tunnel appeared. I didn't hesitate and veered right, noticing this section of tunnel was slightly higher and wider, allowing us to move more freely. Up ahead, a yellow light glowed faintly against the tunnel wall where it branched off to the left. We turned the corner and the tunnel suddenly lit up as it opened up into a small room. We stepped in and I swung my weapon around the room. It was clear.

The room was a small concrete bunker, deep underground, its walls and ceiling stained by decades of groundwater seepage. It stank of shit and the nearly overpowering stench of rotting flesh.

A wooden box sat on the floor on which was placed a small hurricane lantern that lit the space. Next to the lantern was an aluminium camping plate on which were the congealed remains of a half-cooked meal, a fork stuck in it. Next to the box was a small portable gas cooker. Three bottles of water and discarded dehydrated meal packets were scattered across the floor.

On the cooker sat a small camp frypan and I saw with horror that it contained a barely cooked, and half-eaten chunk of flesh. A green sleeping bag lay open and rumpled against one wall, on top of which sat a Polaroid camera. Against the other wall, away from the sleeping bag and food, sat a loosely knotted black plastic bag and a roll of toilet paper. Other than that, the bunker was empty. We were so close but had come up empty-handed. No killer and no Prudence. I was thinking hard about the next move when Joey entered the bunker, her face grim.

'Galahad,' she said softly. 'You need to come with me. There's another bunker.'

I followed her back out into the tunnel and there, off the right, set deep in the dark, was an opening in the tunnel wall. Joey gripped my arm and shook her head. I shone the torch through the opening and, bending low, stepped into the small cavity. There, lying naked and bound on a rancid old blanket soaked in concealed blood, was my sister.

Prudence's eyes were closed, and her mouth was open. I knelt down beside her, cut her bindings and felt for a pulse. It was there, but it fluttered rapidly like the wings of a dragonfly. I played the torch over her ruined body, my jaw clenched so tight I felt a tooth crack. Her eyes were sunken into her skull and her beautiful dark hair was matted and had fallen out in great chunks. The skin of her face was waxy and taut, and her full red lips were pale grey and shrivelled.

Her breasts had been savaged. Knife incisions raked across her chest, and I could clearly see the deep bite marks, one of which had taken a hunk of flesh from her and around which the decaying skin was puckered purple and black. The wound oozed a foul-smelling discharge. The stump of the ring finger on Prudence's right hand was likewise infected and pus had puddled and dried under her hand where it rested on the blanket.

I turned the torch to her legs and froze in place, the gorge rising in my throat.

The outside of her right thigh had been sliced off, and the glistening white bone shone through the purulent infection that had been flesh and muscle. The skin around the wound was bloated and an evil black and red colour, tendrils of black winding down her leg like venomous snakes. I gently prodded it. Hot to the touch, the skin split, oozing thick yellow pus and the stench was unbearable. I knew what I was looking at.

Gangrene was slowly eating away at my sister.

I hung my head, my eyes closed tight against the tears of horror and rage that spilled down my cheeks. I shuffled forward on my knees and raised Prudence's head, gently brushing the lank hair from her face, and bent to lightly kiss her cheek. As I did, her eyes fluttered open, and she moaned. She was mad with blood loss, pain, and fever but I saw her focus on me and a weak smile appeared on her face.

'Daaih lo, *big brother*,' she said, her eyes bright. 'You came for me... I knew you would.'

I swallowed hard. 'Yes, Pru. I came for you. I'm here now and we're going to get you home.'

She shook her head. 'No... I'm dying. I... I know it.' She clenched her eyes tight. 'Oh, it hurts so much Galahad...' Her head lolled and she lapsed into unconsciousness.

I ripped open the pouch on my vest and pulled out the med kit. Against the wounds she had, I knew I was equipped with nothing that would make a difference, but I had to try. Working fast, I tore open a packet of Neosporin powder and sprinkled it onto the thigh wound then swiftly covered it with a gauze compress and wrapped the leg firmly in a wide bandage. I used another large gauze pad on her breast and sealed it with a sheet of occlusive dressing, then took out a sachet of codeine power and tipped it into the small bottle of water I was carrying. I held it to her lips.

'Pru,' I whispered. 'Come back sai mui, *little sister*. Come back to me...'

Her eyes flickered open once more and I could see the flame of life was burning dimmer and dimmer. I held the bottle to her lips.

'Drink, sis. It will help with the pain.'

She weakly raised her head and I trickled the water into her mouth. She choked a little as she tried to swallow and much of the fluid dribbled down her chin. With an effort, she shook her head.

'No, too late... can't...'

'You drink the fucking water Prudence,' I said, my voice sharp. 'Drink it and do *not* give up.. Mum and Dad are watching, and they want you to be brave, to live! Drink it!'

She tried again and, this time, took in a good mouthful then lowered her head.

'Did... did the girl get away? Penny...'

I nodded. 'She did, Pru. We picked her up today and she's in hospital. She's waiting for you...'

'I did what I could... I....' Her eyes shifted to the left and I raised my torch.

On the ground on the other side of the tiny cell lay two lengths of red cord, one of which had been sawed through. A large shard of glass lay beside them. My sister, wracked with pain and slowly dying, had managed to cut the cords that bound Penny. I shook my head.

'You're a hero, Pru,' I said softly. 'You saved her life...' I choked back at the tears as my voice cracked.

Pru smiled faintly, her eyes still closed. 'Not hero, Gal... just a Jones.' The tears were flowing freely down my face, and I cradled my sister's head in my hands. I kissed her then. She suddenly raised a hand and opened her eyes.

'Mom? Dad...? I can see you ...' she whispered. She seemed to listen for a moment then smiled. 'Yes, he will be fine...'

'Pru,' I pleaded. 'Stay with me. Don't leave. *Please*!'

She turned her head to me, a lone tear escaping from the corner of her right eye. 'Be good to yourself, big brother... Live for... for me. I love...'

She shuddered and a deep breath rattled out from between her lips. Her eyes glazed over and her head, resting in the crook of my arm, rolled gently to the side. My sister was dead.

I lowered her head to the ground and closed her eyes with a caress of my hand. Rising, I bent low and left the chamber. Joey was standing there, facing up the tunnel, her Glock held loosely by her side. She looked at me and I shook my head. I couldn't speak, I couldn't think straight. Joey opened her mouth and was about to say something when there was a scuffling noise deep in the tunnel.

We both raised our torches and there, standing in the stygian darkness, his hands by his side, one grasping a large chef's knife, was Giles Tyler.

His face was painted with red mud, and he was shirtless, his muscular frame daubed in stripes of mud that connected strange, swirling, primitive symbols. His trousers were torn and he wore no shoes. I drew my weapon and snapped it up, my finger tensing on the trigger. The killer grinned wickedly.

'So, Mr Detective,' he said. 'You finally put the pieces together. I knew you would turn up eventually. So here we are, the final act.'

I lowered the weapon a little, my finger still resting on the trigger. 'I should have known better, you bastard,' I said. 'But in the end it wasn't so hard. You're no evil genius, you're just another low crim who gave himself up through a series of stupid mistakes...'

The headset came to life in my ear and I reached to my chest to switch off the radio. The movement of my hand broke the spell that had us staring at each other and the killer suddenly spun about and ran off into the dark.

Joey and I snapped off shots, both ricocheting uselessly off the concrete tunnel wall, and I charged off in pursuit, Joey following close behind.

The light from my torch danced crazily over the walls and roof of the tunnel as I ran as fast as I could down its narrow confines. Catching a brief glimpse of the killer in the half shadow world ahead I raised my Glock and fired two shots. The killer stumbled and bounced off the tunnel wall but staggered on and disappeared around a corner. I rounded the corner and ran straight into him, slamming into his muscular body and dropping my torch.

The knife whipped out in a vicious cut but I instinctively reached up with my left hand to grasp his right arm and twisted with all my might hearing his shoulder pop. He screamed foetid breath into my face.

'Has the whore died?' he shrieked as I brought the Glock up, pressing it against his temple.

He rocked his head to the side and kicked out the instant I pulled the trigger and the shot went wide, blowing a puff of concrete grit into my eyes. I fumbled and dropped the Glock. Desperately, I scrabbled for his throat and kneed him hard in the left thigh where my second shot had hit home. He screamed like a banshee, shrill and other-worldly in the confines of the tunnel.

He was brutally strong and I could feel panic start to rise in me as he wrenched his arm free and slashed out with the knife again. I ducked under the strike and reached up to claw his right eye, sinking my fingers deep into the socket and I kneed him again and again in the leg wound, as I again grasped at his knife hand.

He flailed again with the steel, and I felt its vicious blade score across my neck and shoulder, blood instantly running hot over my shirt and down my back.

My left hand finally found and gripped his right wrist, and he gripped my vest, trying to throw me off balance. We were locked in a lover's embrace, face to face, bodies melding into each other, breathing heavily. I kneed him again and lashed out with a headbutt. His head snapped back as his nose shattered and his eyes crossed idiotically in the half-light from the torch at our feet. He dropped the knife but surged into me, his teeth gnashing at my throat.

'Step back, Gal!' Joey shouted, her torchlight pinning me and the killer. 'Let me take a shot!'

I ignored her and shoved the killer up against the wall, gripping his throat like a vice. Grunting with the effort I shook him like a rag doll, slamming his head repeatedly into the concrete wall and I felt his skull crack like an eggshell.

He snarled and stretched his neck out for my throat one last time then collapsed to his knees on the floor of the tunnel, breathing hard, blood bubbling from his nose. I stepped back and smashed the butt of the Glock into his temple and he sagged, eyes unfocussed, his hands flapping uselessly at his side. Scooping up and holstering the firearm, I threw the killer onto his back and Joey stepped forward with a set of cable ties to secure him.

I waved her away with a snarl and put my boot on the killer's throat.

'Any last words...?' I panted.

He tried desperately to drag in a breath, but I pushed harder with my boot.

'You... you won't do this,' he gasped. 'I know you, Galahad. Law and order. Justice. Good shall prevail. That's you...'

I shook my head. 'There's a big difference between the Law and Justice,' I growled. 'The Law will see you doing life in Shek Pik, three meals a day, clean clothes, time in the yard once a day. But what's happening now is Justice. Justice for your victims... for my sister.'

The killer's eyes widened as I pressed all my weight into my boot, and he grabbed desperately at my ankle. I pushed harder and felt his larynx pop and his airway collapse. I stepped back and calmly watched as his eyes bulged and he gasped like a hooked carp, his hands at his neck, willing his crushed throat to take air into his lungs.

His body convulsed and his heels drummed on the tunnel floor, his panicked eyes locked on mine as his face turned red and his brain started to shut down. His bowels gave way and urine puddled dark on the front of his pants. As I saw his eyes start to glaze, at his very last moment on earth, I bent down and spat in his face. It was over.

I looked at Joey who was staring at me, her face unreadable. Switching the radio back on I keyed the mic. 'Tango One, this is Romeo Bravo. Radio check...'

'Tango One, Loud and clear.'

'We're in a subsidiary tunnel,' I said. 'Had comms problems.'

'Tango One, acknowledged. We found the tunnel when we heard the gunshots. We're nearly with you I think. What's the situation?

Still looking at Joey, I keyed the mic again. 'The offender is down, and we have one... deceased victim.'

The Team Leader acknowledged again and ended transmission. Joey stood silently, her hands by her side.

'*What*?' I demanded. 'If you have something to say, *say* it.'

Joey shook her head. 'No. I'm good…'

I pointed back down the tunnel. 'If you have a problem with what just happened, go back there and take a look at Prudence. Take a look at what…' I pointed at the corpse '*that* did to her!'

She shook her head again, her face blank. 'I have no problems, boss. I saw it all. It was self-defence. Plain and simple.'

I nodded. 'Good,' I snarled. I bent and picked up my torch then stalked back down the tunnel to my sister's body.

67

THE TEAM LEADER and two of his men found me in the small chamber where I was sitting cross-legged beside Prudence, gently stroking her hair. They stepped quietly into the cell and the Team Leader laid a hand on my shoulder.

'We need to take her home, Mr Jones. There's a chopper on the way to pick us up. It will be here in 30 minutes. Do you want to help, or should we do it?'

I looked up, surprised there was someone else in the bunker and they were speaking to me.

'What?' I said, sounding dazed. 'Oh... No, I'll do it. But I'll need help to carry her to the LZ.'

The Team Leader nodded 'Of course,' he said as he passed me the heavy-duty plastic body bag. I unzipped the bag and lay it beside Pru then gently took her under the shoulders and moved her torso into the bag, followed by her legs. I arranged her hands by her side and, taking a final look at her beautiful face, I zipped up the bag.

The eight of us then carried both bodies out of the Shing Mun Redoubt to the Landing Zone 200 metres north, all breathing deeply at the fresh jungle air after the hell of the tunnels. On arrival, the team knelt down on the side of the LZ and the Team Leader placed an IR strobe on the upwind side of the Landing Point. Before long we could hear the deep thrum of a Super Puma coming in low over the jungle canopy, and the Team Leader keyed the mic on his radio to talk the pilot in. The chopper landed with a gentle bump, its four-bladed main rotor beating at the jungle and throwing a storm of dust and leaf litter into the air.

Taking one end of Prudence's body bag, I carried her across the clearing with two of the assault team and we gently slid her on to the floor of the chopper, the Loadmaster expertly strapping her body down. I was about to board when I saw the other half of the assault team start to load the other body bag. I turned to the Team Leader and grabbed him by the front of his body armour.

'What the fuck is this?' I yelled, pointing at the killer's corpse. 'Get that off the aircraft. It's not flying with my sister...'

The Team Leader shook his head and started to answer but froze when he saw my hand reach to the butt of my holstered Glock. 'Get it off!' I yelled. 'Right fucking *now*!'

The officer looked at me unblinking as two of his men levelled their assault rifles at me. I started to draw the Glock. The chopper was bucking against the thrust holding it earthbound and the Loadmaster was gesturing wildly at us to board.

Finally, the Team Leader nodded, then waved his men to lower their weapons and drag the killer's corpse onto the ground. Minutes later, Joey, me and four of the assault team had lifted off from the darkened jungle clearing, the Super Puma banking steeply to the left and southwards as it climbed.

As we approached the helipad on The Island, banking in low over Victoria Harbor, I could see the office buildings lit with animated light displays of reindeer and holly, bells and snowflakes. Suddenly fireworks shot into the sky over Central, bursting into the night in a cannonade of green and red. I stared dumbly at the scene for a moment then checked the date on my watch. I turned back to the widow and gazed mutely out across Hong Kong. It was Christmas Day.

68

The clinical stink of the morgue still clung to my clothes, overlaying the stench of the tunnels, as I sat alone in a quiet bar in Wan Chai, a bottle of whisky and a glass on the table in front of me.

I finished the glass and poured another, rolling and lighting a cigarette. I dragged deeply, inhaling the sweet-scented smoke and swirled whisky around in my mouth but I could still taste the cloying stink of the tunnels. The morgue had been a blur and I didn't remember much. An ambulance had met us at the helipad, and I had ridden in the back with Prudence as we passed through the streets of Hong Kong, Christmas revellers crowding the footpaths, their happy faces lit by shop neons and strings of decorative lanterns.

Prudence's body had been wheeled into the morgue and the attendants had placed her on a gurney before removing the dressings I had applied, and gently washing her.

I stood silently, my mind blank, as I watched their ministrations. I couldn't take my eyes off her face, and I kept expecting her to open her eyes, yawn, stretch and sit up. When they were done, the attendants grasped the handle of a cabinet and pulled the drawer open. It slid open silently and they gently lifted Prudence onto the cold steel shelf, covering her neatly with a clean, white cotton sheet, folding it back under her chin. That done, they respectfully stood in a corner of the room and left me with her.

I approached the drawer and looked down. Her face was white and the firm skin of her cheeks and throat had sagged; her lustrous dark hair looked like burnt straw. I reached out and neatly brushed away a strand of hair then leaned over the drawer and kissed her, one last time, on the forehead. The attendants quietly closed the drawer, and I walked out to the office where Joey was waiting.

As I had entered, Joey stood up and Michael Wong put away his notebook, stood and walked to me.

'I'm very sorry, Galahad,' he said. 'Truly.'

I nodded. 'Thank you,' I said, my voice seeming far away.

'You understand I will need to ask you a few questions... but that can wait until tomorrow. I have most of what I need from Miss Loh, she being there the whole time.'

I glanced at Joey, but she didn't react.

Michael went on. 'Miss Loh has provided a statement on the circumstances surrounding the death of the killer...' he paused and looked hard at me. I swallowed hard, my mouth desert dry. 'So,' he said 'it appears to me a case of self-defence on your part, and we won't be pursuing it any further. It would have been good to interview him, but I doubt he would have given us anything so...' He shrugged.

I nodded at Joey. 'Thank you Michael,' I said quietly. 'Yes, it was self-defence. Him or me...' An image of Prudence lying in the steel drawer flashed before my eyes. 'Michael,' I said. 'I don't want a Post-mortem. Please. She's been ... cut up enough. No more.'

Michael Wong thought about that for a moment and nodded. 'Yes, I think that will be fine,' he said. 'The offender is dead, there will be no trial and the facts of Prudence's death are quite clear. I will reflect that in my Report to the Coroner and I am sure the need for a PM will be waived.'

He sighed deeply. 'We still have to find Peter Toh of course,'

Michael said. 'We *will* keep looking for him and I'm sure he will appear somewhere sooner or later. But, as far as the Trails Killer is concerned, the case is closed.'

He had nodded to me in farewell then, and left the office. An unmarked car sat at the kerb outside and Chief Inspector Wong slid into the back seat and it drove away. Joey had hugged me tightly and not said much before she left to check on Penny at Eastern.

Alone and dazed, I had stumbled out of the morgue and into a taxi

Now, in the bar, I filled the glass, emptying the bottle and ordering another. A cigarette burned in an ashtray at my elbow, its smoke curling to the ceiling like dragon's breath. The fresh bottle arrived, and I cracked it open, swallowed the glass of whisky in one gulp, filled it again and swallowed that. I don't remember anything else about that night.

69

THE REST of that week I hid in my apartment, and I drank.

I drank nearly all day, every day, stopping only when I collapsed on the floor, or on the hard tiles of the terrace, after a solitary binge. Alastair, Joey, and Angel made the funeral arrangements around me, calling me now and then to ask my opinion or to tell me what they had done. I hadn't cared and didn't want to know. My lawyer had called me at some stage when I was so drunk I couldn't see and said something about Prudence's Will, but I had hung up on him.

I couldn't sleep, I didn't wash, I barely ate, my clothes stank and, worst of all, I neglected Bors.

In a rare moment of clarity, I had called Jenny Lam, the eccentric woman who ran an animal shelter and from whom I had adopted Bors, and begged her to take him until I sorted myself out. She had agreed but had asked me how long that might be. I have a hazy recollection of telling her 10 or 15 years.

The one bit of good news came the day after our ordeal in Shing Mun. Joey called. She told me Penny was physically fine and the killer had not molested her. The downside was that the kid was traumatised by the experience and by what she had witnessed. It would be a long road back. Joey had ended the call by telling me she did not like what I had become in recent weeks. Nor did I.

The day before the funeral I woke with a hangover and realised, through the fog, there was one more thing I needed to do. I had spoken briefly to Caesar Li a few days earlier and found out Guo Yu-xuan was still recovering in hospital and had not spoken a word to anyone.

Caesar had told me the very brief investigation had concluded Guo had miraculously switched off the CCTV in the corridor outside his cell, had obtained a length of cord, had tipped the steel prison bed on its end, and attempted to hang himself from the back of the bedhead. The investigation was a whitewash; I knew it and Caesar knew it. Someone had got to Guo and tried to silence him. The only two options for who that was were the people behind Guo's attack on Walter Chan, or Chan himself.

Luckily for Guo the prison officer who had strung him up had botched the job and the bed had toppled over against the cell door with a loud clang that alerted other officers on duty. Guo was expected to make a full recovery and would soon be released from hospital, but it was clear his life was in danger. I stumbled to the bathroom, splashed water on my face, swirled some mouthwash and headed to Kwun Tong to visit Guo's wife and child.

70

THE APARTMENT BUILDING in Kwun Tong was small – four floors – and looked derelict. It sat in a narrow street that was oddly quiet with many of the shopfronts boarded up and no one on the street. I looked around and the entire block looked the same.

Everything seemed still and frightened. Blinds were drawn and no laundry hung from window racks, there was no traffic and not a sound could be heard as I approached the door.

With a sudden hiss, a large ginger cat darted out from behind a wooden crate and sprinted away. I jumped and, heaving a deep breath, moved into the doorway. The usual security panel of door-bells and intercom had been torn from the wall and the steel security door was ajar and unlocked. Yellowed and rumpled bits of newspaper blew about in a circle in the small entrance from which a set of stairs ascended into the building.

I could smell the faint odour of cooking which was a welcome sign – someone lived here after all – so I climbed the stairs to the second floor and knocked on the door to Guo's apartment, noticing the mortice lock had been recently replaced in the splintered door frame. I heard shuffling from inside, then the door opened and a female face peered at me over the top of a chrome door chain.

'What do you want?' she demanded in Cantonese, her eyes wary as she looked over my shoulder and down the hallway.

'Mrs Guo?' I asked.

She eyed me again. 'Who's asking?'

I handed her my Hong Kong ID, passing it through the gap in the door. 'My name is Galahad Jones, Mrs Guo. I'm a Private Investigator. I want to help your husband. I have been to see him in prison...'

She passed my ID back and shook her head. 'Don't need help. Go away,' she said as she closed the door.

'Mrs Guo,' I said hurriedly. 'I know there is more to this than your husband is saying. I'm sure there's a reason behind his attack on Chan Yi-chen and that that reason, once I know it, could help secure a sentence remission or even his release... Please, hear me out.'

I stood there in the silence of the dank and gloomy hallway waiting for a response then, with a metallic clink, the door chain was slipped and the door opened.

The woman standing there, her arms crossed defiantly was small and could have been in her mid-thirties but worry and anguish had lined her face, prematurely aging her. Her long hair, pulled back in a severe ponytail, was greying and her lips were tight lines as she looked at me, running her brown eyes up and down. She didn't like what she saw.

'You look like shit, Mr Private Investigator,' she said. 'But you don't look like one of *them*. If you were, you would have kicked the door in instead of knocking.' She pulled the door open and stepped back. 'Come in,' she said.

The apartment was tiny but clean. The main room had a small refrigerator, a sink beside a cook top, and a laminate dining table with three chairs. Pots and a wok lined the bench beside the sink. A single window stared with its cracked and dirty eye across the street into what looked like another abandoned apartment building. An old Chinese timber cabinet held a few glasses, a set of small porcelain bowls, plates and a teapot, next to which an ancient black and white television sat precariously on top of a small side table.

I glanced to my right and noticed two doors, presumably to a bedroom and a small bathroom. Both doors were closed and I sensed someone else was in the apartment. The woman pointed at one of the chairs.

'Sit,' she commanded. I sat and she pulled up a chair across from me. 'You have 10 minutes, Mr Investigator,' she said. 'So start talking. Why are you here?'

Taking a deep breath to calm my thoughts and ease the headache that was cracking my skull, I began.

I told her I had been the one who had tackled Guo during his attack, but that I had always had my suspicions he had not acted alone. I told her I was convinced the attack was orchestrated by a triad and that it was for some wrong Walter Chan had done them. If I could obtain evidence that Guo had acted under duress, it might go well for him. I finished and sat back.

'Can you tell me anything, Mrs Guo?' I asked quietly.

Guo's wife was staring silently at me, her face expressionless then she shook her head and laughed. It was a bitter, fractured sound.

'You have no idea, Mr Investigator,' she said, her voice brittle. 'Triads? Chan, our fine upstanding politician, standing up to them and risking his life? Oh, *diu*! That's hilarious!'

'Well, tell me, Mrs Guo. Tell me what is going on. What is Walter Chan up to and how does it involve your husband.'

Again, she studied me hard, summing me up, her eyes hard and suspicious. I watched her in silence and saw the moment she made her decision. She seemed to deflate at that moment and her head lowered, her hands clasped tightly on the table in front of her.

After a slow count of ten, she lifted her head and called out a girl's name. Yù míng. Jade Brightness. A moment later a small girl entered the room, her head down, eyes lowered as she shuffled up beside her mother, her flip-flops scraping the floor, and gripped the older woman's shirt. The girl was rolling something around in the palm of her clenched right fist.

Guo's wife waved her hand in the air.

'This apartment, this whole block, sits on land that has been rezoned. The developers want to build a hotel, shops and restaurants.

Bars. The problem they have is the block can't just be reclaimed by the government. It's freehold. Each and every business owner, every resident, must agree first to sell. Those that have – and there are many – have received next to nothing for their homes and businesses. But we *won't* sell! This is our *home*!'

The pieces started to slowly fall into place in my foggy mind. Chan was number two in the Development Bureau and was responsible for urban planning decisions. He had to be tied in with the developer, doubtless for a handsome backhander. I felt defeat closing in on me.

While I could understand his attack on Chan, Guo's anger at being levered out of his home in no way mitigated the offence, and establishing Chan's corrupt dealings with the developer would be next to impossible to prove. It was, in fact, a common occurrence in the city. What Guo's wife said next stopped me in my tracks.

'About six weeks ago,' she said, her voice low, 'Chan and two of the developer's henchmen came visiting. My husband was away working and I would not open the door, so they kicked it in. Chan came in and sat right where you are sitting and offered me a price to sell. I told him to fuck his mother.' She sighed deeply and lowered her head again. 'I should not have done that. Chan got angry and then spotted Yù míng in the next room. He got up and... and he went into the room and closed the door.'

I held my breath and my eyes slid across to the tiny girl, standing silently beside her mother. I felt sick and the welcome red rage began to rise again in me. Guo's wife went on.

'I...I could hear her cries through the door,' she said. 'I could hear the blows. It went on for a long time and when Chan came out he was smiling and doing up his pants. He... he raped her.'

She sobbed, an agonising, gut-wrenching sound in the tiny room, and tears streamed down her face. The girl's tiny hand stopped fidgeting.

'Yù míng,' I said gently. 'I am a friend of your daddy's. Can you show me what you have in your hand? Please.'

The girl looked up and glanced at her mother who cuffed away her tears and nodded. Yù míng opened her hand and dropped what she was holding onto the table. It was a single cufflink, enamelled in black and red. I knew instantly what I was looking at. Etched in the enamel, in white, were the same characters I had seen hanging in a frame on the wall in Walter Chan's office. It was a yin jian, or "chop" with the traditional Chinese characters for his name.

I picked the cufflink up. 'May I keep this, Mrs Guo?' She nodded and I pocketed it. 'So that's why Yu-xuan attacked Chan,' I said. 'Mrs Guo, did you report this to the police? Did you take Yù míng to hospital?'

She shook her head. 'Chan told me if we went to the hospital or the police they would kill her...My husband swore me to silence, and I know he will never tell.'

I sighed. My last conversation with Guo now made sense. But there was no evidence. Nothing with which to pin the offence on Chan. He was home free. I rubbed my eyes.

'But,' Guo's wife said, standing and opening the refrigerator. 'I have this.' She reached into the small freezer compartment and pulled out a ziplock bag and handed it to me. The bag was fogging in the room but I could see, inside, was a folded pair of young girl's underwear.

'Is this what I think it is...?' I said.

She nodded. 'I took them off her after they had left and put them in the freezer.'

A thrill of elation coursed through me. Viable DNA in rape cases has been found even on laundered clothing, or clothing that had sat for months in a cupboard. By freezing the specimen immediately after the event, Guo's wife had secured iron-clad DNA evidence of Chan's rape of the young girl.

'I want to keep these also,' I said. 'Trust me: they will be in police hands today and you will have protection as soon as I can arrange it.' I looked hard at her.

'Are you with me?' I said. 'We can do this, Mrs Guo. We can bring Chan to justice and I'm sure a good lawyer – who I happen to know – will secure your husband's release.'

The small woman, crushed by life at Hong Kong's margins, looked at me and smiled bravely. 'Yes, Mr Jones,' she said, slipping an arm around her daughter's waist. 'I am with you. All the way.'

I nodded, slipped the ziplock bag carefully into the pocket of my jacket and stood. I moved to the door and looked back at the woman and her daughter sitting in silence and grief in the small room. I would make this right; I swore to myself. No matter what.

71

THAT DAY HELD one more surprise in store for me. I had stepped out of the MTR at Causeway Bay onto Matheson Street, heading home, when I stopped in the Wan Chai Road Wet Market to grab some Char Siu and rice. I hadn't eaten for nearly two days and my stomach was cramping. I had ordered and was standing waiting, wrapped in my thoughts of what the next day would bring, when I felt a sharp prod in my left kidney, followed instantly by a sibilant whisper in my ear.

'Don't turn around,' Jade Tooth said in Cantonese. I could smell the garlic on his breath. 'You and I have unfinished business, Jones.'

Without a word or a movement, I watched the street stall cook spoon steamed rice into a small styrofoam box. Jade Tooth prodded the knife point in further and I felt it prick the skin beneath my shirt.

'My man Fung has disappeared in Manila,' Jade Tooth hissed. 'And I *know* you were there at the same time. I don't give a fuck how protected you are by 14K, you're a dead man and I promise you I'm going to do it slowly.'

I took the offered package of food, tied up in a small white plastic bag, paid the stall owner and began to turn. Over Jade Tooth's shoulder I saw a beat cop standing on Bowrington Road watching us closely.

'You're scared, Jade Tooth,' I said. 'I can smell it on you. You stink of fear because you *know* you're next.'

Jade Tooth's face cracked in a thin-lipped leer. He was about to speak again when the cop began to move toward us.

'Hey, you two! Break it up!' the cop shouted. Jade Tooth turned his head and palmed the knife, expertly slipping it back up the long sleeve of his shirt. He held up his hands.

'No trouble here, Constable,' he said, then leaned in close to me. 'This isn't over you half-breed bastard,' he whispered, spittle flecking into my face. 'I heard about your whore sister. Good riddance! Your turn now, and soon.'

With a broad smile at the policeman, Jade Tooth turned and walked away toward Hennessy Road. Watching his back, I knew I would never have peace until Jade Tooth had been dealt with, and the germ of an idea started to form in my mind.

72

IT WAS New Year's Eve and the sun shone over Hong Kong on a crisp and cool December morning.

The large trees spreading above the graves in Hong Kong Cemetery were alive with bird song and hundreds of butterflies flitted among the flowers, now and then alighting on a headstone. A Water Dragon emerged from the dense green undergrowth to peer unblinking at the small group of people standing around a hole in the ground, a mound of black dirt beside the grave covered with a green mat.

The funeral was small – Prudence had wanted that – and I was flanked by Joey and Adele, both of whom gripped my hands. Alastair stood on the other side of the grave and, behind him, Angel and Tommy Ho. To Alastair's right stood a small group of people, close friends of Pru's, none of whom I knew. At a respectful distance from the invited mourners stood Michael Wong, his hands clasped loosely in front of him. I glanced at him and he nodded back, his stern face set and eyes hidden behind sunglasses.

The priest stood at the end of the grave, delivering the service in a clear voice that rang around the glade of the dead. I wasn't listening. Instead, I stared fixedly at the dark oak casket lying on the bier atop the grave. I shut my eyes and the priest's words swept over me. It was Ecclesiastes 3:1-4

To everything there is a season, and a time to every purpose under heaven:
A time to be born, and a time to die;
a time to plant, and a time to pluck up that which is planted;
A time to kill, and a time to heal...

Recent weeks had been a time to kill but I wondered if there would ever be a time for me to heal. I didn't think so, which was why I had a large black duffle bag packed and sitting on the ground behind me. The priest finished the reading and gently closed his book, standing back slightly as the gravediggers moved forward, released the planking of the bier, and slowly lowered my sister into the earth. I blinked hard at the tears that ran down my cheeks from behind my sunglasses and bent to scoop up a handful of rich, dark soil as the priest did the same.

The priest dropped the dirt into the hole and it thudded onto the lid of the casket. Joey and Adele flinched next to me. Somewhere in Pru's friend group, a woman was sobbing.

'Forasmuch as it hath pleased Almighty God,' the priest intoned, 'of his great mercy to take unto himself the soul of our dear sister here departed: we therefore commit her body to the ground; earth to earth, ashes to ashes, dust to dust; in sure and certain hope of the Resurrection to eternal life...'

I dropped the soil from my hand into the grave and stepped back as the small crowd started to break up and drift away.

Joey and Adele hugged me and whispered words that I didn't register. Angel kissed me lightly on the cheek and squeezed my hand. She pointed at the bag at my feet.

'You're leaving,' she said, a pained smile on her face. 'Where to?'

'Somewhere not here,' I said quietly.

Angel nodded. 'Well, don't make me wait too long Galahad Jones,' she said before she brushed gently past me and walked away.

Tommy Ho and Alastair both patted me on the shoulder and

Alastair mumbled something about getting pissed. The friend group left without a glance at me and I was alone with Michael Wong. He stepped up and stood in front of me. The gravediggers had removed the green cover and were slowly shovelling dirt into the grave, each thud of soil pounding into me like a punch to the gut.

Michael cleared his throat. 'I'm truly sorry, Galahad,' he said. 'I'm sorry we didn't catch him in time...'

I shook my head. 'It's okay, Michael,' I replied. 'It's not your fault. She was dead from the moment he grabbed her. It was me. I knew him, the clues were there for me to put together but I didn't.'

I pointed into the half-full grave. 'This is down to me...'

Michael nodded. 'Maybe,' he said. 'Maybe not. Anyway, we will talk soon about the Chan case. The bastard was released on bail yesterday – money talks. But the case is solid. He will go away for a very long time...'

I shrugged and Michael turned to walk away. He took two steps then turned back.

'Galahad,' he said. I turned to look at him. He took off his sunglasses and stared hard at me. 'Do something good with that triad money...'

I sighed and nodded. 'I will, Chief Inspector,' I said and turned back to watch the gravediggers hide my sister from the sunlight forever. I rolled and lit a cigarette dragging deeply on the rich scented tobacco and turned my head toward the two headstones on the left of Prudence's grave.

'I'm sorry, Dad,' I said. 'Mum. I couldn't do it. I couldn't look after her. I tried... I really did, but I wasn't good enough.'

I stood looking at my parents' headstones and waited for a reply, something from them that might ease the pain, if only for a moment. Of course, nothing came. I bent and picked up the black duffle, slinging it over my shoulder then turned and walked slowly out of the cemetery. I was leaving Hong Kong, the city of my birth, the city that burned bright inside me, and I didn't know when, or if, I would be back.

EPILOGUE

THE APARTMENT DOOR opened and Walter Chan stepped in, flicking the light switch and dropping his briefcase by the door with a contented sigh.

He moved across the large living room, pausing to pick up a remote and turn on the TV to the local news, before walking into his study. He reached out and flicked at the light switch but nothing happened. Grunting in annoyance he stepped into the darkened room, moving to the lamp on his desk. As he approached the desk, a floor lamp in the back corner of other room snapped on. Walter Chan jumped and spun around. There, sitting in a wing-backed chair, his legs crossed, dressed in a dark, well cut suit, sat a man. He was squat and muscled with jet black hair and a neatly groomed beard.

'Sit down,' the man said quietly in Cantonese, pointing at the chair behind the desk. Chan sat, stunned. The man took a deep breath and exhaled loudly as if meditating. He smiled and Chan's blood ran cold.

'You don't know me,' the man said. 'But I am the last person you will see on this earth...'

Chan whimpered. 'Money! Is it money you want? I have money, lots of it! It's here. Just take it...'

The bearded man shook his head. 'Oh, there is no amount of money you could give me that will stop what is about to happen,' he said. 'But I *will* take everything you have. It will go to the Guo family.'

Chan's eyes widened and the man went on, his voice calm, implacable. 'Ah, I see you recognise now why I am here. That's good. It's good to come to terms with one's guilt before... well, the end.' The man pointed at Chan. 'Open the safe and empty it.'

Hurriedly, Walter Chan stood and slid back a painting to reveal a wall safe, the tumblers of which he spun. Opening the safe, he reached inside and pulled out wad after wad of tightly rolled US dollars, dropping them on the desk.

'Please...' Chan wailed. 'Don't hurt me... I beg you! I have a wife, a child...'

The man stood and took up a large, black sports bag. Shovelling the money into it, he zipped the bag and slung it over his shoulder. Reaching inside his suit jacket, he drew out a SIG Sauer P226 and slowly screwed on a suppressor.

'It has been decided by my boss,' he said 'and by the Chief Secretary...' The man paused when he saw the shock on Walter Chan's face. 'Oh yes, the Chief Secretary! He is one of us. I bet *that's* a surprise!' he chuckled. 'Anyway, the gentlemen have decided that a short sentence in a medium security establishment simply does not fit the crime of child rape. So, here is your punishment.'

With that, Tommy Ho raised the weapon and fired two shots into Walter Chan's forehead. The body rocked back in the chair then slumped forward across the desk, blood pumping dark onto the green leather inlay. The Panda looked at Walter Chan for a moment then picked up the expended cases, switched off the lamps and quietly left the apartment.

~

The pretty young woman shrugged under her rucksack, pulling down on the adjustment straps, to hitch it higher on her shoulders as the track suddenly steepened toward the summit. Choosing a lesser-used side path, the girl skirted the summit contours and descended the hill, the January sun still high and warming her neck as she moved carefully down the rock-strewn track along the spur line. Before long, the track branched off to the left and the girl pushed into the low brush, heading east until she came to the low rock outcrop she had found the week before. She lowered her rucksack and crawled into the small hide hollowed out in the bushes, pushing her pack in front of her. Working quickly but carefully she opened the pack and drew out the Remington Modular Sniper Rifle, unfolded the stock and snapped open the bipod.

Resting the bipod on a level rock shelf she drew a small sandbag from inside the pack, nestled it around the legs of the bipod and tested the weapon's stability. A second small sandbag she put to one side. Satisfied with that, she pulled out the Schmidt & Bender 5-25x56 PM II scope and, flipping the lens caps up, put it to her eye.

Below her, on the crystal clear, blue waters of Sham Wan Cove sat a Maritimo S55 motor yacht, its sleek white hull and cockpit deck swept back in powerful, but aesthetic, lines. The anchor was down and two women, dressed in bikinis, were dancing on the aft deck.

The girl gave a satisfied grunt and clicked the scope home on the rifle's picatinny rail then, taking up position behind the rifle, stock in her shoulder, made small adjustments to the reticle for range and sighting. She then adjusted for elevation, bringing the point of aim in line with the point of impact, followed by a turn or two of the parallax wheel to bring the reticle onto the target image.

That done, she picked up the five-round box magazine and carefully inserted three .338 Norma Magnum rounds, rolling each gently to ensure they were properly seated. She snicked home the magazine, pulled back on the bolt and chambered a round. Adjusting her chest and stomach on the ground, she raised the stock again, snugged it in and settled down to wait. She didn't have long.

A man emerged onto the aft deck. He was dressed in white shorts and was bare-chested. A black-shaded tattoo of a dragon writhed the length of his right arm, with which he waved a bottle in the air while grabbing at one of the women.

The girl glanced up. The shot was a long one, almost 900 metres.

She assessed the wind one last time, using a pennant fluttering gaily on top of the motor yacht to judge direction and speed. Lowering her master eye to the scope, the girl snuggled into the stock of the weapon, her right hand around the grip, bringing the rifle into her shoulder, and she slipped the other small sandbag around and under the rifle's stock, gripping it with her left hand, to further support the weapon.

She sighted on the target. He was swigging from the bottle and swaying his hips lewdly at one of the women. He raised the bottle.

The young woman drew a deep breath, snicked off the safety, and took up the first pressure on the trigger. The man was standing still, drinking deeply from the bottle when the girl let out half the breath then held it while gently squeezing the trigger. The rifle bucked and the shooter smoothly worked the bolt, chambering another round. She didn't need it.

Just under a second after leaving the muzzle of the rifle, the .338 round smacked into the head of the target, blowing it asunder in a wild spray of blood, bone and hair. Jade Tooth's body dropped to the polished timber deck, twitched once and was still.

Chaya quickly broke down the weapon, collected the spent casing and packed her rucksack. After brushing away her hide position with a leafy branch, she shouldered her rucksack and made her way back up the track to the main trail. A little over an hour later she was boarding a ferry in Sok Kwu Wan, bound for Aberdeen.

AUTHOR'S NOTE

Hong Kong is my second home. I have loved the city since I first set foot there. The city has changed greatly in the 35 years I have known it – physically, culturally and, most significantly, politically – but none of that has changed my feelings for Hong Kong or its people, feelings only reinforced and strengthened over the last six years of living there, despite the turmoil the city has recently endured.

There is no newspaper in Hong Kong called *The South China Herald*, but there is a newspaper with a similar name. That is where the similarities with my fictitious newspaper, for which Alastair Chard works, begin and end.

I have always found Chinese names to be descriptive and poetic - you can be sure each given name is carefully chosen to reflect the parents' views (and future hopes) of their children. Chinese naming conventions used throughout 'Dragon's Claw' can sometimes be confusing for the uninitiated. They follow the [FAMILY NAME] [First given name-second given name] convention. The family name (or 'surname') as in English is inherited from one's parents and shared with other members of the individual's immediate family. For example Galahad's mysterious girlfriend YEUNG Mei-ying (first name, incidentally, meaning 'beautiful flower' - see my point about 'descriptive and poetic'?). Readers will note most Chinese characters of this novel have anglicised first names, making their names expressed in written form as [English First Name] [Chinese Family Name] [Chinese given names] so, for example Morris Ngan Fei-hung.

There are a number of reasons for this but, chiefly, it is due to the long British connection to Hong Kong so the adoption of an 'English' first name for business and social contexts, has become somewhat of a tradition. While it's never really discussed, the anglicised first name, in Hong Kong at least, tends to denote the person has a decent education (that also includes the ability to speak English).

There's another, very practical, reason and that is that Chinese forms of address are either very formal or overly familiar, so English first names tend to serve as a 'lubricant' to speed up the process of getting acquainted. Paradoxically, I've always favoured my friend's Chinese names while they prefer me to address them using their English name.

Much has been written about Chinese transnational crime syndicates, commonly known as Triads. The term 'triad' - originally a translation of the Chinese term San Ho Hui (or Triple Union Society) has come to be synonymous with the organised criminal gangs - known as 'societies' - that operate in Hong Kong, Macau and other South East Asian countries. Like the Italian mafia, they are highly disciplined organisations with complex organisational structures created to engage in a variety of criminal activities including trafficking (in both drugs and people), prostitution, fraud, political corruption, extortion, illegal gambling and money laundering.

As this novel depicts, it is not unusual for triads to run, or be connected to, legitimate business enterprises both as a way to further their commercial success and launder their proceeds of crime. Lee Pak-chun's YunCorp does not exist but it easily could. Speaking of

YunCorp, the International Commerce Centre in Tsim Sha Tsui, where I have located YoungCorp's corporate headquarters, is 108 stories high, but with the top floor numbered 118. Floors 119 and 120 do not exist.

There are several references in 'Dragon's Claw' to triad hierarchy and rank systems, that use numeric codes to distinguish positions within the society – this is known as *I Ching*. The leader of the triad is the 489, or 'Mountain Master' below whom report 438 'Vanguard' or Operations Officers. 426 'Red Pole" are the enforcers of the unit and run teams of rank-and-file members known commonly as 'soldiers' but made up of 'Blue Lanterns' (uninitiated members) and '49ers (ordinary members who have been inducted into the triad by the Incense Master (ceremonies officer). The Panda, Tommy Ho, is a Red Pole, and the mysterious and beautiful Angel Yeung, as Galahad found out to his dismay in 'Dragon's Back', is the 432 of the triad, the 'Straw Sandal' or Lee Pak-chun's Liaison Officer.

Just as he was recruited, Tommy Ho wants to recruit Galahad's street kid sentries in the classic method of the triads by seeking out marginalised and troubled youth, taking them under his wing and showing the kids, possibly for the first time, respect and a sense of purpose. It's cynical and manipulative but a very effective recruiting method.

14K and Sun Yee On exist and are two of the most powerful Hong-Kong triads, but that's where the similarity with the people and events of this novel end. Everything I have written about events and people connected with 14K and SYO is fictional and the product of what my friends formerly of HKPF call my 'fevered imagination'.

I recommend the following excellent books for further reading into triad societies in Hong Kong: Peng Wang's *The Chinese Mafia* (2017) is an excellent study on the origins of the societies in ancient China and their rise in contemporary China. Chu Yiu-kong's *The Triads as Business* (2002) is my go-to resource on the rise of the Hong Kong triad.

Professor Morris Ngan is based loosely on a real person who met me twice in Hong Kong and gave me his valuable time to discuss the theories of deviant behaviour, Psychopathy, and serial killers. His help in understanding the aberrant criminal mind was invaluable in shaping my killer and his behaviour. As Morris Ngan says in Chapter Thirty-seven, the study of serial killers and what drives them is 'an immensely complicated subject area', however I would recommend the following as light reading for anyone interested in the subject. *Sociology of Deviant Behaviour* by Marshall Clinard, 1965; *The Diagnostic and Statistical Manual of Mental Disorders*, published by the American Psychiatric Association; a 2020 paper titled *A Behaviour Sequence Analysis of Serial Killers' Lives: From Childhood Abuse to Methods of Murder*, by UK-based psychologist Dr. Abbie Maroño; and finally a rare paper from 1985 titled *Profiles in Terror: The Serial Murderer*, by Holmes and DeBurger

I make a long note about HKPF in Book One of the Dragon Series, *Dragon's Back*, and won't repeat it here

A team of operators from The Special Duties Unit (SDU) features in Chapters Sixty-six and Sixty-seven. The unit, nicknamed the 'Flying Tigers', was formed in the mid-70s by the then-British Hong Kong Government and initially trained by a team from the British SASR and SBS. SDU is made up of three assault teams, a sniper team and a boat team, all of whom are supported by a team of combat medics. The operators in SDU are very well equipped and trained to an exceptionally high standard – it was my great pleasure to have been invited to observe one of their exercises a few years ago and I was immensely impressed by their capabilities and skills.

Finally, while I have tried to be as accurate as possible in all aspects of this novel - much of it drawn from my own experiences - it is a work of fiction and of imagination so mistakes, doubtless, have been made. My Cantonese is rudimentary - despite my best efforts - and Pinyin - the system of Romanised spelling for transliterating Chinese - can often vary. Last, I admit to, occasionally and slightly, altering

Hong Kong's geography, climate and streetscape. In my defence, I only did so where I felt it enhanced the story and allowed me to neatly tie up a narrative point. I apologise to my Hong Kong friends and beg their forgiveness.

Brisbane, Australia
2023

ACKNOWLEDGMENTS

I would like to express my deep thanks to the many people who have supported me along the way, too many to name. First, my beautiful wife of 30 years who has been a rock of support to me – even during the times when my moods and writer's angst got the better of me. Thank you, Liz, for everything! Thanks also to my old dog, Loki, and monstrous white cat, Murphy, who keep me company during the long hours in the study.

Thanks yet again to my old friend, fellow paratrooper and writing mentor, Chris Allen - author of the outstanding 'Intrepid' Series - without whose advice and encouragement I would never have started down this path, let alone stuck to it. Finally, thanks to my old police and security contacts in Hong Kong; good lads all.

ACKNOWLEDGEMENTS

[illegible]

[illegible]

ABOUT THE AUTHOR

A.C. (Andrew) Edwards is a former policeman, paratrooper and Special Forces officer. He served in the Australian Army and operated widely across South East Asia and the South West Pacific, including attachments to the Malaysian and Indonesian armies, and other operational deployments. He retired at the rank of Major.

In addition to his police and military career, Andrew has worked as a security adviser across SE Asia, a close-protection specialist for several Very High Net Worth individuals and their families, and as a Security Contractor in the Middle East and Afghanistan. He was most recently the Regional Security Director for Asia Pacific for a multi-national company but has now swapped the corporate grind for full-time writing.

Born in Singapore, Andrew has lived and worked for much of his life across Asia Pacific. Today, he lives between Hong Kong and Brisbane with his wife, dog and rescue cat.

Book 3 in the 'Dragon' Series, 'Dragon's Eye', featuring Galahad Jones is coming soon...

www.ingramcontent.com/pod-product-compliance
Lightning Source LLC
LaVergne TN
LVHW050920080826
845145LV00001B/143

* 9 7 8 0 6 4 5 8 6 7 3 2 9 *